TINK

Elite 8 Studios Book 3

Emmy Sanders

Beta Reading by Georgia Johnson, Jen & Maxie of Smut Readers Society, and Lauren

Editing by M.A. Hinkle

Proofreading by Ky

Cover Design by Natasha Snow Designs

ISBN: 9781967130023

Content Warning: This book contains the mention of past verbal abuse.

For the Goldies.
Shine bright, beautiful. Don't dim your light for them.

Contents

Chapter 1

ALEX

"Come to Mama, you beautiful beast, you."

"Pardon?" my coworker asks dryly.

I bark a laugh, straining from my prone position to pat Dixon's knee. Even though his eyes are on his phone, his thick eyebrow is raised in begrudging amusement.

He loves me. I know he does.

"Not you, Grumpy Bear. This dick," I reply, flashing my phone screen his way.

Dixon's eyes raise to my device before he can think better of it, and a scowl jumps to his face. "Jesus Christ. Keep your dicks to yourself."

Cackling, I flip onto my back atop one of the many couches in our break room at Elite 8 Studios and swipe through Grizz1330's pictures, which are few. Two, to be exact. There's the aforementioned dick pic and a faceless body shot, and even though both are taken in poor lighting with less-than-professional angles, there's no mistaking I'm looking at one bear of a man.

I want to climb him. Or lick him. Climb him and lick him.

"Are you seriously trolling for dick right now?" Dixon asks in his deep grumble of a voice. "After you just had a scene?"

"It was only blowies," I comment as I glance through Grizz's info. His profile is pretty scant, but it says he's thirty years old—four years older than my twenty-six—and single. "I haven't been properly dicked in a week, Dixie. A *week*."

It's a travesty of epic proportions.

My friend-slash-coworker sighs loudly enough that I don't even have to turn my head to know exactly what expression he's sporting. "Alex, pudding pop, li'l biscuit—"

"Hungry much?"

"—we've talked about this."

"Of course we talk about dicks, Dix. We're porn stars," I retort with an eye roll that, unfortunately, Dixon can't see.

"That's not—" Dixon cuts off. I didn't think he could sigh any louder than the first time, but he proves me wrong. "You know what? No, that's fine. Whatever. You're gonna overshare no matter what I say, so why do I even bother? I have the worst friends."

"Aww, bestie," I say, rolling over enough to take in my six-foot-something behemoth of a friend. "I love you, too."

Dixon shakes his head, pinching the bridge of his nose as Niko saunters into the break room. Although really, this place is more like a lounge. *Break room* sounds sad and utilitarian, but our boss, Jerome, did us a solid when he outfitted this space. There are a bunch of plush couches and chairs, complimentary snacks and beverages, and tastefully erotic nude stills from the studio decorating the walls.

I seriously have the best job.

"Niko," I call out, garnering the Greek god's attention. He may be named Adonis on set, but the man lives up to his moniker, that's for sure. His head swings my way as Dixon's head swings his way. "Your boyfriend is being mean to me." I pout for good measure.

Niko grins widely, strutting over—because yes, the man literally struts every second of every day—and Dixon sighs yet again. That is until Niko lands in his lap. Then Dixon melts, wrapping his arms around his boyfriend's waist. Niko plants a quick kiss on Dixon's short-cropped hair before his eyes cut my way.

"He's mean to me, too. That's how you know he cares," Niko says, bringing a smile to my face and a scowl to Dixon's. Niko pats Dixon's chest. "Ready to head home, griniári mou?"

"Yeah, yeah," Dixon grumbles, but I don't miss the way he tucks his face against Niko's wet curls before the pair of them stand up.

Dixon can humph and grumph all he wants, but we all know how much he loves Nikolas Adamos. From the moment they locked eyes, it was love-disguised-as-hate at first sight. Now, nearly a year after they first met here at Elite 8 Studios, the pair are still going strong, partners on and off the set.

And considering we make adult films—Elite 8 Studios is the gay porn mecca, after all—that's saying something. Not everyone is okay with their love interest fucking other guys. Believe me, I know.

Frankly, I don't see the problem, not as long as there's communication, clearly set boundaries, and consent on all sides.

"You guys go have fun being all cutesy and domestic," I say, waving my hand and returning my focus to Grizz and his truly impressive dick. I open up a new chat. "I have a bear to bait."

Niko snickers. "Have a good night."

"Be safe," Dixon counters.

I pull my eyes up from my phone to send Dixon a reassuring grin. "Always."

Niko gives me a wave before the pair are out the door, and I type out a message via my favorite hookup app—Grindr.

Me: Hi! Love your cock. Mind if I take it for a ride?

I grab a bottled water from the cooler as I wait for Grizz's response. Typing bubbles appear and disappear several times before a message finally comes through.

Grizz1330: Shit. Really?

I snort a laugh, settling cross-legged on the couch.

Me: Really, truly. Too forward?

I know some guys prefer a little more back and forth first—more wooing—but I've always been a straightforward person. I see no reason not to go after what I want.

It takes Grizz a long time to answer again, but I don't mind. I flip through my Insta, smiling at the shenanigans my friends are up to. My phone buzzes after a couple minutes.

Grizz1330: No. First time on here, is all. I appreciate the bluntness. I'd be good with that.

Oh, honey. I bet you would.

Grinning, I type back.

Me: Great! You won't regret it.

I add a few suggestive emojis.

Me: Can you host?

As I'm waiting for his reply, Cas, the newest performer here, comes through the door. He ticks up his chin when he notices me. "Hey, Tink."

"Heya, Himbo," I shoot back lightly, using his stage name since he used mine. "How's it hanging?"

He shrugs, a loopy little smile on his face as he grabs a bag of chips from the snack machine. "Can't complain."

I chuckle. "Mhm." The man looks blissed out. "Good scene?"

He huffs a laugh at my bouncing eyebrows and drops into a seat nearby. My phone buzzes, but I wait to check it. I'm many things, but rude is not one of them.

"Yeah," Cas answers, opening his chips. "I was filming with, uh...shit. I forgot his real name. Teddy?"

"His name *is* Teddy," I fill in, laughing when Cas's eyebrows jump up.

"Seriously?"

I nod, flipping my phone idly in my hands. "Yup. Our sweet Teddy Bear truly is a Teddy. Theodore, technically, but he doesn't go by that."

Cas nods, looking a little lost in thought as he pops a chip into his mouth.

"Don't worry, sugar, you'll pick up everyone's names. It's a lot," I say, figuring that might be what he's worried about. The guy has only been here a short while, and he doesn't film on a full-time schedule. No one's going to blame him for taking a minute to find his footing.

"Thanks," he says, eyes dropping to my phone when it buzzes again in my hand. "That your boyfriend? Girlfriend?"

I raise an incredulous eyebrow. "Girlfriend? Really?"

Cas laughs, shrugging. "I didn't want to assume."

"Honey, there is not a straight bone in this body. Puh-lease." I wave a hand down myself for emphasis—all five-and-a-half feet of me, from my blonde mop of hair to my rainbow-print crop top. "Tink the twink, at your service."

Cas chuckles as he pops another chip in his mouth. "Noted."

"And no," I say in answer to his previous question, swiping my phone open. "No boyfriend. Just a hookup." *Hopefully.*

Cas hums, and my smile stretches wide as I read Grizz's messages.

Grizz1330: Yeah, I can host.

Grizz1330: I had to look up what that meant. I'm pretty hopeless.

Grizz1330: There's still time to back out.

Oh, precious baby. Mama will take care of you.

Me: Not a chance. No fluid exchange, though. That's a hard limit for me.

Gotta stay safe, after all. Especially being a sex worker, I take that responsibility seriously.

Grizz1330: That's fine with me.

Me: We're on then. Send me your address. 10 p.m. work?

Grizz1330: Sure.

He follows that up with an address across town, just on the outskirts of Las Vegas. Popping off the couch, I slip my phone into my pocket.

"Gotta go. Scored a big date," I tell Cas, doing a little shimmy of excitement.

He looks amused. Honestly, that seems to be Cas's default—resting happy face. Is that a thing? If so, Cas has it. The guy is like a friendly puppy, all good intentions and happy-go-lucky attitude behind a killer bod and that sharp-angled, swoon-worthy mug. He's seriously gorge, with chestnut-colored hair, whisky amber eyes, and plump blowjob lips. The cut jawline. The chiseled abs. He's somebody's perfect package.

Not mine, but somebody's.

"Have fun," he says, his chip bag crinkling as he balls it in his fist. He aims for the trash and misses with a groan.

Swiping up the empty bag, I drop it into the can. "I always do," I tell him, sending my newest coworker a wink before heading through the door.

My steps are light as I all but bounce toward the front of the building. I pass Raylin, our cosmetologist—and the woman who removes all my body hair—in the hall, and she gives me a quick hello. As does Nathaniel, the argyle-wearing assistant producer here at the studio. I return their greetings, but I don't stop to chitchat.

I have a date with Destiny.

Is it weird to name a guy's dick before meeting it?

Nah.

Smile on my face, I run my fingers over the neon Elite 8 Studios sign on the wall, the yellow tubing running nearly floor to ceiling, and then I'm out the door, skipping toward my Jeep. Top down, I head toward home, singing along to Rihanna. Love may be on her brain, but something much more fun—*and filthy*—is on mine.

Inside my apartment, I run through my routine: thoroughly washing inside and out, prepping myself while I ignore my aching cock, and then pulling on my clothes. I stick with the rainbow crop top I was wearing before because it's hella cute.

Primped, pressed, and primed, I make sure I have extra-large condoms and lube, and then I turn on my phone's location sharing with my friend and ex-coworker Mal. He gives me a thumbs up in response.

I may like sex a lot. Okay, who am I kidding? I love it. And let's be honest, I have a lot of it, in and out of work. But I'm not about to rush into a stranger's place without taking some precautions.

It's just before ten when I arrive at the address Grizz gave me. His house, which is nestled in a suburb of adorable little

Spanish-style homes, is white stucco with a terracotta roof and arched windows. Even though it's relatively small, the place is well-kept and has the cutest little covered porch out front.

I pull my Jeep up to the closed garage door, check to make sure I have everything I need in my pockets, and then hop out of the vehicle. There's a flicker of movement behind the drape at the front window as I walk up, so I'm not surprised that it only takes a moment for the front door to swing open after I knock.

But when it does—*ho boy*. I just about swallow my tongue.

Look, I'm not that picky when it comes to my sexual partners. There's attraction to be found in everyone, if you ask me. Skinny, large, short or tall. Blonde hair, brown, red. Square jaws, rounded faces, freckles or clear skin. Classically handsome, rugged, nerdy. It doesn't much matter to me.

But if asked if I have a type that gets my motor revving every damn time, that answer is a resounding yes, you bet your ass I do. And this man is *it*. His pictures simply did not do him justice.

Grizz1330 is tall and gloriously beefy. Big all over. In fact, I have to tilt my head back to take him in. He's wearing red plaid, of all things, and I already know he has a deliciously furry chest underneath that shirt. Add in the shaggy brown hair and the big beard and...

Holy mother of dragons.

I truly did snag myself a Grizzly Bear.

"Oh, honey," I say to the man whose eyes are as wide as a deer caught in headlights. "Please tell me you're going to invite me in."

Grizz—cripes, what an appropriate username—stares at me for a long moment before stepping to the side. "O-of course," he stammers. "Come on in."

I shiver a little as his deep but gentle voice settles over me. "Thanks, boo."

Traipsing inside, I kick off my shoes before turning to face my host. Again, I have to look up. Way up. Definitely climbable, this man. *And lickable.* Lickable, for sure.

"I don't suppose you're a lumberjack?" I tease, giving his arm a little stroke and possibly letting my fingers linger longer than necessary.

He looks genuinely confused. "Um. What?"

Oh, sweetness.

I bite my lip. "Never mind. Shall we?"

Grizz doesn't answer right away. He swallows roughly, his lips parting. The man, rather endearingly, seems downright shy. Well, that's all right. I can be bold enough for the both of us.

"Where do you want me?" I ask, giving him the big eyes my fans seem to love. "Couch? Bed? Right here against the door?"

"Uh," he answers, blinking fast. Despite the staring and apparent shock, I can tell he doesn't recognize me. There's always a certain flare, a little *a-ha* moment, when people realize they're looking at Tink, the porn star twink. Grizz doesn't have that. To him, I'm just another man.

And *God*, I love that.

"Bed?" he finally answers, the word sounding like more of a question.

I give him a warm smile. "Sounds good to me, handsome. Lead the way."

He nods a little jerkily and takes half a step before stopping and rubbing the back of his neck. He seems hesitant. Uncertain. "Do you, uh, want something to drink first? I have water, beer, wine?"

Oh Heavens. Am I rushing him?

"I'm okay," I say, giving his arm a soft squeeze. "But if you need a minute before we head upstairs, or if this is too much for you, that's fine. Nothing has to happen if you don't want it to."

He exhales, meeting my eyes full-on. His are brown, framed by dark lashes. They're pretty and, best of all, kind. His hair is a bit of a mess on top of his head, and his beard is bushy, as if he attempted to tame both but they didn't want to listen. But honestly, the whole rough-and-tumble look is a good one on him.

"I want to do this," he replies. "I'm just... I've never..." He shakes his head a little in frustration. "I've never been a casual guy."

"Are you a virgin?" I check.

He shakes his head *no*.

"You've just never hooked up?" I ask.

He nods ever so slightly.

"Okay, that's totally fine," I say, wanting, first and foremost, to set him at ease. "We can go at your pace, sweetness. I have all night."

He looks down at my hand resting casually on his bicep and licks his lips. His face pinches slightly. "I, uh..."

I cock my head.

Attraction isn't the problem; that much is clear. The massive bulge in his pants is proof enough of that. And he says he wants this. I believe him, but his body language is screaming unease. Maybe...

"Or," I hedge, taking a step closer. Close enough to feel his body heat emanating through his shirt. "I could take the lead?"

He puffs out a breath at that, relief flooding his body. "Yes. That."

Oh, darling man. My sweet grizzly. *I am going to wreck you so good.*

Smile a mile wide, I bring my body flush with his, and Grizz's hands land on my hips, the size of them making me nearly dizzy. Big hands are a weakness of mine, second only to big cocks, and this man has been graced with both.

Grizz swallows roughly when I bring my hand to his dick, cupping him through the denim of his jeans. His pupils blow wide.

"Honey," I purr. "It would be my pleasure."

Chapter 2
ROWAN

There is no world—not this one nor any alternate dimension—in which this makes sense. This guy is so far out of my league it's not even funny.

Why did he pick me? Out of all the guys he could've messaged for a hookup, why *me?*

Unaware of my internal freak-out, Goldieboi flashes me a grin that should be downright illegal. Palm on my erection, he squeezes, and I damn near combust on the spot.

How is this beautiful man in my living room right now? I mean, really?

"C'mon, Grizz," he says, grabbing my hand and tugging me toward the stairs. "Let me take care of you."

Fuckity fuck.

I follow him up the stairs.

"Which one is yours?" he asks, his hand so much smaller tucked inside my own.

"First door on the right."

Goldieboi leads me into my bedroom, flicking on the light before he turns and starts to walk backwards, pulling me along toward the bed. There's a smile on his face as his gaze slides down my body, and I can't comprehend how the appreciation I see in those bright hazel eyes could possibly be real.

He lets go of me to pull off his shirt, and the hint of flat stomach I could see earlier is fully revealed as his crop top flies over his head. I gape as he flicks the button on his shorts.

"This okay?" he asks, sliding the material down his legs.

I nod, swallowing, my voice lost.

Goddamn, he's so...small, beautiful, sexy as fuck. He looks breakable compared to me. Like a pixie. How the hell is this going to work?

"I, uh—" I lose my voice as he steps close, running his fingers over my stomach before grabbing my waistband and giving a little tug. He bites his lip as he opens my fly.

"Okay?" he checks again.

I nod, heart beating rapid-fire inside my chest, all my blood rushing south at a fast clip as the backs of his fingers brush against my boxers.

"You seem a little tense. What's your concern?" he asks, leaving my jeans open and setting to work on the buttons of my shirt.

Some part of my brain notes I should be doing something other than standing here like a useless log, but I can't quite seem to get my body in working order. Goldieboi flicks the buttons of my plaid shirt open one at a time, fingers trailing upwards.

"I, uh..."

"Is it because you've never had sex with a stranger?" he guesses.

That's part of it, but mostly it's *him*.

I nod, and he spreads my shirt open, palms smoothing over my chest as he all but rumbles like a purring cat. *Oh God.*

He deftly pulls my shirt off my shoulders, having to reach up a bit to do so. "But you want to have sex with me?" he asks.

I must really look like a mess if he keeps checking. "Yes." Absolutely yes.

He nods, seemingly satisfied with that. His fingers sneak under the hem of my undershirt next, blunt nails raking over my skin.

"God, you're sexy," he rasps, drifting his fingertips over my soft belly.

I shake my head, having no response to that. I'm not sexy. I'm not much of anything.

His brows draw in slightly, eyes pinging up to mine as he canvasses my face. Holding eye contact, he lifts my shirt, going all the way up on tiptoes to pull it over my head. I can't seem to move anything other than my limbs as he all but undresses me like a doll.

Fuck, this is what Manuel always complained about. That I wasn't manly enough. Wasn't assertive.

"Sexy," he repeats. "Big. Solid. Strong."

Goldieboi trails his hand over the hair on my chest before rolling my nipple between his finger and thumb, and my knees nearly give out. My hands fly to his hips on instinct, as if this waif of a man could possibly hold me up if I happened to fall.

My eyes get caught on the slim swath of fabric that passes for Goldieboi's underwear. The material is bright blue and tight enough I can make out every single line of the erection nestled between my thumbs. It's straining upwards, standing at attention. Because of me?

Absently, I run my thumbs along his hip bones.

Goldieboi hums, stepping closer to me, his fingers journeying downward again toward my waistband. "So you want me," he states. "And I want you." He punctuates his point by running his palm over the length of my erection through my boxers. I hiss as he adds, "Badly."

"Yeah," I breathe out, having no other words.

"Mkay, then," he says with a wickedly seductive smile. In one fluid move, he tugs my pants down and follows them to the floor.

Good Lord. Is this real life?

Goldieboi taps my leg, and I lift it enough for him to pull my jeans free. He repeats the motion on the other side, and the moment his eyes laser in on my covered cock, it bobs right in front of his face.

"Hello to you, too," he says, grinning as he runs his finger along the clothed length of me.

I curse, wishing I had something to grab onto.

Goldieboi looks up, a playful set to his face as he grabs the band of my boxers and tugs them down. My dick slaps upright, nearly taking out his eye, and I'd be downright mortified if it weren't for the look of sheer desire that runs over his face. Mouth popping open, he reaches up, taking me in hand as he breathes out, "*Ohh.*"

Boxers pooled around my feet, I watch, utterly rapt and so damn horny I'm seriously concerned about giving the guy a facial on the spot, as Goldieboi pumps his fist over my length slowly. Near reverently.

"Oh, Grizz," he says, eyes flicking up. "I can't even tell you how much I'm going to enjoy having this beast inside my ass."

"*Fuuuck*," I hiss out, bringing my own fist to the base of my cock and squeezing tight to stave off my orgasm.

Goldieboi laughs, looking so joyous and free that I'm momentarily gobsmacked. How is this ethereal beauty here with me, acting like he's enjoying this just as much as I am?

Mercifully, he relinquishes his hold, only to tap the crown of my dick like a pet before standing. In a quick move, he sheds his tiny underwear and bounds over to the bed.

"Do you have supplies?" he asks, sprawling over my comforter like a naughty painting come to life. "If not, I brought some."

"I, uh... Yeah, I do," I answer, stepping out of my boxers. "Drawer."

I point, and he rolls over, flashing his flawless, smooth ass as he rummages inside my nightstand. Giving myself another squeeze, I step to the bed.

Goldieboi rolls back with a couple condoms and a bottle of lube in his hand. He looks over the packaging on the con-doms—checking the expiration dates to be safe, maybe?—and then he pats the bed. "C'mon over. I don't bite." He grins, bouncing his eyebrows. "Unless you ask nicely."

When I don't respond, too caught up in entertaining *that* scenario, his expression eases.

"Grizz," he says lightly, knee-walking to the edge of the bed, less than a foot in front of me. I briefly wonder if I should tell him my real name, but he hasn't given me his, either. "If this is too much, just say so. I—"

"No," I cut in, forcing myself forward. On his knees on the bed, Goldieboi is my height. Tentatively, I slide my hands around to his back, brushing over all that smooth, soft skin. He hums, wiggling closer to me, his hands coming to rest on my shoulders. "I'm in my head. But *fuck*, I do want this. Want *you*. Okay?"

How could I not? The man is sex on a stick. Way too good for me. But maybe I should stop questioning my fortune.

Eyes sparkling, he snakes his fingers up into the hair at the back of my head as he leans forward, lips brushing the shell of my ear. "Then get up on this bed, Grizz, and let me make this good for you. Okay?"

When I nod, Goldieboi leans back, giving me room to join him on top of the mattress. I swing the lightweight comforter out of the way and climb up. And since he mentioned wanting to ride me—*Jesus*—I push my pillows out of the way and plant myself at the headboard.

"Oh, Grizzly Bear," he says affectionately, stalking closer and running his palms up the length of my legs. "You are temptation personified."

What? No. No way.

He's just sweet talking, surely. Trying to make this good for me, when I should probably be the one worried about making this good for *him*.

"You are," he adds, seemingly taking my silence as the rebuttal it was. He grabs a condom, ripping it open before rolling it expertly down my length. I grit my teeth at the feel of his fist briefly working my dick. "The thick thighs. The furry chest. And don't even get me started on this," he says, squeezing my dick. "You have one of the biggest, most mouthwatering cocks I've ever seen in my life. And believe me, I know big, beautiful cocks. It's in my job description."

I have no answer for that. Although it does make me incredibly curious as to what his job is.

"I want to lick every inch of you," he says, eyes raking over my body as he grabs the lube. He gives me a swift grin as he flicks open the cap. "But I'll settle for having you inside of me, instead."

God, how am I possibly going to last long enough for that to happen?

Goldieboi swipes the lube over my dick as I grit my teeth, but he doesn't linger, probably realizing exactly how close I am to busting. My balls feel heavy already, hugging the base of my dick, ready to unload. And every word, every touch from this man, has me inching closer to the edge.

When Goldieboi straddles my lap, my heart takes off, and my palms start to sweat. I have the distinct impression that maybe I'm hallucinating. Maybe, instead of filling in my Grindr profile and happening upon this literal golden ray of light about to lower onto my dick, I'm at the shop, passed out in the service bay because I left the garage door shut with an engine running.

This isn't real. This isn't happening.

My crown makes contact with something tight.

Holy hell, this is happening.

"Wait," I say, my mind snapping to the present. "Jesus, we need to prep you."

Goldieboi's face relaxes, but he doesn't move, hovered as he is over my dick. His slim waist, flat chest, and erect cock make an enticing picture, but somehow, it's the look in those hazel eyes, both gentle and mischievous, that has me reeling.

"I prepped before I got here. I'm good to go," he says. "More than good to go."

"But," I counter, shaking my head, "I'm not small. I should make sure you're stretched."

His grin sets my blood alight. "Sweetness, *not small* is not the way I would describe you. But trust me when I tell you I can handle it, okay? I know my body, and I'm ready for your cock. So please, can I have it now?"

Groaning, I can do nothing but nod.

Goldieboi holds the base of my dick as he gets into position, and I watch, mouth open, breath coming short, as he lowers himself enough for my crown to slip in. The pressure is intense, the heat even more so, but he barely pauses before taking a couple inches into his body and groaning so damn lasciviously it's a true miracle I don't straight up come. I fist the sheets on either side of me, hands clenched tight, as he works himself down, sinking an inch at a time. There's no indication of pain on his face, no grimace or hesitation, just pure, unadulterated lust. His hands move to my chest for balance once I'm halfway in, and when he reaches the root of me, ass pressed to my skin, his entire body rolls in a shiver.

"God," he groans, wiggling his hips in a way that has me nearly going cross-eyed. "*Definitely* gonna enjoy this."

Then, in a motion as fluid as silk, Goldieboi rises up, rolls back down, and does exactly as he promised—he rides me.

I wasn't the best conversationalist up until this point, but with Goldieboi's body strangling my dick, with him bouncing over me in a mind-melting dance, I completely lose my voice. One of my hands settles on his soft thigh, the other smoothing up his torso almost independently from my brain. But when my thumb rolls over Goldieboi's nipple, and he moans out a "*Yes*," I focus my attention there, desperate to hear more of those sounds. Desperate to—hopefully—make him come before I lose it. Because there's no way I'm going to last.

I have never in my life witnessed a more exquisite sight than Goldieboi straddled atop my lap, using my body for his pleasure. Taking my cock as if it was meant to be inside him.

His hands roam continuously—over my neck, through my beard, along my shoulders—before he plants his palms on my chest and rides me like his life depends on it. When I finally manage to pull my gaze away from his pink, pebbled nipples, I find him staring right at me with half-lidded eyes. His lips are parted, his abundance of blonde hair falling over his forehead in messy waves, and I'm fairly certain he must be an angel.

Maybe I did die back in the garage.

"So good," he moans, his words practically slurred as he rakes his nails over the hair on my chest and belly. "Your dick, Grizz. Your dick is so good to me."

I choke out a groan, hips punching up reflexively as a *zing* travels through my body and mind, and Goldieboi answers with a sound that's almost curious. Eyes holding my own, he grinds down on me harder.

"*So. Good*," he repeats slowly, his voice pure sex and breathy with his exertions. "Can feel every inch of you, Grizzly Bear. Every damn inch, hitting me just right. Fucking me *just right*." He leans close, his cock rubbing against my stomach, and I shift my hands to his hips, needing the tether. "Gonna come all over that hairy chest of yours. Would you like that? Want me to show you exactly how good you make me feel?"

"*Jesus*," I groan out, head thunking against the headboard as I do everything in my power to pull back my orgasm. I reach for his cock, but Goldieboi swipes my hand away.

"Not yet," he says.

"I can't last," I tell him through gritted teeth.

"You can," he replies, rolling his hips like a belly dancer. My gaze gets caught there, on the smooth, soft planes of his stomach. On the jut of his hip bones and the gentle definition of his ribs. "You'll last because I'm asking you to. Because I *need* you to. I'm not done with you yet."

I tighten my grip on his body, thrusting harder, every inch of my skin firing as electricity licks over my flesh. Under my flesh. Through my balls and down my shaft. A bead of sweat slides down the side of my face, but I ignore it, tugging Goldieboi down on me as hard as I dare.

"*Yes*," he hisses out, back arching, his hair bouncing as we slap together again and again. "Just like that, Grizz. My big bear. Fucking me so good."

"Rowan," I punch out, my legs practically shaking with the effort to hold back my orgasm. "My name is Rowan."

Goldieboi smiles, big and bright and blinding. "Rowan," he purrs, and the one word—my name rolling off his tongue—is nearly my undoing. "Love your cock, Rowan. Love your furry chest. Your thighs. Your *hands*. Those sweet eyes looking at me like that. So perfect. You're perfect for me."

"Fuck, fuck," I chant, reaching for his erection again. This time, he doesn't stop me, and when I wrap my hand around his precum-slicked dick, I stroke fast.

He drops his head back, groaning, his whole body shivering as he starts to tense. "So good, baby. Just like that. I'm one seriously lucky boy."

I nearly guffaw. Him? He's the lucky one?

I tighten my hand around his erection on the upstroke, and he slams down on me so hard, I see stars.

"*Ah*, yes," he rasps. "You're gonna make me come. Yes, yes, Rowan, *yes*."

His body clamps around me like a vice, and I hold my breath as Goldieboi's cock swells in my fist. I stroke him through it as his cum lands across my stomach and chest, just like he promised, his ass rhythmically milking my dick all the while. And when my lungs draw tight enough that I'm forced to pull in a breath of air, I detonate.

My vision whites out as fire rages along my veins. From the tips of my fingers and toes, from the top of my head, it races inwards, heat jumping along synapses, converging in the very core of me. The pressure mounts, a single second feeling like a lifetime, and then it snaps, all sensation barreling down my shaft as I call out, lost in the throes of the single most powerful orgasm of my life.

Goldieboi rolls his hips throughout it, his ass wringing out every last ounce of my pleasure. His hands bracket my neck, palms hot against my own overheated skin, but his touch is light. And even though I can barely think—can barely *move* after that—I tug him to me. I tug him to me, and he doesn't resist in the least, instead nestling comfortably against my chest, his riotous hair tickling my chin.

My ears are ringing when I come back to Earth, but Goldieboi's murmuring words break through the noise.

"Mm, that was lovely," he says. And, "Want a mold of your dick. Want to lay here all day. So warm. My big grizzly pillow."

I huff a laugh—I can't help it—and he lifts his head off my still-heaving chest to plant a soft kiss over my bearded jaw. My inhale stutters at the simple, sweet gesture.

"Alex," he says.

"What?" I ask, tilting my head down to look at him.

"My name is Alex."

"Alex," I repeat, tasting his name on my tongue. I like it more than I should, knowing, after tonight, I won't have another chance to say it.

This was just sex. Really amazing, mind-blowing sex. But still just sex.

"Thank you," I say, having no clue what else to say, and completely unsure of actual etiquette in these situations. Should I offer to clean him up? A snack before he goes?

Alex laughs lightly at my thanks, pushing himself upright. He holds onto the base of the condom as he lifts off my half-hard erection, wincing slightly with the motion—the only discomfort he's shown tonight. Because of the loss of my dick inside him?

Fuck, I shouldn't like that so much, either.

"Thank *you*," he finally says. "That was just what I needed." He flits his finger down my dick, like a little caress, mumbling something that sounds suspiciously like, "Such a good boy, Destiny." Then he removes my condom and ties it off. I'm so surprised I don't say a word.

"I, uh..." Shit, what happens next?

Alex flops down beside me, placing his chin on his hand and looking up at me with those big hazel eyes. "Want me to go? No hard feelings if you do. *Or*"—he draws out the word—"I could hang around and we could go again in an hour?"

My heart beats a big staccato thump, and a smile jumps to my face as Alex bats his eyelashes at me, his feet kicking lightly behind him.

"Yeah," I mutter, clearing my throat as my eyes wander down the nymph on my bed. "Stay."

Chapter 3
Finn

Fingers resting idly over my keyboard, I look at the script in front of me. It's been a long day of switching between .NET programming language and Java for my two biggest clients, and my brain is fried. Admitting defeat, I shut down my computer and crack my knuckles, followed by my neck.

"I'm calling it, Buttercup. This workday is done," I tell the orchid sitting at the edge of my desk. Her creamy yellow petals, which fade to a bright orange near the middle, are lit in the early evening sun, and I grab the spray bottle I keep nearby to mist her exposed roots. "Gotta stay hydrated, isn't that right?"

She doesn't answer, not that I expected her to.

"Mo, you hungry, girl?" I call out, tromping down the stairs and heading into the kitchen. As soon as I pull my cat's food from the pantry, her telltale raspy purr rattles through the air. She comes running, and I chuckle, measuring her kibble into the dish. The brown tabby weaves around my legs and plants her face in her food, chomping noisily as I give her back a rub. "Love that tuna flavor, don'tcha?"

Mo doesn't answer, either.

Tugging my fridge door open, I swipe my hair out of my eyes and appraise the contents. There's some chicken in there and fresh bell peppers, and I'm pretty sure I have tortilla shells in the pantry still, which means I could make fajitas. That's a lot of work for just me, though.

Unless...

Closing the refrigerator door, I pop my head in front of the window above the sink in my kitchen. Rowan's lights are on next door, and even though his living room drape is drawn, I'm fairly certain I can see a hint of movement beyond it.

Smile on my face, I jog outside and over to my neighbor's house. The door opens not ten seconds after I knock.

"Finn? Hey," Rowan says, his brown eyes creasing with his smile.

It looks like I caught him just getting home from work. He's still wearing his Mike's Garage jean shirt, and the subtle smell of motor oil drifts on the air between us.

I inhale subtly.

"Hey, Ro," I reply, flashing him a smile. "I just wanted to see if you've had dinner yet. I was thinking about cooking fajitas."

His eyebrows pop up. "Oh, really? No, I haven't eaten."

Rocking back on my heels slightly, I wait, but when Rowan doesn't say anything else, I clarify with a chuckle, "Want to eat with me?"

"Oh, yeah, sure," he says, huffing a self-conscious laugh.

I grin wider. God, he's so cute. I just wish I could get a read on what he thinks of *me*.

Rowan's gay; I know that much. He told me over beers the night he and his ex-boyfriend split that he figured out his sexuality in his late twenties. Manuel was his first real boyfriend. They broke up two months after I moved into the house next door, but in the five months since then, even with my flirting and subtle hints, and even with all the time Ro and I have spent hanging out together, I still haven't been able to figure out whether or not I have a chance with the guy.

Manuel was a slip of a man. Thin, proper, expensively styled. And I...well, I'm none of those things.

Maybe going after my neighbor isn't the best idea. It sure could get awkward if things go bad. But from the moment I met Ro, I was a goner. The shy smiles, the beautiful brown eyes, the kind words he has for everyone—Manuel included, even though the guy didn't deserve them. He's so *good*, and I've always been drawn to that. Always gone after those soft souls.

Maybe because of how I grew up? Lord knows neither of my parents were ever *soft*.

But psychoanalysis aside, Rowan just does it for me, plain and simple. And yet, I can not, for the life of me, figure out if I do anything for him.

"Great," I tell him, glad he agreed to dinner. At the very least, he seems to enjoy my company. "It'll just take thirty minutes or so to cook."

"Yeah, okay," Rowan says. He glances over his shoulder, and I notice a smudge of grease near his ear. "I'll clean up first."

I shove down my offer to help and give a nod. "Sounds good. See you soon."

Rowan's mouth tips into a little smile, and as I jog down his porch stairs, he closes the door behind me.

Although our houses are both Spanish-style homes—as are most of the residences in our Nevada suburb—his is done in the classic white and terracotta mix. Whereas mine... I grin up at my bright teal house as I round the path to my door. Mine was painted by the previous owner. It's a big part of what drew me here.

In a sea of arid earth, my house is a shining jewel.

The inside is much the same as the outside—bright colors, eccentric paint jobs—and I've barely changed a thing. I love the mishmash of hues and the colorful tiles in the kitchen and bathrooms. My new home feels alive, and considering it's where I work five or six days a week, the vibrancy of the environment is something I appreciate.

Grabbing a cast iron skillet, I heat the stove and start to prepare the fajitas. I cut the raw chicken into strips. Season. Sizzle on the skillet. Grab a pan. Cut up and sauté the peppers and onion.

I get lost in the process, and before I know it, my kitchen is perfumed in the smells of chili powder, cumin, and garlic.

When my phone pings in my pocket, I check it, but it's only an email. Still no word from my family now that I'm back in town. Dismissing them from my thoughts for the time being, I pack everything into a portable wicker basket to bring next door. Mo doesn't even bother to lift her head from her perch in the living room window when I go.

I give Rowan's door a quick knock before letting myself in—knowing he won't mind since he's expecting me—and then I set everything up at his dining table inside the kitchen. I can hear him moving around upstairs, and I idly wonder what he's doing. Getting dressed, maybe? Still toweling off?

Shaking my head, I try not to let myself entertain those thoughts too deeply. I set out plates, the steaming-hot in-gredients I brought from home, and tubs of sour cream and guacamole. I've just finished getting everything in place when Rowan comes down the stairs.

"Hey," I call out, announcing my presence.

He comes around the corner, his brown hair still damp, his beard glistening with a few drops of water. He changed, and despite the loose style of his jeans, they hug his thick thighs nicely, and his checkered button-down shirt sits snug against his broad frame.

Fuck. I wonder if Rowan would be a gentle giant in bed, too. Or if he'd be wild.

Pushing those thoughts *firmly* aside, I pull out his chair. "Food's ready."

"Oh, wow," he says, walking into the room. His eyes flick to me before landing back on the spread. "You didn't have to bring everything over here."

I wave him off. "It's no problem."

"Do you want something to drink?" he asks, diverting over to the fridge and looking inside. "I have beer?"

"Yeah, that'd be great. Thanks."

Rowan nods, grabbing two beers and popping off the caps. He hands one over and takes his seat, and I plop down kitty-corner next to him.

"I never did ask. Where'd you learn to cook like this?" he questions, loading up a couple soft tortillas with the seared chicken and veggies.

I take a sip of my beer, shrugging. "Picked it up here and there," I tell him, debating how much to say on the topic. I don't exactly want to talk about my past relationships with the guy I'm hoping to date, but I also want to be honest with Ro. "My ex-girlfriend was a chef. We cooked together a lot."

He hums, nodding, his brows drawn in slightly.

What is that pinch for? Did he not like hearing about my ex?

Hope blooms in my chest.

"I know enough basics to get by," he says, "but I can't cook like this. It's really good."

"Thanks," I reply with a grin, glad he likes my food.

I'm about to ask Ro how his day at work went when his phone chimes. Shooting me an apologetic glance—as if I'd mind—he pulls it out of his pocket. His eyes widen as soon as he looks at the screen, and his mouth pops open.

"What is it?" I ask, my curiosity getting the better of me.

Rowan blinks, eyes pinging to me briefly before they land back on his screen. "Uh. Just a message from a...friend. I wasn't expecting to hear from him so soon. Or at all."

"Oh," I say, watching as Ro types something back. I can't help but wonder why he seems so surprised to hear from a friend.

Unless *friend* is code for something else.

My gut tightens, but I don't have time to contemplate that unfortunate potential complication before Ro sets down his phone and gives me his full attention.

"How's your gran?" he asks before digging back into his fajitas.

My smile is immediate. "She's good. I was over there on Sunday, and she was in high spirits. The new aide we hired has been a big help, too. The place was spotless."

My gran was a big part of my decision to move back to this part of Nevada after having been away for nearly thirteen years. I grew up near here, on the periphery of Las Vegas, but I left after my freshman year of college. After visiting this past winter and finding out how much my gran's health was declining, I moved back.

It was a wakeup call, seeing the state she'd been living in for the last year or so. Finding her so clearly neglected by the rest of the family was like a punch to the gut. I felt guilty—still feel guilty—for not checking in sooner. But I'm here now, making up for lost time, and having someone stop by once a day to check on my gran and tidy up a bit has been a big help on the days I'm not there.

I try to visit a few times a week at the very least, even though my gran keeps telling me I should be out living my own life instead of spending all my time with her. As if it's a bother.

"You should come with me sometime," I say without much thought.

Rowan looks at me in surprise, the fajita in his hand forgotten. "I, uh…"

Shit. Yeah, no. Dial it back, Finnigan. This is not a date. We're not boyfriends. Why would Rowan possibly come along to meet my family?

"Never mind," I say, giving Ro a smile to show him it was probably a silly idea anyway. "Just a thought. Are we still on for watching the game on Friday?"

It's kind of become our thing—watching baseball together on Friday nights. Rowan is from Cleveland, so he's a Guardians fan. I just like the tight pants. And hanging out with Ro.

"Yeah, you got it," he says, giving me a little smile.

We finish the rest of our meal, chatting away, and per usual, I look for any hint that Rowan might be into me. Sometimes, I swear I see him checking me out, but other times, he seems oblivious to the attention I pay his way. I don't usually have such trouble reading people, but maybe my problem with Ro is that there's zero attraction on his end, and I'm looking for something that's simply not there.

I know I need to buck up already and ask him, point blank. Otherwise I'll be left wondering and wanting. But that's easier said than done. I don't want to lose Rowan's friendship, either.

Rowan brings our empty beer bottles to the sink when we're done eating, and I casually sidle up next to him with our plates, letting my arm brush against his. He startles before apologizing and giving me more room.

Elbowing him more purposely, I smirk. "I don't have cooties, you know."

He relaxes, smiling as he goes back to the dishes. "I don't know where you've been," he mutters.

Chuckling, I grab a cloth and dry the plate he hands me. It's not that late in the evening, and normally, at this point, I'd float watching some TV. But before I can make the suggestion, Rowan yawns wide enough for his jaw to pop.

"Tired?" I ask him.

He nods, handing me another plate. "Long night. The beer didn't help, either."

"Need me to tuck you in?" I joke. Sorta.

Rowan huffs through his nose. "Thanks again for dinner, Finn."

"Always my pleasure," I answer.

With the dishes washed and dried, I gather everything else back into my basket and head for the front door. Ro follows, his hands in his pockets. He does look tired, those dark eyelashes of his fluttering slowly in a way that makes me want to haul him close and kiss his face off. He has such beautiful, soulful eyes. I wish they didn't look so sad sometimes.

I reach out and give his arm a squeeze. "Take care, Ro. See you Friday."

"Yeah," he says with a sleepy smile.

As soon as the door is shut behind me, I exhale into the hot night air, groaning quietly.

Friday. On Friday, I'll ask Ro out, one way or another. On Friday, I'll get an answer to the question that has been plaguing me.

And hopefully, even if Rowan doesn't want to date me, he'll still be my friend. I don't have many of those around here anymore, and I can't imagine losing this person who, in a matter of months, has become such an integral part of my life.

I like spending time with Ro. Like being there with him. Being there *for* him. He deserves someone who's going to treat him right, and after the little I witnessed of his relationship with Manuel, that person was *not* his ex. Frankly, I don't know how anyone could not love Ro. He's everything right and *sweet* in the world.

And fuck, I want a taste.

Chapter 4
ROWAN

Goldieboi89: Damn, Grizz. You should come with a warning label. I can still feel you.

Neck hot, I stare—for maybe the hundredth time—at the message Alex sent me the other day, followed by the rest of our conversation.

Me: Sorry?

Goldieboi89: HAH. No, don't be sorry, sweets. Never sorry.

Me: You're welcome, then?

Goldieboi89: That's more like it.

Goldieboi89: I had a really good time. Thanks, boo.

He followed that up with a winking emoji, a heart, and...an eggplant? He loves eggplant?

I still don't know. I'm stuck on the fact that Alex *thanked* me, as if there was anything to thank me for when I barely did a thing. Alex was clearly the one running the show. *Both* times. When he rode me, and then after, when he all but offered up his ass while on his hands and knees atop my bed, spurring me on with loud moans and words of encouragement.

Was any of that real? Did he actually mean what he was saying?

"Goddamn, Rowan, yes. Right there. Right fucking there. So good. Perfect. You were made for me."

Me? Or my cock?

Does it even matter? Not like I'm going to see the man again.

Besides, it was obviously just pillow talk. Not that I have much experience with that. Manny sure wasn't very vocal, unless he was expressing his disapproval.

Shaking my head, I get back to work, determined to push both men from my thoughts.

"Heya, boss."

Jumping, I knock my head on the hood of the Prius whose engine I'd been hunched over. Pauly gives me an apologetic wince.

"What's up?" I ask, rubbing the back of my head before realizing my hand is covered in grease. Just great. Story of my life.

I grab a rag from my pocket, attempting to rid the grease from my hair.

"We have a customer up front who needs a belt replacement. She says she was quoted a better price when she talked to Aaron over the phone," Pauly explains with a little cringe.

Aaron has dyscalculia, which is like dyslexia for numbers. This isn't the first time he's messed up a quote, but I know it's not his fault. He's a good worker, and he tries his best.

"Yeah, all right. I'll go talk to her," I tell Pauly.

"Good man, Grizlak," he says, slapping me on the shoulder as I pass.

The customer in question is standing near the front desk when I pass through the door from the service bay into the lobby. Her eyes take a moment to sweep over me, likely taking in my filthy work attire, and I try not to feel self-conscious under her stare.

"Hi," I say, sliding behind the counter and offering a smile. "I'm Rowan, the manager. Pauly said you have a question about your quote?"

"Yeah," the woman says, pointing at the cost estimate Pauly printed out. "This says 190, but the guy on the phone told me 109."

I nod. That tracks. "Not a problem. I'll get that fixed up for you," I tell her, clicking into the computer program to adjust the cost.

"Oh." She blinks a couple times, looking taken aback that I'm not fighting her on it.

The cost of the belt isn't high. It'll just be eating into our labor costs a bit. Not a huge deal.

I print the new estimate and slip it her way across the counter. "Look good?"

She glances at it and nods, smiling my way. "Yeah, thank you."

"Of course," I say as she signs it. "We should have that done in about an hour and a half. Will you be waiting here or should we give you a call?"

"I'll stay here," she says, blinking at me a few more times.

I nod, grabbing the keys she left on the counter. "There are drinks in the lounge," I say, pointing toward the waiting area. "I'll be back out shortly."

"Thank you!" she calls after me. "See you soon."

Pauly has a shit-eating grin on his face when I head back into the service bay.

"What is it?" I ask.

He shakes his head. Pauly is younger than I am—mid-twenties to my thirty years of age—and sometimes, he acts like it. "Man, you're something else."

"Huh?" I mumble, skirting past him to the Prius with its hood up.

He raises a brow. "That woman was trying to burn me alive with the force of her glare, and yet, after two words out of your mouth, she was looking at you like you hung the damn moon."

My head rocks back a bit. "I have no clue what you're talking about."

"That much is obvious, boss," he says. At least Pauly sounds amused by my apparent obliviousness. "It's the puppy-dog eyes, I swear. Those things are irresistible."

I face my coworker. Employee, technically, although it's always felt as if these guys work *with* me, not for me. I'm just the manager. I don't own Mike's Garage.

"Are you telling me I'm irresistible?" I ask in genuine confusion.

Pauly rolls his eyes. "Hah, hah. You know what I mean." I really don't. "And *guy* isn't my type."

"And she isn't mine," I point out, finishing up with the Prius before closing the hood.

"Yeah, yeah," Pauly says, waving me off. Everyone here knows I'm gay, and luckily, no one has a problem with it. Or, if they do, they haven't said a word. "At least we'll be getting a five-star review after this. Check it out."

I follow Pauly's gaze to the windows between the service bay and the lounge. The customer from before gives me a wave through the glass, and Pauly snorts.

"She's just being friendly because I gave her the discounted price," I say, turning away.

"Friendly. Sure," he fires back before lowering his voice. "If friendly includes a side of benefits."

I shake my head, grabbing the woman's keys from my pocket. "Get back to work," I say without venom.

Pauly chuckles as I head to grab her car from the parking lot. One step outside, though, and I'm brought up short. My ex, of all people, is standing twenty feet away beside his sleek black Audi, watching me steadily. He doesn't look remotely surprised to see me. Which, of course he doesn't. Manuel knows I work here.

He's wearing a suit, like usual, looking put-together in that too-perfect way he always had about him. I never did understand what the man saw in me. But, by the end, he made it pretty clear he didn't know, either.

"Manny," I say on an exhale, resuming a slow gait and stopping in front of the man.

"Rowan," he says in his typical clipped voice, as if he doesn't have time for me. He never really did.

"What can I help you with?" I ask. If he's here, there's a reason for it.

He rubs the side of his car. "Needs an oil change."

I cock my head. "There are dozens of shops on this side of the city. Why are you *here?*"

"Careful, Rowan," he says, taking a step forward. Manuel is a good several inches shorter than me, but he's never failed to make me feel small in his presence. And the way he's looking at me now has my shoulders shrinking down without my permission. "Keep talking to me like that, and I'll think you're not happy to see me." The smile he gives me is all shark.

Always the games with Manuel. He's the one who broke things off, even though I was working up the courage to do it myself. Yet this isn't the first time he's made a point of seeking me out. What for?

Closing my eyes briefly, I take a centering breath. Fleetingly, I wish Finn were here. He always knows what to say to make me feel better. But Finn isn't here. And I'm a grown man who should be able to handle my problems, including my ex.

Maybe I should tell Manuel off once and for all, but the truth is I'd rather just get his oil change finished and have him on his way. I hold out my hand, and knowing he's won, Manny hands over his keys.

"Thanks, babe," he says, the word making me flinch. He doesn't stop to say anything else, just heads over to a nearby car, getting into the back before he's driven off.

With a great big sigh, I shove his keys down into the recesses of my oil-stained jumpsuit. Pauly gives me a concerned look as I drive into the bay with the Honda that needs the belt replacement.

"Was that who I think it was?" he asks when I exit the vehicle.

"Unfortunately," I mumble.

Pauly doesn't question me further, and maybe it's because of the vibes I'm putting off. I'd apologize for my bad attitude, except I know Pauly doesn't mind. He's used to me being quiet more often than not.

I'm just finishing up with the Honda when my phone pings in my pocket. I wipe my hands off as well as I can before pulling it out, and a smile jumps to my face.

Goldieboi89: Look, it's you!

Below the message is a video link, and when I click it, there's a baby bear, covered in brown fur. The small grizzly is rolling around on the ground, looking generally adorable.

I shake my head, chuckling.

What does it mean that my hookup is sending me cute animal videos? Is that normal? In fact, we've chatted quite a bit since the other night. I found out Alex is an art student, and I told him I'm a mechanic. Even so, I have no clue how to respond to *this*.

My fingers, however, seem to have a mind of their own.

Me: I'm definitely bigger.

Goldieboi89: Yeah you are.

More eggplant emojis.

Goldieboi89: Cuter, too.

My cheeks heat.

Me: And I have more hair.

Wait, what? I have more *hair*? I'm hopeless at this. Whatever *this* is.

Goldieboi89: Mm, sure do.

He adds a drooling emoji.

Goldieboi89: Gotta get to work. Later, Grizzly Bear.

A little bewildered but unable to stop my smile, I shut off my phone, ignoring the messages from other men on the app. I haven't responded to a single one.

"What's the schmoopy grin for?" Pauly asks, wiping his hands on his coveralls as he walks up. "Got a new beau?" When I take too long to respond, my coworker's eyes bug out. "Wait, seriously? You holding out on me, Grizlak?"

"No, it's nothing like that," I say, shaking my head as I turn toward the front of the service bay.

Pauly falls in step with me. "What's it like, then?"

I glance over at the man I've known going on five years now, wondering if maybe I *should* talk to him about this. It's not like I have anyone else. Well, apart from Finn, that is. But somehow, I don't feel right talking to Finn about this.

It's not that I think my new neighbor would judge me. And I don't get the sense that he's homophobic. He's never acted remotely uncomfortable in my presence, and the only problem he seemed to have with Manny was the man himself, not his sexuality.

And yet... I can't bring myself to tell Finn I finally decided to try something new after my epic fallout with my ex. Maybe it has something to do with my massive crush on the man who resides next door.

Maybe I don't want him to know just how pathetic I am.

Finn—with his height and size similar to my own, ginger-brown hair that's long on top and shaved on the sides, tattoos that cover his torso and arms, and striking amber eyes that can soften or sharpen as needed—isn't the type of person to put up with people's bullshit. And he's certainly not the type of person who'd have trouble in his sex life. I just know it.

Unlike me.

"I, uh, decided to try that app you were telling me about," I say. "The one your cousin uses."

Pauly's eyes widen in recognition. "No shit? Good for you!" He pats my shoulder hard enough to send me a couple inches to the right. "Got yourself some of that vitamin D?"

Groaning, I turn away, continuing my trek toward the lobby.

Pauly laughs, following me. "Sorry, sorry," he says, not sounding it. "But seriously. Get yours."

Stopping, I rub my hand over my face. "I'm not used to this, Hernandez," I say, using Pauly's last name like the guys at the shop do to me. "I've never had a one-night stand before. I've always been in relationships."

There was Manuel. And before him, three different women before I figured out why dating someone who was supposedly perfect never felt...right.

Manuel and I were together for nearly two years, and although the sex was worlds above what I'd been having before, it took me longer than I'd like to admit to realize things still weren't *right*. And even then, I stuck with it, not wanting to give up the taste of validation I found.

Being with a man felt better than being alone.

And yet, one night with Alex blew my entire experience with Manuel out of the water.

How is that even possible? What does it mean?

Maybe fucking around is the right choice. Maybe there's a whole world of gay wonders out there just waiting to be explored.

But then why haven't I messaged anyone else yet?

"You look like Aaron when he's doing the numbers," Pauly says. "Was it that bad?"

Pulling myself back to the present, I shake my head. "No," I admit with a cough. "It was great."

Pauly grins. "Well, great then." He worries his lip before adding, slowly, "So Manuel...?"

"And I are done," I confirm.

Pauly nods, holding out his hand, palm up. "Good. Let me take care of his car, then. I don't know why that asshole had to come here, but he's clearly trying to mess with you. Let me handle it."

I waffle, skimming my fingers over the keys in my pocket. I should take care of it myself. If Manuel finds out I let Pauly do his oil change instead, he'll be pissed. He always was overprotective of that car of his—something I used to find charming.

But I don't owe Manny anything. And I don't really care if he's pissed at me. Not anymore.

Mind made up, I hand the keys over. "Oil change. The good stuff."

Pauly nods, slapping my back as I turn toward the lobby. I make it there this time and check the file to find out the Honda owner's name. "Meredith?" I call out.

She beams, popping out of her seat and heading my way. When she reaches the counter, she clasps her hands on top of the laminate, looking up at me with big eyes. "That's me."

I give her a smile. "You're all set. 109," I say, shifting the card reader her way.

She pays, eyes flicking up to me. "Any chance I could get your number?"

"It's right on the receipt," I say, pointing to our info on the bottom of her finalized workup.

"I meant *your* number," she says, touching my hand as I slide her keys over.

"Oh, uh…" I grab a business card with my extension on it from the rack. "Here you go."

She blinks at me a little as she takes the card, but Aaron rushing through the door pulls my attention away.

"Have a good day," I mumble as Aaron draws up short, seeing the customer in front of me.

Meredith looks a little glum as she walks away, but I turn my focus to my coworker, who seems two seconds away from passing out.

"I'm *so* sorry," Aaron says, swiping his long brown hair behind his ear. "Pauly told me I fucked up another estimate."

I breathe out a sigh of relief as I realize why Aaron is so put out. "It's fine," I tell him, walking up and patting him on the shoulder. "No biggie."

He grimaces. "It kinda is. You know I try not to do the numbers, but no one else was around to handle it, and—"

"Aaron, really. It's fine."

"Take it out of my pay," he says, following as I head back into the service bay.

"I'm not going to do that," I reply.

"Grizlak, *please*. You're killing me here."

That brings me to a stop. I face Aaron, who's looking at me in a beseeching manner. "Why?"

"You're too damn *nice*," he says, startling me.

"It's true," Pauly calls out, waving his hand from his position half-under Manny's Audi.

"And that's a bad thing?" I ask, befuddled.

"No, it's not," Aaron replies, still sounding winded, as if he's been running since the moment he got here for his shift and Pauly mentioned his screwup. "It's just... I don't want to take advantage of your good nature."

"You're not," I say. "You made an understandable mistake. It's my decision how to handle that, and I say you're fine."

"Fine," Aaron returns, eyes skipping around before his face lights up. "I know how I can pay you back."

"How's that?" I ask with some trepidation.

"Huh? What?" he calls out, backing away. "Sorry, gotta get to work. Talk later."

"Oh, Christ," I mutter. "I'm in trouble, aren't I?"

Pauly laughs from underneath the Audi.

At least I have a few things to look forward to. A hot shower when I get home. Friday-night baseball with Finn. And—I realize as a ping comes from my pocket—the one-night stand who won't stop blowing up my phone.

Chapter 5

ALEX

"What do you think? Does this look too disproportionate?" I ask.

Anh turns from her ceramic work and peers my way, pushing up her glasses with the side of her wrist. Her eyes narrow in concentration before widening comically. "Alex." She snorts. "That guy's dick is the size of his forearm."

"Too big then?" I ask with a pout.

She shakes her head. "God, I love you. Definitely too big."

"Yeah," I say a little glumly, erasing the offending appendage. "I'll make his arm bigger."

Anh chuckles, wiping her clay-covered hand on a towel. "What are you working on?"

"Just messing around."

Truth is I should be working on my final project for one of my classes—an illustrated book—but I haven't been able to figure out what I want the story to be about. Until I can settle on a premise, I don't have anything *to* illustrate.

"So the naked dude with the..." Anh waves her hand in a way I take to mean *massive dick*. "That inspiration come from somewhere specific?" she asks, setting the mugs she created on a rack beside the kiln in the corner of the studio workspace we're hanging in.

Anh and I met here at art school almost four years ago, which was, incidentally, just after I started my job at Elite 8 Studios. We became fast friends, and along with a bunch of other art geeks, we frequently visit this open classroom to work on our projects. We also get together every other Sunday for brunch.

Anh puts a few dried pieces into the kiln and sets it to fire before heading to the sink to wash her hands. I hum at her question about my inspiration, glancing at the drawing I'd been working on. It doesn't look much like Rowan in actuality, but my mind was definitely there when I started doodling.

"There's this guy..." I say.

Anh raises an eyebrow. "Isn't there always?"

I snort a laugh. "You know me well."

After washing up, Anh comes over to the ratty old couch I'm lying on and gives my legs a shove. I sit up and set my sketchpad aside so she can plop down next to me.

"I take it this was a hookup?" she asks.

I nod. Anh *does* know me well. If it were one of the guys from work, I would've told her their name. I don't give out personal info about my hookups. Only the fun details.

"And?" she prods, resecuring her dark hair in a ponytail. "Are you telling me he has a forearm dick?"

I bounce my eyebrows.

"No," she says, mouth dropping open.

"Huge. Like, soda-can big," I only half-joke, making a large circle with my hand to demonstrate.

"Mini or regular?" she retorts.

I snort a laugh. "There was nothing *mini* about this guy, boo. It was seriously a work of art. Easily one of the biggest things I've had up my ass apart from double penetration or, you know—" I close my fingers into a fist.

Anh grimaces. "No, I really don't want to know." She cocks her head, though. "Doesn't that hurt?"

Talking with Anh about sex is always interesting. She's ace, and our sex lives couldn't be more different. Anh isn't as...amorous as me, to put it lightly. She's a much bigger fan of toys than real men. But she likes to hear my stories. And I like hers. I've always been very open with her that way. Well, I'm open with most of my friends, if I'm being honest.

"Fisting involves a lot of prep. And yeah, it can hurt a little," I tell her truthfully. "But the euphoria?" I hum. "Worth it."

Fact is, I love the stretch. That moment my nerve endings start to sing. When my body gives up the fight and *too big* becomes *oh my God, yes please more.*

It's bliss. Even with the recovery time needed afterwards.

"I guess, in comparison, a soda can isn't so bad," Anh says.

I snort. "Not at all. This guy's dick? Damn, Anh. It was just right."

"Okay, Goldi-cocks."

That has me tittering a laugh, but as I run through my interaction with Rowan, a sigh escapes my lips. The man *was* divine, but the truth is it wasn't just his cock. I haven't been able to get Rowan himself out of my head. He was so nervous at first, almost skittish. But once he opened up and started to lose his inhibitions, he was glorious. Like an oil painting brought to life.

He made me feel...fond. So damn fond and horny.

After one final reminiscence, I shove myself up off the couch. "Wanna come out tonight, boo?"

The Elite 8 crew meets up every Friday at a club in town called Sublime. It's a great place to dance, shamelessly ogle half-naked men, and find company for the night. And it's a nice way to cap off the week before spending a couple days decompressing.

Anh's only come with me a couple times. She's not much for the club scene, which I can understand.

I seem to have two main friend groups in my life. There are my boys—my brothers—from work. And then, there's my art crowd. Anh falls firmly in the latter. The pair of us make for an interesting duo, truth be told. We're different in so many ways, but maybe that's precisely why we work. We balance each other out.

"No thanks," Anh says, tugging a book out of her bag. "You go have fun."

"Oh, I will," I singsong, grabbing my things and heading for the door.

"Don't get into trouble," she calls after me.

"I make no promises!"

I mean, really. She should know me better than that.

"Heya, trouble."

"Curls!" I call excitedly, practically tossing myself onto my blonde-haired friend. He *oofs*, catching me before we can go tumbling down. "I haven't seen you in *ages*."

"It's been, like, a week," Mal points out.

Oh, that's right. We had lunch together recently.

"Then you're excused. How's Daddy Henrik?" I ask, slipping onto a nearby couch in our VIP section above the dance floor at Sublime. Mal follows me over, kicking up his long legs.

"He's good." He doesn't even bother correcting me on the whole *daddy* thing anymore. Henrik isn't really Mal's daddy. But the older man did start out as a sugar daddy of sorts to my friend and former coworker. "Probably waiting until I get home so he can re-mark his territory," Mal mutters softly.

My ears perk. "Honey, do tell."

He huffs a laugh. "Not giving you the sordid details, you horndog."

"Ugh." I slump. "You're so mean to me."

He pats my head. "Somehow, I'm sure you'll survive. Where are the guys?"

Without asking, I know who he's referring to. Dixon and Niko. "They're down on the dance floor."

"And you're up here?" Mal asks, eyebrow raised.

"I *was* down there," I say. "But…"

Well, even spending the last hour grinding up on a number of sure things, getting hornier by the minute, I couldn't stop thinking about my most recent hookup. With every invitation out of here, my mind flashed back to Rowan and those big, gentle eyes. I thought about our brief night together and the chats we've had since. And I couldn't do it. I didn't want to fuck any of those other guys.

I want my Grizzly Bear again.

"Oh God," I wail, burying my face in the couch. "I've got a crush."

I don't get attached to my fuck buddies. I don't. I've had boyfriends in the past, sure, but it's been a while. And I've always been able to separate sex and romance, which is a good thing in my profession. Rowan was supposed to stay in the casual zone. And yet, there's a suspicious warmth taking up residence in my chest as I think about the big man and his soft words.

"This wasn't supposed to happen," I tell the cushions.

Mal nudges me until I look his way. "You're gonna have to give me more info, small fry. I have no clue what you're talking about."

I appraise my friend, eyes running over his surfer-boy hair and pretty face. There's almost a glow to him, and it makes my insides all fuzzy, seeing him so healthy again. Healthy and happy.

It wasn't just Henrik's doing, the change in my friend. But Mal's fiancé sure is a big part of what puts that content smile on his face and has his skin looking all sparkly, like he's lit up from the inside.

I'm ecstatic for him. I really, truly am. He deserves the best.

And yet there's a pinch in my gut telling me I'm also jealous. Because I don't know if I'm ever going to find that. I stopped dating because it never seemed to work out. Mal jokes about me being a horndog, but it's the absolute truth. I like sex. A lot. Even more so when it's with someone I'm in a relationship with.

To be needed? To be the reason my partner feels so good? That's a high that goes beyond the physical.

And maybe that's why I can't stop thinking about Rowan. Why I want more of him. Because as soon as I stumbled upon that praise kink button of his, the man lit up. Glowed, the same way Mal does now. It was like a lightbulb turned on, chasing away his shadows and illuminating those beautiful brown eyes of his.

I made him feel good. I did that. I gave him brightness, at least for a little while.

And fuck, I want to do it again. I want to be needed like that again. It felt so good.

"Thanks, Mal," I say, shoving out of my seat to my friend's bewildered stare. "You've helped a bunch."

"What did I do?" he asks.

"Love you, boo!" I call out.

It doesn't take me long to grab a rideshare outside of Sublime. I only had two drinks, but I know better than to drive under any influence. Besides, this frees me up to message Rowan—something I probably should have done before heading his way.

Me: Hey, Grizzly Bear! Feel like company tonight?

I tap my foot as I wait for a reply. Worst-case scenario, I'll have the driver bring me back to the club. Best case, I see Rowan again, and who knows? Maybe I'll drum up the nerve to ask if he wants to see me *outside* of the bedroom. Couldn't hurt to try the whole dating thing again, could it?

The neon lights of Las Vegas are shrinking in the rearview when Rowan replies.

Grizz1330: Right now?

I huff a laugh. The man has probably never gotten a booty call before.

Me: If you're free.

Please be free.

Grizz1330: I'm free.

Relief pulses through me, and my cock—now that it knows action is imminent—starts to plump.

Me: Be there in ten.

I add a kissy emoji and an eggplant for good measure so he knows what to expect, and then I settle back in my seat. Rowan's lights are on when the driver drops me in front of his house, and with a skip in my step, I head for the front door. This time it opens before I even get there.

Like a dream, Rowan stands silhouetted by the light spilling out from inside his house. His big body takes up prominent space in his doorframe, and all over again, his presence simply blows me away in the best way. It's the contrast between his size and his inner marshmallow. He could easily be a threatening guy, at probably six-foot-four with all that mass to throw around, but I'm more than sure Rowan would never use his size advantage to intimidate. Even though I barely know him at all, I know that much.

"Hi," I say a little giddily as I step up onto his porch, my smile stretching wide. Butterflies dance in my stomach as Rowan gives me a shy smile in return.

Oof. Yeah. Crush status confirmed.

"Hey," he replies, holding the door open. I accept the invite, sweeping through and kicking my shoes off, and when Rowan closes the door and turns to me, I step close, hooking my fingers under the waistband of his pants.

He swallows roughly.

"I've been thinking," I say slowly, teasingly, as I pull my hands up to toy with the treasure trail running down the middle of his navel, "that I'd like to blow you."

Rowan swallows again, those puppy eyes of his wide. He nods a little staccato before finding his voice. "Yeah. Okay. Yes, please."

There goes that fluttering in my stomach again. *So damn cute, my grizzly.*

Grinning, I lower myself to the floor of his entryway. Rowan watches, barely moving a muscle, as I unzip his pants and tug them down his legs. His boxers are next, and once he's bare, that big, meaty cock of his bobs right in front of my face. I grab the base of it and give a little hello squeeze, and Rowan bucks into my grip.

"*Alex*," he moans, all breath.

Sliding my palms over his hairy thighs, I drink him in. "I wanna see you, Grizz. Take off your shirt?"

After only a moment's hesitation, he does, pulling the garment over his head and revealing those hairy pecs and that enticingly soft stomach. I have the brief mental image of curling around him in sleep, using his body like a pillow.

I wonder if he'd let me.

"You're gorgeous," I tell him, skating my hands up his legs, closer to his groin. He shivers slightly and shakes his head, but I grip his cock and give it a stroke. "Yes, you are. You're gorgeous to me. Say it."

He blinks several times, seeming at a loss. But finally, he speaks the words, voice uncertain. "I'm gorgeous...to you."

Close enough. "Yes, you are," I say, giving him another stroke.

My name this time sounds like a plea. "*Alex.*"

I know. I've got you, big guy.

Pulling a flavored condom from my pocket, I brandish it. "Strawberry," I tell Rowan, giving him a wink before I tear the packet open with my teeth. I roll it swiftly down his length as he curses. I know it's not quite the same feeling with the rubber in place, but regardless, I lean forward and drag my tongue over the tip of his crown. Rowan groans, his cock jerking in my grasp, and that's all the encouragement I need to wrap my lips around him and suck.

Rowan's knees buckle slightly, and I huff a happy laugh around the girth of him, which makes it happen again. He leans his weight against the front door, and I settle in, swallowing him down greedily. Rowan rewards me with a beautifully tortured moan, and I hum, catching those big brown eyes of his as I bob my head. The look of utter rapture on his face has me grabbing my own crotch and rubbing.

"How—" Rowan cuts off, head tipping back against the door for a moment before he snaps his gaze back my way, like he can't bear to miss a moment. "Is this really happening? I can't believe you're here."

And the way he says it, like maybe it really is *me* he wants, not just any mouth, makes my blood sing hopefully. I redouble my efforts, taking as much of Rowan's massive dick into my mouth as I can, sucking, rubbing him with my tongue, swallowing around his head.

"Alex, I can't... God, I can't..."

Rowan's thighs bunch, his ass flexing beneath my palm, so I pull off, releasing him with a pop.

"Where do you want to unload?" I ask, holding the base of his dick with a firm grip. "My mouth or my ass?"

He makes another of those strangled sounds, nodding rapidly.

Smile on my face, I stroke him once. "Which one, Grizzly Bear?"

"I, uh, um. Ass," he decides, cheeks reddening some.

"Thank fuck," I mutter, giving his crown a parting kiss before I let go and stand up. "Couch?"

Rowan nods rapidly, grabbing his clothes off the floor. He follows me into the living room, and since the drapes are already drawn, I don't hesitate to shuck my own clothes, pausing only long enough to grab supplies out of my pockets. Turning to Rowan, I switch out his flavored condom for a regular, pre-lubed one, and then I open a packet of lube to prep myself.

Climbing on my knees atop of the couch, I stick out my ass and look over my shoulder before sliding two fingers into my body. Rowan watches, his mouth open.

"It'll feel even better once it's you," I tell him, knowing that's the truth.

Rowan swallows, eyes pinging between my ass and face. It must be a pretty sight.

"Stretch me?" I ask, dying to feel those massive hands on my body.

He pauses for only a moment, and then he's closing the distance between us, palm settling beside my knee on the couch as his other drifts over my ass. Without a word, his finger joins my own.

I moan out my approval, pressing back on our combined digits. He glides his other hand up to my chest, flicking my nipple, and my lips part on a gasp.

"Yes, Grizz," I moan. "That's good."

When I'm loosened enough and way too horny for any more foreplay, I remove my fingers, give Rowan's hand a little swat, and brace myself against the back of the couch. Widening my stance, I catch Rowan's eye, nearly melting under the heat of his gaze.

"C'mon, Grizzly Bear," I all but coo. "Fill me up."

Rowan groans, muttering a quiet "*Fuck*," before he steps close. Hand back at my hip, he holds me steady, and then, in one quick motion, he notches against me and slams home.

The breath punches from my lungs, that feeling of fullness overwhelming in its intensity. Tingles race across my skin as I briefly wonder if fate—*destiny*—*is* real. If so, I think it brought me here, to this man. His cock is perfection, the feel of his hands gripping me tight even more so. I'm like a doll between his fingertips, and yet I know I'm the one pulling his strings. I know on an instinctual level that this man would do whatever I asked of him, but all I want is for him to hold me close, just like this.

"Don't go easy on me, Rowan," I plead, wanting to feel it. Wanting the memory of this moment to stay with me for days. He pulls me back harshly to meet his thrusts, and I huff out a sound that's part laugh, part moan. "*Yes*, fuck. So good. That's good, baby."

As words fall from my lips—*perfect, you feel perfect, so big, my strong grizzly*—his hips meet my ass time and time again. The slap of our bodies is loud in the room, and with every glide of his cock, with every grunt or groan that greets my ears, my body coils tighter. Before long, I'm all but wrapped over the back of the couch, my head hanging forward, as Rowan rails me into oblivion.

Now would probably be a bad time to bring up going steady, right?

"Alex, I—"

He's close. So am I.

"Give it to me, love," I breathe out. "Give me everything you've got."

Rowan lets out another one of those beautiful strangled moans before draping his body over mine. With one of his knees on the couch and the other foot braced against the floor, he wraps his arm around my chest and thrusts.

It's *Heaven*, all raspy hair against my back and the warmth from his body heating me through. His beard tickles my ear, and I turn my head so we're breathing in the same oxygen, wishing I could kiss him. Wishing...

"Alex," Rowan rasps, sounding desperate. He wraps a hand over mine on the back of the couch, holding tight as his hips piston, as he drags that thick cock in and out.

"Touch me," I beg.

He does. Without hesitation, his hand leaves my own to wrap around my dick, and I know it's only a matter of time until it's all over. My core blazes, flames licking over every inch of my skin, burning me up, dragging me under.

"Gonna come, Ro," I pant. "You're too good to me. Love that cock. Your hand on my dick. Love the way you—" I gasp as he pegs my prostate brutally. "Right there. Yes. Fuck. *Fuck yes.*"

And I'm screaming so loudly, it's no wonder I don't hear the man inside the room until the volume of his curse rivals Rowan's own exclamation of surprise.

There's a beat of ringing, shocked silence in which time seems to stall. In which I catch the stranger's wide, wild gaze. But my orgasm is already barreling down on me, and I can't do a single thing to stop it.

"*Fuck,*" I moan out, my body shuddering as I unload all over Rowan's fist and the cushion in front of us. Thankfully, the couch is covering me from view. There's a grunt from behind me at the very same moment, and Rowan follows me over the edge, the vise-grip of my ass no doubt having kicked off his own release.

It's only a beat—a few seconds at most—but in the stunningly quiet aftermath, I lift my gaze back to the stranger. His chest is rising and falling. Tattoos peek out over the collar of his shirt and trail down his arms, all the way to his fingertips. His dark reddish hair is shaved at the sides, and the top is spilling down artfully. There's a silver ring at the bottom of his lip. A stud on the inside of his ear. And he's big, like Rowan: equally as tall but a little less husky. He's...

"Oh wow," I breathe aloud. "The elusive Ginger Bear."

The stranger's eyes ping to me for only a moment before they land back over my shoulder—exactly where Rowan is standing. And his gaze, filled with so much longing and *hurt*, takes me by surprise. More so than his appearance in the first place. It makes my breath catch in my lungs because there's no mistaking what I'm seeing on that man's face.

Oh no.

What have I gotten in the middle of?

Chapter 6

FINN

I'd been pacing around my house for an hour, kicking myself over the fact that I chickened out yet again. I had hours over at Rowan's place while we watched the game to ask him out. And I didn't do it.

So after berating myself and working up the courage, I marched back over there. Only, when I knocked, Rowan didn't answer. His light was on, though, so I knew he was home and not asleep. When I heard what sounded like a shout, I didn't even hesitate. I pushed open the unlocked door, heart racing.

And then I stepped into Rowan's living room.

"Right there. Yes. Fuck. *Fuck yes.*"

Rowan was fucking some twink into his couch.

I yelled in surprise. Rowan yelled. The little blonde twink yelled—and *came*.

All the while, I...stood there.

And I'm still standing in Rowan's living room, staring at the two very naked men blinking at me owlishly from behind the partial barrier of the couch back. I open my mouth. Close it. Rip my eyes away from the blonde, who's now cringing.

Walk away. Walk the fuck away.

God, I can't.

"I, uh…" Ro begins, his face flushing.

Shit, I'm making him uncomfortable.

I turn away, scrubbing my hands harshly over my face. "I'm sorry," I croak out. "The door was unlocked, and I forgot something. I didn't mean to see…*that.*"

I didn't even realize *that* was happening. I had no clue Rowan invited company over after I left, let alone that he was even *entertaining* again after Manuel.

Have I missed my chance?

My chest aches, and I practically double over.

There's a whispered conversation behind me, and I know I should go—let my feet walk me right out the door. Except I can't seem to move. I'm cemented to the floor, my determination from earlier not getting the memo that now isn't exactly the time to shoot my shot with my neighbor.

Definitely not the time.

There's some rustling as I stand rooted to the ground, and I assume Rowan and the blonde are getting dressed.

"I should go," the blonde says.

"No, don't," Rowan whispers loudly enough that I can hear. "Stay."

"I think you should talk to your…friend?" There's definite question in the guy's tone.

I can't help it. I look over my shoulder, and Ro, who's now fully dressed and zipping up his pants, nods. "And neighbor."

Blondie looks over at me, the sympathy in his eyes making me uncomfortable—too seen. I look away.

"You should talk with him," he says.

Yes, please.

"I just…" Rowan starts. "Don't go, okay?"

Christ. "Maybe I should go," I speak up.

"No," they both say at once.

"I'm going to grab a towel," the blonde says, and then there's soft footsteps jogging up the stairs.

I glance over my shoulder again. Ro catches my eye before looking down quickly, embarrassed or uncomfortable or, I don't know, maybe just feeling as unbalanced as me.

"I..." Don't know what to say.

Blondie comes back down the stairs, taking one sweeping glance of us before shaking his head and beelining for the couch. He wipes up their mess, and then he points my way.

"You, sit down," he says before aiming his sights on Ro. He tosses him the cloth. "And you. Go wash up."

We're both still for a beat before Rowan walks out of the room, cloth in hand. Somewhat reluctantly, I head to a nearby chair and take a seat. Blondie watches me all the while, and I feel like a scorned school kid under his gaze. He settles on the couch across from me, tucking his legs up beside him.

We're quiet as we wait for Rowan to return, but my eyes keep skipping to the spot on the couch where they were fucking. All evidence is gone, but the memory of it is seared into my brain, playing on a loop inside my head.

I barely even notice when Ro enters my field of vision, but Blondie's clap has me startling to attention.

"Okay." The blonde's eyes are on me. "First things first. Hi, I'm Alex."

"Finn," I reply on autopilot.

He aims a sweet smile my way that disarms me somewhat. "Hi, Finn. Nice to meet you."

"Um."

"Right," he goes on, glancing over at Ro, who's looking down at his lap. Alex returns his focus to me. "So you walked in on us fucking."

I nearly cringe. "Sorry," I say with a sigh. "I honestly didn't mean to."

"Obviously," Alex says, waving me off. "I'm sorry you had to see that."

"I..." I what? I am, too?

Alex's face softens. There's that sympathetic look again. What the hell?

Rowan puffs out a breath, and Alex reaches over, squeezing his thigh and then rubbing there. In comfort, surely, but *fuck*. Just seeing him touch the man I've been trying to woo for the past several months without success is like a knife to my gut.

"You okay?" Alex asks Ro quietly.

Rowan squeezes his hand. "Yeah."

They don't let go of one another.

I must make some sort of noise because Alex's head whips back my way. "Grizzly Bear," he says, presumably talking to Ro, "I think you and your neighbor should have a conversation."

Jesus, how much can this guy see? Is it written all over my face?

If that's the case, why the hell hasn't Rowan noticed? Or has he, and he simply doesn't feel the same?

Another knife to the gut.

Rowan looks at me full-on for the first time since I caught him and Alex together, and I try to give him a reassuring smile, but I'm guessing it falls flat.

"Look, it's fine," I say, pushing to my feet. This isn't the time for declarations or any of that. I'm clearly butting in on a...date? "I'll get going. I shouldn't have interrupted in the first place."

Ro makes some sort of aborted, almost wounded sound as I take a step toward the door, and it's enough to give me pause. In the same beat, Alex huffs, stomping my way and then shoving me back toward my chair. "Men, I swear to God," he mutters. When I plop back into my seat, he dusts off his hands and sits down near Ro.

"You saw us having sex," Alex says again. "Not a big deal." He lifts an eyebrow as if challenging me.

I nod.

"We're all adults here," he goes on. "So if there's anything you want to talk about...something you want to get off your chest, maybe? About what you saw? About how you're feeling?" He eyes me again, and when I don't say anything, he sighs.

Rowan looks lost. "Finn, I'm sorry if we made you uncomfortable. I—"

"What?" I cut in, shaking my head. "No. You didn't. You didn't do anything wrong. I'm the one who stormed in here while you two were...you know." I wave at the couch.

Alex rolls his eyes. "Fucking. You can say the word, boo. It's not like any of us here are blushing virgins." He pauses, peering at me again. "Right?"

Rowan scoffs, mumbling, "He's not a virgin."

I can't help but interject. "How do you know?"

We've never talked explicit details of our relationships before.

Ro simply looks me up and down and says, "Please."

My blood ignites.

Alex raises an eyebrow, smirking at Ro, and despite my mind trying valiantly to stick to what Ro's appraisal meant, something in Alex's expression triggers a memory so strong it's like a bomb goes off inside my head. I stare at him. Stare some more. He finally looks my way, cocking his head.

That sultry smile. The blonde hair. That slender figure and delicate features. Those mischievous hazel eyes.

"Oh, holy shit," I sum up.

I know this guy. I've seen him before. He's...

"You recognize me," Alex says, smile turning to something almost sad.

"Wait, what?" Ro says, looking between us. "How do you recognize him?"

"You're—" I say before cutting myself off. It's not my place to reveal Alex's personal business.

But Alex himself seems to have no such qualms. "Tink," he fills in. "That's right, honeybunch."

"What's going on?" Rowan asks again, looking between us.

Alex turns to him, smiling softly and squeezing his thigh again. "I make adult films," he says simply. "Tink, as in Tinkerbell? 'Cause I'm small, blonde, and feisty? You get the idea."

"I..." Ro blinks a couple times. "Oh, okay."

Alex pats his thigh. There's that sad look again.

"Wait." Rowan's gaze cuts my way. "You've seen his videos?"

"Yes?" I say, not sure why he seems so surprised by that. Plenty of people watch porn, and I'm not ashamed of it.

But what comes out of Ro's mouth next is not what I'm expecting.

"You're bi?" he asks, eyes wide as he leans forward onto his knees.

My mouth drops open. "You didn't *know* that?"

He stares at me. I stare back.

"O-kay," Alex says slowly, clapping his hands together once. "We're finally making some progress here. I'm going to grab some drinks. You two"—he waves between Ro and me—"talk about this."

Alex is out of the room before I can blink, and Ro and I just keep staring at one another. Finally, I get my mouth to cooperate.

"I thought you knew."

Ro shakes his head slowly, leaning back and covering his face with his hands. "I...no, I didn't."

"Is that...a problem?" I ask, not sure what to make of Rowan's reaction.

"What?" he says, dropping his hands. "Of course not. Why would I have a problem with you being bi? You know I'm gay."

"Yeah, but..."

"But what?" he presses.

"I've been trying to get you to notice me for months, Ro," I blurt, so much more ineloquently than I'd ever planned. It's like all of my carefully constructed words have gone up in smoke, and now, there's only the blatant, base truth of it, lobbing its way across the space between us like a sack of stones. "I thought, at the very least, you knew we batted for the same team."

He shakes his head again, eyes wide.

Groaning, I sink further into my chair. This is a disaster. This is all a fucking disaster.

A soft voice breaks through my distressed fog. "Here. Drink."

"Thanks," I mutter, accepting the glass of water Alex hands me and downing the thing in one go.

Alex hands Ro a glass, too, but Ro just sets it aside.

"I didn't know," Rowan says, gaze holding mine, apologetic. "I had no clue."

"Clearly."

Ro had no idea I was flirting with him. It's discouraging to have such solid proof of my utter ineffectuality when it came to wooing my neighbor.

"Is that why you're always coming over here?" he asks, face scrunched up slightly. "'Cause you..." He doesn't seem to know how to say *want me* and just points to himself.

"I mean, that's not the only reason," I say, sitting upright. "I like you, Ro. I like being your friend. I just also..."

Christ. I guess I can't say it either.

Ro opens his mouth, words seeming to pour out. "I've had a crush on you since the day you moved in."

I snap my gaze to his, shocked, elated, and full of hope for the first time since I walked back in here tonight. "You have?"

He swallows roughly. "Yeah. Are you kidding?" He makes a motion toward me like that says it all.

"Why didn't you say anything?" I ask, scooting to the edge of my seat.

Alex, I notice, is sitting aways down the couch from Ro now, watching us with a soft, almost resigned expression. And suddenly, I feel terrible for having this conversation in front of him. I'm the one who barged in here, wrecking his night with Rowan. And now, what? I'm stealing Ro right out from under him?

I open my mouth to backtrack or apologize, or—I honestly don't know, but then Ro starts to speak.

"I was with Manny at first," he says, "even though I knew we were ending. And then, I just... I didn't think, even if you liked men, that you'd ever go for someone like me."

My breath catches in my throat.

I always got the sense Rowan's ex said some pretty terrible things to him. I never had proof, and when I pressed Ro about it, he brushed me off. I don't blame him; at the time, he didn't know me from Adam. But I could see it in the way my neighbor would shrink anytime Manuel was in the room. Rowan's ex was like a wolf in sheep's clothing, and I was more than glad to see him go.

I don't know if Rowan's self-confidence was low before Manuel, but I most certainly am not his ex. And the idea that this beautiful, kind man thinks himself lesser in any way has me out of my seat without a moment's hesitation. I dip down in front of him, crouching low with my hands on his knees.

Ro pulls in a short breath.

"Someone like you?" I question. "What, someone caring and gentle? Someone gorgeous and sexy and real? Someone worthy? How could I not go for a man like that?"

Rowan's chest rises and falls, his big brown eyes blinking rapidly, and beside him, Alex squeezes his hands in front of his chest. My gaze slips his way, guilt over this situation yet again intruding, but Alex gives me a thumbs up, biting his lower lip in a smile.

"I didn't know," Ro says again, softly.

"And now?" I ask, heart stalling as I wait for an answer. "Now that you do?"

"I...I don't know," he nearly whispers, eyes flashing toward Alex.

My gut sinks.

I see.

Backing up, I get to my feet, and Alex looks between us with a bewildered, despondent expression. "No," the blonde man says urgently, flapping his hands. "*You guys.* Kiss."

I huff a pained sort of laugh, not sure if it's Rowan's rejection or this whole situation that's most surreal. That after months, I finally tell my neighbor how I feel, only to find out it's too late. That I didn't get to him in time. That he had no clue how I felt. And now, he likes someone else.

And how can I blame him? Alex is a perfect package—exactly Ro's type if his ex is anything to go by. I get it. It sucks, but I get it.

But Alex was right. We're all adults here, and I can act like one. I'll lick my wounds in private and make sure Ro knows we can still be friends—that I'm not going to drop him just because he doesn't return my feelings.

I nod and take another step back, preparing my retreat. But then there's a tug on my hand, and when I'm spun around, Ro is right in front of me.

"Don't," he says. "Don't run."

And then his lips are on mine.

Chapter 7
ROWAN

I hold Finn in place, my fingers tangled in the hair at the back of his head. His lips are soft—so much softer than I expected.

And the kiss. *Fuck*, this kiss.

It's exhilarating. Intense. And full of a sort of startled hunger that gnaws at me, leaving me wanting more.

Is it Finn's hunger or my own?

All I know is I couldn't let him go. I couldn't let him walk out the door thinking I didn't want him. Who wouldn't want Finn? The man is too good to be true.

But all of this is happening so fast. This confusing heap of a night has me feeling like I'm spinning off my axis. And I'm painfully aware that Alex is sitting nearby, watching me kiss another man.

I pull back from Finn, but I don't yet let go.

"Please don't run," I repeat, squeezing the back of his neck and making sure I don't hide the *want* from my eyes. He deserves to see it. If he's truly been interested in me all this time, he deserves to know I want him, too. "Just give me time to sort through my thoughts."

Because yes—I want Finn. Of course I do.

But also...

"Well, it looks like my job here is done," Alex says, pushing off the couch.

"Alex," I say, my gut hollowing.

"Walk me to the door," he replies, holding up his phone as it pings in his hand. "My ride's here."

Shit. I didn't even realize he'd called one.

Alex steps around me, giving my neighbor a big grin. "So nice to meet you, Finn."

"You, too, Alex," Finn responds, giving me a helpless sort of look that mirrors my own bungled emotions.

I follow Alex to the door, not sure what to say or do. Not sure if I *should* say anything. He slips on his shoes, and then he stands up, hand on the doorknob.

Panic hits, and I reach for him. "Alex, wait. Don't go. I'm sorry. I shouldn't have—"

"Hey," he interjects softly, stepping close. He pats my chest in a way that speaks of affection, not condescension. "It's okay. You did nothing wrong, Grizzly Bear. You know I was encouraging the both of you."

I do. Alex was clearly pushing us together from the moment Finn showed up, but I don't understand *why*. Or how he understood.

"Yeah, but—"

"But nothing. I'm happy for you," he says, his hazel eyes kind, his voice sincere. "He seems like a great guy. Smokin', too."

I huff a laugh. Understatement.

Alex lowers his voice. "I'm glad I met you, Ro. We had a really good time together, didn't we?"

I nod.

"Right," he says, smile faltering ever so briefly as his hand shifts over my chest, the motion akin to a caress. "But we both know that's all we were supposed to be—a good time."

I nod again, even though the sentiment feels like lead in my belly. Heavy and wrong.

"Take care, Grizz," he says, his hand falling away.

"Alex, wait." I'm not ready for this to be the last time I see or hear from the man. "Could we... Could we be friends?"

Alex's face lights up, his smile reaching his eyes. "I'd love that."

He squeezes me around the middle before I can protest, not that I would, and I hug him back, my nose pressed to the top of his head. I subtly inhale his scent. He still smells a little bit like me, and he fits so perfectly in my arms.

When he steps away, I'm not quite ready to let go, but I do. He's almost out the door when he stops one more time and turns around.

"Hey, Rowan?" he says softly. "I don't mean this like a good-bye because now that we're friends, there's no getting rid of me." I chuckle a little wetly at that, and he smirks. "But just so you know... You're lovely."

My heart patters away, his compliment making me slightly short of breath. I nod, swallowing down the lump in my throat. Voice a little hoarse, I tell him, "And you have a beautiful heart, Goldieboi."

He huffs a small laugh, biting his lip. Then he wiggles his fingers, and in a flash, he's gone.

My chest deflates.

"Goldie boy?" Finn asks quietly, stepping up beside me.

I nod, turning to find my...friend? Neighbor? Something more?...watching me, those liquid gold eyes of his assessing calmly. That's Finn. Always calm. Always steadfast.

It helps soothe me some.

"His username," I explain. "We met on an app."

Finn winces slightly. "Ro, I'm so sorry for getting in the middle of you and Alex. It was never my intention. I didn't even know you were seeing someone."

His tone is clearly apologetic, but I shake my head a little, heading back into the living room. Finn follows.

"We weren't seeing each other," I explain. "Not really. We just hooked up. Twice." Three times? "I barely know him."

"Really?" Finn asks, claiming a spot next to me on the couch. He glances briefly at the back cushion, as if remembering what he walked in on earlier tonight, and my face flushes. "You two seemed, I don't know...cozy?"

"I guess so? He was really easy to be around," I admit, thinking of how quickly Alex alleviated my nerves. Something about his confidence and, frankly, shamelessness was calming in its own way.

He made me feel...free.

"Ro," Finn says quietly, garnering my attention. He slips his fingers through his own hair, idly brushing the strands into place, and the ink on the back of his hands stands stark in contrast to his auburn locks. "You seem to like him."

Do I? In a way, of course. How could anyone dislike Alex? He's pure sunshine. If sunshine flirted with the devil. I do like him.

But Alex just made it clear he was after one thing when it came to me—sex. And now, that time has passed.

Thinking of anything further than that is moot.

"He's not looking for a relationship," I say, well aware I'm skirting the real answer.

Finn watches me closely, something he does often, I realize. How did I miss that glint in his eye? How is this man possibly into *me?*

Finn looks the epitome of a badass, if said badass were a computer programmer with flower tattoos. If his hair were shorter, surely it could stand as a mohawk. But as is, the top hangs long, sometimes in front of an eye, sometimes styled neatly back. It's an edgy look that's right on par with the colorful ink covering his skin and the piercings on his face.

But the entire affect is tempered by his gentle, golden brown eyes and the fact that Finn, more often than not, is smiling. You can't watch that man coo to his cat, mist his plants, or hear him talk about his gran without thinking he's anything other than a complete and utter softie.

"Ro," Finn says lightly.

"Sorry," I mutter, snapping back to attention. "What did you ask?"

"I asked if I should head home," he says, eyes creased in concern.

"I don't know," I admit. "I'm all over the place right now." I wave toward my head, and Finn nods, seeming to understand.

"Why don't we table this for now? We can get some rest and tomorrow, after you've had some time to think everything through, we can talk. What do you think?"

I nod, rubbing over my eyes, realizing my lids feel heavy. How late is it? "Yeah, I think that's a good idea. Thank you for, you know...being so understanding about all of this."

"No need to thank me for that," he says, squeezing my thigh.

I gaze down at that hand resting on my leg and take in the *zing* that travels instantly up my body.

Finn lets go, and I swallow roughly. He gets up without a word, heading toward the door.

I feel...scattered. Like everything is slipping through my fingers before I can close my fist. Even though I know Finn isn't leaving me. I'm not *losing* him.

But fuck, it's like time is moving too fast. This whole night has upended what I thought I knew of my current situation. And now, doors are opening that I never imagined would unlock. And others are closing, too far from my grasp to even stop them.

Finn *likes* me. Somehow, he's wanted me for months. I should be thrilled.

And instead, I'm just...spiraling away.

A warm hand cradles my cheek, and Finn's face comes into focus. "Just to be clear," he says softly, the cadence of his deep voice comforting, "I want to date you, Ro. Be boyfriends. All of it. I'd very much like to show you what the two of us could be. I hope you'll give me that chance."

I nod mutely.

"Okay." He plants a gentle kiss to my cheek, and then he's gone.

"Boss. Boss. *Grizlak.*"

"Huh?" I ask.

Pauly gives me a look. "Jesus. Where's your head at? Shop's locked up. You gonna get outta here?"

"I, uh..." I look down at the phone in my hand.

Goldieboi89: You would not BELIEVE the day I had. Glitter everywhere.

Me: Art stuff?

Goldieboi89: You'd think so, but no. Mishap at the studio. It's like sexy disco Armageddon in here.

And then...

Goldieboi89: What do you call a wet bear?
Me: No clue. What?
Goldieboi89: A drizzly bear! *laugh-cry emoji*
Me: You're ridiculous.
Goldieboi89: And you love me for it. Admit it.

My pulse fires. "Finn wants to date me," I blurt, pocketing my phone.

Pauly's eyes widen. "Your neighbor?" he asks.

"Yeah."

"Well dang. That's good, right?" Pauly says, slapping my shoulder. He's a slapper, Pauly.

I nod. I told Pauly about Finn after Manny and I split, so he knows a bit about my neighbor. At the time, Pauly was worried about me being alone, but I said I wasn't. That I had Finn. I guess he picked up a lot from my tone because he's asked me about the man more than once in the past several months.

"Yeah, it's good. I just... I didn't see this coming," I tell my friend. "I had no idea he was even interested in me like that."

"You never do," Pauly says, lips twisting. "So what are you going to do about it?"

"Say yes, I'm pretty sure," I admit.

"What's holding you back?"

I squeeze the phone that's resting inside my big jumpsuit pocket, a certain lithe blonde entering my mind, with his laughing smile and wicked sexiness. I didn't have time to think about what he said while Finn was over—the fact that he makes adult films—but I've thought about it plenty since last night. It explains Alex's—Tink's?—confidence in the bedroom. Why he was so good at reducing me to a puddle with a single word or touch.

It explains all those sweet and dirty things he whispered or moaned my way and how they affected me so. He knows exactly what he's doing. The guy makes people want him for a living. I wasn't anything special.

And he said he doesn't want more. That we were only a good time.

So what's holding me back?

"Nothing, I suppose," I answer.

I've liked Finn for a while, after all. It was lust, at first, when I caught sight of him dragging his belongings into his house for the first time, muscles straining, hair bright in the sun. And then that attraction turned into something much more affectionate as I got to know him better. My crush on the man blossomed once my relationship with Manny was dead and buried, and I only held it back because I didn't think Finn would reciprocate my feelings.

But he does. So it should be a no-brainer.

I can make something solid with Finn if I give us a real chance. He doesn't want casual. He wants us to be *boyfriends*. That was never an option with Alex.

So why does my heart feel like it's being pulled in two directions?

"Let's get out of here," I tell Pauly, tugging my phone free before stripping off my protective jumpsuit and tossing it in the laundry.

He watches me a little oddly, but once I meet him at the door, his smile is back in place. "Have a good night, boss."

With the boss thing again. I shake my head. "Night, Pauly."

The drive back to my house doesn't take long, but my thoughts are thick inside the cab of my truck. I end up rolling down my windows, letting in the arid heat, as if that would help.

I mean to head inside and wash the shop off me before going over to Finn's, but as soon as I park inside my garage, my feet take me one house over. I knock on Finn's door like he does so often to mine, and when he answers, the man's grin has my pulse skyrocketing in a second flat.

"Hey, Ro," he says happily. "Do you want to come in? I made lasagna."

"I, uh, need to wash up," I tell him, waving to myself, although I'm sure Finn can see the remnants of my day on me somewhere. I never can manage to stay clean, even with the jumpsuit on over my clothes. "I just wanted to come over first and say...yes."

God, I can't believe I managed that last part without stammering.

"Yes?" he asks, head tilting adorably, hair flopping to one side.

"Um. To dating you. To giving us a shot."

His grin widens.

Christ, how? How does he want me this much?

Finn steps forward, invading my space on his porch. Even though it's still sunny out, the little fairy lights strung on the underside of his awning are on, giving the front of Finn's home a whimsical feel that fits with the teal exterior and colorfully potted cacti to the sides of the door.

It fits with *him* somehow, as if this place were made for someone as colorful as Finn himself.

"Ro," he says, hands gliding up my arms and sending goosebumps over my skin despite the heat. "I can't tell you how happy that makes me. You're sure? That I'm the one you want?"

I blink in confusion. I thought we already covered this yesterday. That Alex wasn't interested in a relationship. Even if he was, would I—*could* I—pick him over Finn?

"I don't want you to have regrets," he adds softly.

I take a deep breath before slipping my hands around to Finn's lower back. His muscles are strong under my grip, and my insides jumble every which way. "Finn, I want you. I have since I met you. I'm not going to regret this."

He breathes out in relief, although his eyes are still creased somewhat. He opens his mouth, licks his lips, and then shakes his head a little. "Okay," he finally says, voice solid. "In that case, I'd really like to kiss you now. Unless you don't want that."

I shake my head once. Of course I want that.

And Finn, because he understood that shake meant *yes* and not *no*—because he *gets* me—slides one of those large palms up to frame my face. And then he's kissing me.

He tastes like marinara sauce and smells like cinnamon, and his lips against mine short-circuit my brain. I go offline, utterly surrendered to this new yet familiar Finn standing in front of me. The one holding me tight. The one systematically drowning out every single one of my doubts while simultaneously lighting up each square inch of my skin.

The one who, now that he's been given the green light, is claiming my mouth as if he already owns it.

I didn't realize before how much Finn had been holding back around me. Now, his hesitance is gone.

Finn releases me much too soon, and if his little smirk is anything to go by, he knows exactly what I think about that. I don't doubt I look more than a little dazed.

"Go wash up, Ro," he says gently, his thumb brushing my cheek before he lets go. "And then come have lasagna with me."

I nod, but my body doesn't move.

"Go," he repeats with a chuckle. "Otherwise, I'll be dragging you up to your shower myself, and I won't be leaving."

Oh fuck. Oh fuckity fuck.

When I don't immediately respond, way too caught up in entertaining that enticing scenario, Finn cocks his head a little. "Ro?"

I can't find my tongue. *I want that.* Want him. Badly.

Say it.

I chicken out.

"I'll, uh, be right back," I manage, turning to head down the porch stairs.

"Can't wait," he calls after me.

Me neither.

Cripes. Is this real life?

Chapter 8
ALEX

"Ugh," I groan for the millionth time today, dropping my forehead against my arm.

Dixon prods me with his fork. "Are you dying?"

"Think so," I say, rubbing my stomach.

"Wait, really?" he asks. "What's wrong?"

Despite my mopey mood, I smile at the genuine concern in my friend's voice. Bringing my head upright, I find him appraising me with worried eyes.

"I'm fine," I say, taking a breath and puffing it out. I use my fork to poke at my little wilted salad, but then I push it away, not hungry anymore. "I think I'm just having withdrawals."

Dixon's eyelids narrow into slits. "What kind of withdrawals?"

Rolling my eyes, I shove his arm. "Not *that* kind." Dixon is a total mother hen, and I have no doubt he'd have something to say if I were doing drugs. "I lost my new toy, and I'm being melodramatic about it. Shocking, I know."

Although I send an internal apology Ro's way for referring to him as a toy. He's much more than that, of course, despite the man being fully on board with me using his cock like my own, personal, flesh-and-blood dildo.

The reminder sends a little shiver down my spine. I can still recall the feel of him inside me, that fat cock searingly warm, filling me up so good there wasn't room for anything else. He was delightful, my Grizzly Bear. All big, furry, and desperate to please.

I sigh again.

"You? Being dramatic? No," Dixon says deadpan, going back to his lunch now that he knows I'm not really in peril.

The truth is I'll be fine. I may have lost Rowan right on the cusp of finding him, but I don't need a man to complete me. To fuck me? Heck yeah, honey, sign me up. But I'm perfectly happy on my own without a boyfriend. There are plenty of men out there to play with. More the merrier, right?

My gut twinges, and I rub it again.

"Your graduation is next month, isn't it?" Dixon asks, done with his food now.

I nod. "That's right."

I'm not surprised Dixon remembers. He's remarkably attentive, even though he likes to act aloof.

"Good for you," he grumbles almost entirely under his breath.

A slow smile spreads across my face. "Grumpy Bear, is that a compliment?"

He grumbles some more.

"It *is*. You're proud of me," I exclaim happily. "Admit it. Tell me how you're a proud papa."

He crosses his arms and leans back in his chair, his posture completely at odds with what comes out of his mouth next. "It *is* a big deal, Alex. You went after the degree you wanted, and you got it. *Are* getting it. That's admirable." I gape, but Dixon isn't done. "I *am* proud of you for that."

Biting my lip, I throw back my chair.

"God, no," Dixon complains.

"Too late," I cry. Clambering onto my friend's lap, I hug him tight, hiding my face over his shoulder. I refuse to let him see the suspicious moisture in my eyes.

My parents are supportive in their own distanced way, but they don't understand me. Not really. They never got why I switched my degree to Fine Arts, and they weren't on board at first. I think Dixon is the first person to outright say he's proud of me.

I didn't realize how much those words would mean until I heard them.

Squeezing my beast of a friend with all my might, I tell him softly, "Thank you, Papa."

He groans, as I knew he would. "Get off me, you sprite."

"One more minute."

Dixon sighs, wrapping his arms around me in return. And that's precisely how Niko finds us.

The long-haired man stops still, grinning at the sight of his boyfriend caught in a comforting embrace. Without a word, he pulls his phone from his pocket and snaps a pic.

"The fuck was that click?" Dixon asks quietly.

"Nothing," I whisper.

Dixon turns his head, and the moment he catches sight of Niko with his phone out, he flings me from his lap. I cackle as Niko comes over and hugs Dixon from behind.

"I hate you all," Dixon mutters half-heartedly.

"No, you don't," Niko replies, planting a kiss on his cheek.

My phone takes that moment to buzz, and I ditch the rest of my salad before grabbing the device off the table. There's an alert from someone named FinnAgain on the Instagram account I use for Tink. A shock of red hair in the profile pic has me tilting my head in confusion as I pull up the message.

FinnAgain: You're surprisingly easy to find. I hope you don't mind me messaging you out of the blue, but I was hoping we could talk. This is Finn, by the way. Rowan's neighbor.

As if I couldn't tell as much. I click into Finn's profile for a moment, surprised to find a mishmash of orchid and cat pics. *Huh*, that's interesting. As is the fact he messaged at all. I wonder what the man could possibly want to talk to me about. Presumably something regarding Rowan.

Me: Hey, Ginger Bear. I'm all ears.

I mumble a quick goodbye to Dixon and Niko, who are chatting amongst themselves, before heading from the room to get ready for my scene this afternoon. I'm filming with Trevor today, one of my favorite performers to work with simply on the grounds of his truly porn-worthy cock. I'm always left satisfyingly sore after our scenes together.

But thinking about Trevor immediately makes my mind jump to Ro. Because Rowan's cock, although similar in length to Trevor's, is even thicker. And fuck was the stretch amazing.

A size queen? Me? *Noooo*.

My buzzing phone pulls my mind from the gutter.

FinnAgain: Could we talk in person? Maybe meet for lunch when your schedule allows? My treat.

I think over Finn's request as I change in front of my locker, pulling on my outfit for today—skimpy AF nurse's scrubs that barely cover my ass.

In the end, I can't think of a reason *not* to meet with Finn. If the guy is going to be around Rowan a lot—which seems likely based on how I left things—then I should probably get to know him, too. I was serious about being friends with Rowan. I like the sweet man, and even if I can't have him for myself, I want to see more of his shy smiles and maybe help him come out of his shell a little. It only makes sense to be friendly with his potential boyfriend, too.

Not that I'm jealous or anything.

Okay, not much.

Me: Sure. I won't turn down a free meal. Tomorrow?

FinnAgain: That works. Thanks, Alex.

Me: You got it. Now I gotta get to work. Very important business, you see.

I snap a quick selfie of myself in the tall mirror inside the locker room and send it along with my message, grinning like a fool. I can't imagine Finn would mind the half-scandalous pic. The others on Tink's profile are much more revealing.

FinnAgain: My nurses have never looked like you.

I bark a laugh.

Me: No? That's a shame. I have great bedside manner.

I add a wink and an eggplant emoji. Then, finding a stethoscope, I send that, too.

FinnAgain: You're not supposed to give your patients a heart attack, you know.

Me: There, there. Nurse Tink will make it better.

FinnAgain: I have no doubt.

I snort.

Me: Ooh, is that an invitation? Need a little mouth-to-mouth resuscitation?

Really, though. The man is making it all too easy to tease.

Setting my phone aside, I quickly brush my teeth at the sink. The door opens behind me while I'm at it, and I see my partner for the afternoon walk in. Trevor gives me a little nod in the mirror before stripping down and stepping into a shower stall.

FinnAgain: You're trouble, aren't you? I can see why Rowan likes you.

That gives me pause.

Me: What do you mean?

FinnAgain: He needs a little levity in his life. The man bears the weight of the world on his shoulders, and he doesn't understand that he doesn't have to.

I don't know Rowan well, that's true, but that does sound like him. Serious and responsible.

I'm glad, based on the tone of Finn's messages, that he doesn't seem to have a problem with me bringing that levity to Rowan's life. With *staying* in Ro's life. I don't know many men who wouldn't be at least a little jealous of an ex-lover hanging around the guy they're interested in. I expected to have to reassure Finn that I wouldn't go anywhere near Rowan again *like that*—that I wouldn't make a play at him now that he's taken. And honestly, I wouldn't have minded having to do so. I'm glad for the two of them. I am. It's obvious they have a connection already.

But now, I'm wondering if Finn isn't the type of person to feel threatened by another man in his territory. If, maybe, we could all be friends.

FinnAgain: I don't mean to keep you. I'll text you about lunch. Have fun in your scene.

Me: Later, Ging.

I'm pensive as I finish getting ready for my shoot, which doesn't take long. I washed up when I first got to work, so a visit to Raylin is all I need to look fresh-faced for the camera. Shortly after, my scene with Trevor, aka Bruiser here on set, goes off without a hitch. He fucks me over an examination table, and it's hard and punishing, and I come like a geyser.

But for the first time in a very long time, while my scene partner is inside me, my mind is stuck somewhere else.

Finn and I meet the next day at a little deli that has fresh-made fountain soda and sandwiches the size of clubs. As soon as we sit down and I dig into my meal, I groan appreciatively.

"Fuck," I moan around my bite. "I love me some carbs."

Finn watches me curiously, unwrapping his own sandwich. "Sounds like it."

I chuckle around my mouthful of food.

"Are you always this ravenous?" he asks, taking a much more subdued bite of his own lunch.

"On off days, yeah. I have to be careful about how I eat," I admit.

Finn doesn't look particularly happy to hear that. "Why?"

I gulp down some fizzy lemon-and-lavender-flavored soda before answering him. "For a couple reasons. For one, you do *not* want to go into a scene bloated. It doesn't look or feel good. Believe me. And for another, I have to stay regular. It's kind of part of the job description."

Finn thinks that over for a minute, his beautifully golden eyes narrowed shrewdly as he chews. He really does have fantastic features. All the copper coloring is striking.

"Because you're a professional bottom?" he finally asks.

Ding ding.

I throw an exaggerated wink his way. "You got it."

He nods, although his mouth is downturned a bit. "Sucks that you can't eat whatever you want."

I shrug. I'm used to it, and it's not like I'm dieting with the intent to lose weight. It's just part of my regimen.

"What's it like?" he asks.

"What?" I mumble around my food.

"You know," he says, waving a hand slightly. "Your job."

Ah. "You mean having sex for money?"

"Well, yeah," he answers, cool as a cucumber.

Frankly, it's refreshing that he even wants to know. Generally speaking, the people I meet who know me as Tink never ask questions. They dance around me, like they don't want to know anything real. Anything of substance. Like they don't want to imagine me as an actual person with thoughts and feelings and aspirations of my own that don't include being plowed into the nearest semi-hard surface.

And it's fine. I get it.

But it's nice to talk to someone who's not uncomfortable discussing the ins and outs of what I do. The *why* of it.

"People don't usually ask," I tell him.

"I didn't mean to—"

"No, it's fine. I'm glad you did," I cut in, not wanting Finn to mistake my comment for reprimand. "I don't mind talking about it, actually. I like sex. I like it a lot."

"Most people do," he says with a little smirk before wrapping his lips around the straw in his drink.

I quickly pull my gaze. "Sure, plenty of people do," I agree with a chuckle. "I just mean... For me, it's the perfect job. I get to do something I love. But...it *is* a job, you know? I'm putting on a show, always. I'm happy to do it. It's a lot of fun."

"But?" he asks.

"Yes, there are a lot of butts," I say emphatically. "I love those, too."

He huffs a laugh, shaking his head. "No, I mean it sounded like there was a 'but' in there."

I poke at the pickle sitting beside the remnants of my sandwich. "No buts," I answer. "I love my job."

He looks at me a little dubiously before nailing the problem on the head. "And when you date? Is it a problem?"

I blow out a breath before snapping half the pickle off in my mouth and chewing.

"Yikes," Finn mutters, visibly moving one hand to cover his junk. "Remind me never to piss you off."

My eyebrow wings up, and I lean forward, a grin on my face. "I didn't realize my mouth around your cock was a possibility, Ging."

He bites his lip, shaking his head good-naturedly. "Not what I meant."

"Fine," I say with an exaggerated sigh, my insides fizzing happily when Finn chuckles. The feeling falls a little flat when I think back to what he originally wanted to know. "To answer your question, I don't date much anymore."

"Hm," he says.

"Hm?" I ask. "What's 'hm?'"

Finn is watching me with something heavy in his gaze, and it nearly makes me squirm. Why is he looking at me like that—like he's trying to pick me apart?

For that matter, why did he invite me here? We haven't talked about that yet. Except... If Finn is here to talk about Rowan, maybe this all circles back to him?

Like a slap, it hits me. "You're wondering about me and Rowan, aren't you?" I ask. He tilts his head a little, and my indignation rises. "It's not some game to me, fucking around with guys, okay? Yeah, I work in porn, and yeah, I have a lot of sex outside of that. But I treat my partners with respect. Always. Even if it's only for one night."

"Alex, that's not what—" Finn cuts off, brushing his hair back from his face. The motion causes it to cascade to one side like a waterfall of burnt leaves. "I'm not judging you, and I'm not concerned about what it was you and Rowan got up to."

My ire dissipates. "Oh. Then what...?"

Finn plops his elbows onto the table, leaning forward and cutting straight to the heart of me with his fiery gaze. "Do you not date because that's the way you want it—or because you don't have a choice?"

Chapter 9
Finn

Alex looks like an anime character, all big, bright eyes in his boyish face and hair flopping every which way. He blinks at me owlishly.

"I..."

His non-answer is answer enough. Rowan was wrong—it's not that Alex doesn't *want* a relationship. It's that being a porn star makes it difficult for him.

Acid burns through my gut at the thought of this lively creature being rejected, even casually, by the men he pursues. It's not like I even know Alex. I don't. Not at all. But even I can see the fragility hiding behind those smart hazel eyes.

The man wants to be loved.

Damn it.

My internal debate lasts only a moment. No matter which way I spin it, there's only one right thing to do.

If Alex wasn't looking for more in his life right now, I would simply apologize for what went down the night I barged in on him and Ro. I still feel badly about my intrusion, and it would be easy to use that as an excuse for why I called him here today.

But it's not the whole truth.

The truth is that I could see something on Alex's face that night. He covered it well enough, masking his feelings with a smile, even while he was walking out the door. But his disappointment and resignation were palpable.

And Ro... Well, Ro had near hearts in his eyes every time he glanced Alex's way. There was definitely something there... Before I unintentionally tromped through the middle of it.

I've wanted Ro for a while now. That's true. But I never wanted to hurt anyone in the process of getting him. And I'm fairly certain I did just that. I hurt both these men.

But maybe there's a way we all win.

"Alex, look," I say, laying my hand tentatively on his arm. He doesn't move or flinch, so I give him a squeeze. "I'm going to ask you a question, and all I request in return is that you're honest with me. I won't be upset at whatever answer you give."

"Okay?" he says tentatively.

I ease out a breath, taking my hand off his arm. "Are you interested in Rowan?"

Alex opens his mouth, as if ready to instinctively deny any such thing. But then he seems to reconsider, holding my gaze for a long moment. "I do like him."

I nod, dropping my head slightly, and Alex rushes to assure me.

"That doesn't mean I'm going to act on it, Finn. I wouldn't ever—"

I shake my head. "It's okay, really."

Alex looks dubious, and I understand the confusion. Here I am telling him I don't have a problem with him lusting after my boyfriend.

But the truth is... I don't.

"Ro and I are dating now," I make clear, and Alex nods. "But...I don't have a problem with you pursuing him, too."

Alex's mouth pops open slightly. Honestly, it's strangely satisfying to have shocked a porn star.

"What?" he asks.

"If you want *more* with Rowan, I think you should tell him," I clarify.

Alex shakes his head, almost like a shiver. "Why...why would you encourage me to do that? Why would you be okay with it? For Rowan?"

"For him," I admit. "For me. And for you."

"I don't understand," Alex says, and I can't blame him.

I sit back in my seat, running my hands through my hair and then holding onto the back of my neck. "So much of my life has been a competition. My parents were always pushing me and my siblings to be the best. To come out on top. There was an immense amount of pressure to never mess up, to have perfect grades, to go to the best colleges and graduate top of our class, to join the family business. We're lawyers," I explain, twisting my lips and sitting forward. "I hated it, Alex. I hated all of it, but I went along with what they wanted because it was what I was supposed to do."

"I get that," he says softly. "The weight of parental expectations. So what changed?"

I huff a laugh, smiling a little. "My gran smacked me upside the head and told me life was too damn short to do what I'm supposed to. She told me to live. And fuck, I did."

I left my lackey position at my parents' company. Switched my degree after my freshman year of college. Moved away. Inked my skin like I always wanted to and learned who *I* was for once. I changed the entire course of my life, all because my gran knocked some sense into me. The only thing I regret is not keeping better tabs on her while I was gone.

"My point is," I say, "I know what it feels like to be crammed into a shape that never fits your skin. I don't know how you feel about polyamory, but for me, I don't believe monogamy is a requisite for a healthy relationship." It sure never made my parents happy. "Forcing Rowan to commit to only me isn't going to make us last. You can't..." I wave my hand in the air, trying to come up with words. "You can't trap a heart and expect it to have room to fly. But trusting Rowan—being open and honest and communicating our needs—will give us a fighting chance. It doesn't have to be a competition, Alex."

He blows out a breath, kicking one leg over the other and looking out the window of the deli for a moment.

I know I need to give him some time to think, but I add one more thing.

"I'm going to tell Rowan the same thing the next time I see him, but if you and he want to make a go at it, I won't stand in your way. I just ask that you respect our relationship, too."

Alex meets my gaze, nodding once.

It's almost six o'clock when I finally shut down my computer for the day, not having accomplished much after my lunch with Alex. I had too much on my mind, mulling over what I want to say to Ro. I have no clue if he'll be on board with a poly arrangement. If not, I won't push it, of course. I simply want to give him the option.

There's a part of me that wonders if I'm being foolish. I finally have Rowan all to myself, and what am I going to do? Invite another man in.

But I meant what I said to Alex. I'm sick of competitions and doing what I'm supposed to. That never made me happy. Ro has become the brightest point of light in my life. Ever since I moved in and met that beautiful man next door, *he's* made me happy. I want to do the same for him.

I want him to have everything he deserves.

As I'm filling Mo's food dish, Rowan's lights come on. *Here we go.* I give my loudly purring cat a rub, and then I check my reflection in the microwave, finger-brushing my hair into place and running my hands over my stubble to make sure it's not too overgrown. Half a minute later, I'm standing in front of Ro's front door, knocking gently. He opens it quickly thereafter, and I come face to face with that shy smile and those gorgeous, brown eyes of his.

My chest swells like a balloon.

"Hey," Ro says warmly.

"Hey yourself," I reply, stepping in close and winding my arms around his midsection. I'm still not quite used to the fact that I *can* do this now. Rowan, I notice, is still in his work uniform, and he smells like motor oil and man. I run my finger over a smudge on his cheek. "Can I kiss you?"

He bites his lip, an entirely unconscious gesture that draws my gaze nonetheless. "You don't have to ask anymore, Finn."

Pulling in a breath of oil-tinted air, I lean forward, slotting my lips to Ro's. He makes this soft sound—so very delicate and wanting—as he goes pliant against me, and my insides light up. I've dreamed of moments like this.

"Finn," he says softly, lips brushing mine as he speaks.

"Mm?" I answer, tilting his head back and sweeping my tongue inside his mouth.

He answers a little breathlessly. "I'm getting you dirty."

"Mm."

He gasps as I draw his lip into my mouth and bite lightly. "I should...should shower," he says when I let him go.

"Mhm," I rumble, that imagery sending my mind haywire. Ro wet and dripping. Ro stark naked. Ro's body covered in soapy bubbles and my own two hands.

Regardless of how that picture makes my cock plump, I take a step back, not wanting to push Ro before he's ready. He blinks as I give him some space, lips parted slightly, as if he's coming out of a daze. For someone who outwardly looks so rough and gruff, Ro really is quite the opposite. It's times like this when that becomes more apparent than ever.

"Go shower, Ro," I tell him softly, running my fingers over his beard. "I'll be here when you're done."

And then we can talk about this whole poly thing.

"I, um, yeah," he responds, turning slowly with a look of...defeat on his face?

Wait, what?

"Hey," I say, halting him with a gentle hand on the arm. "What's wrong?"

He opens his mouth, not saying anything but slanting his eyes toward the stairs, and it hits me.

"Ro," I say gently, sliding my hand to the side of his neck. I run my thumb over the pulse point there, feeling his heartbeat. "Do you want me to come upstairs with you?"

He exhales in relief, eyes dipping closed and shoulders dropping. "Yes. Please."

Aw, fuck, baby.

I'd been trying to let Ro set the pace between us, afraid I'd come on too strong if I did or said all the things I've been wanting to. Because *hell*, there is a *lot* I want to do. Things I've been aching to do for months now. But clearly, holding back was a mistake.

I'm not sure if Ro's insecurity to voice his own needs has anything to do with Manuel, but I don't want Ro, even for one second, to think I don't want him *always*.

"I'd love nothing more," I tell him sincerely, squeezing the back of his neck. "I hope you have a big shower." We're two big men, after all.

Rowan huffs a laugh, nodding slightly and looking infinitely lighter than he did a moment ago. He holds out his hand, and I grab on.

As I follow Ro up the stairs palm in palm, my steps feel weighted. Slow, almost. Like my brain is cataloging the moment as something of importance and slowing it down for careful and concise filing. His bathroom is to the left at the top of the landing, across the hall from a sparsely outfitted spare room, and his master bedroom is to the right. Ro leads me straight to the bathroom, flicking on the light once he's through the door. Then, he turns toward me, his gaze down. Cautious, still.

"Did you know," I say, bringing us toe to toe and sliding my hands over Ro's hips, "that the first time I laid eyes on you, I had a visceral urge to tear off your shirt?"

"Really?" he asks in clear surprise.

"Mhm," I say with a nod, drifting my fingers up to the buttons on his work shirt. I flick the top one open. "I thought, 'Hot damn. That is a man I'd love nothing more than to get naked and sweaty with.'"

Ro's eyes drop to my lips as I free another button. His mouth is parted gently, chest rising and falling.

"And then, the more I got to know you, the more that urge intensified," I admit. "But also changed. I wanted to do a lot more than get naked and sweaty with you."

"Like what?" he asks, his voice a little ragged.

I unbutton the rest of his shirt, a little smile tugging at my lips, the same way something tugs deep within my ribcage. "I wanted to hold you. And know you." Ro's eyes flash, once again, in surprise at that admission. "I wanted to fuck you senseless. And then wrap you in my arms until morning."

"Finn," he says, not protesting in the least when I pull his shirt down his shoulders and off of his arms, leaving his hairy chest on display. In fact, he barely seems aware of it with the way his entire focus is trained on my mouth, as if he's reading the words directly from my lips. As if he needs the confirmation that they're real and not inside his own head.

"I don't know what all that man said to you," I voice, knowing he'll know exactly who I'm talking about. I have to swallow down the lump in my throat before going on. "But he was *wrong*. You are wanted. Just as you are. For just who you are. Understand?"

Ro nods, his eyes finally lifting enough to catch my gaze. There's a little moisture there. A little bit of disbelief. But also hope. And fuck, I want to feed that hope until it grows wings. Until it can stand on its own.

Dropping into a crouch, I hold Ro's gaze as I open his pants. As I pull them down his legs. As I remove every last piece of his clothing until he's bare in front of me. His cock is half-hard, a weighty presence between his legs, and I finally drag my eyes away from Rowan's own to take in its impressive girth.

"Fuck, baby," I mutter, my breath ghosting over his crown. He shivers, hardening further. "You are such a gift."

"Finn," he says again, almost a plea.

Pushing upright, I lean into the shower stall to turn on the water. "Hop in, Ro," I tell my man.

He does as I ask, waiting until the water is hot enough before slipping under the spray. As soon as the last of my clothing hits the floor, I follow.

Ro's eyes roam over me greedily, *freely* for maybe the first time. At least, it's the first time I've felt the weight of his stare. It travels over me hotly, from my shoulders and chest to the ink wrapping down my arms. My stomach, lower still to my cock.

It stops there, his gaze, and Rowan chokes out a gasp. His eyes fly to my face before returning to my erection, and then he ducks his head, as if trying to get a better view. With a chuckle, I grab my shaft and angle it flat against my body so Ro can see the underside.

"You're...pierced," he ekes out, one of his hands reaching forward and stalling. "Christ, Finn. How many are there?"

"Five," I answer, tapping my finger against the small metal ball at my slit and then the one that sits at the base of my crown. "This is one piercing. A Prince Albert. And these"—I trace the four horizontal barbells that run down my shaft—"are a Jacob's Ladder."

"Fuck," he says. "Did that hurt?"

I shrug. "Wasn't pleasant."

"I..." Rowan's fingers twitch at his side. His gaze is hungry, and yet, he's still hesitating.

"You can touch me anytime you want," I say softly, stepping close. "I will always want your hands on me, Ro."

He shudders, exhaling as he reaches forward and wraps his fist around my length. He pumps me, his thumb traveling along my ladder piercings. I'm hit with a blast of euphoria so strong, it's a wonder I stay on my feet.

"What does it feel like?" he rasps.

"Sensitive," I answer, puffing out a breath as I drop my face to Rowan's shoulder. I nip him there, tasting the subtle sweat on his skin that hasn't yet been washed away.

"And for...for your partners?" he asks.

Lifting my head, I can't help but smirk a bit as I catch Rowan's gaze. "For you? Hopefully good." He swallows, and I lean forward, catching his lip and sucking it. "Let me show you?"

He nods in a little jerk, and insides thrilling, I press Rowan until his back is against the shower wall. The stream of water cascades down our sides as I wrap the two of us in my fist. Rowan inhales sharply as I give our trapped erections a pump, his hand coming around my bicep like a vise. On the first pass of my fist down our lengths, his breath stutters. And when I add in a thrust of my cock against the underside of his own, his head thunks against the wall.

I can't tear my eyes away from Rowan's expression as I jerk us together, rutting against him in tandem with the movements of my hand. His eyes are closed, but I don't mind. The look on his face, the utter rapture, is worth every single day I've spent moving toward this moment. Making Ro feel good, making him feel like *that*, is what I've wanted for so very long.

Rowan's cock is like granite in my hand, hard and ready to blow. I have no doubt there will be many moments to savor this man. Countless instances where I can show him exactly how I feel by taking him apart piece by piece, slowly and methodically. But this isn't one of those moments. It's fast, and it's urgent, and when Rowan's eyes open and his head tips toward mine, I wrap a second fist around us and latch my mouth to his. Ro tenses, his fingers digging into my arm almost painfully as he stutters out a choked moan against my lips. His dick pulses, so impossibly big against my own, and then he's spilling over my fist in forceful, jerking spurts.

My own orgasm is already barreling down on me, but when Rowan slips his hands to my ass, urging me against him, I lose it. My release flashes through me like lightning, searing and hot, and I shudder as I unload between our bodies, my mouth pressed tightly to Ro's. My entire body tingles in the aftermath—my lips, my balls, my toes even—and I give Ro one final lingering kiss before easing back.

The moment I let our dicks go, Rowan's arms come around me like a band. Much to my surprise, he kisses my cheek and then tucks his face over my shoulder. I welcome the embrace, slipping my arms behind him, too, insides melting as we lean together against the shower wall.

"Okay?" I ask gently.

He nods. "Yeah. That was, uh…"

Something big. A shift between us at long last.

"Yeah," I agree, closing my eyes as the steam from the shower swirls around us like mist. Pulling back a fraction, I catch Rowan's gaze. "Hungry?"

He nods.

"How about we finish washing up and then have some dinner?" I suggest. "And after that… Well, I'd really like to spend the night, Ro, if that's something you'd be comfortable with."

"Yeah?" he asks, a smile blossoming on his face. "I'd like that."

"Good," I reply, stepping back and giving his ass a gentle slap before grabbing Rowan's body soap. "I hope you have a big bed, too."

Rowan chuckles, and I make a promise right then and there to do everything in my power to hear that sound as often as possible.

Chapter 10
ROWAN

It's been a while since I've spent the night with someone. But unlike Manuel, Finn slides right up against me as soon as we're beneath the covers. Chest pressed to my side, he wraps his arm around me without a single word, and I barely breathe, too afraid to shatter the moment.

"I hope you're a cuddler," Finn says, kissing my shoulder.

A nod is all I can manage. I am now.

When my body finally releases its tension, I tuck my arm over his, liking the feel of his coarse arm hair underneath my fingertips. I trace the ink on his skin lightly, and Finn seems to enjoy it, judging by the soft hum that comes from his lips.

"There's something I wanted to talk to you about," Finn says after a moment.

I turn my head, and he leans back slightly so we can see each other more clearly. "Okay?"

Finn's lips press together, as if he's trying to figure out what to say. Or how to say it. I'm about to go into panic mode when he gives me a little smile that instantly sets me at ease.

"Have you ever been in a poly relationship?" he asks.

"I...no," I answer, not having expected that question at all.

"I haven't either," he says, "but I've suspected for a long time that I'm poly."

I have no clue what to say to that. Is Finn telling me he wants an open relationship?

"I think..." he begins carefully, his words slow and measured, "people have a great capacity to love. Monogamy is the norm in our society. And there's nothing wrong with it. But I think there's more than one way to commit to someone. To love them."

My mind skips over the L-word, positive Finn is speaking in general terms. But the rest gives me pause.

"Are you... Are you telling me you want multiple partners?" I ask.

"No. Not at all, actually," Finn says. "Right now, there's only you, and I would be perfectly happy being with *only you*, Ro. I don't *need* more partners. What I'm trying to say is that it's a concept I'm open to. So..." He blows out a breath and gives my shoulder another quick kiss. "If there's another person you're interested in romantically, a certain *blonde* maybe, I would be okay with you dating him, too."

My mind reels. "You want me to date Alex?"

Finn huffs a tiny laugh. "I'm saying if you want to date Alex, you have my support. But if you want to keep our relationship between only the two of us, I support that, too."

Finn runs his fingers along my chest as my shock renders me silent. My first thought—my very first reaction—is one of hope. And immediately on its heels comes immense guilt. I shouldn't want anyone but Finn, should I? He picked me. He wants me. And I want him, too.

But Finn is telling me he could be in a poly relationship. He's saying that if I want *others*—want Alex—that would be okay.

What do I do with that?

I've never, not once, considered having more than one partner in my life. Never thought of a future with multiple men. Is that something I'd want?

"Ro," Finn says quietly, his fingers at my chin. I turn my head to take him in. His eyes look like burnished gold in the low light of the lamp, and the little ring in his lip shines, bringing to mind the way the metal felt against my mouth when Finn kissed me. "I like you. A *lot*. I need you to know that. I have plans when it comes to you and me."

That admission helps settle me. Warms me, even, to know Finn is already thinking of our future together. Why I caught this man's eye, I'll never know, but I won't lie and say I don't think of those things, too. What a future could look like with him.

So how would Alex play into that?

"I think we could have something pretty great," Finn goes on, his voice quiet. He looks so handsome lying there in my sheets, his expression open and sincere, that my heart kicks. "I think we could have that regardless of whether we're two...or something more. Just think about it, okay? It's entirely up to you. I'll be happy either way."

And, somehow, I believe him. I believe what he's telling me is the truth.

But what do *I* want? And does it even matter if it's not what Alex wants, too?

"Should we get some sleep now?" Finn asks.

I nod, and Finn shifts, practically straddling my body to turn off the lamp on my side of the bed. When he resettles, he's even closer than he was before. Lying on his side, Finn is a solid presence against me, his arm thrown over my chest, his leg wrapped around my own. And even though I'm positive I won't get any rest with the thoughts running circuits inside my head, with Finn's steady breathing beside me, with him holding me tight, my mind goes quiet, and sleep comes for me swiftly.

Goldieboi89: Hey, Grizzles. Wanna go dancing tonight?

I stare at Alex's message, my insides flopping around like a fish.

Do I want to go dancing? No, not really. I don't need that embarrassment in my life. But I do want to see Alex again. I haven't seen him in person since *that night*. And ever since Finn brought up the possibility of being poly, I haven't been able to get the bubbly blonde out of my head.

I've been thinking. Wondering.

Wishing, just a little.

I feel guilty even contemplating the proposal. I mean, Christ, could I actually date two guys? It sounds so outlandish. But Finn is the one who suggested the idea in the first place, so realistically, I know my guilt is misplaced.

And then there's the question of *why*. Why does Finn want me to consider this? What does he get out of it?

Why is he so damn...perfect?

None of it matters, though, if Alex doesn't want to date *me*. And that's the rub. That's why I've been working up the courage to see him again. I have to know if what I thought I was feeling toward the man is still there, and I have to know whether or not he could possibly feel the same.

He said we were a good time. But maybe, *maybe*, if I asked him outright, he might say yes. Could I be that brave?

Definitely not while dancing. Besides, it's Friday. And Friday is baseball night with Finn.

It's five o'clock when I finally wipe my grease-stained hands off on a rag and pull my phone back out of my pocket. I don't open my text thread to Alex, though. I message Finn.

Me: How would you feel about extra company tonight?

Before I've had a chance to put my phone away, Finn is calling. Butterflies rush through my stomach at simply seeing his name on my screen, and for a moment, I marvel at how, even from afar, the man can make me feel so good.

I accept Finn's call, walking off to a quieter area of the service bay. "Hey."

"Hey, Ro," he responds warmly. "You want to have people over tonight?"

"Just one," I say, my nerves suddenly igniting. Finn said he was good with me and Alex being friends *or* more, but how would it work with all of us spending time together? "I was, uh, thinking about inviting Alex over."

"Oh, sure," he says easily.

"Yeah? That'd be okay with you?"

"Ro," he says with a little huff that sounds like laughter. "Yes, that'd be fine. You don't need my permission to invite people over."

"Yeah, but..."

"Even Alex," he adds, sensing my concern.

"Okay," I say on an exhale.

"Okay then. Pizza tonight?" he asks.

"Yeah, that'd be great. See you soon."

Finn makes a noise of happy agreement before ending the call. When I slip my phone back in my pocket and turn around, Pauly is there. He bounces his eyebrows at me. "That your man?"

I open my mouth to say yes, but then it hits me—how would I even explain it to people, if I were dating more than one man?

Before I can get my mouth in working order to answer Pauly's question, Aaron comes bounding up. His hair is held back with a bandana, and he's sporting a smile. "Hey, boss. What's your favorite fruit?"

My favorite fruit?

"Pineapple," I answer. "Why?"

"No reason," he says, turning and jogging away just as succinctly as he arrived.

I look over at Pauly, who only shrugs. "No idea. But hey, listen. I'm happy for you, okay? You deserve a good boyfriend."

I catch his unspoken words. *Unlike Manuel.*

But do I deserve two boyfriends? That isn't a question I ever thought I'd be asking myself.

"Thanks, Pauly. Have a good night," I tell my friend.

"You, too," he replies, boxing me on the shoulder.

Once Pauly heads off, I grab my phone to message Alex.

Me: How would you feel about baseball instead?

Goldieboi89: Like...playing it? I'm good with balls, but I dunno...

A laugh hits the back of my throat.

Me: Not playing. Finn and I are watching a game tonight. Want to come over?

His response takes a minute.

Goldieboi89: Do I need to be in uniform?

My eyebrows pop up.

Me: Do you have a uniform?

Goldieboi89: There's one somewhere around here. It's a little short, though.

Short? On Alex? What is it, a kid's size?

Me: No uniform required. Just yourself.

Goldieboi89: That, I can always bring. What time does sportsball start?

Chuckling, and with a little nervous energy strumming through my veins, I text Alex the info for tonight. He responds with a thumbs up emoji, a baseball, and...a net?

It isn't long before I'm closing up shop and heading home. Finn is already inside when I arrive, having made good use of the key I slipped into his pocket yesterday, and the instant I step through the door from the garage to the kitchen, he's there, swooping in to claim my lips.

I sink against the cupboard, my cock plumping as he clasps the back of my neck tight and shifts his knee between my own, bringing us flush together.

He's so *affectionate*. So demonstrative in a way I'm entirely unused to. Will I ever get used to it? I hope not. I hope it's always this thrilling. This comforting.

"Welcome home," he says against my lips, sending a frisson of want through me so strong I nearly lose my footing.

Home.

As if that's a place we belong together. As if that place is *him*.

"Fuck, I want that," I mutter. *Aloud.*

Finn cocks his head, an amused smile playing on his lips. He misconstrues my statement, however, glancing down at where our crotches are snugged together. Where the hard evidence of his arousal is pressed pointedly to my hip.

"You want that?" he asks, voice all low and raspy.

My brain blips.

I want that, too.

"Alex is coming over," I say quickly, knowing if I don't put a stop to this, Finn and I are going to end up naked in the kitchen. Quite possibly with me finding out exactly how those piercings along his dick would feel inside of me.

I've never done that before. With anyone. Regardless of how much I've wanted it.

Finn breathes out, brushing his hands down my chest. But he doesn't look upset. Instead, he smacks a kiss against my lips before backing up. "Pizza should be here soon."

I nod, pushing off the cupboard and heading for the stairs on wobbly legs. After washing quickly, I get dressed in clean clothes and head back downstairs. Finn is in the living room when I get there, and he flashes me a smile just as there's a knock at the door. Diverting that way, I puff out a breath and relax my shoulders.

It's merely Alex. The man I had a two-night stand with. The guy who sends me cute animal videos and corny jokes and random messages twenty times a day. Nothing to worry about.

When I pull open the door, I'm promptly smacked in the face with the reality that there's *everything* to worry about. The man is beaming at me in all his tiny glory, wearing the shortest pair of athletic shorts I've ever seen and a mesh, see-through jersey.

I promptly choke on my own spit.

"All right?" Alex asks in concern, stepping forward and patting my back as I cough.

I nod, waving him in. "Uh, yeah. Fine."

"I couldn't find the baseball uniform," he says, "so I had to make do." He sets down the bag in his hand before toeing off his shoes.

"Yeah, um. You look nice," I manage.

"Thanks," he says brightly. The grin on his face hits me over the head like a sledgehammer.

I absolutely still want this man.

Swallowing, I pick up the bag he brought. "What's all this?"

"Oh! Hot dogs and champagne," he says. "I figured I'd bring a little bit of the club to baseball night."

Alex smiles as he says this, but my stomach plummets. *Shit.* I didn't even think about my invite wrecking his plans. Would he rather be out dancing?

"Alex, I'm sorry," I say. "I didn't mean to take you away from your night."

He waves me off.

"No, really. If you'd rather go dancing—"

"Grizz," he interjects, patting my chest once to get my attention. His eyebrow is raised, and the look on his face has me snapping my mouth shut. "One thing you should know about me is that I never do anything I don't want to do. I wouldn't be here if I didn't want to be, okay?"

I nod.

"And secondly,"—he gives me another pat—"when a boy offers you his hot dog, you smile and say thank you."

I huff a laugh, and Alex winks.

"Thanks, Alex."

"Mhm," he says before walking past me and rounding the corner. "Hey, Finn!"

"Did I hear something about wieners?" my boyfriend replies.

Alex cackles, and by the time I've followed him into the living room, he's diving onto the smaller of the two couches, making himself right at home.

"How's work?" Finn asks, braver than me.

I still haven't been able to bring myself to ask Alex about his job, even though I did do a little bit of Googling before I realized looking up Tink was *not* a good idea. Not unless I want to see the man naked. Again.

Although maybe now I do.

Alex doesn't seem the least bit perturbed by Finn's question. He grins, tucking his legs up beside him. "Great! I had a DP scene today."

I choke harshly—*yet again*—and nearly drop the hot dogs I'd been placing out on the table beside the pizza. Finn gives me a knowing smirk while Alex laughs.

Jesus. Double penetration. How the hell does he fit two cocks up his ass? Realistically, I know it's possible. And yet it seems improbable. He's so small.

Glancing over at him, I remember how easily he took me. Against my will, my mind flashes to our first time, when Alex rode me. And then I wonder... Could he have taken Finn, too?

Inhaling through my nose, I lift the champagne bottle in my hand and ask, a little too loudly, "Drinks?"

"I'll grab glasses," Finn says, standing up and disappearing into the kitchen.

I set the champagne onto the coffee table beside the food, and when I glance up, Alex is watching me, his gaze thoughtful.

"I don't have to talk about it if it makes you uncomfortable," he says.

I ease out a breath, sitting down on the couch Finn vacated. "You talking about your life doesn't make me uncomfortable, Alex," I tell him as truthfully as I can.

I'm just...trying to work through this mess in my head.

"Does it bother you, knowing what I do? Do you...regret it?" he asks.

I inhale sharply, understanding he's asking whether or not I regret us hooking up. "No. I don't regret a thing," I tell him firmly. How could I? "You helped me feel good again when I hadn't for a long time. I'll never regret that."

He smiles, although it looks a little sad.

"I'm glad it was you," I add softly as Finn reenters the room, three stemless wine glasses in his hands.

Alex's gaze cuts to Finn, but Finn doesn't comment on what I said as he sets down the glasses. He takes a seat next to me, close enough for our thighs to touch, and then he squeezes my leg—in support? As he pops open the champagne bottle and pours three glasses, my heart starts to pound, so many *what ifs* rolling around inside my head.

Could I really do this? Could I date two men? Isn't that selfish? Would people understand?

But when Finn unmutes the TV for the start of the game and Alex makes a sharp noise of surprise, my tumbling thoughts take a backseat. Alex leans forward to the very edge of the couch, his champagne held aside in one hand.

"Oh. My God," he says.

"What?" I ask in alarm, looking between him and the TV screen. What did I miss?

He pans over to me slowly, eyes as wide as saucers. "Ro, honey. You undersold this baseball thing. Look at those *pants*." Alex points in dramatic fashion, and Finn barks a laugh from beside me.

"Why do you think I watch this game?" Finn says to Alex, who looks at him with glee.

"Wait," I cut in, looking at Finn. "You like baseball, though, right?"

Right? We watch baseball all the time.

Finn leans his shoulder against mine, eyes sparkling. "Ro, I watch baseball because I like those pants. And because I like *you*."

Alex squeals as the camera zooms in on the pitcher's behind, and my heart takes off again, stampeding away. I'm stunned and disoriented.

He's been watching it for me all this time?

"Lord have mercy, those *glutes*," Alex gasps. "Finn." He waves his fingers Finn's way without looking. "Hand me a dog."

Finn chuckles, putting a hot dog on a plate before passing it Alex's way. Alex doesn't even break concentration as he shoves the end of it in his mouth and takes a large bite.

"I think," Alex says slowly as the first pitch is thrown, "I'm gonna like this game."

Chapter 11

Good Lord, the pants. Why did no one tell me about the *pants?*

"Oh, oh! Flexed ass cheek," I call out. "Drink."

Finn takes a sip of his champagne, and I giggle maniacally—I can't even help it. It didn't take long for Finn and I to develop a baseball booty drinking game. It might be my new favorite thing.

"First baseman crouched," Finn points out. "Drink up."

"This is the best," I comment to no one in particular before sipping my bubbly. "Go team!"

Rowan shakes his head, looking bemused. He also seems to be the only one following the actual game. He and Finn are snuggled up together on the larger couch, Finn with his arm around Ro and Ro with his hand on Finn's thigh. They're damn adorable, and it only hurts a little seeing them so cozy and obviously in the early stages of puppy love.

I want that. I miss affection and connection outside of sex. Finn said he wouldn't mind me having that with Ro, but I have no clue how Rowan feels about it. He hasn't mentioned anything yet, even though Finn assured me they talked.

Should I say something first? Should I even interject myself into someone else's relationship when there are so many other men out there to date?

But I want that one.

Ugh, it's true. There's something about that big grizzly that won't let me be. I've always been monogamous in my relationships outside of what I do for work, but maybe that's where I've been going wrong. Mal said something like that to me once, when we were talking about my lack of romantic success. That perhaps I'm simply not a *one man* kind of guy. I thought he was joking at the time, but now, I think he might be onto something. Because the men I've dated always wanted me to be someone I wasn't. Even before I started doing porn, monogamy didn't work out so well for me. Apparently, *some guys* don't like having a nympho boyfriend. Whatever. I'm over it. Mostly.

But maybe, if I were in a polycule, none of it would matter. Maybe Ro really could be mine. And Finn's.

Glancing up, I catch Finn's gaze on me, and I realize I'd been looking at where they were connected on the couch. I give him a little smile before hopping out of my seat.

"Gonna use the loo," I chirp, setting down my mostly empty glass of champagne.

Once upstairs, I relieve myself and send a text to Dixon.

Me: If you hypothetically were single and had a chance with this guy...let's call him Mikolas...but he was with this other guy, but the other guy told you to go for it, would you go for it?

Dixon: What.

Sighing, I text Anh.

Me: Do you think I should join a polycule with Soda Can Guy?

Anh: Holy crap. That would actually be perfect for you.

Me: Right? That's what I was thinking.

Anh: Uh, yeah. Go for it, babe.

Me: I'm so glad you get me. Thanks, honeybunch.

Nodding to myself, and feeling better after talking to Anh, I head out of the bathroom. I'm gonna go for it. What do I have to lose?

When I get back downstairs, I'm not prepared for the sight that greets me, but *oh*, is it a welcome one. Finn is leaning over Ro, Ro's chin in his hand. Their lips are locked, and seeing the pair of them together, even in an act so relatively innocent as kissing, has all my blood rushing south.

It's Rowan who notices my presence first, his gaze catching mine when his eyes flutter open over Finn's shoulder. He jerks back, but Finn looks unrepentant when I plop down on the smaller couch across from them.

"Don't stop on my account," I tease, only half-joking. "That was hella hot."

Finn clears his throat, smirking, but Rowan looks at me with wide eyes, as if unsure of what to do. *Would* they let me watch? For that matter, if Ro and I were dating, would Finn and I keep our distance? Or would we work together like a team? I certainly wouldn't be opposed to that. The man is ginger fire.

Rowan exchanges a look with Finn, and Finn raises an eyebrow. "Up to you," Finn says.

Ro looks back my way, licking his lips once.

Holy smokes, is he... Is he going to ask me first?

"Alex, uh," he says a little shakily. "I was wondering, um..."

Rowan cuts off, looking down, looking *unsure*, and my pulse trips.

My sweet, precious Grizzly Bear.

"Ro, would you go out with me?" I ask clearly, not wanting him for one moment to feel insecure about what my answer would be.

Head whipping upwards, baseball game forgotten, Rowan looks at me with those big puppy eyes. "Really? You'd want to...?"

I nod, grinning widely and bouncing in my seat. "I really would. I'm sorry for making it sound like that wasn't something I was interested in before. It's just that... Well, I could see you and Finn already had something together, and I didn't want you to worry about me. But yes, I'd really, really like to be yours, Ro."

"I thought it was only me," he says. "That, whatever it was I was feeling, was only on me."

"Oh, Grizzly Bear," I breathe out. "I feel it, too."

I've had a lot of partners in my life, and truthfully, there's not much that's novel anymore. But something about this man has been pinging around in my system ever since we met. He's different, and I don't know why that is. Chemistry? Magic? Good old-fashioned *like*? Whatever the reason, I feel it, too—this thing between us. And I'm not ready to dismiss it.

"Wow," Ro nearly whispers, glancing Finn's way. Finn rubs his thigh, giving Rowan an encouraging smile. Rowan turns to me next, voice a little stronger. "Then, yeah. My answer is yes."

My smile is so wide I have to bite my lip to temper it. "Yeah? Does that mean I get to kiss you now?"

Please. Oh, pretty, pretty please.

Rowan looks at Finn again, eyes wide, and he's barely started nodding before I'm out of my seat and jumping into his lap. He catches me easily, arms holding me tight, and when I crash my lips into his for the very first time, it's like the finest champagne. Bubbly and bright and *delicious*.

I kiss him hard. One smack. Two. A long, lingering minute where nothing exists but Rowan's mouth on mine. It's only the swelling of that thick cock beneath my ass that finally drags me from our bubble. There's a lot we'll have to discuss before taking this any further.

One thing's for sure, though.

Leaning back, I catch Rowan's lust-filled, dazed expression. "Oh, Grizzly Bear. I'm gonna do so many dirty things to you."

Finn barks a laugh from beside us, and Rowan blushes. Hard.

Oh, how I love that blush.

Sighing, I set my sights on Finn next. "And Ging," I say sweetly, "if you ask nicely enough, maybe I'll even let you watch."

This time, it's Finn who chokes on nothing.

Satisfied, I jump up, giving Ro a tug. "C'mon, lover. It's halftime or intermission or something. Let's dance."

"What?" Rowan asks in surprise, even though he follows me to the middle of the living room.

"You heard me." I pull my phone from my pocket, set Miley on level ten, and then wrap my arms around my new beau. "I brought the club to sportsball night, so now, you have to dance with me."

Rowan looks alarmed, but he lets me place his hands on my ass—the damn things stretch all the way across—and when I start moving back and forth, he moves tentatively with me.

"Get over here, Ginger Bear," I tell the man with the soft smile on his face. "Grizzly's backside is woefully unprotected."

Finn flicks his lip ring with his tongue, smiling wide before he pushes off the couch. He stalks over and wraps his arms around Rowan from behind, notching his chin over Ro's shoulder. And just like that, my big grizzly starts to relax. Eyes closed, he sways to the music, and for four immeasurable, perfect minutes, we dance. Just the three of us.

I have a feeling it won't be the last time.

I'm strutting through the halls of Elite 8 Studios Monday morning when I catch sight of Dixon. Beelining his way, I give my friend a little shove once I'm close enough, and he nearly drops his latte in his surprise.

"You big jerk!" I say with no malice whatsoever. "Why didn't you tell me about baseball pants?"

His eyebrows predictably rise. "What now?"

"Baseball pants, Dixon. You're supposed to be my friend. I know you watch sports."

"Alex, sugar plum, swizzle stick—"

"Don't you dare give me adorable nicknames right now."

"You're not making sense."

I huff. "The tight white pants, Dixon. With the dirt streaks and the butts," I say, motioning for emphasis. "They're glorious, and you can see *everything*. And I didn't know. But now, thanks to Grizz—not *you*—I do. And now we're dating."

"You and...baseball pants?" Dixon asks.

An affronted sound leaves my lips. "Are you even paying attention? Me and Grizzly Bear! Cripes. It's like talking to my dad."

"I...don't know how to take that," Dixon says flatly.

"You're not invited to the wedding," I shoot behind me as I walk down the hall.

Luckily, nothing can mess with my mood right now. I'm on cloud nine.

Up ahead, Teddy walks out of Raylin's room, a towel around his waist. The man started working here a few years back, and frankly, I adore filming with him. He's kind and gentle on set, and for a short while, I even had a crush on the bear of a man. What can I say? Physically, he's totally my type. But that only lasted until I realized our preferences off set weren't exactly compatible.

Teddy Bear needs someone a little more...compliant to toss and boss around. And *compliant* is not a word I would use to describe myself.

I jog to catch up with him. "Hey, Teddy."

He stops and waits for me, that white towel the only thing protecting his modesty. Not that any of us here care one whit about nudity. "Hey, Alex. How's it going?"

"Not too bad," I reply, following Teddy into the dressing room. He heads over to his locker, pulling off the towel in the process. "Excited for our scene today?" I ask.

Teddy raises an eyebrow at my question before holding up the outfit he's been given: a ripped-up pair of jean shorts and a baseball cap.

I snicker. "Truck driver never looked so good."

He shakes his head, a sardonic smile on his lips. "What'd you get?"

Heading to my own locker, I open it up, laughing when I see the single garment hanging inside. "A coat. *Just* a coat. No wonder I need to hitch a ride. I'm probably freezing."

"Oh Lord," Teddy says, chuckling as I flourish the short trench coat in front of him.

Looking at the garment, I get an idea. "Hey, can you take a picture of me?"

Teddy holds out his hand, accepting my phone, and I quickly shuck off my clothes, pulling the coat on after.

"Do I want to know?" he asks.

"Probably not," I admit, striking a pose and letting the coat peek open just so.

Teddy huffs a laugh, dutifully snapping a pic. "Look okay?" he asks, handing the device back.

Grinning, I nod. "Perfection."

Me: Think this outfit is missing anything?

I attach the photo to my message and send it to Grizz's number. We finally stopped communicating through Grindr. Rowan doesn't answer right away, but I'm not surprised. Sometimes it takes him a bit to respond when he's at work. Before I put my phone away, I shoot him one more message.

Me: P.S. I'm excited for tonight.

Ro, Finn, and I are getting together after work to hammer out the details of our poly arrangement. Honestly, I'm shocked I never thought to try this before. With my lifestyle, exclusivity is a problem. I'm committed to the guys I date—not that there have been any lately—but there's always going to be my work. And it's an issue. The men I've been with never saw me as boyfriend material, or they couldn't handle the nature of my job.

I understand it on some level. And I was starting to accept that the traditional happily ever after wouldn't be in my cards. But geez, I've never been the traditional type anyhow, and it didn't even occur to me to go a different route.

Maybe I just needed a certain Ginger Bear in my life to get the ball rolling.

When my phone starts to ring, I make a grab for it, excitement curling in my belly. But it's not Rowan. It's my mom.

"Hey, Mom," I answer, tying my coat shut. I can't talk to the woman who birthed me while I'm half-naked.

"Hey, hun. Is this a good time?"

"I'm a little busy, but I have a few minutes," I tell her.

She hums. "Okay, I just wanted to check with you about your graduation. You haven't sent us the date yet."

"Oh, right." I reach for my school bag only to remember I left it back at my apartment since I knew I'd be heading to Ro's tonight. "I don't have the info on me, but I'll text it to you later."

"Okay, hun. How're you otherwise? Doing okay?"

I huff a little laugh. "I'm fine, Mom."

"Have enough groceries?"

I roll my eyes. "Yep. My fridge is fully stocked."

"Okay. I'll let you go. Send me that info."

"Will do. Love you."

"Love you, too," she says.

Teddy's grinning at me when I hang up.

"Not a word," I tell him.

"It's cute," he says, standing there in his tiny denim shorts with a baseball cap on backwards.

I point his way. "Don't test me. I know your kryptonite, *Daddy*."

Teddy's eyes flash, and with a wry grin, he motions his lips sealed.

"Now c'mon," I say, adjusting my coat tie. "We have a scene to get to."

Teddy shuts his locker. "Ready?"

"Please. I was born ready," I shoot back.

My phone buzzes as I'm putting it away.

Grizz: I don't think you can call that an outfit.

Grizz: And I'm excited for tonight, too.

Grizz: Can't wait to see you again.

A grin on my face, I close my locker door. It's a damn fine day.

Chapter 12
FINN

"Okay?" I ask Rowan. The man is standing near my front window, watching for Alex's arrival. He's been on edge ever since he showed up a few minutes ago.

"Yeah," he says, although he sounds distracted.

"Hey," I say, stepping close and wrapping my arms around him from behind. Some of his tension melts away. "It's going to be fine."

"Theoretically, I know that," he says quietly. His chest rises, and then he whooshes out a breath. "But inside my head, I'm worried this is a mistake. I'm worried you're going to regret...sharing me."

"Oh, baby," I say gently, walking around until I'm in front of the man. I pull him back into my arms. "I wouldn't have suggested this if I thought for even a second it would hurt you and me. I'm so damn wild about you, Ro. I don't think you even realize. Unless you tell me to get lost, I'm not going anywhere, okay?"

He nods, but his gaze pings over my shoulder, and he worries his bottom lip. Grabbing a hold of his chin, I snag that lip between my own, and Ro makes a soft sound before going pliant. He leans into me, whimpering slightly, and I pour every single reassurance I can muster into the space between our mouths.

"I'm not going anywhere," I repeat.

This time, Rowan's gaze stays on mine when he nods.

The sound of a car door draws our attention out the window, and we look just in time to catch Alex strutting up the short walk to the porch, a yellow Jeep parked behind him. He sees us in the window and waves exuberantly before disappearing from sight. A second later, there's a knock.

"Ready?" I ask.

Ro looks a little more confident this time when he says, "Yeah."

I head to the door, opening it to a cheerful-looking Alex. His eyes are wide and excited as he steps inside and looks around my brightly colored home.

"Hey, Finn. I love your place," he says enthusiastically. Much to my surprise, he steps forward to give me a quick hug.

"Thanks," I reply. "How was your day?"

Alex kicks off his shoes before tapping his chin. "Mm. Well, I picked up a truck driver and blew him through a rest stop glory hole. So there's that."

Rowan steps into view as Alex says this, and his eyes shoot wide.

Alex titters. "My scene today," he clarifies, his gaze softening as he steps over to Ro. He throws his arms around the bigger man without hesitation, eyes closing as he rests his cheek against Rowan's chest. "Hey, Grizzly Bear."

"Hey, Goldie," Ro says back, tucking his face against Alex's hair.

My chest warms in an instant. *Fuck*, they're so sweet together.

When Alex steps back, he catches sight of Mo in my living room window, and with a gasp, he bounds that way. "Kitty!"

With a snort, I follow. "She's not very friendly without food," I admit.

But Alex isn't to be deterred. He holds out his hand for a moment, and when Mo doesn't bite it off, he pets her head gently. And Mo, the little rascal, leans right into it.

"What's her name?" Alex asks, cooing over my usually standoffish cat.

"Mojave," I answer. "Mo."

"Like the rattlesnake?" he asks. "Or the desert?"

"The snake," I respond. "You'll see why."

On cue, Mo's purring kicks up in volume as she stands up on top of her window perch to rub against Alex's hand. The raspy noise sounds more rattlesnake than cat, and Alex laughs as he scratches along her back.

"Oh my gosh. She's the cutest. You're the cutest. Yes, you are," he says, picking Mo up and bringing her over to the couch. The brown tabby doesn't make a single fuss, and once Alex sits down, she puts her front paws up on his chest and rubs her face all over his chin. "Oh, honey. You're mine now. Yes, you are. The sweetest, bestest girl."

Ro clears his throat as Alex says this, looking away, and a bright spot of red blooms up his neck.

What the...

Alex doesn't miss Rowan's reaction, either. He keeps petting Mo as he smirks Rowan's way, and then he whispers to my cat, "Someone's jealous, isn't he? But he doesn't need to be. He's the bestest, too. My big, sweet Grizzly Bear. So good to me. Such a good boy."

Oh.

Oh, fuck.

Adjusting myself, I watch as Ro's flush spreads up his cheeks. Damn, okay. He definitely likes that.

"C'mon, boys," Alex says, smiling at the pair of us standing near opposite ends of the couch. "Take a seat."

Alex shifts to one side of the couch, giving Ro the option of sitting in the middle. We've barely sat down when Alex launches into it.

"Okay, so how is this going to work? Are we keeping everything separate?" he asks, motioning between himself and Ro and then me and Ro. "Or are we going to, you know—" He mushes his hands together before resuming Mo's pets.

Huffing a laugh, I shrug. I appreciate his bluntness. "I suppose we can do whatever you both are comfortable with. Alex, I wouldn't mind spending time with you. I think that might make this easier—if we don't worry too much about splitting things up."

Alex nods. "I'd like that. But I wouldn't have a problem if you two want to be alone sometimes, too. Frankly, I can be a bit clingy and a lot horny, so you're going to have to let me know if it's too much."

Rowan coughs, and I cover my laugh with the back of my hand. Squeezing Ro's thigh, I say, "I don't think he's going to have a problem with that."

Ro shakes his head slightly. "I, uh, would like it if you two got along. Would it just be...us, though?" he asks, motioning between us all. "Would there be others?"

"Others in the relationship?" I ask, and Ro nods. "I'm not looking for anyone else, but I think that'd be something to be open and honest about. If any of us are interested in adding someone to the relationship, we talk about it first."

Alex nods, grabbing Ro's hand and squeezing it in his own. "You know what my job is," he says gently. "Pure exclusivity is not something I can give. But I don't want relationships with the men I work with, and if we're doing this—if I'm with you—then I'll be *with you*. I won't be hooking up with other guys. I think Finn is right, and we're going to have to be really open with one another. But as far as I see it, there's no one but you and me." His lips twist a little before he adds, "Well, and Finn, 'cause you're kinda a package deal."

Alex sends me a little wink, and I smile in response. His answer was perfect, as far as I'm aware.

"So, the three of us?" Ro asks, looking between Alex and me.

"The three of us," I answer.

Alex squeals a little, disrupting Mo, who'd been resting on his lap. She jumps to the ground, swinging her tail in agitation before sulking over to the window and launching onto her usual perch.

"This is so exciting," Alex says, bouncing a little in his seat. "Can I kiss you again? Because I really want to kiss you again."

Ro's breath hitches, but he nods immediately, and Alex swings onto his lap. The smaller man threads his fingers into the hair at the back of Rowan's head, and from one blink to the next, they're lip-locked. It's surprisingly soft for how exuberantly Alex jumped into it, but as soon as his mouth meets Ro's, the pair float. That's the best way I can think to describe it. There's this moment, this excited suspension, and then softness follows. Mouths meet like the wind over trees, gentle, a gasping breeze.

It's so damn sweet, so *intimate*, that I know I made the right choice suggesting this arrangement. I know Alex is going to be a wonderful partner to Ro, just as I will. And if we really can work out a way to be comfortable around one another—which I don't see being an issue at all—then I know I'm going to be able to enjoy many more moments just like this one.

I know not everyone approves of polyamory, but I don't understand it. How can loving big and whole-heartedly ever be wrong?

When the pair break apart, they look at one another. Alex's face spreads into a wide grin, and Rowan looks so besotted I can hardly look away. Neither makes a move to part when Alex settles more fully onto Rowan's lap, turning to me slightly, as if he's trying to make sure I'm included.

"We should probably talk about protection," Alex says. "I'm on PrEP, and I get tested bi-weekly for my job."

"Rowan and I just got tested, too," I say. We went earlier this week to make sure we were safe to move on to more than the handjobs we'd been doing. "All negative."

"Okay," Alex says, blowing out a breath. "In that case, I'd be good with dropping the condoms for oral if that's something you're comfortable with"—Ro swallows roughly at this, and Alex pats his chest—"but it's not without risk, so you should consider that. Condoms for anal, on the other hand, I feel strongly about using. The risk to you is higher. And I'd also feel a lot better if the two of you were on PrEP. I trust the guys I work with, but you never know. Accidents happen."

I appreciate how factual Alex is being about all this. I've always been a relationship kind of guy, so I haven't been taking PrEP out of precaution, and I doubt Rowan has either, but I'm glad Alex is putting our safety first.

"I'll call to get a prescription set up," I say.

Rowan nods. "Me, too. And I'm okay with using condoms for anal sex," he says, blushing cutely.

"Same with me," I agree readily. "Whatever you think is best."

"Good. Thank you," Alex says, rubbing his hand over Ro's chest almost lazily, like he was doing with my cat.

"Now that that's settled, how about some food?" I ask.

Alex perks up. "Yes, please. I'm famished."

Shaking my head, I push off the couch. "Life of a porn star."

"Don't I know it," he groans, giving Ro a sweet little peck on the cheek before jumping up and following me to the kitchen. Rowan follows, too. "But I have a feeling you're going to spoil me rotten, aren't you?"

I huff a laugh, turning off the oven that was set to warm before opening the door. "Damn straight."

Alex grins, peeking at the dish I set atop the stove. "Are those enchiladas?"

"Mhm," I hum.

Alex groans. "Fuck me sideways."

"Is that an offer?" I joke.

Alex winks, and Rowan heads to the cupboard to grab plates. He sets the table, and I smile at the domesticity of it all.

This is what I've always loved about being in a relationship. Don't get me wrong; I love sex, too. But it's everything that happens outside of that—all the little moments you share, the familiarity you build together—that makes the rest of it feel more meaningful.

It's love. Growing to love someone is quite possibly the most magnificent thing a person can do.

When the three of us take our seats, I start dishing up plates.

"So," Alex says, planting his elbows on the table. "I know Rowan here plays with crankshafts all day, but what do you do, Finn?"

Setting the spatula aside, I chuckle. "Short version, I code."

"Oh yeah?" Alex asks before taking a bite of his food. He moans so lasciviously, even I have to shift in my seat.

"Yeah," I answer. "I work remotely and can set my own hours, so it's a pretty great gig. I have an office upstairs."

Alex nods. "I wouldn't have pegged you as a computer guy."

"No? Why's that?"

He lifts a brow, and Ro snorts. "Because," Alex says slowly, waving his hand up and down my frame, "all that."

"The tattoos and piercings throw people off, Finn," Ro says.

Alex nods, agreeing. "It's true." His eyes flit from the ring in my lip to the piercing in my tragus. Then they drop to my hands. To the ink there. He takes his time looking me over as he chews, and I nearly squirm again, feeling hot under his assessing gaze. "Are those flowers?" he finally asks.

Nodding, I push my sleeves up a little higher and hold out my arms.

Alex leans closer, one finger trailing over the many varieties of orchids decorating my skin. "Oh wow," he says, voice soft. "They're so pretty."

"You should see upstairs," Rowan says.

"What's upstairs?" Alex asks, looking between us.

My lips twitch as I hide my smile. "I'll show you after you eat your dinner."

"Meany," Alex pouts, but he goes back to eating.

Rowan shoots me a little smile.

When the three of us finish up and the dishes have been put away, I find Alex bouncing at the entryway to the living room. "Now?"

"Sure," I say with a chuckle, grabbing Ro's hand as Alex shoots off up the stairs. We follow at a more sedate pace, and when we reach the second-floor landing, Alex is exactly where I expected him to be.

"Woah," he all but whispers, stepping toward the wall of floor-to-ceiling windows that look over my tiny back lawn. But it's not the view he's impressed by. It's the dozens of orchids sitting shelved in front of the glass.

Alex runs his fingers lightly over the leaves of a Dendrobium. It's not in bloom at the moment, but the plant is littered with buds ready to open to a bright white. All of the plants here are in various stages of growth. About half sport flowers in shades of pink, purple, white, red, even orange and yellow. The rest are simply leafy green.

"His gran was an orchid grower," Rowan tells Alex, stepping up beside him. He lifts a Phalaenopsis bloom, handling the pink flower delicately. "Finn inherited her collection."

"How old are these?" Alex asks.

"Some of them are over a decade," Rowan says. "He takes very good care of them."

Ro glances back at me, his expression so fond my throat gets tight. Sometimes I forget how well my neighbor, now boyfriend, knows me. It doesn't feel like we're only starting out together. It feels like we're jumping in halfway down the road.

"This one is my favorite," Ro tells Alex, pointing to a Brassavola orchid that recently finished its flowering phase. The shoot is cut back now, and it's storing up energy for new growth. "When it blooms, the flowers are white, mottled through with pink specks, and five green points grow out behind each one. It looks like hearts dancing among the stars."

"Oh," Alex breathes out, leaning his shoulder against Ro's arm.

My chest gets tight.

These two—they're so polar opposite when it comes to the physical. Ro: big, bulky, and brunette. Alex: small, slim, and blonde. Yet they fit against one another perfectly. There's a kindredness there. A similarity of spirit.

They're both dreamers.

And I know, in this moment, that regardless of how this thing develops between us, I'll do everything I can to make sure Alex feels welcome here. To make sure Ro knows I'm not going anywhere.

These men, they're gentle souls.

And now, in a way, they're both mine to tend to.

Chapter 13

ALEX

When I look over my shoulder at Finn, this man I have so much to learn about, his expression makes me a little weak. He looks...fond and so very protective. If those two things could be bottled together, it'd be Finn, standing there in his tattooed, red-haired glory, arms crossed in front of him, eyes soft and hazy.

I get the sense he'd go to great lengths to protect Ro. I only hope he continues to see me as a companion, not a threat.

"These are wonderful," I tell him, looking back at the rows of beautifully cared-for plants on glass shelves in front of the window. "I can't even manage to keep a cactus alive."

Finn huffs a laugh, coming closer. "They're not so bad," he says, turning one slightly, fussing like a proud papa. "Not if you listen to what they have to say."

"How do you listen to a plant?" I ask dubiously.

Finn picks up one of the orchids and points to the roots sitting above the potting mix and those running down beneath the clear plastic pot. "The roots talk to me."

Rowan shoots me an amused grin. "Green roots are happy roots," Rowan says at exactly the same time as Finn.

I snicker as Finn rolls his eyes affectionately. Finn gives Rowan's ass a slap—*Papa, indeed*—before replacing the orchid on the shelf.

A little more hot and bothered than I should be while looking at plants, I turn away. "I should probably head out. It's getting late."

"You don't want to stay the night?" Finn asks, like that's simply a given.

Is it? Would he really not mind?

"I... No, that's okay. Next time," I answer.

Truth be told, I don't think these two realize exactly how smothering I can be. I've always been a little gung-ho about my relationships. It's not the same when I'm fucking around casually. I don't let my emotions get involved then, same as when I work. But when I like someone—when I allow myself to truly fall in with someone—all bets are off. They're mine, and I goddamn treasure what's mine.

I know Ro—and Finn, for that matter—are going to see that side of me eventually. But cripes, we *just* started out. I'm trying to have a little chill.

Do I want to stay the night? Of course. Do I want to move my things in and join our bank accounts? Yes, that, too.

But I'm well aware I'm *too much* for most people. I have the track record to prove it. No guy wants that kind of intensity right off the bat.

I can be cool. I can rein it in...a little—no matter how much I want to drop to my knees right here and worship my new boyfriend's cock condom-free in front of *his* boyfriend and his boyfriend's extensive collection of orchids.

One does not do such things on day one of officially dating.

"Besides," I say, "you guys probably want some time for yourselves."

Which I'd also be fine with. It makes sense that Ro and Finn might want it to be just the two of them at times, and that's not something I'll take to heart.

Ro exchanges a brief look with Finn, his brow creased. They do that silent communication thing that speaks of shared history.

"Stay," Ro says, those big brown eyes out in full force. "We want you here. Please?"

Gah, a boy can only withstand so much.

"Okay, Grizzly Bear. I'll stay."

Rowan smiles, holding out his hand, and with a skip, I grab on. It's still a little too early to actually sleep, so the three of us head back downstairs to watch some TV. Finn encourages Rowan to pick, and he chooses this adorable documentary about penguins that is too cute for words. The three of us sit all in a row, Grizzly Bear in the middle, and with that big, comfy body to snug up against, I fall fast asleep before the end credits roll.

When I come to, it's light out, and I'm in a bed the size of Mississippi.

"Holy smokes," I say, starfishing as wide as I can. My fingers don't even reach the sides of the mattress.

"Alex?" a voice calls gently, moments before Finn's head pops around the corner. "Hey. I thought I heard you up."

"Ginger Bear, I could get lost in here," I say, rolling myself into a burrito in Finn's fluffy blue comforter.

He chuckles. "I'm a big dude. I need a big bed."

I come up for air, raising an eyebrow his way. "Lots of big dudes could fit in here."

"Well, then, it's perfect for us, isn't it?" he says.

Us. I smile.

"Is Rowan awake, or is he lost somewhere in here with me?" I ask.

Finn laughs again, his eyes looking otherworldly as they shimmer like gold. The man should be an eye model. Is that a thing?

"He left for work a while ago," Finn says. "I was working, too." He points down the hall, presumably to where his office is located.

And apparently, I slept through it all. I must have been more tired than I realized. Either that or I really trust these men.

"Don't let me interrupt," I say, forcing myself from my cocoon of warmth. "I'll be out of your hair shortly."

"No rush," Finn says. "There's an extra toothbrush in the bathroom if you need one."

"Thanks," I say, stretching one last time as Finn heads back down the hall. With a content sigh, I slip out of bed and head to the bathroom.

As Finn said, there's a toothbrush waiting for me on the counter. I pop open the package and use Finn's toothpaste to brush my teeth. When I see myself in the mirror, I chuckle. I look like a rumpled mess, but I guess that's what happens when you sleep in your clothes overnight.

Maybe I should leave a few things here or at Ro's.

Nope, too fast. Rumpled is fine. It's a good look.

Before I go, I swing by Finn's office. He's standing in front of his desk—which is elevated higher than a sitting desk—typing away.

"I'm heading out," I tell him.

He turns my way and nods. "All right. See you soon?"

Couldn't keep me away. "Count on it."

Finn gives me a smile, and I head from the room, down the stairs to where I find Finn's—I mean *my*—adorable cat, Mojave.

"Such a sweet girl, aren't you," I coo, loving her up. She starts to purr loudly, rolling onto her side on that window perch she seems to adore so much. "You love me best, don't you? It's okay. I won't tell."

Mojave purrs her assent.

"Bye, you little rattlesnake."

The sun is already high in the sky when I head out Finn's front door. I need to swing by the studio today, but that visit shouldn't take long. Then, I should probably work a bit on my art project.

Smile on my face, I turn the ignition. Only nothing happens.

"Well, that's not great," I mutter.

I try again. Nothing. Nada.

"Fiddlesticks."

Huffing out a breath, I jump down out of my Jeep and head back into Finn's house. The man is exactly where I left him, and when I give his open office door a little rap, he looks at me in surprise.

"Itsy-bitsy problem," I say with a wince. "My Jeep won't start."

Finn's lips twist slightly. "Good thing we know a mechanic, huh?"

I chuckle as Finn pulls his phone from his pocket.

"Anywhere you need to be quickly?" he asks. "I can give you a ride."

"Nah," I say, shaking my head and plopping into the chair in the corner of Finn's office. "I have a waxing appointment, but I can do that anytime."

Finn raises a brow, eyes pinging to me before he goes back to typing. "Bet that's a pain."

"Literally, yes. Ray is a beautiful sadist who makes me look good."

"I'm not sure I could handle your job," Finn replies, eyes on his phone. "All right. Ro said he can come by around one."

"That works. You don't mind me hanging around until then?" I check.

"Nope, of course not," he answers. "In fact, wanna go for a walk? I need to move for a minute."

I hop back out of the chair. "Sure."

Finn locks up his house as we head outside, and then he leads us left, down the sidewalk that lines his residential neighborhood. The area is quiet this time of day, but it's pretty. A lot of the yards are done up in the typical grassless desert landscape style. Lots of stone, cacti, perennials, and shrubs.

"Mind if I ask a question?" Finn says after a minute of walking.

"Shoot."

"Why were you hesitant to stay last night?"

My head whips his way so fast I almost miss a step. I didn't expect him to call me out on it or even really notice.

With a shrug, I tell him, "I didn't want to be an imposition."

Finn watches me for a moment as we walk side by side, and I meet his gaze. His hair is curling slightly in front of his forehead, and that enticing little lip ring winks in the sunlight. "I call bullshit."

I bark a laugh. "Really?"

"Mhm. What's the real reason?" he prods.

"Well, shit, Ging. Not gonna get much by you, am I?"

"Nope," he answers.

Expelling a breath, I collect my thoughts. I guess, maybe, honesty is the way to go. "People like me in small doses," I say. "Like tickling. Or peppermint schnapps. I'm a lot, and sooner or later, I'm too much for most people. Too much effort. Too much everything. I guess I was hoping to delay the inevitable by holding back just a little."

"Alex," Finn says, stopping me with a gentle hand on my arm. He guides me around until I'm facing him with nowhere to run. "Give us all you've got."

"Pardon?" I ask in surprise.

"You heard me. Don't hold back."

My pulse starts to sprint as Finn stares me down, challenging me to...what? Show him and Ro exactly who I am? Am I really ready to do that? Will they still want me if I do?

"You might regret it," I say.

Finn's lips twist up at the corner, and he flicks that ring in his lower lip with his tongue. "I don't think I will."

Oh.

Finn resumes his walking pace, and I fall back into stride next to him, mind spinning. We're quiet for several long minutes as we enjoy the scenery and stretch our legs. It's nice. I don't get a chance often to simply *walk*. Or maybe it's that I never make the effort.

Of course, ten minutes later, I know exactly why that is. "I'm out of shape," I complain.

Finn gives me an eyebrow raise. "I sincerely doubt that."

"You can be thin and out of shape, Ging," I tell him. "I'm not used to exercising these muscles. The type of flexing I do is not usually exhibited in polite company."

Finn barks a laugh. "I'm polite company?"

"You're company. Now be polite and carry me," I joke.

Finn gives me his back, squatting down. "Hop on."

I come to a grinding halt. "Seriously?"

"I'm offering, aren't I?" he asks. When I still hesitate, he notches his head. "C'mon, Goldie. Get your ass up here."

With a grin and a little whoop, I climb up Finn's back. The man is sturdy as all get out, and I wrap my arms and legs around him like the little koala I am.

"You've done it now," I warn. "I'll be demanding piggyback rides at all times. Kitchen to living room? Piggyback ride. Bathroom to bedroom? You're my man."

Finn chuckles, wrapping his arms back to support me from underneath. With a happy little sigh, I tuck my chin over his shoulder.

"You smell like cinnamon," I note. "Is that a ginger thing?"

Finn shakes his head, rumbling with laughter. "It's not a ginger thing. I just like cinnamon gum."

"'Cause you're red hot? Oh, no, wait. That's not the gum. 'Cause you're a big red?"

He chuckles again, muttering, "Oh boy."

"Regretting it yet?" I ask, a tiny sliver of doubt intruding despite Finn's clear amusement.

He turns his head. "I regret nothing."

With a little smile on my lips, I point out, "Your back might be regretting it in about ten minutes."

"Right. Because you weigh so much."

I snort.

"C'mon, trouble," the man says, entirely unconcerned. "Let's head back."

When Finn and I get back to his house, I begrudgingly dismount from my new pony and settle at the kitchen table with some printer paper Finn so graciously supplies. While he goes upstairs to work, I lose myself in sketching. It's about one o'clock when Finn calls out, "Hey, Alex? Ro's here."

I grab my paper and fold it neatly into a square before pocketing the drawing. It's not that I don't want either man to see it, per *se*, but it *is* a nude sketch of two dudes going at it. Two bears, to be precise, who look suspiciously like Grizz and Ging.

Hmm. Wonder where that inspiration could have possibly come from.

"Coming," I call out before snickering to myself. *Not yet.*

Finn and I end up at the front door at the same time, and when we head outside, there's Ro, our boyfriend, bent over the front of my Jeep, checking the engine or...something. His shirtsleeves are rolled up, a little bit of sweat glistening at his brow, and those jeans of his fit him just right.

"Damn," Finn and I say at the exact same time.

I look his way, grinning. "This is exactly how a good scene would start out. Excuse me, Mister," I say all breathily. "Something's wrong with my engine. Can you help me? I'll repay you however you want."

Finn plants his hands on his hips. "Come on. You can do better than that."

I gasp. "'Scuse you, I do this for a living."

Finn shakes his head and clears his throat. When he speaks, his voice has dropped a good octave. "Sir. I've been having issues with my driveshaft. Think you can...give me a hand?" He flips his hair back.

"Well fuck, Ging. Where've you been hiding that?" I ask, fanning my face. Because of the *heat*. It's Nevada, for cripes' sake.

"Alex?" Ro calls out. "Your battery is dead. I can grab a new one from the shop real quick and replace it if you'd like?"

"Can I watch?" I call back.

He tilts his head. "Uh, sure?"

I give him a big thumbs up. "Finn, got any lemonade around here?"

Chuckling, Finn heads back inside, and I plop myself down on the porch step, not at all displeased with how this day is turning out.

Chapter 14

ROWAN

"So once I reattach the positive and negative terminals, it should be good to go," I tell Alex.

He nods at me. "Uh-huh. Uh-huh."

"Want to give her a crank?" I ask, wiping my palms on a cloth.

Alex continues to nod, his gaze roaming my hands and forearms.

"Alex?" I prompt.

"What?" His eyes snap to mine. "Oh, yep. Okie-doke."

Rounding the Jeep, Alex climbs in. When I give him a thumbs up, he turns the ignition, and the vehicle roars to life. Alex grins widely before turning it back off and climbing down.

"Fuck," he says, heading my way. "Competence is hot."

I nearly swallow my tongue at the look in Alex's eyes, and when he reaches me, he doesn't hesitate to pop up on his tiptoes and grab the back of my neck. He tugs, his request clear, and I bend to meet him, powerless to do anything but.

It's no less surprising than the first few times, the softness of his lips against my own. Alex kisses like sunshine and marshmallow fluff, and it's so addictive that I don't want to ever come up for air. He hums against my mouth, his tongue playing lightly along the seam of my lips, and his hands roam lazily over my neck and beard. Mine are glued to his back. To the soft swell where ass meets spine. My thumbs find his skin, and I stroke the silky smoothness.

It feels like a lifetime ago that I had this man naked in my bed, even though the memories are fresh in my mind.

Alex shivers against me, tugging my hair gently before pulling back half an inch.

"Later…" he says like a promise, brushing my lips with his, "you're going to feed me that big cock of yours. And let me tell you, Grizz. I can not *wait* to have your taste on my tongue."

"Fuck," I mutter.

Alex kisses me with a grin before popping back onto the balls of his feet. "I need to take care of a few things, but I'll be back later."

"Uh, yeah. Okay," I say, nodding and dazed.

"Thank you for fixing my baby, baby." He pops his hood down and sends me a little wink before jumping into his Jeep. With another wave, he backs out of my driveway, and then he's off.

"Fuck," I say again, adjusting myself. When I glance back at the house, Finn gives me a wave from his office window. Even though I can barely make out the man, I swear he winks.

Triple fuck.

How am I ever going to get through the rest of this day?

"You like pork?" Aaron asks, startling the crap out of me.

I look up from the invoices I'm filing, wondering what the heck he's up to. "Sure, I like pork. Why?"

He shrugs. "No reason. By the way, Old Mike stopped by earlier while you were out. Said he's really impressed with how things have been running."

"Really?" I ask, my insides swelling with pride. Mike, the owner of the garage, doesn't come around too often, but I've always liked the man. He started this place decades ago and only retired four years back when I moved into the management position.

I suppose I should've taken his absence as a good sign—that he trusted me to get the job done in his stead—but I always worried a little bit about his radio silence. It's good to hear he's happy with how I'm treating Mike's.

"Are you really surprised?" Aaron asks, smiling at me a little crookedly. "You're a great boss to have, Grizlak."

"Thanks, Aaron," I mutter. "I appreciate it."

"You betcha. See ya later."

"Have a good night," I reply.

As Aaron heads out of sight, Pauly pops his head into the office. "Hey. Can I get Finn's number?"

"My Finn?" I ask in confusion.

"Do we know another Finn?" he shoots back.

I file the last invoice into the cabinet beside me and push the drawer closed. "Why do you need Finn's number?"

Pauly waves his hand dismissively, coming into the room. "I just have a computer question I figured he could help me with."

"O-kay," I mumble, pulling my phone from my pocket. Finding Finn's contact info, I pass it over, and Pauly copies it into his phone.

"Thanks," he says, giving me an obligatory shoulder slap before heading from the office.

"Is everyone acting odd today, or is it just me?" I question aloud.

Checking the clock, I let out a breath of relief when I realize it's late enough for me to lock up and head home. I do one last sweep through the service bay and reception area, shutting off lights and cleaning up a couple stray tools, and then I'm out the door.

By the time I pull into my driveway, Alex's Jeep is already there. I pass by, driving into my garage and shutting the automatic door. A text waits on my phone.

Goldie: At Finn's.

With a smile on my face, I head upstairs and shower the shop off me as quickly as humanly possible. My cock has been half-hard all afternoon after my short run-in with Alex, but I ignore it as best as I can, soaping off efficiently and rinsing clean. Dried, dressed, and impatient to see my guys—*shit*, that's wild—I head next door to Finn's.

As soon as I step inside, I can smell something delicious cooking, which is no surprise. I think there's onion and bell pepper, but it's not the same smell as when Finn made fajitas.

"Honey, you home?" Finn calls out from the kitchen, and my smile stretches even wider.

Shoes off, I round the corner, finding Finn in front of the stove and Alex sitting up on the counter beside him.

"Hey," I say, looking from one man to the other.

Is this my life now? Is this, somehow, my future?

Finn gives me a smile while simultaneously scrambling eggs, but it's Alex who pulls my attention when he drops down from the counter and strides over to me like a tiny hunter on the prowl. The moment he's within touching distance, he tugs me down by my beard and connects his lips to mine. I *"oomph"* into his mouth, but Alex doesn't miss a beat. Pushing me back until I'm stabilized by the pantry door, Alex kisses me like a man on a mission. There's still that sunshine. That marshmallow fluff. But there's also heat, and it sears me from the inside out, bringing my half-hard cock to full mast in three seconds flat.

Alex's hands roam over me—my arms, my chest, my neck—and then, before I can even process the implications, he's leaning back, tucking his fingers underneath the waistband of my jeans.

"Ro, baby," he husks. "Do you have any objection to Finn seeing you get a blowjob?"

My breath gets lost somewhere deep within my ribs, and my eyes shoot wide, meeting Finn's gaze as his head whips our way. The whisk in his hand suspends over the bowl of eggs, forgotten.

"N-no," I choke out, surprised by the pure bolt of lust that shoots down my spine at that prospect. Am I into exhibition? Or is it just because it'd be Finn who'd be watching?

Alex shifts his hand over my erection, the pressure more of a tease than anything. "Finn?" he asks, never taking his eyes off me. "Thoughts?"

"Pro," Finn answers in an instant, setting down the whisk and turning our way.

Green light given, Alex doesn't hesitate. He squeezes me through my jeans and then promptly sets to work removing the obstacle. My head swims as he tugs down my pants and underwear in one swoop, and when he takes my rigid cock into his hand, saying a quick, "Hello again, big boy," my vision nearly whites out.

I grab the pantry door behind me, more turned on than I've maybe ever been, and with a wicked grin, like he knows it, Alex drops down and swipes his tongue over the tip of my dick. My head hits the pantry door.

"Fuck, you taste good," Alex says, as if he truly thinks so. As if he loves having my cock in his mouth as much as I love it being there.

I can't manage a single word.

Alex cups my sac as he draws his tongue along the underside of my dick, flicking beneath the head before sucking me between his lips. I knew, from before, that Alex was talented with his mouth. That he could take me further than anyone else I've been with. But without the condom in place, I can feel the heat of him more succinctly. Can feel the velvety press of his tongue teasing my shaft as I hit the back of his throat. Can feel the vibrations of his moan like a train rumbling over the track.

It's too much. Too good.

"Alex," I groan, sliding one hand through his hair, holding onto the doorknob of the pantry door with the other. He winks. Goddamn winks while he's on my cock with his eyes watering and his cheeks rosy bright.

I forgot... Somehow, I forgot how damn potent he is.

Alex pulls back, replacing his mouth with his hand, jerking me. "Gonna give me your load, Grizzly Bear?"

Another groan.

"Mhm," he hums, flicking his tongue over me like a cat. "You'll be good for me, won't you, baby? You'll give me what I want."

And fuck, that does it.

Alex slides his lips back over my cock, suction strong, tongue unrelenting, and my balls draw up tight. My gaze shoots to Finn, needing to find him, needing to know what he thinks. He's standing off to the side, watching raptly, chest rising and falling, the evidence of his arousal tenting the front of his pants. And I lose it.

Muscles locking up tight, I start to unload down the back of Alex's throat. He slides off me some, milking just my crown as he jerks off my base, and the rest of my release splatters across his tongue.

"*Shit*," I croak, thighs shaking, fingers clenched a little too tightly in Alex's hair. Once my motor functions are up and running again, I loosen my grip and smooth his mane back from his face. Alex releases my dick with a gentle pop, and, sitting back on his haunches, he gives me a grin.

"Missed that, Grizz."

Really? Did he really miss this with me?

Alex stands up, leaning close with his hands on my chest for support, and then he's smacking a kiss across my lips. "I'm still hungry," he says casually. "Finn, anything I can do to help with the frittata?"

Alex flounces off toward the half finished food, and I stand there, completely brainless. It takes me a moment to realize my pants are still down.

A hand grabs my chin. "Fuck, that was hot," Finn says, tugging me in for a rough kiss. He winks before sidling up next to Alex, who's washing his hands.

Managing to scrape together a few brain cells, I tug up my pants and zip them closed, and then I head toward the stairs to clean up.

Staring at myself in the bathroom mirror for a good long minute, I contemplate this massive shift in my life. The fact that I have not one, but two men downstairs who want to be with me. Who want to spend time with me and, somehow, against all odds, are attracted to *me*. They don't treat me like a burden. They don't act annoyed by every little thing I do, like I'm not of any use. They don't tell me to be more manly or assertive or to be anything other than myself.

I don't know how to take that. I don't know how to trust it won't slip away.

I spent a lot of my life feeling adrift. Back when I lived in Ohio, when I was in grade school, I was the kid who was okay at everything but not great at any one thing. I was big, but not good at sports. Smartish, but not enough to get A's. I didn't even know what I wanted to study in college.

Then my parents passed away in a car accident when I was nineteen, and I was lost without them. Without a family—a home—to go back to, I dropped out of college and left.

I couldn't explain why I ended up in Nevada, other than a feeling. I drove the old Chevy my dad and I had fixed up—I always did like cars—to Las Vegas, and when I saw a hiring ad for Mike's Garage, I applied on a whim. Landing that job was my first piece of feeling *home* again.

But I still didn't have a family. The women I was with never felt right. *I* didn't feel right, until I started to really examine why that might be. Then I found Manuel, and I had hope.

But he carved me out and left me hollower than before.

It's hard to feel confident in myself when I've never succeeded at much of anything. Fixing cars is the one thing I've been good at in my life. In every other way, I feel hopeless. I know I'm not conventionally handsome, and with Manny's words still ringing in my head, I feel unlovable, too. Unworthy.

Deep down, I know that's not the case. And if I want to keep these men, I have to be open. I have to believe this isn't a passing fancy. I have to show them how much I care, even if the prospect of being truly vulnerable again scares me like none other.

This is Finn and Alex, two men who've been nothing but kind to me. Two men who deserve the world, including a partner who gives it their all. I can't wait around for it to end, or eventually, it will.

When I get back downstairs, Alex and Finn are almost exactly where I left them. Making sure I don't bump any food prep in the process, I wrap my arms around Alex's shoulders to his chest, hugging him from behind. He makes a soft, curious sound, but he tilts his head, leaning back into me with a smile on his face. I kiss that smile.

"I'm glad you're here," I tell him. "I'm glad I found you."

Alex bites his lip, looking so damn adorable, I kiss him again. Keeping one arm around my pint-sized boyfriend, I reach for Finn. His expression is soft, all his hard edges tempered by the look in his eye, and I brush my thumb along his lip, over his piercing.

"Thank you for trusting in us," I say.

Finn gives me *that smile*. The one I've noticed ever since I let myself look. "Easiest thing I ever did," he says.

Damn. This man.

Leaning forward, I replace my thumb with my lips. Finn tastes like the peppers he was cooking for the frittata. "I want you to fuck me later," I tell him.

Alex gasps, and Finn groans, his hand tightening at the back of my neck.

I haven't been able to stop thinking about it since the moment I saw Finn's dick. I've never bottomed—Manuel didn't want to top me—but I've played around some. Enough to know I enjoy being fingered.

Finn and I have been taking it slow, but I'm more than ready for this man. I want to know what it feels like to have that ribbed cock inside my body. I want to know what it feels like being stretched and coveted. What it feels like to be taken and filled.

I may have a hard time trusting that I deserve these men, but my trust in Finn was never in question. I have no doubt he'll take care of me. That he'll treat me right. And seeing the flash of desire crossing his features, the darkening of his amber eyes, I have no doubt he wants me, too.

Finn holds my neck tight in his grip, that hard edge taking over as his arousal spikes. I love the way he becomes more dominant—more assertive—when it comes to sex. Finn isn't a pushy guy by nature. He's immensely considerate and not in the least bit overbearing. But when he's turned on, all bets are off. He takes exactly what I want to give him.

It's the quality Manny always asked of me in the bedroom. But dominant *isn't* me. It never was, and I couldn't force it.

Luckily, my men seem to like me for exactly who I am.

"Ro, honey," Finn says, voice like gravel. "Have you ever..."

"No," I answer. "I haven't. But you won't hurt me."

"No," he says firmly. "I won't. I won't ever hurt you."

And I understand what he's saying. I understand, and I try my damndest to let myself believe. Not in Finn, but in myself. To believe I deserve good men. *These* men.

"Please, *please* tell me I get to stay for this," Alex says, voice whisper-soft, as if he doesn't want to disturb the moment. "I mean, you can say no, of course. I'll respect that. I know not everyone is as comfortable as I am with—"

"Alex," Finn cuts in. "Stay."

"Oh, thank fuck," Alex breathes.

Finn raises an eyebrow, making sure I'm okay with that. I nod. Of course I am.

Finn's smile is all wickedness. "Dinner first," he says, voice pitching low. "Then dessert."

Alex moans.

Agreed.

Chapter 15

Finn

Dinner drags. At least, that's the way it feels. None of us say much, but the looks being passed around speak volumes, and the sexual tension could be cut with a plastic spoon.

Alex is the first to set down his fork, and Ro immediately follows.

"Finn," Rowan says, the sound like a plea, and *fuck*. Resistance isn't even an option.

"Bedroom," I answer. We need the space for this. Ro deserves a bed.

Both men scramble up, and Alex grabs Ro's hand, tugging him toward the stairs. After a deep breath to calm my overexcited nerves, I follow.

I can hear Alex giggling before I've even turned the corner into my bedroom, and when I finally step into the doorway, I have to pause. Rowan is standing near the bed, and Alex is kneeling on it. The pair are facing each other, a big smile on Alex's face and a shy one on Ro's.

My heartstrings draw tight, pulling. Urging me forward.

Maybe it should be odd, having Alex here the first time I fuck Ro. I'm sure some people would think so. It's such an intimate moment, after all. But it feels like the most natural thing. Seeing Alex and Rowan earlier in the kitchen was a gift. I didn't feel like an intruder. I didn't feel unwelcome. I felt like I was being offered a window, a glimpse into the connection that's uniquely theirs.

I had wondered what it would be like to see the two of them together, considering I *have* watched Alex's videos in the past. I thought it might be the same, like I was watching porn. It wasn't the same at all. I don't know if I could describe it if I tried, but Tink was nowhere to be found down on my brightly tiled kitchen floor. That was all Alex.

It's the same man who's here now, grinning at me as I step into the bedroom. The same man who has a heart two sizes bigger than most.

Alex gives Rowan a quick kiss before sliding to the head of the bed. He settles on his knees, bouncing slightly, like he's in for a show. I guess he is.

Stepping up to Ro, I pull the man into my arms, putting us toe to toe. Eye to eye. "You're sure?"

"I'm sure," he answers, blowing out a breath before tugging off his shirt in a move bolder than I'm used to seeing from him. As if he needs me to know he's confident in this. "You'll make me feel good."

"Fuck, baby," I mutter, skimming my fingers over his chest hair and down to his navel. His trust in me is humbling. "I'll make you feel so good."

Rowan lets me undress him the rest of the way, and when I'm down on my knees and his cock is free, bobbing in front of my face, I lean forward to give it a kiss. Ro exhales, his hands threading through my hair, and I hum, looking up in time to catch his lustful gaze. I give him a teasing caress before standing.

"On the bed, baby," I say softly. "Just relax for me."

Alex makes an appreciative little sound, as if he likes the sound of that. He's gnawing on his lip, eyes roaming over every inch of Ro as the man climbs up onto the mattress, and when Alex sees me looking, he shoots me a wink. I can't help but smile in return.

The guy is damn adorable, and honestly, his clear affection for Rowan is the main reason I was so okay with this particular poly arrangement to begin with. I can tell how much Alex cares for Ro. It endears me to him even more.

I make a quick trip to the nightstand to grab supplies, and when I shuck off my shirt without finesse, Alex inhales sharply. It dawns on me that he's never seen how far my tattoos extend, so I stand tall and toss my shirt aside, letting him look his fill.

"Wait until you see the piercings," Ro says, his eyes traveling over me like molten lava.

Alex cocks his head, but then his eyes shoot wide as Rowan's implication sets in. His gaze drops immediately to my crotch. "Oh, Ginger Bear. What are you hiding, naughty boy?"

My erection kicks up at his words, as if begging me to let it free and show him. Licking my lips, I oblige, tugging my pants down first, and then, slowly, my briefs.

Alex leans forward on a gasp, unapologetic about his blatant perusal of my dick. "Well, fuck me. Aren't you just full of surprises?"

I huff a laugh. "I aim to please."

Alex's grin turns lascivious. "Of that, I have no doubt."

Shaking my head in amusement, I climb atop the bed and make my way to Ro. I shove him flat on his back and fall over his body, bringing us an inch apart. His eyes blow wide.

"We're going to take this slow," I tell him. "There shouldn't be any pain."

Rowan nods, and when he lifts his chin in a silent request, I catch his mouth, tangling us together. It's a kiss I can feel down to my toes because it's *Rowan*. The man I've been steadily falling for since the moment I set eyes on him. And now...now he wants me to take him. *Claim* him. He wants me to have something no one else has. It's almost too much.

I make my way down Rowan's body slowly, mapping his skin, worshiping every inch of him the way he deserves. His hairy chest. His broad nipples. His soft belly, and the freckle on his left hip. When I finally arrive at his cock, Ro is panting. I take him into my mouth without further teasing, loving on his crown and giving him a good, long suck. He groans, dropping his legs wide, hand reaching out for Alex. It lands on the man's calf, and Alex strokes over Rowan's arm as I flip the lube open and wet my fingers.

As I trail my lubed digits back behind Rowan's balls, he plants his feet on the bed, giving me better access. His body is pliant, relaxed as I stroke over his hole. I take his cock back into my mouth, toying with him gently as I massage his opening. And when his body feels soft enough to slip just the tip of my finger in, Ro doesn't tense at all. His breath catches, but he pushes back on me, and I slide in up to the second knuckle.

"God," he breathes out.

"Okay?" I check.

He nods rapidly.

Easing my finger in and out, I fuck Ro gently.

"You're doing so good, Grizzly Bear," Alex coos from beside him. "Look at you."

Ro whimpers slightly, but his cock kicks a drop of pre-cum onto my tongue. *Damn*, he really does love that praise.

After a few minutes of stretching and adding my own words of encouragement—*Good, baby. So tight. So sweet*—I slowly ease my finger out of his body and press in with two. I leave them at the first ring of muscle, lapping his cock as I wait for his body to relax. It only takes a moment, and then I'm sliding inside that snug heat once more.

"Are you feeling it?" Alex all but whispers. "That spreading ache? That fullness? That craving for more?"

Fuck.

"Fuck," Ro agrees before nodding his head. A blush spreads up his chest and neck, and Alex hums, stroking his hand over Ro's furry pec.

I twist my fingers, loosening, searching, and when Rowan moans, long and low, I know I hit jackpot. I rub his prostate relentlessly, easing up on his cock, and Ro squirms beautifully.

"Oh God. Oh God. *Finn*," he begs.

"I know, baby."

"I can't—"

I hush him gently, pulling my fingers free. Relubed, I press in with three. Rowan tenses slightly, so I drag on his cock, giving him time to adjust.

"You're almost there, Grizzly Bear," Alex says. "You're doing so good. So good for Finn. So perfect for us."

Ro moans again, latching onto Alex's arm, and my chest swells.

When Rowan's body gives up the fight, I slide my digits in. His stuttered inhalation greets my ears, but he takes my fingers so well. I give his big mushroom crown one more suck before leaning back and watching my fingers disappear into his body.

This man laid out before me. My neighbor turned friend turned lover. This delicate soul in a lumberjack body.

He's mine. And he's beautiful.

I run my palm over his thigh, digging my fingers into muscle and hair as I stretch him for my cock. His eyes meet mine, thickly lashed and bright.

"Beautiful," I say aloud, needing him to know. "I'll give you everything you need, Ro. Anything you ask of me."

Rowan doesn't say a word, but the look in his eyes speaks volumes. He watches me patiently as I remove my fingers and roll on a condom. But as soon as I'm done, he reaches for me, and I fall over his body, finding his lips once more. He kisses me in desperation and hope, and I feed it back to him, those heartstrings of mine so tight they could snap. They vibrate inside my chest, a tune of Ro and me. A song of us.

When I reach blindly for a pillow, Alex passes one over, his hand colliding with my own. I shoot him an appreciative glance as I urge Rowan to lift his hips so I can slip the pillow beneath his body. Once he's settled, I notch against his entrance.

"Ready, baby?"

"Make me yours," he says softly.

"Oh, Ro," I reply. "You're already mine."

Ro's body clasps me like a glove as I press inside his hole, but my crown slips in with minimal resistance. I hold there, trembling slightly as I check in with my man. He nods rapidly, and I work inside of him slowly, each inch a mile of pleasure. When my balls finally rest against Rowan's plump ass, my entire body breaks out into goosebumps.

"I'm good," Rowan says before I can even ask. "Really good. Fuck me, Finn."

"Yeah, baby," I respond.

He moans with that first drag of my cock inside his body, and my very being lights up in a rush like a star-swept sky.

"Oh, darlings," Alex whispers, his voice oh so soft. But I hear him, and I can't help but wonder what he sees. What he feels.

"Your boyfriend likes this," I tell Ro, sure of that at the very least. "He likes watching you get fucked."

They both moan, and when I snap my hips harder, my name rasps off Ro's lips. I love the sound of it way too much. That "*Finn.*" I want to hear it again and again and *again*.

"What does it feel like?" Alex asks. He's sitting back at the headboard again, giving us space, but his cheeks are flushed and his hand rests above the waistband of his shorts, fingers toying gently over his skin. "The piercings—what do they feel like?"

"Fucking amazing," Ro chokes out, his breath punching from his lungs as my balls slap his ass. His arms are wrapped around me, hands holding tight, and his cock is hard and leaking against my stomach. "Fuck. It feels... *Finn.*"

I know.

I meet his lips, and for several long moments, we're a tangle of body, nerves, and fire. Like shooting stars. Like the softest of blankets. Like all things good and *exhilarating* wrapped into one. Like a welcome home.

Soft moans remind me of the other man here, and without overthinking it—without worrying about what's proper or how things are *supposed to be*—I lean back and motion him in. Alex looks at me in surprise, but then he crawls forward, hand wrapping around Rowan's cock as he leans in to kiss his boyfriend.

The two are lovely together—a perfect fit—and as Alex's small fist works Rowan's erection, his body tightens around my cock.

"I'm gonna—" Ro chokes out.

"Come for us, Grizzly Bear," Alex says against his lips. "Show Finn how well you can milk his cock."

Rowan groans, my pace falters, and then, in an inevitable bang, Ro comes undone. His body tugs me in with his climax, and his cock shoots his release across his abdomen and chest. Alex strokes him through it, and I can't do a thing other than hang on for the ride as I come, hard and desperately, into the condom.

Alex releases Rowan's cock as I fall forward, and he moves aside without a word as I seek out Rowan's mouth. I have the strangest urge to tug Alex back in—to include him in this—but I don't. I kiss my boyfriend like my life depends on it.

When I finally release Rowan's mouth, I lean my forehead against his. There's so much I want to say. Too much. And maybe too soon. So I settle for something simple.

"How'd you like your first time bottoming?"

There's a beat of silence, and then Rowan is laughing. His body tightens around me once more as his chest shakes, and with a hiss for my oversensitive cock, I grab the base of the condom and slowly pull out. Ro looks utterly debauched when I sit back on my heels, so boneless and satisfied that I can't help but laugh with him.

"I think," Alex says, mouth in a cheeky grin, "if he can't speak, you did a good job."

Rowan nods, and the three of us exchange another chuckle.

"Now," the blonde says, bouncing his eyebrows, "I'd say this definitely calls for cuddles. But first, I'm going to take a shower and jerk off. Anyone wanna join me?"

Rowan's eyes meet mine, twinkling, *happy*, and I grin.

I think this—*us*—is going to work out just fine.

"Okay, so explain this to me again," Alex says from the passenger seat of my vehicle. "You grew up here, but when you moved away, your family stayed?"

I nod.

"But no one looked after your grandma?"

I nod again.

"What the fuck?" he succinctly summarizes.

"It's just as much my fault as theirs," I say, taking the turn off the highway that'll bring us to my gran's house. "I should have kept in touch better. Visited more than once a year. Made sure she was okay."

Although, as far as I was aware, she *had* been doing okay. Her health decline was a recent development.

"Maybe so," Alex concedes, "but I don't really blame you, Finn. They were *right here*. They should have been checking in."

It's the same argument I've gone round and round a million times. I should have done better, but they should have, too.

"Either way, we have a home health aide who stops in now, and that's been a big help," I tell Alex. "Gran may need more permanent care in the future, but I don't think we're there yet."

He nods, blonde hair bobbing.

I was surprised when Alex said he wanted to join me today. It's Saturday, but Ro went into work—as he does some weekends, rotating the shift with his employees. Alex was hanging around and jumped at the chance to meet my gran. Lord knows why, but I wasn't about to complain about the company.

Alex is easy to be around.

It's only another minute before we reach the house. There's a vehicle parked off to one side of the driveway, so I park on the other. "Ready?" I ask.

Alex nods, and the pair of us get out of my car. As we're heading up to the front door, it opens. But it's not the aide I was expecting to be here.

It's my sister.

"Finnigan," she says in surprise that mirrors my own. She closes the door behind her before walking toward us.

Alex turns to me, mouthing *Finnigan?* With a huff, I nod.

"Fiona. How're you?" I ask.

"Fine," she says, running her eyes over me quickly. "You have more tattoos now."

"I do," I answer simply.

"Who's this?" she asks, gaze pinging over to Alex.

Fiona has red hair, same as me—whereas our other two brothers are blonde—and like I'm used to seeing on my sister, it's tucked up into some kind of complicated twist. She looks exactly the same as I remember, even though it's been a few years since I saw her last.

"This is Alex," I tell my sister, placing my hand on his shoulder. "My boyfriend's boyfriend."

There's a pregnant pause in which Fiona digests that bit of information, her face carefully neutral. "Pardon?"

"You heard me," I say.

Out of everyone in my family, Fiona was the one to take my bisexuality best in stride. Even though she, like my brothers and our parents, are all about their image and standing in their social circles, she never seemed to have any inherent problem with my sexuality. I appreciated that at the time, but now I'm wondering if her open-mindedness only extends so far.

I'm expecting a polite brush off or maybe shock, but when Fiona's face draws down in genuine concern, I'm a little baffled.

"Finnigan," she says quietly, as if Alex won't hear even though he's standing directly beside me. "I thought... Didn't you want a big family?"

"I'm sorry?" I ask, thrown off by the apparent leap in topic.

"I thought you wanted kids," she says. "How will you raise kids if your partner has..."

"Another partner?" I fill in for her.

She nods, but Alex pulls my attention when his hand lands on my arm. Looking his way, I see big eyes and a lip tucked between teeth.

That lip pops free. "You want kids?" Alex asks softly.

Christ. What is going on right now?

"I mean, I always envisioned that as something I'd like if my partner wanted a family, too," I admit.

Alex's face goes all soft, and then he turns to Fiona, practically puffing up his chest. "If Finnigan has kids, I will be the best uncle-dad they could ever ask for. And those kids will be damn lucky to grow up in a household that teaches them about all the different possibilities of what a family can be. They will be loved. *So* loved. Finn will make a wonderful father."

Oh fuck.

Alex squeezes my arm before stepping up to Fiona, hand outstretched. Fiona accepts his palm with a slightly bewildered expression.

"It's nice to meet you, Fiona," Alex says. "I'll leave you two to talk."

Fiona nods. "Nice to meet you, too," she mutters.

Alex takes a step past her, presumably to head in to meet my gran without me because he's fearless like that. But then he turns around and rushes back over. Voice quiet, he says, "Quick, what's your last name?"

"O'Conner," I answer around a laugh.

Alex nods, and then he's off. When he disappears into my gran's house, Fiona turns to me, brow raised.

"Your boyfriend's boyfriend?" she asks. "Not yours?"

I scrub my hand over the back of my neck, trying to get my bearings. "What are you doing here, Fi?"

Fiona sighs, but she does look a little abashed as she clutches her purse to her side. "I haven't come around enough. I'm trying to do better."

"I'm not going to lie—that's a surprise," I tell her.

"Yeah, well, maybe if we saw each other more often than once every few years, there'd be fewer surprises between us." She looks away quickly after she says this, but I don't miss the hurt in her eyes.

"You're right," I admit, wondering if my moving away was harder on my sister than I realized. "We haven't been a family in a long time, have we?"

Fiona blinks a few times before shaking her head.

"Why didn't you text me back, Fi?" I ask softly. I thought, out of everyone, she would have returned my messages when I moved back to town.

Fi looks down, hand twisting around her purse strap. "I'm sorry, Finnigan. I was...occupied."

"Well," I hedge, "would you and Leonard like to stop by for dinner? You could meet Rowan. My actual boyfriend."

"Leonard and I aren't together anymore," Fiona says, finally meeting my eye. "We divorced. That's what I was occupied with."

"Oh, Fi," I say sadly. I didn't see that coming. "I'm truly sorry. I wish you would have told me."

"I didn't want to burden you," my sister replies.

"You're not a burden," I say. "*Christ*, you're my sister. I know... I know I left, but that was for my own reasons. I've always been a phone call away."

She lets out a small sigh, lips pressed tight. "I know that. I do. It's just...everything is different than it used to be."

I can't disagree with her there. A lot has changed since we were younger. I'm certainly not the same person I once was, and I expect that's true for Fiona, too.

"I'd like to meet your boyfriend," Fi says. "And maybe we can catch up."

"Yeah," I answer. "I'd really like that."

Somewhat stiltedly, I offer my sister a hug. We were never huggers, my family. But Fiona steps forward, wrapping her arms around me in a brief embrace.

"I like him, by the way," she says, stepping back. "The blonde one."

I huff a laugh. "Yeah, he's something, isn't he?"

My sister watches me for a moment before clearing her throat. "All right. Well, call me about that dinner?"

"You got it," I tell her. "See ya, Fi."

"Bye, Finnigan."

As she heads off, I look toward my gran's house. I can't see Alex inside, but I can imagine him there just fine, charming my gran's socks off, no doubt.

Does Alex want kids? Could he see himself with a big family? He'd be a good parent, I bet. He has this way of making you feel good. Of making you feel *secure*.

There's a lot I don't yet know about this man who shot into my life like a bright ray of light. A lot I have to learn.

But I'm excited, I realize, to do just that.

Chapter 16
ALEX

"Oh my gosh, look at this one," I say, pointing to a picture of a toddler-aged Finn standing in a kiddy pool, completely naked. "Look at that little butt!"

Mrs. O'Conner joins in my laughter, and after a moment, she turns the page of the photo album. She points to another picture with her wrinkled, slightly bent finger. The woman has clearly seen many a day, but she has a strong spirit, and I'm already in love.

"This one," she says, tapping the photo, "is my favorite."

I take a closer look. There's little red-haired Finn again, but he's... "Is he riding a pony? Naked?"

"Always naked, that one," she says with a great big guffaw. "Always skirting the rules. His parents had a fit every time he pulled off his clothes, but I just snapped a picture."

"This is delightful," I say, storing up a million mental snapshots of this beautiful experience so I can tease Finn mercilessly later.

"He's a good one, our Finnigan," his grandma says softly, the fondness evident in her tone.

"Yeah," I agree. "He really is, isn't he?"

"Oh, Jesus," Finn groans, coming through the front door at long last. "The pictures, Gran? Really?"

His grandma titters, not in the least bit perturbed by Finn's supposed irritation. Finn shakes his head, but his eyes are smiling when he meets my gaze. I give him a grin, so damn charmed—by Finn, by his gran, by *all* of this. And when Finn exhales softly, crossing his arms casually in front of his chest and tilting his head in a way that seems to imply, *Really, Alex? You, too?*, my heart damn near skips.

Oh. Since when did we start talking without words?

"While you two conspire against me," Finn says, "I'll go get drinks. Ginger ale for you, Gran. Alex?"

"Same for me," I reply. "I like a good ginger."

Finn pauses on his way to the kitchen, shaking his head before continuing on. I watch his retreating form, my stomach doing funny little hops.

"Ready to see his teenage emo phase?" Mrs. O'Conner asks.

"Oh my God," I whisper-hiss. "I've never been more ready for anything in my life."

When Finn and I leave his grandma's house two hours later, my mind is buzzing. Which means, as soon as he starts the car and pulls out of the driveway, my mouth starts to run away from me.

"Do you think it could really work?" I ask. "Kids in a situation like ours? I know I defended it to your sister and all, but if you haven't noticed, none of us has a uterus. Which means we'd need to go with surrogacy or adoption or even fostering. But would those agencies approve a situation like ours?"

"Alex," Finn says calmly.

"No, I know. We're new. Like, *super* new," I agree. "But Finn, you want *kids*. That's just the cutest thing *ever*. God, I could see you with kids. I could see it so hard. It'd be adorable. Like you with your cat."

Finn chuckles, gaze shifting to me quickly before he refocuses on the road.

"But realistically, is that even an option?" I ask, rolling my thoughts over out loud. "And cripes. I'm twenty-six, Finn. And you've got to be in your thirties."

"Thirty-two," he confirms.

"See? Thirty-two. And Rowan is thirty. You guys are probably ready to start a family. And here I am, possibly in the way of all that. Maybe it would be best if I—"

"Alex," Finn says, his voice tinged with a hard edge I'm not used to hearing from the man. "Don't. Whatever you're about to say, don't say it."

"But—"

"No," he says, putting on his blinker and turning off into an abandoned parking lot. He stops the car out of the way of traffic and faces me. "This isn't something we have to worry about yet. You're right—we *are* new. This situation is new. But it won't do us any good to end things before they've had a chance to truly begin, all because of some vague hypotheticals we haven't even discussed as a team yet."

My breath leaves me in a rush, and I nod.

Finn softens his gaze. "If, down the road, the idea of kids turns into a reality we're ready to face, we'll figure it out. Okay? Somehow, we will."

"You're right," I say, my pulse coming down. "You're absolutely right."

"I usually am," he says with a little smirk.

"Gosh, Finnigan. Have you always had this big of an ego?" I joke. "Was the red hair blinding me?"

Finn lets out a big laugh, and with the way the sun is shining in through the window behind him, he really does blind me for a moment. With his hair set on fire and his mouth in a wide, happy grin, and with those tattoos peeking over the collar of his shirt and winding down his arms and the backs of his hands, he's a sight.

The rare and mighty Ginger Bear. Scarcely seen in the wild, and yet, somehow, I lucked into a friendship with one of my very own.

"Finn," I say seriously, "if it does get to a point where we run into an issue, you and Rowan could marry."

"Alex," he says, that trepidation back in his voice.

"I know. *New,*" I repeat, moving my hand in a repetitive little circle. "But you and Rowan have known each other long enough to know you work at some level. There's a stability there. A foundation. My lifestyle...it could be a problem, Ging. That's the simple truth. We both know it."

Finn doesn't refute my claim, but he looks like he wants to.

"I'm just saying—if it came down to that, I wouldn't have a problem with it," I tell him.

"Alex," he says again, rubbing his hand over his face. "Are you asking me to marry your boyfriend?"

His delivery has me breaking into a fit of laughter, and Finn's face twists into wry amusement.

"You didn't get down on one knee or anything," he mutters.

Aw, is our Ginger Bear a romantic?

Finn sighs heavily before going on. "Look. I appreciate what you're trying to do, but we're not there yet. Not even close. And if—*if*—some combination of us were to get married in the future, I think the person getting married off should have some say in the decision."

I huff. "Yeah, I suppose you're right."

Finn raises an eyebrow, as if to say, *Didn't we already cover this?*

I roll my eyes. *Yeah, yeah.*

Ugh, we're doing it again, aren't we?

"Why don't we stop and grab some ice cream," Finn says, starting the car. "There's a shop nearby I used to go to as a kid. Unless"—he pauses, looking over at me—"you can't eat ice cream right now?"

"So considerate of you to check in with me and my digestive tract," I tease. "But I would absolutely love some ice cream."

"Let's do it then," he says, pulling back out onto the road.

It only takes a couple minutes to get to the little ice cream shop with its massive cone-shaped sign above the entrance. Finn opens the door of the establishment, and a bell jingles overhead.

"After you," he says.

I bat my lashes at him. "Such a gentleman."

Finn bites his lips, shaking his head a little. "Not really," he mutters ever so quietly as soon as I'm through the door.

It takes everything in me not to react to *that*.

Oh my.

Instead of responding, I appraise the ice cream choices. "What does Ro like?"

"Chocolate almond," Finn says instantly.

"Oh really? Why am I not surprised our guy likes nuts?"

Finn chuckles, and it makes me feel all glowy inside. Why do I enjoy getting such a reaction out of the man?

"And what do you think I like?" I can't help but ask.

Finn cocks his head, tongue doing a distracting dance with his lip ring while he thinks. The way he gives the question due consideration, as if I'm worth the effort, makes that glowy feeling get a little too hot.

"Vanilla," he finally answers.

Well, shit.

"How'd you..."

My sentence peters off as Finn steps up to the counter, and the employee that had been waiting on us approaches. Finn holds my gaze for a moment. "Because despite what I'm guessing most people assume, you appreciate the simple things in life." He turns to order, and I gape. "Pints of chocolate almond, vanilla, and pistachio, please."

My breath comes a little short as we wait for the employee to scoop up and package our ice cream to go. I'm not sure what it means that this man can see so clearly to the heart of me.

"Ready?" Finn asks, bag in hand.

I nod, and we head back to his car. The drive back is peacefully quiet, and even though Finn parks in his own driveway, we divert Rowan's way. His lights are on, so he must be home from work already.

Before we get to his door, and before I can forget, I tell Finn, "I want to go again. To see your gran. She's wonderful."

Finn gives me a soft smile. "That's nice of you, Alex. Thanks."

"Of course," I say. It certainly was no hardship getting to know the woman. I don't have any grandparents of my own—they all passed when I was young—and Finn's grandma was a genuine delight. As Finn opens Rowan's door, I add, "She reminds me of you, you know."

"Really?" he asks, kicking off his shoes.

I do the same. "Mhm. She's...sassy."

Finn barks a laugh, looking back at me with a sassy grin of his own.

"Uh-huh," I say, pointing at his face. "You two are the same."

He shakes his head a little, but I think he's secretly pleased to hear me say so.

"Ro?" I call out, looking around. The man appears at the top of the stairs, dressed only in jeans. A towel rests in his hand, and his hair is damp, dark, and clinging to his head.

My mouth dries up in an instant.

Finn steps up beside me, making an appreciative sound, like a low, growly "*mmm*," and I nod. *Agreed*.

"Hey," Rowan calls. "I'll be down in a minute."

"We brought ice cream," I tell him, snatching the bag from Finn's hand. "I picked chocolate almond for you because I had a hunch it was your favorite."

Ro smiles, even though he looks confused, and Finn makes an affronted sound. "*Hey*," Finn hisses, swiping at me, but I sidestep his hand.

"We'll wait for you," I tell Ro before hightailing it into the kitchen.

Finn has a faux-menacing look on his face as he follows. "That's not fair."

"All's fair in love and war," I singsong.

"And, what, we're at war?" he asks, lips curling in amusement. He stops on the other side of the sink from me, kicking his hip against the counter as I grab spoons from the silverware drawer.

"No, baby," I tease. "We're all about the love here."

He crosses his arms, lips pursed tightly, and I give him a beaming smile before sashaying over to the table. Really, people should sashay more often. It feels marvelous.

Rowan steps into the kitchen as I'm setting the ice cream onto the table, and I head his way as soon as my hands are free.

"Hi," I say, stopping in front of him.

He looks me over, eyes casing my face as if he's simply enjoying *seeing* me for the first time since this morning, and my little twink heart nearly bursts out of my chest.

"Hey," he replies, tugging me close.

With a grin, I pop up on my toes and meet Ro's lips. Smooth. Sweet.

I melt.

When there's a swat on my ass, I back up with a gasp. Finn swoops in, grabbing the back of Ro's neck and hauling him in for a kiss. I stutter out a laugh. *Touché.*

After Finn is done mauling my boyfriend's face off, he leans close to his ear, whispering something.

I gasp again. "What are you telling him?" He better not be ratting me out for the ice cream.

Finn just shoots me a wink before pulling out a chair for Ro and then taking one of his own. With a humph, I pull out my own seat and plop down at the table, handing out the pints to their owners.

"So, ice cream before dinner?" Ro asks, his lips tipping up as he lifts the lid of his chocolate almond.

"Mhm," I answer, swiping some vanilla off my spoon. "We're daring like that."

Finn chuckles.

"Hey, Ro. Do you want kids?" I ask.

Both men choke a little, and Rowan's eyes shoot wide in surprise. "I, uh... Well, I guess so, yeah. I always thought it'd be nice to have a family."

Insides turning to goo, I glance over at Finn. He's staring at Ro with all sorts of dreams in his eyes. I can see it, and it makes me damn happy that these two men might be able to have that someday. Family like that.

Maybe I could be a part of it, too, in a way.

"Where's this coming from?" Ro asks.

I shrug a little, shoveling another spoonful of vanilla ice cream in my mouth. "Just curious."

Finn looks a little relieved. Truth be told, I think he half expected me to propose for him. I snort at the thought.

"Alex," Ro says.

"Mm?" I hum around my spoon.

"Do you?"

"Do I what?" I mumble.

He tilts his head a little. "Do you want kids?"

"Oh," I say, my insides doing funny little fuzzy things. "Yeah. I think I'd really like that someday."

Rowan nods once, a smile on his face, and the three of us continue to eat our ice cream.

Yeah.

Someday.

Chapter 17

ROWAN

A limb hits my gut, waking me from a dead sleep, and then there's a muttered apology, followed by a thump on the floor. Peering my eyes open, I blink a few times, taking in the sunlight streaming through the window of my bedroom.

I must have slept in.

Alex's blonde head pops into view as he gets up off the ground. He hops on one foot, tugging his sleep shorts off as he heads to my dresser. Opening the second drawer from the top, he pulls out a pair of pants—since when are his pants in my dresser?—followed by lime-green underwear. He tugs his current pair of briefs off and starts to get dressed as I stare in confusion. A shirt comes out of the drawer next, and he slips it over his head.

Alex tosses his underwear in my hamper before he notices me watching. Quietly, he heads my way, dipping low once he reaches the bed. "I'm meeting some friends for brunch," he says softly. "Didn't want to wake you two."

Turning my head, I find Finn behind me. The morning fogginess is starting to dissipate.

Alex leans in, giving my cheek a smooch, and then he waves before heading out the bedroom door.

Finn makes a soft sound behind me, and then his arm wraps around my middle.

"Finn?" I say quietly, in case the man is still asleep.

"Yeah?" he mutters, voice gravel.

"Did Alex move in?"

Finn chuckles, his arm tightening. His lips ghost along the back of my neck before he answers. "You didn't notice?"

"I, uh..."

Shit, how'd I miss that?

"He reorganized half my closet," Finn adds before yawning. "Took my sock drawer, too."

"What'd he do with your socks?" I ask.

"Rolled them up neatly and put them in my underwear drawer."

"Huh," I say.

I suppose it makes sense. Alex has been spending most of his time over here lately—either at my place or at Finn's. In fact, when was the last time he slept at his own apartment?

"He went out for brunch," I tell Finn.

He hums near my ear, and I shiver, so he does it again.

"How's your gran?" I ask. I forgot to the other day, which makes me feel terrible, but there was Finn, Alex, ice cream, and then cuddling on the couch, and it completely slipped my mind.

"She's good," Finn answers. "Thanks for asking, Ro."

"I'm sorry I couldn't come. Tell me when you go next. I'll try to be there."

"It's okay," he says, hand rubbing over my arm. "I know it doesn't always work out with your schedule."

He likes to go during the day, when his gran has more energy for a visit. "Still. Let me know."

He nods against the back of my head. "I will," he says before kissing my neck gently. "I like this."

The subject change throws me. "What?"

"This," he repeats, running his nose along my neck. Goosebumps erupt over my skin. "I like waking up with you. Being able to touch you whenever I please."

"Yeah?" I ask, voice a little breathy.

"Mm," he answers. His hand trails along my arm again. Lower. Slips over my stomach.

I tense. I try not to, try to remind myself who it is behind me, but it happens before I can tell my brain to shove off.

Finn notices. Of course he does.

"Ro," he says gently, trailing his fingers over my skin. My happy trail. My belly button.

"I know," I say, hiding my face near my pillow. I should turn my head and look at him, but I can't. "I know you don't care. I just..."

His fingers still, but only for a moment. Then he resumes his lazy exploration. "Don't care?" he asks.

"About..." *Fuck.* "My body."

His inhale is audible, and then his breath ghosts over my shoulder. "I do care," he says with force and conviction. And suddenly, my gut is swooping in a way that leaves me feeling dizzy, and not in a good way.

Finn curses, and then he's on the move. He lands in front of me, those golden eyes inches from my own, and grabs my face in a gentle hold.

"I do care," he repeats, voice a little choked. "I care. I like you, Ro. And I like your body. It's not something I'm looking past. It's not something I ignore. I *see* you." He pauses, eyes flickering between my own. "I see you, and I like what I see. I always have."

My breath stutters, and I have no idea how to respond to that. Does he really?

"Ro," Finn says slowly, closing his eyes for a moment. "Did he hurt you?"

There's no doubt in my mind that he's talking about Manny.

"He was always careful when I was around," Finn adds. "But *fuck*. I'd see the way you acted when he was there. Like you were just waiting for a blow."

"He wasn't physically abusive," I manage to say.

He breathes out at that, but he doesn't look entirely relieved. "But verbally?"

I nod slightly, and Finn's jaw clenches. He climbs back onto the bed, curling in front of me when I scoot back to give him more room.

"I wish I could go back and punch him in the face," Finn says matter-of-factly.

I choke out a laugh. "No, you don't."

"I do," he argues. "I should have trusted my gut and done something."

"And what would you have done, Finn? We barely knew each other at the time, and Manuel and I were already on the outs. If anything, I'm the one who should have stood up to him."

Finn shakes his head. "You didn't do anything wrong. He was the one in the wrong."

"He was, wasn't he?" I agree. "Which means it wasn't your fault, either."

Finn sighs, tugging gently on my beard.

"I was with him for nearly two years," I practically whisper, ashamed of that fact.

Finn's lip quivers, and he squeezes my arm, fingers denting my flesh. "How bad was it?"

"It wasn't bad at first," I admit, swallowing around the tightness in my throat. "It really wasn't. Then it was little things. A grievance. A slight. I should have walked away when it started, but he was saying things that I already thought to be true. So it was easy to believe him."

And *God*, the way Finn looks gutted, as if it happened to him.

"Ro," he says quietly. "I wish you didn't believe you're anything other than perfect. I wish you could forget every single word he spoke to you."

I smile a little at that. "You're helping me with that. You and Alex."

"Are we?" he asks, leaning closer until the tip of his nose touches mine. He closes his eyes. "Are we really?"

"Yes."

"Good," he says softly. "Good." His eyes open again. "Can I show you something?"

Curious, I nod, and Finn rolls away. He pads around the bed, and I follow him with my gaze, taking in the sway of his ass beneath his sweats, his tattooed chest and arms, and the ginger trail leading down his stomach. *Fuck*.

When Finn comes back, he has his phone in hand. He taps away for a minute before flipping the screen around my way. There, on the device, is an Instagram page filled with pictures of a dark-haired, burly guy in various stages of undress.

"What is this?" I ask in confusion, looking up at Finn.

He nods toward his phone. "See that guy? That's Teddy, one of Alex's coworkers."

I look back at the screen. The man is large, hairy-chested, and...hell. "He looks kind of like me."

"Yeah, he does," Finn says, scrolling down so I can see more of his pictures. "Fans love the guy. In fact, a *lot* of queer guys like bears like you, Ro. Guys who are big and soft and hairy. I know I do."

"I..." I shake my head a little.

I always felt like a bit of an outlier. The guy who was larger than average. I don't have chiseled muscles or facial features. I never saw men like me on the covers of magazines or starring in TV shows. I know I'm new to the whole gay scene, but before there was Manny, there were women. And most seemed to glance over guys like me.

I've never felt desirable for my body.

But here Finn is, telling me he likes these things I always thought were negatives. The qualities Manuel preyed upon. My ex always knew the best places to pick. The sore spots that would fester under the slightest provocation. And he enjoyed that, I realize. He liked to pick, pick, pick.

I know the things he said aren't all true. In theory, I know that, and I've been trying hard to retrain my frame of mind. To accept myself as I am. But that's not an easy process, despite my best intentions.

Yet Finn wants me. He likes me. He likes my body. And isn't that what Alex was saying from the get-go, too? The way he practically fawned over me. The words he so freely gave. I didn't believe it at the time, but maybe they see something I don't.

Maybe I need to look harder.

"Thank you, Finn," I say seriously, unsure how else to explain what it means to me that he cares so much about how I feel. That he wants to make sure I know I'm wanted.

Finn simply nods, tossing his phone onto the nightstand before he snuggles back against my body. Not in any hurry to move from this precise spot, I let myself enjoy the comfort of his arms.

"Hey, Grizzly Bear. What's your last name?"

I look down at the blonde man in my lap. We're lounging on the couch, which is where we've been ever since Alex got back from brunch. It's been nice, enjoying a rare day off where none of us had work or classes to get to. At the moment, Alex's head is across my legs, and *his* legs are over Finn's lap. Finn, for his part, doesn't look remotely perturbed by this. His bowl of popcorn is balancing on Alex's legs, one hand on the man's calf as we watch a movie.

"Grizlak," I answer.

Alex blinks for an extended moment before barking a laugh. "Seriously?"

I shrug.

"Well, geez. I guess that explains your username, huh?" he says. "I just thought it was blatant advertising."

Finn snorts at that, and Alex shoots him a little grin.

"You can't tell me it's not perfect," Alex says before twisting his head my way and patting my chest. "A true Grizzly Bear."

"Kids at school did use to call me Grizz," I admit.

Alex's expression softens. "Were they mean about it?"

"Not really," I tell him. "It was more like a fact. I was big, even then."

Alex nods against my legs, hand still stroking my chest. It's distracting. "You would've starred in this boy's fantasies if I'd known you back then," he says.

"Really?" I ask, a little curious about that. "Did you always know you were gay?"

His face scrunches cutely. "Pretty much. I liked boys from the moment I was old enough to *like*. Did you know early on?"

"No," I say, shaking my head. "Didn't figure it out until a few years back."

Alex gasps lightly. "You're a baby," he says. "A baby grizzly. And now, you're all mine."

Damn, he sounds happy about that.

"What about you, Finn?" Alex asks.

Finn nods and finishes chewing his popcorn before saying, "Came out as bi in high school. My folks were *not* pleased."

Alex makes a disgruntled sound. *My thoughts exactly*.

Finn shrugs, though. "I didn't let their judgment get to me. And I left not long after that. Started living my own life."

"Good for you, Ging," Alex says before pointing to his mouth. Finn shoots a piece of popcorn his way, and Alex snags it, chomping happily.

I huff a laugh, looking between these two men and the way in which they're connected. They're so casual with their intimacy, and I wonder if they even notice it. Do they see what I see?

"What's your last name, Alex?" I ask, stroking my fingers through his hair. He leans into the touch, practically purring.

"Monroe," he answers. "Not as fabulous as Miss Marilyn, but I do all right."

I scoff. "More than all right, Goldie."

His face goes all happy and soft. "You're good for a boy's ego, Grizz."

Ditto.

"Is it terrible that we didn't know these things about each other?" Alex asks with a little frown.

"Nah," I answer. "We've got plenty of time to figure it all out."

He seems to like that answer if the way he strokes my beard is anything to go by.

"Finnigan," Alex says after a moment, voice contemplative. "Did you get all of your piercings at once or space them out?"

"Really?" Finn replies with a huff. "That's what you want to know?"

"Yes. Inquiring minds and all," Alex says, poking Finn's leg with his toe and disrupting the nearly empty bowl of popcorn in the process.

Finn grabs the bowl and sets it aside. "You seem quite invested in my dick, Alex."

Alex squawks, not quite a denial. "For your information," he says, "I'm invested in all dicks, not just yours."

"Yeah?" Finn asks, squeezing Alex's calf. "A passion of yours?"

"Yes, it is," Alex answers, unrepentant. "And the two of you have two of the most exquisite dicks I've come across in my many years of research."

Finn runs his thumb over my ear, giving me a little smile. "Ro does have a particularly large cock."

Alex huffs a laugh as I flush. "It's fucking massive, yes it is. Such a good cock," Alex says, patting my lap.

Christ.

"And you," Alex goes on, poking Finn with his foot again, "are impressively pierced. Not a common find, you know. So yes, of course I'm curious. Did you have to be hard to get those done?"

Finn smirks. "Wouldn't you like to know?"

"Uh, yes," Alex says simply, looking at me for backup. "I *do* want to know. It's why I asked."

Finn snorts before getting up off the couch, and Alex sits up, watching his departure.

"Finnigan!" Alex calls out. "Get your ass back here and tell me about your dick!"

Finn laughs loudly from the kitchen.

They like to tease each other like this. Flirt, I think. I don't know if that means anything. But if there is something there, surely they'll figure it out. Won't they?

"Rowan," Alex says with a moan, tucking himself back onto my lap, head at my chest. "Make your boyfriend be nice to me."

I chuckle to myself as Finn yells, "I'm plenty nice."

I run my fingers through Alex's hair again, and he really does purr. It reminds me of Mojave. "I'll be nice to you," I say gently.

Alex looks up at me, a smile on his face, before he closes his eyes with a hum. "You spoil me." He's quiet for a moment, sort of nuzzling against my chest, and I almost think I hear him say, "Might just have to keep you," but it's so faint, I can't tell for sure.

Nevertheless, my heart speeds up, and I run my hand through his blonde locks again, thinking that sounds pretty perfect to me.

In fact, I don't think it gets more perfect than days like this.

Chapter 18

ALEX

When Monday morning rolls around, I begrudgingly leave the comfort of the two bears' homes to go to class. It's not that I'm unenthusiastic about my coursework as the end of term approaches, but yeesh. It's getting harder and harder to leave. Which is probably a problem. Most definitely a problem.

I'm getting far too attached.

"Give us all you've got."

Hm. Maybe not.

After my lecture wraps up, I head to the open work studio to put some solid effort into focusing on my final project. Of course, the moment I get there, that plan gets derailed by one of my very favorite people.

"Anh," I say happily, hopping her way. Her fingers are deep inside some sort of clay creation, stretching the malleable material at the rim in a way that reminds me of what I do for my day job. "Jesus, boo. I hope you bought that vase dinner first."

Anh looks up, a scrunched smile on her face as the clay stops spinning. "It's a pitcher," she says.

My brows pop up. "Looks like a catcher to me."

She blinks at me a couple times before dropping her head forward and laughing. "God, Alex. I mean I'm making a *pitcher*, not a vase. Like, for pouring drinks?"

I cackle, flopping onto one of the old, ratty couches nearby. "That makes a lot more sense," I admit, pulling my sketchbook and pencils from my bag. "So what's new? I haven't seen you in a few days."

"Try a week," she says, pushing her glasses up with the back of her hand.

"Really?" Has it really been that long?

Anh starts her clay wheel back up. "Mhm. Soda Can Dick keeping you busy?"

"Oh God, we've got to stop calling him that," I groan. The poor man would probably be mortified. "His name is Rowan."

Anh's face goes all soft as she gives me another smile. "You named him. Must mean it's something serious."

"Yeah," I say with a loopy little grin. "We're dating for real now. He's so sweet, Anh. I just want to cuddle him all the time. And fuck him. Cuddle and fuck him."

"So romantic," she teases.

I sigh. Isn't it?

"He doesn't expect things of me," I say quietly.

"What do you mean?"

"He knows I work in porn," I answer. "But he didn't when we met. And...I don't know. It's like he sees me as a normal guy. To him, I'm just Alex. His Goldie. He doesn't care about all the rest, and he doesn't need me to put on a show. He doesn't expect me to show up as Tink so he can fulfill some porn-star-screwing fantasy. He's just happy when I show up as me."

"Oh, Alex," Anh says softly.

"I *know*. I really like him," I admit. "I like being with him. I like the way he makes me feel."

"And the other guy?" she asks, shaping her pitcher as it spins on the wheel.

"Yeah, that's um..." Something. How do I describe Finn and our situation when I'm not even entirely sure what it is? We agreed to date Ro separately, but the three of us have been spending way more time together than I anticipated. And Finn has seen Ro and me having sex on numerous occasions, same as I've seen of them. I've never been one to worry about modesty, but Finn and Ro don't seem to have any issue with it, either. At least, not when it comes to sex. Which there's been a lot of.

But there's also the dinners and playing with Finn's cat and spending nights at either Finn's or Ro's and cuddling on the couch. Hell, I've barely been at my own apartment since that first night they invited me to stay.

It doesn't feel like me and Ro plus Ro and Finn. It feels a lot like it's truly the three of us.

"Alex?"

"Yeah, the other guy is great," I say because that much is true. "And Christ, Anh." I lower my voice as another student comes into the classroom. "You should see that man's dick. It's more adorned than a Christmas tree."

"What?" she shrieks.

"Shh," I say around a laugh. "He's hella pierced."

"On his *dick*?" she whispers harshly, face doing something complicated. "What would that even feel like?"

"I don't know, but I'd love to find out," I admit.

"Alex," she admonishes with a smirk.

"Hey, you're the one who brought it up," I point out. But then I groan, covering my eyes. "I know I shouldn't be thinking about it, but I can't help it. I'm a curious being, Anh. You know this about me. And Rowan seems to really like it. The piercings, I mean."

When I peek through my fingers, Anh's eyes are big. "I don't need to know how you know that."

Laughing, I lock my lips and throw away the key. "Okay, next topic. What's been going on with you?"

She shrugs. "Got a new vibrating dildo."

"Anh!" I gasp in delight. The guy at the other side of the room looks our way, and I slam my hand over my mouth.

"Chris Humsworth and I are getting along just fine," she adds.

I lose the battle with my laughter. "Oh, God, boo. I love you so much."

She looks mighty pleased.

When I've finally stopped giggling, I make sure to tell her, "Send me the brand of that dildo."

This time, it's Anh laughing.

I do manage to get a little bit drawn in my sketchbook, but once again, it's two beefy men in various stages of undress and flirtation. Not something I can put before my professor. I'm running out of time to pick a topic for my story.

It doesn't have to be long, the book, but I still have to write and illustrate the whole freaking thing. And if I don't settle on a theme soon, I really might have to turn in these scandalous bear drawings I've been amassing.

Wonder what Professor Hughes would think of that.

Really, though—this *is* the type of thing I'd love to illustrate. Gay men. Men of different shapes and sizes. Sex. Love.

But I can't do that for my class, can I?

When it's time to head to work, I close my sketchbook and pack up my belongings. Anh left a little while ago, but there are a couple other students in the workroom when I exit, and the halls are packed as I head out of the art building. I swerve around the other students heading to and from class and make my way to my Jeep where it's parked in a nearby lot.

It's hard to believe I'm almost done here. That, in a few short weeks, I'll have graduated. I'm more thankful than ever that I decided to follow my dream instead of my parents'. Accounting would have paid the bills, but it wouldn't have fed my soul.

When I get to work at Elite 8, Jerome, our boss, is standing outside his office talking to Nathaniel, the assistant producer. He waves me over as he finishes his conversation, and by the time I get in front of the man, Nathaniel is walking off toward the studios.

"What's up?" I ask.

Jerome, who looks like a silver fox-leather daddy combo if I ever saw one, cants his head toward his office. "Delivery came for you."

"For me?" I ask in surprise, following him through the door.

Jerome waves toward his desk, where a vase of flowers sits. The arrangement is full of maybe two dozen stems of various blooms, and they're all in shades of yellow and white. I don't know the names of the different flowers—I never did inherit my mom's green thumb—but it's beautiful. It looks like a little ball of sunshine.

"This is for me?" I ask a little shakily.

"There's a note with it," Jerome says.

Stepping forward, I pluck the card sticking out of the arrangement and open the envelope. Inside is a handwritten note.

"For Goldie. Thank you for bringing light to my life. I hope I can give a little back to yours. From your Grizzly."

"Oh my God," I say, wiping my eyes quickly.

"Everything okay?" Jerome asks with some trepidation.

"Yep," I answer cheerfully, shooting him a grin I hope doesn't come off as maniacal. Based on his worried expression, I'm not sure I pull it off. But cripes, how am I supposed to keep it together right now? Grabbing the vase of flowers, I hug it to my chest and make for the door. "Thanks, Jerome."

My boss nods as I pass him by, and I head down the hall, debating where to go. Break room? Locker room? I end up diverting down the hallway toward a row of small suites we use for solo sessions and private meetings, glad when I find one unoccupied. Shutting the door, I take a moment for myself.

The bouquet is fragrant under my nose when I sit down. After a big sniff, I set it on the coffee table in front of me and look closely at every single flower. There's bright yellow and softer, buttery cream. There's golden and stark, bright white. Even a couple in shades of light orange. Every single bloom is different, I realize. And there *are* two dozen. Twenty-four carefully picked stems. Twenty-four flowers that reminded Ro of me.

I swipe at my eyes again.

Grabbing my sketchpad and the colored charcoals from inside my bag, I start to draw. My fingers fly like mad, cataloging the arrangement in front of me. Recreating every hue. Capturing every detail. I know I don't have much time—I still have to shower before my scene with Cas—but I'm determined. And fifteen minutes later, with my fingers bled in yellows and green, I pack my bag back up and grab my vase of flowers.

There are a couple guys in the locker room when I enter. Cas, getting ready for our scene together. And Emil, a psych major nicknamed Felix here on set. The guy is a super-cute nerdy type.

"Woah, who are those from?" Cas asks, unabashedly standing in the nude as he towels off his wet hair.

"My boyfriend," I answer with a smile. I set the vase on the bench seat in front of my locker, making sure it's right in the middle so it won't fall off.

"You're dating someone?" Emil asks, slipping his own book bag inside his locker. His looks a lot heavier than mine.

"Yeah. Wanna see?" I pull out my phone as Emil comes over, and it only takes me a moment to find a photo of Ro, Finn, and me on the couch. I took this one the other night when we were all cuddled up before bed. Ro isn't looking at the camera. He's looking at me, a small smile on his face as I grin for the picture.

"He's the one with brown hair," I tell the guys.

"Oh damn," Cas says, peeking over my shoulder. "The way he's looking at you."

"I know," I breathe out.

Emil nudges my arm. "Who's the other guy?"

"That's my...Finn," I answer.

"He single?" Cas asks.

I cough a laugh. "Actually, no."

Cas shrugs, and after one more happy sigh and longing glance at my phone, I shut it off. Emil heads toward the showers, and I put my things away before grabbing my toiletries bag. I can't resist giving my flowers one more sniff, and then I grab a towel, turning toward the stalls. That's when I realize Cas is still standing there, completely naked and looking lost in thought.

"You okay?" I ask him.

He startles slightly before giving me a rueful smile. "Yeah, fine. I just, uh... Never mind. It's stupid."

"Hey, no," I say, stepping close and giving his arm a little squeeze. "What is it?"

"I just..." He blows out a breath and shrugs. "I want a guy to look at me like that."

My heart clenches. I work with the biggest softies, I swear.

"You'll find that," I say. "You're a catch."

He shrugs again. "I know I'm pretty," he says in a way entirely devoid of pride or vanity, almost as if he's regretful about the fact. "But guys don't look at me like that. Ever. I want someone to see me. You know?"

"Oh, hun." I give Cas a hug, nudity be damned. "I do. More than you know."

He squeezes me back, and for a moment, that's how we stay. Embraced in the locker room. One of us wearing his birthday suit.

"This is awkward, isn't it?" Cas finally asks.

"Shh," I tell him. "We're ignoring the elephant between us."

He chuckles before stepping back. "Thanks, Alex. You're a pretty great guy, you know that?"

"Aw, sugar." I sock his shoulder. "I do know that, but it's sweet of you to say so."

Cas chuckles again, and with a wink, I head toward the showers.

Poor Cas. He's used to being overlooked, and I get that. It's easy to be the center of attention and still not be seen.

My stomach swoops as I start the shower and strip. Somehow, I think I found *two* men who look beyond my surface. Who don't see Tink, the porn star. But who see Alex, and who want him around. I'm still trying to figure out what that means in regards to Finn, but with Ro, I know I've found the sweet, sexy, submissive bear of my dreams.

The man sent me flowers, for cripes' sake. There's no getting rid of me now.

As I wash up for my scene with Cas, my thoughts tumble over. I want to thank Ro for his gesture—for showing me I was on his mind—but a text isn't enough. Not for this. I need to do it in person.

Luckily, I know just where he'll be when I'm done with work for the day.

Chapter 19

ROWAN

Goldie: Hey Grizzly Bear, are you out at your work-place?

Me: Yeah, why?

Goldie: Didn't want to cause a scene.

A scene? What does that mean?

"Hey," a voice calls. A voice I know well.

Spinning, I catch sight of the tiny blonde fireball coming my way right before he takes a flying leap. Thank God I don't have anything in my hands because the next moment, I'm catching Alex in my arms as his lips collide with mine. He smacks a kiss against me hard before pulling back, looking at me, and doing it again.

He tastes like candy. Like Chapstick, maybe. I never liked that on women. On him, I love it.

"Ro," Alex says, arms and legs tightening around me as he buries his face in my neck.

I manage to find a word. "Hey."

When I look over, cognizant of where we are, Pauly is giving me wide eyes. He's not the only one who noticed Alex's arrival, but Freddie, one of our part-timers, goes about his business, and Aaron gives me a little smile before tucking his face back away in the engine he's working on.

Not that I care if they see a little PDA between me and Alex, but wow. I'm sure not used to that sort of thing.

"Are you okay?" I ask when Alex doesn't come up for air.

He nods. "You smell nice."

I huff a laugh. "Do I? I probably smell like motor oil."

"Like it," he mumbles, lips tickling my skin.

Shivering, I ease backwards and sit onto one of the swivel chairs near the small desk in the service bay. I pull Alex with me easily, settling him on my lap with his legs to either side of my body. He lifts his head once we're planted.

"Thank you," he says, looking me in the eyes. Two simple words, but the way with which he says them is profound. Heartfelt. He means them. I can see it, and I can hear it.

"You got the flowers?" I ask, face warm.

He nods slowly. "No one has ever given me flowers before."

"No one?" I ask in surprise. How can that be?

He shakes his head. "It's not just the flowers, Grizz. It's the fact that you were thinking about me, and that you wanted me to know."

I swallow roughly.

"I like that you think about me," he says quietly.

"I haven't stopped since the moment you showed up on my doorstep."

"Oh, Grizz," he sighs. "You're such a sweetheart, you know that? How did I luck out finding you?"

His smile is soft, his hazel eyes shining. So often, they look light brown. But up this close, right now, I can see the green that makes up half of his irises. His face is so delicate, so precise. Beautiful features and soft skin. The perfect little chin. He's captivating.

But it's not just the physical. Alex is so *kind*. And I think that's a big part of what drew me to the man after he upended my life like a meteor crashed down to Earth. I needed kindness after Manuel. I needed someone to tell me I had worth. And Alex did. He does all the time. Finn is the same.

Is it okay to let myself have that? With Alex? With Finn? Is it okay to just...believe them and let the rest of it go?

"What is it?" Alex asks, seeming to sense my shift in mood.

I shake my head, hesitant to put voice to my thoughts because I know they're not healthy. I know it's my own insecurities giving me doubt. Always with the doubt.

But Alex won't be deterred. He cups my face in his hands, fingers on my cheeks. "Tell me," he asks.

"Sometimes," I say, swallowing involuntarily, "I don't know why you're here with me. I'm only...me."

Alex's face falls. "Oh, Ro," he says. "Let's get a few things straight right this instant. Or, at least as straight as a couple gay boys can be." He huffs lightly. "You're not *only* anything. You're so many wonderful things."

"Alex, I—"

"Please," he says. "Listen to what I have to say."

I shut my mouth.

"When I think of my ideal partner, I think of someone nice. Of someone soft in here." He taps his chest, right over his heart. "I think of someone who wants me, extras, frills, and bonuses included. I think of someone who *needs* me. I like being needed, Ro."

I nod, throat tight.

"Are you getting it?" he asks, his face inches from mine. "Do you see?"

I nod again.

His ideal partner sounds a lot like me.

"You're exactly my type, Grizzly Bear. Inside and out. I *love* your body. I love your soul. I love this face and the way you smile at me. I love all of your hair, and, frankly, I love your cock."

I cough lightly, head whipping sideways to check on the whereabouts of the employees in the service bay. Luckily, no one is paying us any mind.

Alex gives me a little smirk when I look back his way, but then his expression sobers. "I don't want you thinking you're not good enough for me, sweetness, because you're exactly right for me. But I don't mind saying it again and again until you believe me, okay?"

I squeeze Alex to me, and he makes a happy little sound.

"Love your hugs, too," he says.

Love everything about you, I think to myself.

Clearing my throat a little, I force myself to pull back. "I need to wrap up a few things around here. Do you want to meet me at home or stick around?"

Alex doesn't even comment on the fact that I said *home*. He simply gives me a smile.

"I'll stay while you work," he says. "Fair warning, though, watching you do mechanic things makes me horny. So you'll have a very frisky twink on your hands later."

I cough. "That's, ah... Yeah, okay. Not opposed."

"No?" he says, a teasing smirk on his face. "Gonna help me out with that? Gonna stuff me so full of that big, gorgeous cock of yours that every time I sit down tomorrow, I'll think of you?"

"Jesus," I hiss, glad, at the very least, that Alex kept his voice down.

He leans close, lips at my ear. "You'll make it feel good, won't you, Grizz? Love when you're inside of me. Can't get enough. Such a good cock. Such a good boyfriend."

Fuuuck.

What is it about that word? Every time Alex tells me I'm *good*, my brain turns to mush.

I nod repeatedly, wanting to be good for Alex.

He pats my chest, a wicked gleam in his eye, and I will my erection down, reminding myself I'm at work. Luckily, Alex jumps off my lap before things can get out of hand.

"Okie-doke," he says. "You better get to it before I start humping you in front of your coworkers. I'll just sit here and be cute until you're finished."

As if he could ever *not* be cute. "There are drinks inside if you're thirsty," I tell him, voice a little raw.

"Oh, I'm thirsty, all right," he says, giving me a wink.

Not sure what to say in response to that, I nod and head toward my last job of the day—installing new brake pads on a Mazda. Pauly corners me as soon as I settle in to work.

"Who's that?" he asks, crouching down beside me.

"Alex."

"O-kay," he says slowly. "And who's Alex?"

"He's, uh...the guy I met on Grindr. We're dating now," I tell him as little cotton balls bounce around inside my chest.

Pauly is quiet for a moment, and I spare him a glance. "What about Finn?" he finally asks.

"We're dating, too," I say, continuing to work but bracing for...I'm not even sure what. I can't imagine Pauly would give me shit for dating more than one guy, but this is entirely new territory for me. I've never known someone who was in a poly relationship, and I've certainly never waded into those waters myself before.

Pauly nods slowly as he digests my news. "They both know?"

"They both know."

"Well, shit, Grizlak," he says, slapping me on the knee. "When you go for it, you *go* for it, huh?"

"I...sure?"

"He's small," Pauly muses, and I bark a laugh.

"Don't let that fool you," I tell my friend.

"He's waving at me," Pauly whispers before waving back. "What do I need to know before I go introduce myself?"

I huff a laugh. That's a question without a short answer.

It doesn't take long before I'm finishing up for the day. After storing my tools and filing the Mazda's keys away for the owner tomorrow, I find Pauly and Alex shooting the shit near the service bay doors.

"Ready to go?" I ask Alex.

He grabs my hand in his, swinging it lightly. "Ready. It was nice meeting you, P-dawg."

"Back at ya, Alex. I'm sure I'll see you around." Pauly shoots me a little wink and a smile. I take that to mean he approves. "See ya, boss," he adds.

"Night," I reply before Alex and I head out toward our cars. "Meet you back at the house?"

Alex nods, going up on tiptoes to give me a quick kiss before we get into our respective vehicles and drive back to my place. The moment we step inside and the door closes behind us, Alex pulls me into the living room and shoves me down on the couch, his intention crystal clear.

I guess he wasn't kidding about the whole frisky twink thing.

I lick my lips as Alex tugs off his shirt. "I should probably shower first," I point out weakly.

He shakes his head. "No. I like you like this," he says, climbing onto my lap. His touch is soft as he feathers his lips across my cheek. "Can I ride you?"

I puff out a breath and nod.

Alex's movements are slow as he begins to methodically undress me. First, my pants. He flicks the button and drags the zipper down before sliding to the floor and tugging them gently off my legs. Then my boxers, which he removes with the same intentional care. My cock is hard, aching between my legs, and Alex gives it an appreciative once-over before settling back on my lap and unbuttoning my work shirt.

"Can anyone see in here other than Finn?" he asks, nodding toward the lone window on the other side of the room.

I shake my head.

"Can I open the drape?" he asks.

"You want Finn to see us?" I check, excited by that idea.

Alex nods, pulling my shirt down my arms. "Then he'll know to come over."

"Yeah, okay," I say, my voice all breath.

Alex slips off my lap and takes a step back, holding my gaze as he strips off his shorts, leaving him standing in only a pair of tight, baby-blue briefs. He rubs his cock through the material, his eyes roaming over my body.

"Have you ever watched my videos, Ro?" he asks.

I shake my head before switching course and nodding slowly. "Kind of? I, uh...looked you up. Looked Tink up after you told me about your job," I admit. "I watched half of a video, but I didn't..." I blow out a breath. *Honesty*. "I didn't want to see you with them. I didn't want to know if..." If I wasn't anything special.

Alex lowers his briefs, slipping them off his legs one at a time without saying a word. His cock, like him, is slim, dainty, and mouthwatering. He steps over to the window, completely unabashed in his nudity—confident in his own skin—and then he opens the drape.

Once he's exposed our position on the couch should Finn look through his kitchen window, he walks back over to me, condom and lube packet in hand that he pulled from his shorts. Kneeling on the couch, he settles over my lap once more, and his hands come up to frame my face.

"If you'd feel comfortable watching a video sometime, I'd like for you to see what I do," he says, fingers drifting over my beard. "Who I am at work? Tink? He's not who I am with you."

Alex reaches down between us and strokes my cock, pumping it once, twice, three times to full hardness.

"With you, it's never an act," he goes on. "I'm not pretending; I don't have to. The things I say? The way you affect me? That's real, and it hits me in here." He taps his chest before rolling a condom down my cock.

I can barely breathe, but I nod. Alex rips open the lube packet, and, grabbing my hand, he spreads the moisture on my fingers. Heart pounding rapidly, I take my cue as Alex goes up on his knees, and I reach underneath his body to prep him.

"Give me two," he says.

I oblige.

"Grizzly Bear," Alex moans, riding back on my fingers as I stretch him. "I need you to believe that sex with you means something more. I need you to know that the things I want from you? I don't want those things from the men I work with."

I nod in a little jolt as Alex gently pulls my hand away and positions himself over my cock. He barely pauses before lowering his body, taking half of me in one go. My breath stutters, and with a roll of his hips, Alex seats himself fully.

He groans, pausing there, head dropped back and hips shifting almost imperceptibly, as if he simply wants to *feel* me. When his gaze drags back to mine, he loops his arms around my head and starts to ride me. Slowly.

"I don't want them to hold me at night," he says, eyes piercing. "I don't tell them how perfectly made for me they are. Because they're not. I'm given a script, and I do my job, and sure, it's fun. But it doesn't *mean* more than that. You, Grizzly Bear. You mean..." His breath punches out as I tug him down on me harder. "You mean *so* much more."

I inhale a shaky breath, nodding again. I feel dazed, as if I'm in a dream.

Alex doesn't break eye contact as he works himself on my cock. As he drags us both closer to orgasm. My hands on his hips span so much skin, and it makes me feel...powerful. It makes me feel capable of protecting this man. Of protecting his heart.

And I realize, as I glide my thumbs upwards until they rest over Alex's nipples, that he's bared so much of himself to me already. He's trying to reassure me that I'm important to him. That sex, to him, is not the measure of what makes a relationship strong. He can get sex from anyone. But he wants me. *Needs me* for more than that.

He needs someone who's there for him at night. He wants someone nice, he said. Someone who sees him as he is and loves him for it. Someone who accepts him. Respects him.

He wants *comfort*. He's not asking for anything more. But *fuck*, he deserves that and so much more.

Alex moans when I roll his nipples between my fingers, and his hips pick up their pace.

"The truth is," I say, gliding one hand around to Alex's lower back so I can rut into him harder, "it doesn't matter to me that you're with other men. Because you still picked *me*. You chose me. I never asked to be the keeper of your body, Alex. All I want is..."

"My heart," he says quietly. So quietly.

He's right.

Picking Alex up, I take him down to the couch and settle over top of him. His eyes are shining, and his legs wrap around my hips.

"You're perfect for me, too, you know," I say quietly, fucking into him with a hard thrust, the way I know he likes it. He gasps, and I give him another. "You make me feel...strong." Capable. *Worthy*.

"You are," he says, hands running up my arms, fingers digging into muscle. His hair flops on every slam of my body into his. "My big, strong Grizzly Bear. Fuck, baby, you're gonna make me come."

I drop my head, kissing his temple, smelling his sunshine hair, giving him more. Giving him *everything*.

"Oh, Ro," he moans. "Oh, God. Just like that. So good. So fucking *deep*. You were made for me. I'm not ever going to give you up."

"Alex," I breathe, his words suffusing me with warmth. I punch into him harder, spiral higher, and that's when my eyes catch on Finn standing at the edge of the room.

Alex turns his head when I do, inhaling sharply. "You came," he says.

Finn licks his lip, nodding. His gaze is dark, hand resting idly over his crotch, and he looks *ravenous*.

My pace falters, but Alex urges me on, hands scratching at my back. "Don't stop," he tells me fiercely before his gaze latches onto Finn. "Do it, Ging. Get yourself off. Let us see that pretty cock."

And *fuck*, a jolt travels through my body at that. Finn lowers his zipper without hesitation, taking out his pierced dick. He works his cock over with abandon, and Alex's sounds turn frantic as he meets my thrusts. I try to pull my orgasm back—try to rein myself in—but it's impossible. I'm too far gone, and I need these men there with me when I fall.

Alex gasps as I shift his hips, pegging him just right. His mouth opens on a wordless prayer, and not a moment later, his cock is jerking against my stomach. Relief hits, strong and heady, as warmth floods the space between us, and I absolutely lose it. With Alex tightening around me and Finn coming apart before my eyes, I grab the armrest and grind my way home, shivering, shaking, as my release flows from me like a dirty benediction. *Hallelujah*.

I float for a moment. There's darkness and starlight. And then the sun. Alex gazing up at me, smiling.

His heart is in that smile.

And when I look over, Finn is wearing a similar expression.

This, I think, is exactly how it's supposed to be.

Chapter 20
FINN

When I see Rowan and Alex through the kitchen window, all spread out on the couch, the view opened up just for *me*, I can't get over there fast enough.

They look like...

Like everything I secretly want.

When I step into the room, Alex is moaning a litany of praise. "Oh, God. Just like that. So good. So fucking *deep*. You were made for me. I'm not ever going to give you up."

"Alex," Rowan breathes, his ass cheeks flexing as he fucks Alex into the couch.

It's a visual that has my cock jumping straight to attention.

It doesn't take long for the pair to notice me. "You came," Alex says, and my heart jumps—*flies*—at how damn pleased he sounds by the fact.

He truly wants me here, doesn't he? I'm not just window dressing.

"Do it, Ging," the blonde says, his face awash in pleasure. "Get yourself off. Let us see that pretty cock."

Oh God.

I don't need to be asked twice.

Unzipping my pants, I pull myself out swiftly, wrapping my hand around my length and groaning as Rowan's gaze rakes over me. He's close. I can see it in the tension around his eyes. In how his muscles are bunching and the sounds that are coming out of his mouth.

Alex seems to be teetering on the edge, too. And he's not only focused on Ro. He's watching me, as well. It makes me feel…

A whole lot of things.

When Alex's mouth opens on a gasp and Rowan starts grinding against him as if he's never felt anything more exquisite in his life, it's all over. My entire body shudders as I come, and I catch my release in my palm.

For a moment, as I watch Alex and Ro come down from their own highs, I wonder *what if.* Could we…?

But then Alex sighs, drawing my attention away from my thoughts. "I don't want you to move," he says softly to Ro. "I know you have to. But I don't want you to. I want to keep you inside me all night."

That's an image that has me shivering from head to toe.

"Maybe someday?" Rowan asks.

Alex's smile dips at the corner, and he shoots me a little glance. "Not while I'm doing porn."

Ro nods, grabbing a hold of the base of the condom and easing out of Alex's body. As they get themselves in order, I step out of the room, washing up in Rowan's kitchen. I can still hear their conversation, though.

"I'm sorry," Alex is saying. "I know it's not ideal."

"Hey," Ro replies. "I have no complaints. If we always use condoms, I won't have any complaints."

I smile at that. Rowan is such a good man.

"Okay, Grizzly Bear," Alex says with an audible sigh that sounds like contentment.

When I get back to the room, Rowan is brushing Alex's hair back. He kisses the blonde's forehead sweetly.

"Why don't we wash up real quick?" Ro suggests.

Alex nods, and the pair get up off the couch.

"I'll start dinner," I say.

Rowan shakes his head. "Don't. I'm cooking tonight. You need a break."

"Really?" I ask, stepping close, uncaring that the two are a bit of a sweaty, cum-stained mess. *Fuck*. That's pretty hot, actually.

"Really," Ro says, hands along my biceps. "Want to shower with us?"

"Abso-fucking-lutely," I answer.

Alex grins, and the three of us make our way up the stairs. Ro ditches the condom in the trash and starts the shower while I undress, and Alex hops in before it's even heated. He dances around a bit, his arms around his stomach.

"Oh fuck," the little blonde says. "It's cold."

Laughing, I step into the shower and wrap my arms around him without thought. His eyes shoot wide, but he smiles as I block the water from his body. Alex and I have never touched *each other* while naked before, but it doesn't feel the least bit strange. And since Alex clearly doesn't mind, I won't let myself either. Ro steps into the shower after us, smiling our way.

As the water heats, I rub my hands up and down Alex's arm—his other is plastered to my stomach—and once steam is swirling in the air, I let go. I grab my shower gel to wash up, and they do the same.

The three of us are quiet for several long minutes, but we move around each other like a choreographed dance, exchanging soft smiles and heated looks. I'm the first to step out of Rowan's large shower, and I dry off and put my clothes from earlier back on, since they're clean enough. Ro heads to his room to dress, and Alex follows. The blonde has been steadily leaving more and more possessions both here and at my place.

Honestly, I don't mind that one bit.

Downstairs, Rowan heads into the kitchen, and when he bodily shoves me from the room, I take the hint and settle in front of the TV. Alex joins me, bouncing onto the cushion right next to mine. I put on a cooking show I like to watch but turn the volume low.

"How are classes going?" I ask Alex.

He brightens before his face falls into a sort of scrunched frown. "Good, mostly. I think I'm going to miss being in school."

"Really?" I ask, turning toward him. "I was glad to be done."

He shrugs, stretching his little body out until his feet are on the coffee table. They barely reach. "I like having a reason to do art."

"You can still have a reason after you graduate," I point out. "Isn't that why you got an art degree to begin with?"

"I mean, yeah," he says with a chuckle. "It just might take me a while to make a living out of it, you know?"

In a way, yeah. I don't know how it will be for Alex and art, but I know, for me, it took a little time to find the right fit with my programming. I like where I am now, working from home and able to pick and choose which projects I take on. I'm lucky to have such flexibility. I know that.

"I think you'll figure it out," I say. Alex is bright.

"Thanks, Ginger Bear," he replies, giving me a smile. "I still have to decide what I'm doing for my final project, though."

"Oh, yeah? What's it about?"

"I have to illustrate a book. Something short," he says.

"Like a fairy tale?" I ask.

Alex looks over at me, mouth falling open slightly. He blinks a few times. "Huh."

"What?"

"No, I just hadn't thought of that," Alex says. "I don't want to do a children's book, but...why not an adult fairy tale?"

I shrug. "Sounds good to me."

Alex wiggles his toes, nodding slowly. "Hm." After a moment, his smile turns a little sly. "So, you've seen my videos."

I huff a laugh. "I have. Where's this coming from?"

"Ro and I were talking about it earlier. About me doing porn and...well, how it's different for me in my personal life."

I nod, understanding what he's talking about. "Yeah, you're not the same in your videos."

"Exactly," he says, turning to me in excitement and swatting my arm. "I'm glad you can tell the difference."

"Yeah?" I ask. "Why's that?"

Alex bites his lip slightly, seeming to think over his words before speaking. "I think...you see me as I am."

My breath punches from my lungs, chest seizing tight.

But Alex doesn't give me a moment to respond to *that*. He nudges my arm, and his eyebrows dance. "Which is your favorite?"

"What?" I ask, laughing a little incredulously.

"Your favorite scene," he says. "C'mon, I wanna know."

"Oh, Jesus." I run my hand over my eyes.

Alex isn't to be deterred. "Is it the one where I get plowed inside a space shuttle? That seems to be a crowd fav."

"That one didn't even make sense," I point out. "The physics alone were problematic."

Alex cracks a laugh, falling back on the couch. "Good point. Okay, how about the Christmas spit-roast?"

I cough, eyeing the troublemaker. That *was* a good video, and judging by Alex's mischievous grin, I can tell he knows I think so. I mean, really, though. The man looks damn fine getting stuffed from both ends.

Shit.

"As hot as that was," I say slowly, "it's not my favorite."

"No?" Alex asks, canting his head.

"Nuh-uh." I lick my lips. Clear my throat. "The, uh, fisting is."

Alex's eyes widen before, astonishingly, a blush spreads across his cheeks. He smiles quickly, however, covering his initial reaction with a wicked sort of grin.

"Oh, Ginger Bear," he says, leaning toward me and speaking softly like he's imparting a secret. "I do believe I've got your number."

"Hey, guys?" Ro calls out. "Do we want broccoli in the pasta?"

"Yeah, baby," Alex calls back, eyes still on me.

"All right," Rowan says.

Alex settles into his seat, facing the TV, and mouth dry, I turn up the volume. I watch the screen unseeing while Alex's words tumble over and over inside my head.

"It'll be fine," Alex says, smoothing Rowan's shirt. "You look hot."

Ro fidgets, tugging at the hem of the tight black tee Alex picked out for him. It hugs him beautifully, and I think that's why Rowan is so self-conscious about it. Although he shouldn't be.

Going up on his tiptoes, Alex leans close to Ro's ear. "All the gay boys will be eating you up."

Rowan huffs, but his posture relaxes, hands gliding over Alex's hips. "I don't want them."

"No?" Alex asks with a little smile, popping back flat on his feet. "Just me and Finn?"

Ro's eyes meet mine. "Just you two."

Alex hums, heading back to my dresser. He grabs a pair of tight pink pants from inside before walking to my closet and plucking a semi-sheer white shirt off a hanger. The next second, he's changing, clothes falling away, leaving him nude before he's covered once more. I've seen the man naked plenty of times by now, but I still have a hard time keeping my eyes averted when he's in such a state.

Alex and Ro are so very different on the outside, but I'm starting to realize my appreciation for both runs deeper than that. And I have yet to figure out how to handle that development.

Alex adjusts his shirt collar in the mirror. The entire thing is see-through enough that I'm not sure why he's even wearing it in the first place, but I suppose that's part of the tease. Since I'm already dressed in a simple white button-down, I head Ro's way, slipping my hands around my boyfriend's middle.

"Okay?" I ask him.

Rowan nods, but he looks nervous.

"I'm sure Alex would understand if you don't want to go," I say quietly.

But Rowan shakes his head quickly, turning in my grip so we're face to face. "I want to do this. It's just dancing. If I embarrass myself, then so be it. But Alex…" He glances over his shoulder, and my gaze follows his. Alex is spritzing something into his hair. "He really wants me there. I can tell. It's not a sacrifice to spend the night with the guys I—"

Rowan cuts off, but I have a sneaking suspicion I know exactly what he was going to say, and it sets my pulse racing through my veins like wildfire.

I lean close, running my lips along Ro's cheek, right above his beard. "We'll have a great time," I assure him. "Just think. It'll be a whole night of edging, and then we'll come back here and fuck so hard we forget our own names."

"Finn," he says on a breath, his hands tightening on the sides of my shirt.

"You boys ready?" Alex asks, a cheeky little smirk on his face as he watches us both.

Ro nods resolutely. "Let's dance."

Alex drives us in his Jeep, insisting he'll stay sober tonight. The club, Sublime, is lit up in typical neon fashion, with a bouncer outside and a line running down the street. A few people eye Alex with obvious recognition as we walk past, and I realize this is his place. His people, in a way.

I think tonight is about more than dancing.

The bouncer lets us pass, and Alex all but drags Ro and me inside where the crowd thickens. Music infiltrates the space, blasting through the speakers, booming through the soles of my shoes, and guiding the throng of bodies on the dance floor. Alex leads us to the bar first.

"Drink?" he asks over the noise.

Rowan nods. "Tequila?"

Looks like he needs a little something to settle his nerves.

I place my hand on his lower back. "Same," I tell Alex.

Alex nods and leans his entire body over the bar to get the bartender's attention. More than one pair of eyes shoot to Alex's ass, and *fuck*, I can understand why. Those pink pants are practically painted on his slim form.

The bartender heads right Alex's way, leaning across the space to give him a little hug. Everyone here seems to know the blonde minx.

After a short minute, Alex turns back around, two shot glasses in hand. "Cheers!" he yells.

Rowan and I accept our drinks, clinking them together before downing the liquid. Alex hands us another each, and I laugh.

"You're big boys," he says with a wink.

Shots emptied, Alex starts to sway to the music. He takes a step backwards, motioning Ro and me to follow. I keep my hand on Rowan's back as we make our way toward the dance floor. The bass thumps around us, and colored spotlights roam slowly over the people dancing in the middle of the club. With the lights set low, it'd be easy to get lost in here. Lost in the moment. Lost in the sea of bodies and *want*.

Alex tugs us right into the thick of it, his shirt flashing in multicolored hues as the lights move overhead. People press in on us from all sides, and I can tell Rowan is nervous. That he doesn't really know what to do. So I give him a gentle nudge forward, planting myself at his back as Alex closes in on his front, protecting him. Sandwiching him between us like we've done before.

Rowan relaxes some as I wind my arms around his stomach and tuck my chin over his shoulder. He turns his face into me, his beard rasping over my lips, and Alex's hand bumps into my hip as he grabs a hold of Rowan. Alex may be a slight man, but his personality is anything but small. He doesn't hesitate to grind up against Ro, looking effortlessly sexy as he does so.

It's impossible to talk, so none of us try. We communicate wordlessly through movement and touch. Alex garners a lot of attention, but each time some guy approaches, he politely brushes them off. He doesn't seem to want to be anywhere but with us.

My cock sits hard against Rowan's ass for what must be an hour before Alex motions us off the dance floor. The breather is welcome. He winds down the hall to a roped-off staircase further blocked by an employee, but as the man sees Alex, he slips into a smile and opens the rope right up. Alex gives the man a pat on the chest as we pass, and upstairs, we emerge onto what looks like a private balcony. There are couches, chairs, and tables set all around, as well as several men milling about and a server in booty shorts, a tray of drinks in his hand. It's marginally quieter up here.

"C'mon," Alex says, pulling us toward a couple of couches where a few men sit. When we get close, they notice Alex, giving him a cheer.

"Small fry," one calls out, holding up his drink. He has long, brown hair and is tucked up next to a big man I recognize as one of Alex's costars, Dix.

"Did you miss me?" Alex teases. He slides up next to Rowan, practically plastering himself to Ro's side. "This is Rowan, my boyfriend," he says before reaching over and grabbing my arm. "And this is Finn."

The men look between us, the long-haired one smiling. Alex points to him. "That's Niko. Next to him is Dixon. They're in *lurve*. And this is Kipp," he says excitedly, hopping over to a man with short, dark hair, who grins widely. "I haven't seen you in forever, Kipper. What've you been up to?"

"Oh, you know. The usual," Kipp says, shrugging.

"So, being your awesome self?" Alex shoots back.

Kipp chuckles as Alex takes a seat on the open couch. He motions both of us over.

"Alex, you're one lucky SOB. You know that, right?" Kipp says, tone light, even as he shakes his head a little.

"How so?" Alex asks, unceremoniously hopping onto Rowan's lap as soon as the man takes a seat. Rowan catches him easily, holding onto the smaller man, and Alex sprawls his legs over my thighs.

"I can't even find one Mr. Right," Kipp answers. "And here you are with two."

Alex doesn't correct him that I'm not technically his. He looks first at Rowan, and then at me, and he says, "Yeah. I am pretty lucky, huh?"

Chapter 21
ALEX

Rowan and Finn have another drink while we take a break in the VIP lounge at Sublime. And when Lonny, one of our usual servers, eyes the pair of them with obvious interest, it doesn't even bother me. *Yeah, that's right. My bears are hot.*

Bears. Plural.

I can't stop thinking of them that way. Somewhere along the line, Finn stopped being Ro's neighbor and boyfriend, and he became...my friend. And then my something more.

At least, I want us to be more. I'm pretty sure Finn feels the same.

"I'm a little envious," Emil says, pulling my attention.

"You, too?" I ask, assuming he's talking about the bears seated next to me. They're side by side on the couch, Finn's hand trailing steadily higher up Rowan's thigh. It's hot.

Emil cocks his head in confusion.

"Wait, envious of what?" I ask.

"That this is your last year of school," he says.

Whoops. I might have missed a bit of our conversation. I give myself a little mental slap. *Rude.*

"How much do you have left?" I ask.

"Another year of undergrad," he answers. "And then there's my master's. Plus my doctorate, if I decide to go that far."

"Yeesh," I say. "How do you get through all that without a mountain of debt?"

"You don't," he replies a little glumly, taking a sip of his drink.

I appraise my coworker. Emil has always been a little private. Not standoffish, but he doesn't go out of his way to be a part of group functions or friendships. He's polite, but distant. I don't know him as well as I maybe could.

"Is that why you got into porn?" I ask. Money is a big motivator.

Emil pauses, the tip of his straw in his mouth. He looks at me, glasses a touch askew on his face, and it's more than obvious the answer to that question is no, but he hesitates. What doesn't he want to tell me?

"Hey," Finn says, squeezing my leg gently to get my attention. A *zing* travels straight to my cock at the simple touch.

Ho boy.

"What's up, Gingersnap?" I ask, pivoting his way.

He leans close, his lips at my ear as he speaks quietly. "If you want to do any more dancing, now might be the time. I think Rowan's reaching his limit."

I look past Finn to our Grizzly Bear. I think Finn's right. The man looks a little tired and wary, as if he's reached his cap of peopling for the day.

I give Finn a nod before turning back to Emil. "Wanna dance, boo?"

He shakes his head. "Not right now. Go on ahead."

"If you're sure."

He nods again.

Grabbing Finn's hand, I give the man a little tug. He gets off the couch, giving Ro a tug, and the three of us head back downstairs into the throng of horny bodies. I catch sight of some of my coworkers down here on the dance floor. There's Dixon and Niko, grinding on each other with love in their eyes, the cuties. Cas, eyes closed, doing his own thing amidst a sea of admirers vying for his attention. Even Kipp is down here, dancing with some cute twink with pink hair. And Teddy... Oh. Teddy is watching Kipp like a damn hawk.

Well, hello.

Finding a space amongst the crowd, I come to a stop and turn to my guys. Like before, Finn and I press Rowan between our bodies, and like before, the bear of a man starts to relax, as if being cushioned in the middle of us is a comfort to him.

Knowing we'll head home after this, I can't help but tease Ro a little bit more than I did earlier. I run my hands over his body slowly as we dance, straying closer and closer to where his cock is tenting the front of his jeans. His responding rumble is low, and when I finally brush my fingers over the denim trapping his erection, caressing lightly, his eyes shutter halfway closed.

I love how I affect him.

Spinning, I give him my backside, and his hands close immediately over my hips, fingers digging in as I grind back against him. He's so tall he's basically rubbing his erection against my lower back instead of my ass, but *dang*, he doesn't seem to mind. And neither do I. I wind my arms up, grabbing on, barely able to clasp my fingers behind his neck.

And then...then another set of hands close over my waist, and lips press against my knuckles.

Oh. Oh damn.

My knees go a little weak.

The music is loud, but I can feel Rowan's moan vibrating through my body. Feel Finn's lips brushing over the sensitive skin of my fingers. Feel two sets of hands gripping me tight. Holding on for dear life.

Spinning, I dislodge their hands and go up on my tiptoes. Mouth at Ro's ear, eyes on Finn, I say, "Let's go home."

Both men nod.

The abrupt loss of sound as we exit the club is jarring. My ears ring in the absence of noise, the traffic a subtle background track compared to what was inside. None of us say a word as we walk down the street to where I parked my Jeep. It's as if we're under a spell.

The drive home—to Rowan and Finn's neighborhood—seems to simultaneously fly and crawl. I park in Ro's driveway when we arrive, but the three of us head toward Finn's place by unspoken agreement. The silence carries until the door shuts behind us and I catch sight of Mojave at the window perch.

"Sweet girl," I coo, beelining her way. The guys can wait one minute.

Mo purrs as soon as she sees me coming. She really does sound like a rattlesnake, all raspy with an underlying buzz to her vocals. She pushes up into my hand, accepting scritches against her cheeks and chin, and then weaving back and forth so I don't miss her spine.

"Such a little attention whore, aren't you?" I say, chuckling when she places her front paws on my chest and rubs my chin. "Yes. Yes, you are. That's right. My good, sweet girl."

When I give Mojave one last pet and finally turn around, my breath catches.

Rowan and Finn are standing nearby. Just like at the club, Finn is behind Rowan, his arms around the man, his chin sitting over his shoulder. And both men are looking at me softly in a way that has nothing whatsoever to do with sex.

Taking a step closer, I let my eyes trail to Finn. "Are we going to keep pretending nothing is happening here?"

Finn blows out a slow breath before stepping out from behind Rowan, putting them side to side. His eyes trace me for a beat before his hand reaches for Ro's. He threads their fingers together before speaking.

"We said we'd talk if any of us wanted something about this arrangement to change," Finn says, eyes on me before he turns to Rowan. "Love, would you mind if I kissed your boyfriend?"

Rowan's inhale is sharp, matching my own, but he doesn't look the least bit surprised. He blinks Finn's way before turning to me, and the expression on his handsome face floors me. *Acceptance.* Did I expect anything but?

"I think you should ask him yourself," Rowan says, his permission evident.

Finn looks my way, opening his mouth, but I'm already in motion. He doesn't let go of Ro's hand as I collide into his body, but his arm comes around me like a band. We hover there for the quickest of beats, staring at one another, me up on tiptoes, our lips an inch apart. My hands are in Finn's hair, arms stretched as high as they can go. His arm tightens around me, a light squeeze.

And then there's no space between us at all.

Finn's kiss is completely different from Rowan's. It's more demanding, and it tastes like cinnamon and spice. His lip ring brushes against me like a smooth caress, like a reminder of what's waiting down below, and his tongue is relentless in its pursuit to turn me to mush.

I'd gladly be a pile of horny mush for these men any day.

When we pull apart—oxygen a necessity—Finn's eyes are burning gold. Flickering flames. I want them to consume me.

"Are we doing this?" I voice, eyes roaming between these two men. "Are we...three now?"

Neither asks what I mean. They get it. Rowan bites his lip, looking at Finn. Finn nods slowly. Rowan smiles. I smile.

"Oh wow," I say.

I guess our tiny polycule just became a triad.

"Upstairs, babies," I tell my men. *My men.*

We move up the stairs in a sort of trance. I can still feel the beat of the club in my veins, like I've been laced with a sort of buzzing electricity. It guides me to strip inside Finn's bedroom, moving my body slowly to the music inside my own head. I can feel their eyes on me from behind, watching each article of clothing as it falls away from my body. It amps me up. Excites me to have their focus.

When my briefs finally fall to the floor, I turn. Finn is behind Rowan again, stripping him, peeling his clothing off the same as I had been doing to my own. Both of their eyes are on me. Rowan's gaze is lustful as he stands there obediently, completely at ease as Finn divests him of his clothes. It makes my chest sing that Ro seems to be accepting the submissive side of himself. He doesn't look nervous, as he did in the beginning. He looks...settled.

When Finn strips Rowan's pants and boxers down, presenting the man like a gift, I approach, closing my hand around Ro's impressive girth. He's a true beast in my fist, meaty and veined. He doesn't fit fully in my hand; not even close. My Grizzly Bear is plain hung.

I drop to my knees as Finn begins tugging off his own clothes, and I roll my tongue over Ro's crown, humming as he fills my mouth and invades my senses. Dragging my lips up and down his shaft a few times, I reacquaint myself with his taste and smell. I toy with his crown. Lick. Suck. And then I take him into my throat.

Ro's moan punches from him—one of my favorite sounds—and his fingers find my hair. Another set of hands land lightly on my back, trailing downward, and I realize Finn is behind me, crouched low to the ground. His fingers tease my hips, my stomach, my navel, leaving bubbles of anticipation in their wake. One hand stays there, at my belly button, but the other...the other slides lower, wrapping around my cock and giving a slow, smooth tug.

I moan, shivering as Finn's lip ring catches the lobe of my ear. His teeth follow as his fist jerks me in lazy, corkscrewing motions. I can't help but glance down. The ink covering the back of Finn's hand is like art, wrapping around me and coloring me in waves of blissful relief. Rowan groans above me, his eyes certainly on what's happening below, and I run my palms over his thighs. All that thickness and hair makes me dizzy.

"C'mon," Finn says gently before his touch feathers away.

A sigh rolls through me, and I lean back, letting Ro's dick pop from my mouth. When I look up, Finn is there, holding out his hand. I grab on, a little flutter dropping through my stomach as our palms connect, and Finn tugs both me and Rowan to the bed. We land together in a heap of bodies and light laughter, none of us much caring about the slight sheen of sweat on our bodies from dancing at the club. Our minds are elsewhere.

Finn grabs the back of Rowan's neck once we settle, pulling him in and kissing him before reaching for me. Our mouths and tongues meet, back and forth, greedy and demanding, and I stroke the cock in my hand. Finn's. The piercings drag along my palm, almost a tickle of sensation, and Finn groans, punching into my grip.

One day...one day very soon...I'm going to find out *exactly* how these piercings feel inside me.

When Rowan's hand curls around my hip, tugging gently, I roll his way, settling between him and Finn. He kisses me, my Grizzly Bear, tasting of tequila with a hint of Finn's cinnamon, and instantly, I'm an addict. I suck on his tongue, wanting more, wanting all of it, and he rewards me with another of those stuttered moans.

When Finn shifts behind me, spooning my smaller form, my pulse kicks in excitement. He guides his erection between my legs, and, with an encouraging moan, I tighten my thighs around him, giving him the perfect sleeve to fuck into. He attacks my neck, sucking kisses along the tender skin at the top of my spine, below my ear, at the edge of my shoulder.

With Finn curled behind me and Ro tucked in front, I feel like I'm floating, suspended in the most perfect cloud.

My men. My bears.

Touch comes from every direction, and it's almost too much to follow. Rowan spans his hand across my chest, his thumb at one nipple, his pinkie at the other. Finn's hips gently slap my ass, his breath ghosting near my ear. We're a mess of need and want, hands and tongues. And when Finn reaches forward, taking Ro's erection in his fist, it hits me someplace deep. The three of us, tied together. Finally.

Not a word is spoken as we rut, kiss, and fuck fists and thighs. As we explore each other for the first time as a throuple. We seem to move as one. An endless dance. An unspoken treaty where the end goal is clear.

Togetherness.

One of my hands rests on Finn's thigh as he moves behind me. The other holds Ro's face. My dick rubs against Finn's fist as he jerks Rowan off, and occasionally, Finn switches his grip to me, stroking me surely toward orgasm.

Bliss.

Finn's lips brush the side of my neck, so I turn my head, snagging his mouth as Rowan circles his thumb over each of my nipples in turn. I groan, fingers digging into Rowan's chest, and Finn releases my mouth, grabbing Ro's hair to tug him in for a sloppy kiss of their own. My throat gets tight, watching these two men come together, mouths, tongues, breath as one.

So lovely. So very mine.

We're a tangled knot of limbs and bodies, and I don't want it to ever end, but when Rowan reaches down to encircle the both of us in his fist, I know we won't last much longer. Finn grabs my hip, fucking my thighs harder. His cock rubs along my balls, the length of it hard and heavy between my legs. He groans, pace hastening, but it's Rowan who comes first when Finn joins his pumping hand over our lengths. Our grizzly spills in hot spurts over his fist and my abdomen, and like a domino effect, Finn and I fall.

Finn detonates with a punched-out groan, his release dampening my inner thighs and some landing on Ro's leg. And as their combined fists tighten over my still-hard cock, my own orgasm washes over me like a sudden rainstorm. It drenches me all at once, every muscle in my body tightening, sensation pooling low and sweet. And then, like thunder, it rolls out.

I choke out something unintelligible as I come, but all I know, all I feel, are the hands stroking me. The palms running over my skin. The flutter of lips and the soft whisper of voices as aftershocks make me shiver.

I tuck my face to Rowan's chest, breathing heavily as something inside of my ribcage squeezes oh so tight.

"Goldie," Finn whispers, stroking my back.

I nod. I know.

Reaching back, I find a hand, and I tighten my grip in Finn's. Rowan kisses my hair, nuzzling the top of my head.

"I think," Ro says slowly, rubbing his palm up and down my arm, "we might've broken him."

I chuckle a little hoarsely, lifting my head at last. Ro gives me a smile.

"I'm going to regret it when we wake up plastered together just like this, but can we not move?" I request. "I want to stay right here."

For as long as possible.

"Yeah, Goldie," Finn says softly, grabbing the corner of the fitted sheet that came loose with our tousling. He wipes us up as best as he can.

I close my eyes as he works, feeling Rowan's soft breaths puff above my head. When Finn is done, he tucks his arm over me, and I let out a sigh.

Cocooned in perfect warmth, my mind drifts. I have the fleeting thought that I'm going to have to explain this to my parents—that I'm seeing two men. But it's a passing concern, unable to take hold as my grizzly and my ginger hold me tight.

I don't know that I've ever felt as perfectly content as I do in this moment.

I'm not sure anything could screw it up.

Chapter 22
Finn

"Well, this is new," I say, crossing my arms and leaning against the wall outside my office door.

Alex looks up, a sheepish smile on his face. "Do you mind? I brought it over from my place."

I blow air out of my nose, walking over to where a massive beanbag chair sits in front of my orchids on the landing at the top of the stairs. Alex is sprawled stomach-down on top of it, a sliver of his skin visible above the waistband of his fitted shorts and a sketchpad set out in front of him. His shirt, I realize, eyeing the dimples above his ass, is cropped short.

What a wonderful thing to find on my break.

"I don't mind," I say, crouching low beside the beanbag.

Alex rolls onto his back, and my eyes drop to his exposed stomach. "Enjoying the view?" he asks with a grin.

My lips twitch. "Mm. I like that I can look now."

"You could have looked before," Alex says, stretching in a way I'm positive is intentionally enticing.

Maybe that's so, but I think I was denying my attraction to Alex for quite some time, not ready to admit there was more there. Why, I'm not sure. Maybe I didn't want to take away from Ro. Maybe I was simply waiting for the time to feel right.

"Do you have class today?" I ask.

Alex shakes his head before closing his sketchpad and setting it on the floor.

"Working on your project?" I guess.

"Trying," he says with a frown. "I still haven't nailed the idea."

"You'll figure it out," I say, sure of it. "Wanna walk with me?"

Alex nods, reaching up and wiggling his fingers. Standing, I take his hands in my own and tug him to his feet. He's so much smaller than me, just a slight thing. But as much as I love Rowan's big, burly body, I equally appreciate Alex's slim one, all smooth lines and dainty features.

I could toss him over my shoulder if I wanted and cart him away.

The idea makes me smile.

"What are you working on right now?" Alex asks as we head out the front door.

It's hot today—in the mid-eighties—so I roll my sleeves up to my elbows as I answer. "A web application for a library in Utah."

"Really?" he asks, looking over at me with a scrunched smile.

"Really," I answer. "I'm creating an updated system for their lending library."

"Huh," Alex says. "I don't understand how all that works. All the...script or whatever you call it. Whenever I catch a glimpse of your computer screen, it looks like something out of *The Matrix.*"

"Well," I say with a chuckle. "It would make sense if you were a programmer. You just have to know the language."

"Is that like the orchids?" he asks, squinting against the sun. "You speak to flowers and computers?"

I huff in amusement. "I'm a man of many talents."

Alex waggles his eyebrows, and I snort. Always the innuendos with this man.

The feisty blonde hops a step, bouncing lightly. "I'm curious what your piercings would feel like on my tongue," he says, apropos of nothing.

My throat catches, and I clear it. "Yeah?"

"And in my ass," he adds, almost thoughtfully.

My dick makes it clear I would *not* be opposed to Alex finding that out.

He smirks, the wicked little thing. "You're already ribbed for pleasure," he stage-whispers because apparently, he's decided to torture me on this walk.

"Christ, Alex," I mutter, training my eyes forward for a moment so I can regain my equilibrium. A sprinkler is on in the yard we're passing, and it mists water down over the succulents and flower beds. "You're dangerous, you know that?"

He laughs quietly next to me. "I did warn you."

"So you did," I say, meeting his gaze.

Alex tentatively seeks out my hand, and when I give him a squeeze, he keeps a hold of it as we walk side by side past the houses on my street. It feels so natural, his palm tucked against my own, and I wonder at it.

Were we always headed here? Was it inevitable?

"What's your family like?" I ask. There's a lot about this man I don't yet know.

Alex shrugs a little, swinging our hands lightly between us. "They're okay. Very...average? That feels terrible to say," he says, shaking his head a little, "but it's true. Typical all American family with a middle-class income and a white picket fence surrounding a two-story home. My parents are stable, and they love me. But they don't really get me. They worry about my choices."

"Your job?" I ask.

"They don't actually know about the porn," he says, grimacing slightly. "Honestly, they don't need to know. I think they'd expire from shock."

"Oof."

"Yeah," Alex says slowly, still swinging our hands. "Art school has been difficult for them. They were concerned about my future and my finances. They don't realize I'm already...well..." He huffs a little. "They don't know I'm already loaded."

I smile at that. Good for Alex.

Not because he has money, but because he made something out of a career many people wouldn't understand. I'm sure Alex gets judged plenty. I'm glad to hear, at the very least, he's swimming, not sinking.

"What would they think about all this?" I ask. "Us?"

Alex's face falls briefly, but then he gives me a little smile. "I don't know, truthfully. It'll probably take them a while to come around. I think they'll support me—*us*—eventually. But they're not going to get it."

I hum lightly. My parents wouldn't either. But my parents aren't a part of my life anymore, so it doesn't really matter. Fi, though...

"I was thinking about inviting my sister over for dinner," I say.

"Tonight?" Alex asks.

I shrug a little. "If she's free."

"We should make enchiladas," he says excitedly. "The ones with the green chiles. Oh! Or burgers. Or *oooh*, no. Biscuits and gravy." He moans decadently, and it's all I can do to ignore the fissure of *want* that sound sends down my entire being. "Although I do have a scene tomorrow, so I'll have to go easy."

He pouts a little at that, and I know better than to lecture Alex on the dietary confines of his job. He's an adult who can make his own choices, and it's not like he's unhealthily skinny.

But I do want to kiss that pout. So that's exactly what I do.

Giving Alex's hand a tug, I swing him around and bend low to slot my lips against his. He makes a sound of surprise, but then his hands are around the back of my neck, holding tight, and his tongue sweeps enthusiastically into my mouth, the velvety surface of it sliding alongside my own. He's like C-4. An explosion of fire and energy.

"Ginger Bear," he husks, that nickname he uses for me. There's ownership in his tone, and I love that. I love that I'm his *anything*. His Ginger Bear.

I brush my nose against his before leaning back. "You really want to cook with me?" I ask. He did say *we*.

He nods, eyes pinging between my own. "Is that okay? I'm sure you won't let me burn the kitchen down."

My lips twitch, and Alex grins, eyes bouncing to my mouth for a moment. Lingering there. He's still holding my neck, his arms stretched high, and my hands are on his hips. Holding him feels good. Right.

"No, I certainly won't," I assure him. "I'd love to cook with you."

Alex seems oh so pleased with that. He steps back at last, and grabbing ahold of my hand again, we continue walking.

"I'll call her when we get back. Fiona," I clarify.

Alex's head bobs. "I can run to the store if we need any groceries. Does she like wine? I can get some wine. Maybe chocolates, too?"

"Are you trying to bribe my sister into liking you?" I ask in amusement.

Alex smiles a little crookedly. "Think it'd work?"

I huff a laugh. "She already likes you, Goldie. You have nothing to worry about."

"Does she really?" he asks, swinging my hand. "I've never had a sister before."

My breath gets caught in my lungs at the implication of that statement. *Christ*, the things that come out of his mouth sometimes.

"Come on," I say, leaning down so Alex can climb on my back. "Let's go menu plan."

Alex squeals, jumping onto my back, and with a gigantic smile, I walk us home.

"Ro is gonna shower real quick, and then he'll be right over," Alex calls out, sounding as if he's kicking off his shoes in the entryway.

"You didn't want to join him?" I call back from the kitchen.

"Please. If I did that, there'd be no *quick* about it, and your sister is on her way."

I snort. Fair point.

Alex comes around the corner as I'm slipping the pan of biscuits we made into the oven. "Mm," he hums. "Those look good."

"They'll taste good, too," I reply, lowering the heat on the burner where the gravy is cooking.

"Assuming I didn't mess them up," Alex says.

"You didn't," I assure him. "You did great."

He beams.

"So, chocolates... Yay or nay?" he asks, pulling a giant box of truffles out from behind his back.

I bark a laugh. "Let's see how the night goes."

Alex nods, sticking the chocolate inside the pantry. A moment later, the front door opens and closes, and then Rowan steps into the room looking freshly showered.

Alex hums happily. I do, too.

Bounding over, Alex tugs Ro to the table, plopping him into a seat and then climbing onto his lap. "So how are we doing this?" he asks the both of us. "Are we easing your sister into the fact that we're all fucking like bunnies? Or, you know, are we going to be subtle about it?"

"You're capable of subtlety?" I tease, laughing when Alex tosses a cloth napkin my way.

"I can be respectable," he says with a sniff.

"Just be yourself, Alex," I say, shaking my head slightly. I give the sausage gravy another stir before turning off the heat. When I look back at the two at the table, Alex's expression is soft, and his eyes roam over me slowly. Not in a lascivious way. Simply like he's...looking.

"I told Pauly, my friend at the shop," Ro says. "That I was seeing you both."

"How'd he take it?" I ask, claiming the chair beside them.

"He was really cool about it," Rowan answers, a little smile on his face. "Sometimes I wonder what my folks would think. About everything that's happened. My life. This."

Alex's lips turn down a bit. "They're gone?"

Ro nods, and I reach over, squeezing his knee. I was already aware that Ro's parents passed away when he was still in his teens. Even though I didn't know him back then, he told me it was hard on him.

"Sorry, Baby Bear," Alex says softly, rubbing his cheek against Rowan's shoulder. Ro tightens his arms around the man. "What were they like?"

"Really...great," Rowan says slowly. "I think they just wanted me to be happy."

Alex sighs softly at that before a knock at the door brings our conversation to a temporary halt.

"I'll get it," I say, pushing out of my seat.

Fiona stands with her hands clasped together when I open the front door. She looks different, her hair down for once and her clothes more casual than the pressed workplace attire I'm used to seeing her in—the same type of clothing she was dressed in that day at Gran's.

"Fi," I say, holding the door wide.

She walks in, giving me a little smile before her eyes sweep through my living room. "Thanks," she says. "This place is...colorful."

I snort a laugh. "That it is. Come on in. Rowan and Alex are in the kitchen, and dinner's just about ready."

Fiona sets her purse on the little table beside my door before following me into the next room. Alex is no longer on Rowan's lap, but the pair are seated close together. Ro looks a little nervous. A little shy, unsurprisingly. But Alex has a beaming grin on his face.

The small blonde pops up first.

"Hi, Fiona," Alex says, coming over and giving Fi a quick, tight hug she's entirely unprepared for.

"Hi," she responds, eyes wide when Alex releases her. He has that effect on people. "It's nice to see you again."

Her gaze flicks to Rowan next as he steps her way, and I place a reassuring hand on the small of his back.

"Fi, you've met Alex," I say, giving proper introductions. "And this is Rowan."

"The boyfriend," Fiona fills in, accepting the hand Ro holds out.

Ro blushes slightly. "One of them. Nice to meet you, Fiona."

"You, too," Fiona says, gaze flicking to me in question.

"Yes, Alex and I are dating now, too," I say, deciding to get that out there right off the bat.

"The real kind," Alex adds, attaching himself to my side. "Not just like bunnies."

Fiona looks confused, and I bite my lip.

"Bunnies date?" she asks.

"No, bunnies f—" Alex cuts himself off. "...udge. You know what? I think I heard the timer."

Alex peels away, pretending to check inside the oven, and I give my sister a shrug. Rowan's shoulders shake slightly in my peripheral vision.

"We're having biscuits and gravy," I tell Fi. "I hope that's okay?"

"Sounds great," she says, taking a seat at the table. "So how've you been? Really?"

Hitting the hard stuff, I see.

Since Alex is watching the actual timer like a hawk, I pull out a chair across from my sister and slide the one next to me out for Ro.

"I'm good, Fi. Leaving was the right choice for me. But I'll admit, in recent years, I *was* feeling a little lonely. I think that's why it was so easy to come back here."

Ro subtly squeezes my leg underneath the table. I link my fingers with his.

"And now?" she asks, as if the obvious isn't in the room with us.

"Now, I'm not so lonely anymore," I answer.

Ro gives me another squeeze.

Fiona nods, tucking some of her dark red hair behind her ear. "Have you talked to Mom and Dad at all since coming back?"

I puff out a little breath. "I left a few voicemails, but they haven't returned my calls, and I didn't really expect them to. I'm done trying, Fi. I'm the black sheep of the family. You know that. Mom and Dad don't want me sullying their reputation."

Fiona doesn't even try to refute my claim. To my corporate lawyer family, I *am* the black sheep.

"Dillon and Conner?" she asks. Our brothers.

I shrug. "No word from them either. They stopped responding to my texts years ago."

And considering they've always been not-so-subtly disapproving of my lifestyle—aka being queer—I'm not in any hurry to reconnect. Fi and Gran are all I have left. And I'm okay with that.

Fiona nods slowly, her eyes downcast. "I'd like it if we could, maybe, try to be friends again. Like we used to be when we were kids."

"I'd like that, too," I tell her truthfully. I always was closest to Fi. Out of everyone, I thought she felt a little of what I did. That pressure to conform. The wrongness of it. But then she followed in our parents' footsteps and, over time, we drifted apart.

I'm glad she's here now. And I don't want my sister to feel alone, not like I did. On the heels of her divorce especially, she could use family. Friends.

We could be that for her.

Before the timer has a chance to ding for real, Alex shuts it off and opens the oven door. He pulls the biscuits out and sets them to cool. He and Ro had been quiet while Fiona and I caught up, but now the blonde ball of energy bounds over, scooting onto my lap without a care in the world. He loops his arms around my neck as he gives Fiona a smile.

"Do you like brunch, Fi?" he asks her. "I do brunch with some of my friends from art school a couple times a month. I could let you know the next time we go."

My sister looks taken aback by the offer, but she quickly smiles. A genuine thing. "Yeah, I'd like that."

"Great," Alex says, pulling his phone from his pocket. He hands it to my sister. "Enter your number, and I'll text you."

Oh, Goldie. Sweet boy.

I smudge a kiss against his forehead.

"Are we ready for dinner?" Alex asks.

"I'll get it," Ro says, standing up. He heads over to the counter and uses a spatula to slide the biscuits onto a serving plate as Fiona hands Alex back his phone.

"So," my sister says, a coy little smirk on her face. "Alex, Ro, tell me all about yourselves. How did you meet my brother?"

Alex and I share a look. His hazel eyes sparkle, and I can tell he's remembering the *exact* moment we met in Rowan's living room. The moment that, at the time, felt almost unbearably uncomfortable. And yet, now, looking back, all I remember is Alex and Ro together, naked behind the cover of the couch, both sweaty and blissed as they found their release.

A clatter near the counter tells me Rowan is remembering the same thing.

"It's...complicated," I hedge.

"Oh?" Fiona says, clearly curious.

"Well, you see," Alex begins, a Cheshire Cat grin on his face. I groan quietly. "It all started with Destiny."

Chapter 23
ROWAN

"I just...I don't get it," Alex says, gesturing to the TV. "Why nine? Ten innings would make much more sense."

"Well, the Knickerbockers—" I start to say.

But Alex cuts me off, waving both hands in the air. "I'm sorry, hold up. The *Knickerbockers?*" He spins on the couch, facing the stairway and calling out, "Finnigan! Get your ass down here."

"Huh?" Finn calls back.

"Ro is teaching us baseball," Alex shouts. "Something about knickers." He stills, panning slowly my way. "Wait. Is that the name of the pants?"

His eyes are wide, and I can't help but laugh a little.

"Well, technically, yeah," I answer. "They're called knicker-bockers."

Alex catapults over the back of the couch. "Finnigan! They have a name," he yells, running up the stairs.

Oh Lord.

I chuckle, taking a sip of my beer as Mojave gives my leg a sniff. I offer her my hand, but she turns tail and curls up in Alex's vacated spot instead. I try not to take it personally.

As I wait for my boyfriends to get back downstairs for Friday-night baseball, I notice a blanket along the back of the couch that wasn't there before. And now that I'm looking, there's a new picture on the bookshelf, too. A photo of the three of us—me, Alex, and Finn. Getting up, I take a better look. Did Alex do this?

I glance around. There are a few pairs of shoes in the entryway that most definitely aren't Finn's. A basket of throw pillows near the couch. And a photo on the wall that looks suspiciously like body parts. Or hills.

When did this happen? Should I be concerned that the little blonde is slotting himself into both of our spaces like he was always meant to be here? Because all I feel is...contentment.

A laugh comes from the direction of the stairs before Finn appears, walking down slowly with Alex on his back.

"To the kitchen, Ginger Pony. I need a drink," Alex declares, tugging on the shoulder of Finn's shirt as if he's directing a horse.

Finn stops cold. "I draw the line at being called a pony," he says dryly.

"Ponies get ridden," Alex retorts.

Finn inhales a breath before heading toward the kitchen. Alex mimes cracking a whip, and my smile stretches my cheeks wide. When the pair come back into the room, Alex is grinning, and he nudges Finn my way.

"To our man, Ging," Alex says.

Finn doesn't hesitate. He carries Alex over, but he keeps Alex turned away while he grabs behind my head with one hand and tugs me close. His lips collide with mine, tasting of beer and cinnamon, and I inhale every ounce of Finn that I can.

I will never get sick of this. Never stop wanting this.

Finn's lip ring drags against my bottom lip tantalizingly slowly before he steps back and angles his body. Alex doesn't skip a beat. He leans in and takes his turn tasting my lips. It's playful and bubbly and full of that marshmallow fluff, and my insides fizz like soda water.

"Mm," Alex hums, smacking one final kiss against my cheek before scrambling down Finn's back, a wine cooler in his hand. "All right, Grizzly Bear. Teach us about these knickers."

Alex plops down on the couch, patting the cushions beside him. Finn takes a seat on one side, I sit on the other, and Alex manages to sprawl across the both of us without spilling his drink. When Finn's fingers brush against my shoulder, I look over, catching the fondness in his gaze as Alex starts rambling about knickers and "What the hell are bockers, anyways?"

It's perfect. So perfect. So utterly right. And I wonder, vaguely, if it's even real or only a dream.

If it is a dream, I don't want to ever wake up.

"Shit. Damn," I mutter, shaking out my hand as my finger throbs.

"All right?" Pauly calls, setting down his tools before walking over.

"Yeah. Fine," I say, turning my hand this way and that. My finger is going to swell, that's for sure, but it doesn't feel broken.

Pauly purses his lips, and his eyes narrow slightly. "Did I see that right? You just shut your hand in the hood?"

Sighing, I nod before grabbing the bottle of coolant I just emptied into the vehicle in front of me.

"You shut your hand...in the hood of a car," Pauly repeats.

"Go on," I tell him. "Have your laugh."

"I'm not gonna laugh," Pauly says, following me over to the service bay sink. I ditch the empty bottle of coolant and run my hand under cold water for a minute. "But I am going to ask what the hell has you so distracted."

I give Pauly a look.

"Ah," he says knowingly, lips tipping into a grin. "Your men. Keeping you up at night? Doing the horizontal tango? Gotta say, Grizlak, seems like a lot of parts flying around."

"Pauly," I groan, refocusing on my hand.

He chuckles, slapping me on the back. I *oof*.

"No shame in the game," he says, turning to walk away.

"Hey, Pauly?" I say before he can get far.

He stops. "What's up?"

Turning off the tap on the sink, I ask, "Do you think I have a distorted view of myself?"

Pauly cocks his head before walking closer. He sits his butt on the desk nearby and crosses his arms. "Yes."

"Well, shit," I mutter, grabbing a cloth to dry my hands.

"I've been saying it for years," Pauly says, not unkindly. "You don't think highly of yourself. And look, a certain degree of humility is a good thing. But...remember that woman from a few weeks back with the invoice adjustment? She was hitting on you, and you had no clue."

"Why would she possibly have been hitting on me?" I ask.

Pauly holds his hand out, and then he waves it up and down in front of me.

I shake my head. "Pauly—"

"This is what I mean," he says, kicking off the desk and stopping a couple feet in front of me. "You can't even fathom it. You know, this is why I really hated Manuel. He fed your low opinion of yourself. He wasn't good for you."

"No, he wasn't," I agree quietly.

"I'm glad you can see that now," Pauly says. "But Christ, boss. It's like, because you're this big guy, you think that makes you unlovable. Most people in the world are *not* models, you know, contrary to what the media makes us believe. We're real fucking people with acne or large noses or an abundance of body hair. And there's nothing wrong with that," he says, throwing his hands in the air. "None of that shit even matters; that's the thing. What matters is surrounding ourselves with people who value and appreciate us. And whether or not you want to believe it, you're a catch. You caught yourself two boyfriends, didn't you? What do you think that says?"

Puffing out a sigh, I look up at the ceiling of the service bay. Exposed ductwork runs across the space, and it reminds me of the maze my pet rat had when I was ten. My dad helped me build that maze. I'd forgotten all about it until now.

"Why do you think it's so hard for me?" I ask, pulling my gaze back down to Pauly.

He shrugs. "We're human. Humans are a mess of emotions and flaws. We're just trying to make sense of everything in this world. And maybe," he says slowly, "it's easier to think you don't deserve the things you want in life because if you never have them, they can't be taken away."

I rub over my chest. "Fuck, Hernandez."

Pauly steps close, squeezing my shoulders. "I know you lost your family. But now you have us. You have us, and you have those guys of yours. You're not alone anymore."

Throat tight, I tug Pauly in, and he hugs me fiercely, slapping my back a few times for good measure. My chest constricts, but it's the good kind of ache.

"I don't know what this is," Aaron says, appearing at our side and wrapping his arms around the both of us, "but it's going to be okay."

"Fuck yeah," Pauly says, slapping Aaron on the back, too. "No toxic masculinity in our shop."

The three of us stand that way for a moment longer before breaking apart. There's a sting in my eyes, but I don't even care.

"Thanks, guys," I mutter, feeling monumentally lucky to be where I am right now. Not just in Mike's Garage with men I've come to think of as brothers, but here in life. In a place where I feel warm and welcome. Where I feel like, for the first time in a long time, I'm allowed to be happy. Allowed to have hope.

"Anytime, boss," Pauly says, shooting me a wink before he grabs Aaron by the shoulders.

The two start walking off as Aaron asks, "So, what'd I miss?"

"Well, you see," Pauly starts, voice getting quieter. "Grizlak got himself a couple boyfriends."

There's laughter in my throat when I get back to work. And even though my finger is throbbing something fierce, it's not enough to counteract the *lightness* flowing through my veins. It feels like a good day.

Especially when a text comes through from one of my favorite people.

Goldie: What do you call a freezing bear?
Me: Oh boy. I bet you're going to tell me.
Goldie: A brrrrr! *laugh-cry emoji*
Fuck, I love that man.
Fuck.

I love that man.

Oh, wow. Wow, wow.

Me: Are you working today?

Goldie: Yeah, I have a solo scene this afternoon.

He adds a winking emoji and an eggplant to his text, followed by a spray of water?

Me: See you tonight?

Goldie: Or sooner.

Another winking emoji.

A ring inside the service bay—signaling there's a customer up front—distracts me away from Alex's texts, and I slip my phone in the pocket of my jumpsuit. With a little flutter of something soft inside my chest, I lift my head, looking through the glass windows leading into the lobby.

And that's when everything goes to shit.

A heavy stone drops into my stomach as my gaze collides with that of my ex's. As if summoned from my conversation with Pauly or maybe from the universe itself as a great big *fuck you*, Manny gives me a shark grin and a wave. Feet weighted, I trudge toward the front of the shop. I briefly debate grabbing Pauly to deal with my ex instead, but I think better of it at the last moment. Not only would it fuel Manny, but I can handle this on my own.

I think.

The bell above the door jingles when I pass into the lobby, and Manuel watches my every move as I walk his way, his eyes shrewd and calculating. I wonder what he could possibly want this time. Why he's here to undoubtedly harass me. Why he can't just *stay away*.

"Rowan," he says.

Has his voice always been that cold? Or was it warm once? Did he ever care for me at all?

I slip behind the computer, putting the standing-height counter between us. "Manuel."

Manny rests his forearms on the laminate, leaning close. "Aren't you going to say it's nice to see me?"

"Do you want me to lie?"

Manuel's eyes flash at the words that slipped from my mouth, and he cocks his head. A predator, that's what he reminds me of. "Really, Rowan? Must you be so crude?"

I let out a sigh, so over this. "What do you want, Manuel?"

"My car feels like it's listing to the left," he says, sliding his Audi's keys across the counter.

"I'll take a look at the suspension," I reply, pocketing the keys.

Manuel looks victorious, and I immediately regret the decision. I should have sent him to another shop.

"Thanks, babe," he says, shooting me a wink.

"Don't," I say roughly, my heart tripping over itself in a way that feels like it's being skinned on the ground.

"Don't what?" he retorts, leaning close again.

"Don't do that. Don't call me that, like it means something."

I've never talked back. Never defended myself to Manuel, and I can tell he doesn't like it.

"Really, Rowan?" he hisses. "You're telling me what we had was meaningless?"

"It was to you," I say. "Or, at least, it meant the wrong thing. You never even liked me, did you?"

He scoffs, rolling his eyes in a way I can tell is meant to be condescending.

"Ro, Ro, Ro," he says, tsking and shaking his head. "There you go again, putting yourself down."

"Stop it," I grit out.

Manuel stands to his full height, which is still less than my own, and stalks around the counter. I refuse to budge. Refuse to move away from this confrontation.

"Watch. Your mouth," he says, voice so very low. He wouldn't dare speak to me like this if anyone else were around. He always saved it for when it was just him and me.

It used to scare me. It used to make me feel small and weak because that's exactly how he wanted me to feel. He wanted power over me. He *still* wants power over me, I realize. *That's* why he keeps coming here. That's why he won't let me go, even though we split.

He's a small man, trying to feel bigger. But he only has power if I give it to him.

"I'll have your vehicle diagnostic ready within an hour. There are drinks over there if you're thirsty," I say, stepping around my ex.

I'm only a foot away when his voice causes me to come to a grinding halt.

"Don't you walk away from me, you big fucking oaf. I gave you two years of my life. You should feel *lucky*. Who else would want a weak, fat, sorry excuse for a man like you?"

The hammer hits hard, and with a whoosh, my breath vacates my lungs.

Fuck.

Chapter 24

ALEX

I peek through Finn's office door, biting my lip as I contemplate whether or not it'd be a good idea to sneak in there while he's on the phone. Heading back to the kitchen, I pull a strip of paper off the notepad on the fridge, and I scribble out a quick note. Then I tiptoe back to Finn's office.

He's still on the phone when I enter, and I carefully slide the note onto his desk in front of him, watching as his eyes swing down to read what I wrote. They ping to me next, brows furrowed in confusion as he goes on about timelines and Java-something-or-other.

My instructions were simple. ***"Give me back this paper if you want me to stop."***

Grin on my lips, I slip to my knees and slide under Finn's tall, standing desk. His eyes widen further as my hands tug at the waistband of his pants, but he doesn't make a move to stop me. My pulse thrums in giddy excitement as I pop the button open and ease the zipper down as quietly as I can manage. Finn's speech falters, but he composes himself quickly, carrying on his conversation as I pull his pants down to his thighs with glee.

I've been thinking about Finn's cock nonstop since I saw the thing. It's gorgeous. A true one-of-a-kind. And considering I'll be heading to work soon for a solo session with a new dildo we're promoting, I figured now would be the perfect time to finally explore Finn's piercings in detail. That way, I'll have plenty of fresh spank bank material to guide me through my shoot.

Finn doesn't protest in the least when I drag his underwear down below his balls. "Uh-huh, uh-huh," he says to the caller on the other end of the line as his hand sifts down through my hair.

I purr like a cat before scooting forward and getting my first taste of Finn. The metal of his Prince Albert hits my tongue first, and I swipe at it greedily. Finn's cock, which was only half-mast when I pulled it free, stiffens further, hardening in my hand, and when I smooth my lips over his crown, gliding my tongue across both ends of the piercing there, Finn's hand spasms in my hair.

"I, uh...yeah, that should be doable," he says above me, eyes shuttering closed as I suckle on the end of his dick.

Fuck, he tastes like spice and steel.

Popping off his crown, I explore his shaft next, running my tongue up the ladder piercings on the underside of his cock. Eight little balls in four rows of two tickle the surface of my tongue, and I groan, keeping the sound low as I stuff Finn's dick back in my mouth. I'm eager to feel those ladder rungs against my lip, and as I lower slowly, there they are—smooth metal and a tantalizing glide that's reminiscent of the way his lip ring drags against me when we kiss. My entire body breaks into a shiver at the feel.

I can't wait to try out his piercings in my ass.

Finn's hand tightens in my hair again, and whatever he's saying flies right past my ears as I start working his length over in earnest. It feels almost barbaric, all those metal rods through the frenum along his shaft. But I can just imagine how wonderful they'd feel dragging over my rim as he stretches me wide, and it's enough to have me rubbing the heel of my palm against myself through my shorts.

Finn's hand hits his desk lightly—just a little bang—but he doesn't hand me the paper, so I keep going, sucking and tonguing and taking him into my throat. He's velvet and steel, spice and man. And now, he's *mine*.

Ginger Bear stutters out something above me, and I hear, "Yeah, we'll talk soon." Then there's a clatter of his phone and both of Finn's hands are tugging my hair. "Goddamn it, Goldie."

I hum.

"Fuck," he says, thrusting gently into my mouth. "Fuck, fuck."

I hum again, and a burst of precum hits my taste buds as Finn groans above me.

"Gonna come," he warns.

Sucking harder, my eyes water as Finn's cock slides deep. He grunts, grinds against my lips, and then he's coming undone.

Ungh.

My eyes practically roll back as Finn unloads down my throat, but I pull partway off before he's done, needing a taste of him. His breathing is harsh above me, and those amber eyes of his burn. When he finally stops spurting against my tongue, he loosens his hands in my hair and breathes out a long sigh of relief.

I pull slowly off his cock, giving his crown one last lick before I sit back on my heels.

"Good God, Ging," I say, tucking him carefully away inside his underwear and then pulling up his pants. "You're packing a hazard, you know that? It's a good thing I don't have my tonsils anymore."

There's a brief pause, and then Finn is barking a laugh. I'm sure my answering grin is smug, but he doesn't seem to mind.

"Trouble," he murmurs, shaking his head.

I send him a wink.

"C'mere," Finn instructs, tugging me upright. He's careful to pull me forward first so I don't bang my head on his desk, but then his mouth is greeting mine before my feet have even found footing. He groans, a nice long "*mmm*" against my lips, before pulling back and brushing my hair from my eyes. His face is full of something soft. As is his touch. And it sinks deep inside my stomach, warming me like a furnace.

"Like the taste of yourself on my tongue?" I tease.

Finn's eyes heat, and he chuckles, shaking his head once again.

"I have to get to work," I tell him, squeezing his arm before taking a reluctant step toward the door. "But I'll be back later."

Finn nods, combing his disheveled hair away from his face with one hand. I try not to let my gaze linger too long on the way his muscles pop with the motion. "There are sandwiches made up in the fridge," he says. "Grab one for lunch. And...if it's not too much trouble, could you drop one off for Rowan on your way to work?"

My heart pitter-patters away in my chest, and I honestly wouldn't be surprised if my eyes were shooting literal hearts. I skip back his way, and up on tiptoes, I give Finn another smacking kiss on his cheek before backing toward the door.

"Thanks for taking care of us, Ging."

Finn gives me a little smile, as if to say *it's my pleasure*, and I blow him a kiss before turning into the hallway. In the kitchen, I find the sandwiches Finn was talking about wrapped in little brown paper bundles, and my heart does that happy dance again. I grab one for me and one for Ro, and then I'm out the door.

Mike's Garage is right on the way to Elite 8 Studios, so it's no bother for me to stop there. I pull into the lot, humming to myself, and once I park, I grab one of the sandwiches to bring to Ro.

There's a pep in my step and a lightness inside my chest as I open the door to Mike's, but all of that falls flat when I catch part of the conversation I stumbled in on.

"Don't you walk away from me, you big fucking oaf," the man is saying to Rowan, whose shoulders are hunched, even though he's turned away. "I gave you two years of my life. You should feel *lucky*. Who else would want a weak, fat, sorry excuse for a man like you?"

Oh, *hell* no.

"Grizz," I call out, dropping the sandwich on the chair beside me before running for my man.

He turns, eyes wide in surprise, and I don't stop until I'm jumping up into his arms. He catches me easily, hands under my thighs, and I bring my lips to his.

I kiss him with everything—*everything*—pouring my reassurances into his mouth. Telling him without words, showing him, that he is wanted and beautiful and mine. That this fuckwit behind me is *nothing*. Nothing compared to him.

That we're the lucky ones—Finn and me—to have this lovely, honorable, perfect man in our lives.

His arms shake, but his grip on me is resolute.

"You're mine," I tell him after pulling back just a half-inch from his face. "You are mine, and I am yours."

His eyes flutter closed, and he nods ever so slightly.

Raising my voice, I say, "I hope you don't mind me stopping by, baby, but Finn made us lunch. Such a good boyfriend, isn't he? Can't wait to fuck both your brains out later." I slide down Rowan's body, patting his chest before turning to the man I deduced is Rowan's ex, Manuel. "Oh, sorry. Didn't see you there."

The man shoots daggers at me with his eyes, but I refuse to give him any more acknowledgment than he deserves. I've known guys like him, and being ignored is a greater hit to his ego than any mean words I could lob his way.

"I'll let you get back to your *customer*," I tell Rowan, walking slowly over to a chair and slinking into it, winking at my guy as I swing my leg over the armrest.

He shakes his head slightly, but his eyes are bright as he gives me a smile.

"It'll be about an hour," Rowan says to Manuel, who looks like he wants nothing more than to stick around and finish whatever bullshit he was spewing at Ro a minute ago. But he looks over at me, and with a rough shake of his head, he stalks off, out of the shop.

"He's a megadick," I say, swinging my feet back to the ground and pushing out of the chair.

Rowan blows out a breath, nodding, and I step close, wrapping my arms around my Grizzly Bear.

"Okay?" I ask, hoping my voice doesn't betray how damn pissed off I am. And worried.

Rowan nods again, nuzzling against the top of my head. "Better now."

My chest squeezes.

"You're not an oaf," I say vehemently against Rowan's chest. "Or weak. Or any of those things he was saying. You're wonderful."

"You know," Ro says quietly, his palm rubbing over my back, "I'm starting to think you're right."

"Damn straight I am," I reply, looking up at my man. He has such dark lashes. Such pretty, warm eyes. "You don't deserve that. No one should talk to you like that."

He doesn't respond, but the vulnerability in his expression makes me want to wrap him so fully in bubble wrap that his ex's words can never again reach his ears.

"It's not your fault," I add.

He nods. "That, I know."

Blowing out a breath, I snuggle back against his warm, soft chest. "I really did bring you lunch. It's on that chair behind me."

"Thanks, Alex," he says, running his fingers through my hair. I close my eyes, savoring the touch.

"Mm. I don't wanna go."

"But you have work," he says.

I nod, reluctantly ungluing myself from my bear of a boyfriend. "Will you call or text me if you need to? I don't care if I'm filming, Ro. I'll give my phone to Jerome, and if you call, I'll answer."

"Alex," he says softly.

"Please. Just promise me," I all but beg.

He nods, sighing. "Promise."

"Good." I give his chest a pat. And then another because it really is such a lovely chest. "See you later?"

"Don't think I could get rid of you if I tried," he teases, which makes me smile so damn hard my face hurts.

"You're catching on, sweetness." I wrap my arms around him one more time, giving him a big squeeze. "Okay, gotta go."

I'm halfway to the door when Ro says, "Hey, Alex?"

I stop, pivoting. "Hm?"

"What does the eggplant mean? In your texts."

It takes me a moment, but when I realize what he's asking, I bark a loud laugh, and then I'm giggling for a good handful of seconds before I can manage words. "God, Ro. I love you so damn much."

Ro's eyes go wide, and in the split second of silence that follows, I realize exactly what I said. But I don't take it back. I can't.

"I know what you mean," Ro says, letting me off the hook. But he doesn't need to.

Damn. He really doesn't need to.

"See you tonight, Grizzly Bear," I say, sending him a kiss as I back away.

He blushes a little, looking down at his feet, and I push out the door, heart skipping wildly. It's not until I'm in my Jeep that I realize I didn't actually answer his question.

I pull out my phone to text him.

Me: It's dick, Ro. The eggplant is dick.

After another good chuckle, I message Finn.

Me: Manuel was at the shop. If you have time, Ro would probably appreciate a visit this afternoon.

Finn responds immediately.

Finnigan: Thanks for the heads-up, Goldie. I'll stop by.

I let out a sigh of relief, glad that Finn can be there even when I can't. This triad thing has loads of perks.

Next, I text Pauly.

Me: P-dawg. Rowan's a-hole ex showed up. I would not be upset if you accidentally dropped fish guts inside his air vents.

P-dawg: Jesus fuck. Thanks, Alex. I'll deal with him when he comes back.

Nodding and glad that's taken care of, I head off to work. I'm still feeling a little off-balance, a little jittery and amped, as I get ready for my solo scene. But by the time I've showered and am sitting in front of Bill and his camera, my thoughts center themselves. I think about my guys. About Ro and Finn and the pierced cock that sat on my tongue earlier today. I imagine it's one of them sliding inside my body, fucking me with slow, broad strokes. And when I spill over my fist, dildo still lodged in my ass, it's their names sitting on the tip of my tongue, unsaid.

Bill gives me his stamp of approval, letting me know he captured everything he needed for the video, and I clean myself up with the tissues nearby before wrapping a big, fluffy robe around my body. I'm halfway back to the locker room to shower yet again when Trevor steps out of Studio 2, fully dressed with a little stack of cards in his hand.

"Alex, hey," he says, beelining my way.

"Hey, Trevor," I return.

He hands over a card, and with some curiosity, I take in the gold-embroidered invite.

"My husband and I are renewing our vows this Saturday for our fifteenth wedding anniversary," he says, easy as pie. "Cast and crew are invited."

"I..." Wait, what?

"See you there?" Trevor asks, giving me a smile.

I nod, mouth hanging open.

"Great," he says, turning and walking off.

I look back down at the invite. Trevor is *married?*

Trevor. Aka Bruiser here on set. The man who's six and a half feet tall, likely over 300 pounds, and is built like a professional wrestler. The guy who's worked here longer than any of us, who fucks like a freight train and has the stamina of a seasoned porn star. My coworker who's surprisingly sensitive and kind beneath that hard exterior of his. One of Elite 8 Studios' most popular tops has been married for *fifteen years?*

"You have a husband?" I call out to Trevor's retreating form. "Trevor!"

He doesn't hear me, and I can do nothing but laugh. I'm amazed and giddy and so dang *happy* for some reason I can't quite name, so I laugh.

And I just keep laughing.

Chapter 25
ROWAN

"Hey," I say gently, easing down onto the beanbag chair beside Alex's. I bought a second for the space earlier this week after noticing how much time Alex likes spending here in this little area full of flowers and light.

"Hey," he responds happily, reaching out and squeezing my leg. He has his sketchpad in his lap and a plethora of colored pencils beside him. On the page he's working on is a drawing of an orchid. He's captured it to a T.

"Am I disrupting you?" I ask.

He shakes his head, the back of one of his pencils sitting between his lips. "No. I'm just..." He makes a slight sound of frustration before flopping backwards. "I only have a week left to finish this project, and I have no clue what I'm doing."

"Can I see?" I ask.

Alex hands over his sketchpad, and I flip through a few pages. There are flowers and... *Oh*.

"Is this...me and Finn?" I ask, feeling a blush rise up my neck as I take in the rather scandalous image in front of me. It's clearly two men going at it, one pressed against the wall with his leg hitched up, the other in front of him, face tucked against the first man's neck. It looks a hell of a lot like how Finn fucked me in the kitchen earlier this week.

I clear my throat, the resurfacing memories making my dick hard.

"Kind of?" Alex says, eyes squinted before he exhales hard enough to ruffle his hair. "Yeah. I mean, obviously, it's you two. It wasn't supposed to be, but every time I try to start my project, I keep drawing...you."

Wow.

I flip through a few more pages. There are more nudes, but there's also me and Finn cuddling on the couch, the two of us surrounded by a sea of flowers, a close-up of us kissing.

"Alex," I say softly, flipping through the pages. "Where are you?"

"Huh?" he asks, head lolling my way.

"Where are you in these pictures? All I see is..."

"Two bears?" he fills in, grinning at that.

"Well, yeah. But these pictures are missing something pretty important. Where's our Goldie?"

Alex stills, his gaze going unfocused. With a little gasp, he sits upright and begins gathering the colored pencils around him in a rush. "Holy shit. That's it."

"What is?" I ask.

"That's it! Oh my God, Ro." Alex hops up, shoving his supplies into his bookbag before plucking the sketchpad from between my fingers. "You're a genius." He grabs my cheeks, smacks a kiss against my lips, and then takes off.

"Where are you going?" I ask in alarm.

"The art building," he calls back, his footfalls padding down the stairs.

Uh.

"What'd you do?" Finn teases, appearing in the hallway with an amused smile on his face.

"Scared him off, apparently," I say, adjusting my weight on the beanbag. I don't know how Alex manages to look so graceful in these things.

Finn snorts before walking to his wall of orchids and checking over his flock like a mother hen. He pulls a tray from beneath the shelves and starts lining some of the orchids on top. Then he grabs a watering can and begins soaking the plants, careful to avoid leaves and flowers.

"I used to talk to them a lot more," Finn says. At my clear confusion, he clarifies, "The plants. Mo, too. Obviously, they never talked back. But I realized, just now, that I don't do that as much."

"No?" I ask.

"No." There's a little smile on his face as he continues watering his orchids. "Because you're here now. You and Alex."

I don't even know what to say to that. *Thank you for inviting me into your life? I'm so glad I'm here? I'm so glad you want me here?*

"This place—the house and its floors and its walls—called to me the very first time I walked in here," he goes on. "It was colorful and energetic and came chock-full of memories that weren't my own. It was this idea of what I wanted. A full, vibrant life." He falls silent for a moment. "But now, I think it's alive again. Because we're here, all of us, making new memories. I really like that, Ro. I like it too goddamn much."

"Why too much?" I ask gently, getting out of the beanbag chair and kneeling beside Finn and his plants.

He looks over at me, his face half a foot away. His eyes, so golden, are creased, almost in worry. But there's something else there, too. Something burning and bright. Something fragile but *warm*. So very warm.

And suddenly, I understand why he's afraid.

"Finn," I say, running my palm over the arm closest to me. His shirt is rolled up enough for me to skim my fingertips along the colors there. Over the tapestry of flowers and *life* he inked into his own skin. "I didn't know you liked me because I never let myself look."

"What?" he asks quietly.

"I never let myself look," I repeat. "When you moved here, after Manny and I split and the two of us became friends… I thought, if I truly looked at you, you'd see the want in my eyes. And I didn't think you'd want me back. So I didn't let myself look."

Finn slides his hand over mine on his arm.

"I see you now, Finn," I say quietly. "I see you, and I see how very much you love me. And that doesn't scare me."

His lip twitches, a little movement almost like a tic, and he squeezes my hand tightly. "It doesn't?" he asks.

"No. I think…we were both searching for family. Don't you? A family of our own. I think we found that in each other. You. Me. Alex." I turn my palm upwards, curling my hand against Finn's. "It's not too much, all of this. And it's not going to disappear. I believe that. I'm choosing to believe in that."

"Ro," he says quietly, grabbing the back of my neck and tugging me forward. His lips meet mine softly. A press of wishes and hope.

And maybe I don't fully understand it—why these men chose me. Maybe I never will.

But don't we all deserve love? Above all else, shouldn't we hold onto that tight when we find it?

I sure know I'm not letting go.

When Finn and I break apart, the feel of his kiss stays with me like hot cocoa on a winter's day. It tingles my lips, warm and delicious.

"Your birthday is coming up," Finn says, throwing the words out casually and giving me a cheeky little grin. "Anything you want?"

I shake my head as he starts loading his watered orchids back onto the shelves. "I have everything I need," I say.

His eyebrow raises. "Hm."

Finn grabs the heavy tray of water off the ground and carries it toward the bathroom. I follow, staying in the hall as he dumps it into the sink.

"I do have a favor, however," I say, thinking of something that's been on my mind ever since Alex brought it up.

"What's that?" Finn asks as he rinses his hands.

"Would you watch porn with me?"

Finn pauses, biting his lip as he looks my way. "Anytime, baby."

I huff a little laugh, stepping aside as Finn comes out of the bathroom with his tray. "I meant one of Alex's. Tink's," I amend.

I'm ready to see it. I'm ready to look.

Finn returns his tray to its place below the orchids, and then he stands upright, facing me with a soft expression on his face. "Of course," he says. "Want to do that now?"

"Yeah," I answer with a nod.

Finn grabs his personal laptop, and we head into the bedroom, sitting side by side against the headboard of his king-size bed. He pulls up the website for Elite 8 Studios, does a search for "Tink," and then there he is. My boyfriend—*our* boyfriend—dozens of times over on the screen.

Oh wow.

"Too much?" Finn asks, looking at me in concern.

"What did I say?" I reply, reaching over to scroll down through the videos. "Not too much."

I stop on one that looks...comfy. Alex and his costar are stretched out on a couch, the other man spooning him from behind. I click it.

The video opens on a sort of buildup scene. Alex and the man are sitting upright on the couch, not touching. They're watching TV, but they keep glancing at one another. Eventually, they scoot closer together, and when the other man places his hand on Alex's leg, Alex says, "We shouldn't," but it lacks luster. He says something else about how his brother wouldn't approve. Ah, a brother's best friend sort of thing. And then they're kissing.

The first time I watched a video of Alex, all those weeks ago, I turned it off at around this point, before it could get any further than kissing. My heart had been pounding, and I kept thinking, *What if that's me?* What if I'm that guy? A prop in a show. And everything I thought had been building between us, everything I'd been hoping for, was just a lie?

But I know better now. I know Alex cares for me, that he may very well be falling in love with me.

It doesn't bother me that he has sex with other men. I just didn't want to be another in that line. I wanted to be more. I wanted his heart. I believe Alex when he says what we have means more. And now I'm ready to see it for myself.

On the screen, the other man follows Alex—no, Tink—down onto the couch. His hand slips over Tink's crotch, and Tink moans, arching into the touch. That's not Alex's moan. It moves fast from there. Clothes come off. Hands roam. They're naked. Touching. Using mouths. Before long, the other man is fucking Tink.

Finn reaches over, curling his palm against my leg in support.

"It's okay," I tell him. And I mean it.

It's clear to see that Alex—the man himself—is hard. That he's enjoying this with his costar. But *fuck*. There's something so different about it. It's manufactured. A play.

Even so, the sight of my boyfriend naked doesn't leave me unaffected. My cock thickens as Tink squirms. As he throws his head back against the couch they're on. As the other man, who I've barely paid any attention to, hitches Tink's leg up so the camera can get a close-up of where they're fucking.

"It's hot," I say slowly, my heart thudding now for a reason that has nothing to do with nerves. "But it's not the same. It's an act."

"Yes, it is," Finn says, squeezing my leg.

We watch another video. One where Tink is washing a car in shorts that leave the bottom of his asscheeks exposed and a tight white shirt that's drenched in minutes.

"Holy cow," I say, shaking my head. "He does this sort of stuff for work?"

It's so elaborate, and I briefly wonder at what must happen behind the scenes to pull off a shoot like this.

"Look at his smile," Finn points out with a chuckle. "He's having fun."

"Yeah," I agree, smiling as Tink dumps a bucket of sudsy water over himself. My voice dries up when he bends over and the camera focuses on his ass. *Heck*.

Finn and I watch quietly for a few minutes as some neighborhood boys show up on screen to enjoy the show that is Tink the twink.

"People want him," I voice aloud, thinking not of the guys in his scene but of all the men out there who watch these videos like we're doing now. Who fantasize about having Tink for themselves. Who covet him for his looks. Who know nothing of the man himself.

"Yeah," Finn says, laying his head against my shoulder. "But he wants us."

"*Oh*," I say quietly.

I knew that. I did.

But it didn't really hit me the same as it is now.

Alex wants *us*.

Alex, the man who likes to draw. Who wears tight shorts and cropped shirts because they make him feel cute, and because he enjoys the way Finn and I stare at him. He's the man who's so effortlessly confident in himself and his body, but also the man who's not afraid to showcase his heart on his sleeve. He's bold. And maybe not fearless because who is? But he puts himself out there nonetheless.

He's learning how to cook. He's kind to cats. And he jumped into this relationship with the same enthusiasm he has for life. He went in with both feet and that big heart, and he draped himself over every corner of our worlds. With his clothes and his possessions and *himself*.

He's offering himself.

They say love makes you a fool. But fuck, I don't think that's true.

I didn't have love with Manuel. There was a time when I thought *maybe*. I thought we could be heading there. I wanted so badly to have that with someone that I overlooked *who* that someone was.

But love. Real love. I think it makes you brave.

I think it makes you strong.

I think it coats you like a shield and hands you a sword, so that you never have to fight alone.

I feel braver with these men than I've ever felt before. I don't feel alone. And I don't feel unworthy of the weight of their love because like that shield and that sword, it protects me.

Maybe I'll always be a little insecure. A little overweight and shy. But like Pauly said, none of that matters.

Being worthy of these men... Maybe it simply means loving them the way they deserve.

That, I know, is something I can do.

Chapter 26

Alex

I don't stop drawing for days. At least, that's what it feels like. Every spare moment, I'm working furiously on my final project. At one point, Anh finds me in the art building and shoves a bag of food in my hands. Finn does something similar when I'm at his place, forcing a bowl of soup under my nose at the kitchen table and not leaving until the contents are gone.

By the time Saturday afternoon rolls around, I'm stiff, my fingers are cramped, and I couldn't be happier.

That's it. Holy shit, that's it.

A text comes through as I'm stretching out the muscles in my hand.

Mal: Are you coming to Trevor's vow renewal?

Me: Of course! Wouldn't miss it.

Although, crap, I have to hurry.

Me: Save me a seat, Mal pal. Running late.

Taking one last glance at my finished project, I sigh in relief. And then, I bust my ass.

I'm at my own apartment for once. I came early this morning, having extracted myself from the warmth of Finn's bed and the two men occupying it. Despite having migrated most of my belongings over to Ro and Finn's places, my fancy clothes are still here. Plus, I didn't want them to see my finished book quite yet.

A speedy shower is in order, and then I primp and polish myself to a metaphorical glow. Hair styled, forest-green suit in place, I grab my things and head out the door.

Trevor's house is far outside the neon and bustle of Las Vegas. The neighborhood is quaint, and large hedges give the front of his home privacy. I park along the street where other cars are lined, and then I walk up to the door. There's a sign that says to head around back.

Soft music filters over the air as I step into the backyard. White chairs are set up in rows, and a large trellis covered in pink flowers and soft, sage-colored greenery sits in front of it all. The grooms aren't there yet—thank goodness—but I spot the top of Dixon's head immediately in the crowd, followed by Mal's blonde curls, and I swerve that way.

I flash Mal an appreciative smile and a quiet thanks as I sink into the seat he saved for me, and then I slide my arm around Dixon's.

Dixon looks over at me with a frown. "The fuck did you come from?"

"Your dreams," I say softly, ignoring Dixon's answering sigh. Niko gives me a wave from around Dixon's big chest.

"You made it just in time," Mal says, looking back at the house as the ambient music cuts out. "It's starting."

The crowd hushes as the double doors at the back of the house open. A man wearing a simple black suit comes out first, walking to the front of the trellis and waiting, but all eyes stay on the doors. The music starts back up again, but this time, it's an eighties hit—"Heaven Is a Place on Earth"—being played over the speakers. I bark a quiet laugh as a few other people chuckle or smile fondly.

Trevor appears first, standing in the open doorway and looking to the side. Like the officiant, he's wearing a black suit, but it's cut to perfection and topped off with a black bowtie. There's an expression on his face I'm not used to seeing from the man, and my throat gets instantly tight.

His husband appears next—Isaac, as the invitation said. He's so much slimmer than Trevor and wearing a blue plaid suit. His hair is red, reminding me immediately of Finn, and his angular face is sporting an identical smile to that of his husband's. His bowtie, I note with appreciation, is pink.

The two link arms before turning to face the crowd of gatherers in their backyard. There are so many people here I don't recognize, but a lot I do. Nearly everyone from Elite 8 Studios turned up. But beyond that must be family and friends of Trevor and Isaac's. It's bizarre, seeing the evidence of my coworker's private life laid out before me. All these people likely know a different side of Trevor than I do—the Trevor who lives in this quaint, lovely home with a man who clearly owns his heart.

The two reach the trellis as the singer belts about not being afraid anymore, and they situate themselves opposite one another, hands clasped together as the song comes to a close.

It's quiet for a moment before the officiant speaks.

"Welcome, everyone," he says, a big smile on his face. "As most of you know, Isaac is my cousin. I had the privilege of marrying these two lovebirds fifteen years ago, and I'm honored to be standing here today as they renew their vows." He pauses to smile at the grooms. "A lot has changed in the past decade and a half, but there are some things that haven't. Isaac and Trevor's taste in music, for one." The crowd laughs at that, and I chuckle, too. "And the love these two share—that hasn't faltered in all the years they've known one another. Anyone can see it. I mean, just look at their goofy faces."

There's more laughter at that, and Isaac shakes his head, cheeks slightly red. Trevor, for his part, hasn't once taken his gaze off his husband.

I swipe at my eyes.

"But we're not here to listen to me lecture," the officiant says. "Instead, let's hear what the grooms have to say."

Isaac takes a deep breath before rolling his shoulders back and looking at Trevor. "Cuddle bug..." he starts.

"*Oh my God*," I whisper, grabbing Mal's arm and shaking it. Mal snickers quietly next to me.

"Nineteen years ago," Isaac says, "I met this guy in college. He was sitting in my spot in the library, so big he nearly took up two seats"—more laughter at that—"and I..." Isaac shakes his head. "Oh, how I hated him."

Trevor booms a laugh, lifting Isaac's hand to his mouth and kissing his knuckles.

"Oh, fudge," I mumble, rubbing at my wet cheeks.

"I hated him on sight," Isaac goes on, a little grin on his face. "I thought, 'Oh, great. Here's this big, dumb jock here to fuck up my routine.' I was wrong. So very wrong." He sighs, his lips quivering slightly. "He was kind. And smart. And patient with me, even when I stomped up to him demanding he move. I'd never been more wrong about a person in my life. Never been more *glad* to be wrong."

Isaac takes a quick moment to compose himself.

"Trevor... Since the moment we met, you've been on my side. My biggest cheerleader. My cuddle bug," he adds softly. "You supported me through graduate school. Through the loss of my mother. Through all the hard days and all the good. I feel so fortunate that you came into my life. That you stayed in it, even though we both know I can be a right moody bitch in the mornings. And in the afternoons. And sometimes in the evenings." The crowd laughs again, and my smile wobbles. "Thank you, love. I can't wait to spend another fifteen years with you."

Trevor leans in, kissing Isaac sweetly before stepping back. There's moisture below his eyes that he doesn't even attempt to wipe away or hide.

"Brat," Trevor says softly.

I squeeze Mal's arm tighter. "Oh my *God*," I whisper-squeal.

Isaac hiccups a laugh, and Trevor's smile grows. "You were—and still are—the most beautiful man I've ever laid eyes on."

Oh, damn it.

Mal hands me a tissue. Grateful, I rub it over my eyes.

"You say I supported you," Trevor goes on. "But the way I see it, we've held each other up. You're my partner in every way. My debate partner, all those nights we stay up discussing the merits of Emerson or Descartes. My sous chef in the kitchen and, on occasion, head chef."

The crowd laughs at that, and Isaac groans. "Not a very good one."

Trevor shrugs, nonplussed by his husband's apparent lack of cooking skill. "You're my partner in life, Isaac. And I couldn't have asked for a better man by my side. I love you."

"I love you, too," Isaac replies, his eyes shining.

For a moment, no one else speaks a word. Then there's a whoop from the crowd, and someone shouts out, "Kiss him, you fool!"

Laughter rings out, and Trevor and Isaac gravitate toward one another like magnets. I give up on wiping my face as the officiant guides them through a repeat of their wedding vows. When all is said and done, "Heaven Is a Place on Earth" starts playing once more, and hands held high, Trevor and Isaac walk back down the aisle, matching grins on their faces.

"That was..." I say, sighing, not even finishing my sentence.

"Yeah," Mal responds as people start filtering out of their seats, joining the grooms near the tables of hors d'oeuvres and punch. We stay put, and Mal gives me a little nudge.

"It *is* possible for guys like us," my friend says.

"What do you mean?" I ask, even though I have an idea what he's talking about. He found his own Isaac, after all.

"You could have this," he answers. "I know it's something you were resigning yourself against lately. But...with the right person? The right people? You could have your happily ever after."

"Yeah," I say with a little sigh, thinking of Rowan and Finn. Thinking of the lack of jealousy and the fact that not once have they asked me to change. "You know what? I'm pretty sure you're right."

Mal looks happy about that, giving me a quick squeeze of a hug, which I heartily return. We stay at the reception for quite a while, and I learn Isaac is a professor at one of the nearby colleges. A professor and a porn star. Who would have thought?

I don't blame Trevor for keeping his life private, but I *am* glad he included his work family in this moment. I'm glad to see, with my own eyes, concrete proof that love and family is possible in our line of work. With the right person.

The right people.

When I leave, I take a moment to call my mom from inside my vehicle. It's not that I've been avoiding this conversation, but I need to give my parents a heads-up before they come down for my graduation. I don't want to blindside them with this new development in my life.

My mom answers on the second ring. "Hi, hun."

"Hey, Mom. How're you and Dad?"

"Good," she answers as the background noise on her end of the call lowers. I'm guessing my dad turned down the TV. "Everything okay with you?"

"Yeah, I'm good," I tell her. "I just have something I wanted to tell you guys."

"Okay?" she says hesitantly. And then, "You're on speaker-phone."

"Hey, Dad."

"Alex," he greets, sounding just as curious as my mom.

Blowing out a breath, I begin. "So you'll be here in a couple weeks for my graduation, and I wanted you to know before then that I'm in a relationship."

There's a brief pause, and then my mom says, "Okay? That's great, hun. Will we meet him?"

"That's the thing," I say slowly, chewing the inside of my cheek. "There's two of them. I'm in a relationship with two men. But I would really like you to meet them both."

Another pause, longer this time.

"Two men?" my dad asks, sounding understandably confused. I doubt he or my mom even know polyamory is a thing.

"Yes," I say calmly. "Rowan and Finnigan. They're really wonderful. I think you'll like them. Ro is a mechanic, and Finn does software development."

Another long pause. My parents aren't even talking to each other, but I assume a lot is being said with looks.

"Alex," my mom finally says, her tone one of a concerned parent. "I'm not sure how you want us to react to this. This isn't...normal."

I blow out a quiet breath. Her comment is exactly what I was expecting.

My parents aren't bad people, and I know they love me. But I have nothing in common with either of them. When I was younger, I sometimes wondered if I was a changeling, dropped into the home of these people who were so fundamentally different from myself.

When I started liking pink and dressing up in my mom's heels, my parents were bewildered. My being gay shouldn't have been a shock, but when I came out, they acted like it was this massive bombshell they were entirely unprepared for. They didn't agree with me choosing a future in art instead of a stable career in accounting like my dad, but they came around over time.

Hopefully, having two boyfriends is something they'll adjust to, as well.

"It may not be what you're used to," I respond, trying to keep my voice even and reassuring, "but sometimes people are in relationships that involve more than one partner. It's not as unheard of as you might think."

"But," my mom sputters.

"Alex," my dad cuts in. "I think what your mother is trying to say is that she's worried. We both are. What will people think? What about your future?"

"I don't care about not being able to file joint taxes," I say with a little huff, having a strong suspicion that's exactly where his mind went.

"But what about kids?" my mom asks, and it sounds as if she's close to tears.

Crap.

"We'll figure it out," I tell her.

My dad makes a displeased noise in the back of his throat, and I speak up before either of them can say another word.

"Look," I say firmly. "I knew this was going to come as a shock to you, and that's why I wanted to let you know now. I want you to meet my boyfriends. I know that sounds unusual to you, but all I ask is that you keep an open mind. What's more important—what people think or the fact that I'm happy?"

They're quiet at that, and my throat feels tight as I go on.

"They make me *so happy*," I say. "They're wonderful men. I know you'll love them if you give them a chance. If I send you some information on polyamory—which is having romantic relationships with more than one person—would you read it? Would you think about it?"

"Yes, Alex," my dad says. "We'll read it."

I breathe out a sigh of relief. "Thank you. They'll be there at the graduation. I'd really like for you to meet."

There's a shaky sound on the other end of the line before my mom says, "We'll let you know."

That's about as good as I was hoping for.

"Thank you," I say. "I love you guys."

"We love you, too, Alex," my dad says before my mom makes a soft sound I think is agreement. "Talk soon."

"Okay, bye."

The line goes dead, and I plunk my phone into the cup holder.

"They'll come around," I say to myself. I think they will.

During the drive back to Ro and Finn's neighborhood, I think about my guys. About Ro's gentleness and Finn's inner fire. About how perfectly they balance each other and me.

I think about Trevor's vow renewal, and the look on his and Isaac's faces. I think about how they've made it work, despite their relationship being outside the bounds of traditional monogamy.

I think about what *I* want. What I want my life to look like. And the men I can't imagine losing now that I've found them.

When I walk into Finn's place, he and Ro are seated together on the couch. They both look up when I step inside, twin heads swiveling my way. Two smiles appearing on such different faces.

Ro is the first to speak. "Hey there."

"Hey," I breathe out, toeing off my shoes.

"You look nice," Finn says, the corner of his mouth tipping up as his eyes trail over my body and the suit that does, admittedly, fit me like a well-cut glove.

"Thanks," I say, stepping around to the front of the couch. They follow my path with their eyes.

"Something wrong?" Ro asks, head tipping slightly to the side.

"Nothing," I say truthfully.

"Then what is it?" Finn asks, leaning forward and reaching out for me.

I take his hand, letting Finn guide me onto his lap. With Finn beneath me, I look over at Ro and lay my hand on his chest. "I want you," I say simply. "I want you to stretch me with your cock. And then"—I look over at Finn—"I want you to fist me."

Both men inhale sharply, and Finn's dick kicks up beneath my ass.

"Alex," Finn says slowly.

"I trust you," I reply, watching as Finn's eyes darken. Watching as his expression turns to one of rapturous hunger. "I've never been fisted outside of the studio. I want that with you, Finn. I want to experience that with you both."

Finn and Rowan exchange a look, and I know they're not going to tell me no.

"You'll tell me what to do?" Finn asks.

I nod, breathing out in relief. "We'll go over it beforehand. Every step. We'll talk it through. And then," I say, leaning close to Finn's ear, even as I look into Ro's puppy brown eyes. "Then you'll stretch me wide and fit your hand inside my ass."

Ro licks his lips, and Finn's hands grapple for my waist, holding tight.

"Sound good to you?" I ask with a grin as I lean back.

Finn nods, his chest rising and falling with his deep breaths.

I step off his lap, holding out my hands. "C'mon, then. Let's go get ready."

Chapter 27

FINN

My heart pounds double time as Alex finishes up in the bathroom, getting himself ready for my fist. Ro is in there with him, and every once in a while, I hear a giggle.

For the tenth time, I glance over the information on the webpage we covered when Alex gave me a step-by-step rundown of what would happen. Of how to make sure he was experiencing only pleasure, no pain.

I know I told Alex the fisting scene I watched was my favorite, but I never anticipated having an opportunity to do it myself.

I'm so damn hard I could hammer nails.

The door opens before long, and Alex steps through, Ro behind him. He's already naked, his lithe body on full display, and I blow out a breath as he approaches, trying to temper my nerves.

"Okay?" Alex asks.

My breath becomes a laugh. "Me? You're the one who's about to have a fist up his ass."

Alex grins mischievously. "Can't wait." His grin shifts into something softer, and Alex climbs up over my lap, gently setting my phone aside. "You know what to do. You'll be fine. *I'll* be fine. Dixon is available in case you need to call."

I nod. I know that already. We talked about having his friend and coworker on standby in case something goes wrong. In case I freak out or who knows what. It helps, but I'm still nervous. Nervous and excited.

Alex smooths his palms down my arms, fingers lightly tracing the lines of my tattoos. He looks so ethereal sitting there naked on my lap. All glowing, smooth skin, messy blonde hair, and bright hazel eyes. He looks like an angel.

An angel I'm about to defile.

Alex brings his lips to mine without a word, tasting of toothpaste and something like cherry. He's so much softer than me, so much smaller, but it's Alex who gives me a shove until I lay on my back. And it's Alex directing me to discard my clothes.

Rowan undresses at the same time until he's standing naked beside the bed, his cock hard and pointing forward, as eager as my own. His eyes, though, are swimming with something much gentler.

I urge him closer with my fingers.

Ro climbs up on the bed as Alex attacks my cock, running his tongue up my ladder piercings before taking me into his mouth. My groan is immediate, and I reach for Rowan's erection, my hand automatically mimicking what Alex's mouth is doing to me. I tighten my grip, tug, pull Ro down to me. His mouth meets mine, and it's like coming home.

The three of us. Connected. Perfect.

Alex's hand joins mine in wrapping around Rowan's cock, and we pump it together the way we so often do when we're all joined like this in bed at the end of the night or early in the morning hours. The three of us moving together, sometimes in pairs, sometimes all at once. Rotating, shifting, giving and taking pleasure in turn.

We already discussed the order tonight—not something we usually bother to do. I'll come first to take the edge off so I'm clearheaded when inside Alex. Ro will be next, as he readies Alex for my fist. And Alex is positive he'll orgasm with my hand inside his body.

I'm not convinced I won't be hard again by the time that happens.

Alex works his tongue and lips over me with purpose, paying special attention to my piercings where I'm most sensitive. He laps at them, presses them with the tip of his tongue, scrapes his teeth over them lightly, making a soft *tink* sound each time. Meanwhile, his hands roam. Dragging over my torso, scraping nails along my legs. He's a master at multitasking.

Ro focuses his attention at my mouth, kissing me as if he has all the time in the world for it. And it feels that way. Like we have unlimited time for this. He's supple and sweet, and he moans when I twist my palm over his crown, spreading the precum there.

Alex's hand slips away from Rowan's cock, and the next second, there's pressure below my balls. He rubs the skin there, two fingers stroking my perineum as my sac rolls against his palm. It's too much. Too much sensation. Too much *everything*. So when my cock glides along the back of Alex's throat and his lips press against my groin, I can do nothing but surrender.

My orgasm rushes through me like lightning. Like a whole damn thunderstorm. I moan into Ro's mouth, holding the back of his head firmly as my other hand fists Alex's hair. Alex pulls back, humming as I continue to spurt, the last vestiges of my release coating his tongue. He rubs my thighs as my body relaxes, and slowly, I let him and Ro go.

"Ungh," I manage.

"You're up, Grizzly Bear," Alex says, crawling over my body to gain better access to Rowan. He settles on my lap, over my softening dick, as he brings Ro in for a kiss. Cheeky as ever, he asks, "Can you taste him on my tongue?"

Rowan groans, nodding, and Alex kisses him again. I grab one of the condoms already on the bed and roll it down Ro's cock as Alex grinds against my hip. The blonde slips off me after a moment, pulling Rowan down atop him.

We even discussed this—that Ro would fuck Alex missionary so that Alex could focus on relaxing his body as much as possible.

They settle directly beside me on the bed, and I turn on my side to enjoy the show, running my fingers over Alex's smooth stomach first, trailing over to Rowan's hip, over the coarse hair on his thighs and then up to the downy softness on his ass.

"You two are beautiful," I tell them, my chest squeezing in happiness when Alex gives me a beaming smile and Ro looks shyly pleased.

Other words sit at the tip of my tongue, but I hold them back. This isn't the time.

Alex's legs fall wide, and he tugs Rowan forward, squeezing the globes of his ass. "C'mon, baby," he says softly, offering himself. "Fill me up."

Ro reaches for the lube, and I pump some onto his hand. He slicks himself quickly and then notches against Alex's entrance. Already prepped, Alex's body welcomes him in with ease, stretching around his girth, accommodating the thick dick seeking admittance. Alex's eyes feather closed, and I stroke over his arm as Rowan comes to a seated position inside our boyfriend. Ro moves slowly: long, easy glides of his cock as discussed. Nothing too hard. Nothing punishing. My fist will be enough of that.

Alex's eyes are closed to slits, mouth parted slightly as he watches Rowan fuck him. Ro holds the blonde's waist with one hand, running the other over Alex's small nipples. When he swivels his hips, stretching, loosening, Alex moans.

"Fuck, Grizzly," Alex says, his voice like a song. "That's so good. Stretch me open. Fuck me with that beautiful cock. Get me ready."

Ro twists his hips again. "Like this?" he asks.

"Just like that," Alex moans, chest rising into Rowan's touch. "So good. So fucking good. Love your hands. The way you take care of me. Love your cock. Your perfect, mammoth cock."

Alex reaches for me as Rowan fucks him a little harder, bouncing the smaller man gently on the bed.

"Yours, too," Alex says, eyes blinking at me through his haze of lust. "Love both your cocks. I'm one lucky bitch. Best cocks in all the land, and they're mine."

I huff a laugh despite the circumstances, and Alex grins. His grin melts into another moan as Rowan finds his prostate.

"Not too much," Alex says, warning him off.

Rowan nods, going back to his stirring strokes, and Alex hums, licking his lips.

"Mhm. Fingers," Alex says.

Pumping some lube onto my hand, I reach beneath Rowan's gently pistoning dick. Alex cants his hips up further, grabbing under his knees, opening himself up wide. Ro slows, pausing halfway inside Alex to give me room to maneuver, and with some astonishment, I watch as my finger slips in beneath his cock.

We all groan.

"Fuck," I mutter, moving the digit gently. Rowan shivers above me.

I keep my finger in place as Rowan tests another couple strokes. Alex nods rapidly.

"Mm," the blonde hums. "Another."

Pulling back out until just the tip of my finger remains, I add a second, pushing them in slowly. Alex's eyes close again, and the tendons on his neck stand out as the back of his head rolls against the comforter. He makes an unintelligible sound, all reedy and broken, and Rowan blows out a breath, his body strung tight.

After a long moment, Rowan pumps his hips again, and I can feel him throb against my hand.

"Can't last," Ro says hoarsely, his strokes slow and measured.

"'S'okay," Alex replies, eyes slits as he watches us. "Come, Grizzly Bear. You did so good. Just what I needed. Always what I need. Perfect for me, baby. Such a good boyfriend."

Rowan's breath hitches, and he punches into Alex with a little more force. His cock swells against my fingers as he starts to come, and I'm momentarily stunned to feel such a thing from inside Alex's body. Rowan grinds shallowly a few times, face awash in ecstasy, Alex's name on his tongue.

When he stills, I glance at Alex's cock. Hard, straining, leaking like mad. His sac is drawn up tight, and he's biting his lip as if it's taking everything in him not to come. He looks almost grateful when Rowan slips from his body, and for a moment, I stare, transfixed by the sight of his hole, open and waiting above my two digits.

"Finn," Alex says immediately, and with a shake of my head, I hop to, pumping more lube onto my hand and filling him with four. He sighs, his body going lax.

He told me what to do. What to expect. He said, at this point, his body would be loose, ready for my fist. But I don't think anything could have truly prepared me for this moment as Rowan shucks his condom and gets into place behind Alex. Ro helps Alex scoot up the bed, and I move with them. Alex lays his arms over Rowan's legs, head near his stomach, and we slip a pillow under his hips. All the while, I keep him plugged with four fingers.

Once Alex is settled, his body relaxing into the pillow and bed and Ro himself, he gives me a tiny nod.

"It's okay," Alex says, voice a little slurred already. "You know what to do."

Throat tight, I swallow, looking down at where my hand is resting inside Alex's body. Taking a breath, I coat myself in more lube—lube, lube, lube; that was the number-one instruction—and bring my fingers nearly all the way out. Tucking my thumb into my palm, making the width of my hand as small as possible, I press forward.

It's surprisingly easy, sliding five fingers up to the first knuckle of my thumb. Alex's body took more than that when Rowan's cock was still inside him, so I don't know why I'm surprised. But watching my entire hand start to make its way into Alex's body leaves me a little breathless.

Alex's mouth is open when I glance up at his face, but his eyes are shut, and his head is leaned back, hair sweaty and disheveled over his forehead. I add some more lube and press a little further. My hand makes it up to where my fist is widest, and then I meet resistance.

"Alex?" I say softly.

He gives me another tiny nod, not responding verbally.

I pump my hand slowly and gently, pressing a little harder each time my fist meets his rim. I keep my hand narrowed, fingers straight, and my pulse is a steady constant in my head and my ears as I focus. I check in with Alex constantly, gaze switching between his face and where I'm entering him. All the while, Ro runs his hands soothingly over Alex's body. His chest. His arms. Sifting through his hair.

When it happens, I'm not expecting it. I push, there's resistance, and then—there's none. My hand slips fully inside Alex's body, and he swallows me whole, his outer ring of muscle settling against my wrist like a hairband.

I freeze, looking up at Alex's face. He's gone. Blissed. And apart from the smallest moan as I move my hand ever so slightly inside of him, he doesn't move or speak. He told me. He said he'd be too euphoric to do anything at this point other than take what I give him, but it's sobering seeing it happen. Witnessing it for myself. Seeing the evidence of the trust that exists between us.

The fact that Alex believes in me *this much*—that he knows I won't hurt him, that he's confident in my ability to take care of him—is humbling. And it sets my blood and my body on fire. It's a burn. A flame. Searing me with something permanent and awesome.

I pump my fist slowly, watching as my wrist disappears inside Alex's body. He moans above me, legs twitching, stomach and chest rising and falling with his breaths. I keep my thrusts shallow, pulling back occasionally to stretch Alex's rim. He said he likes that best. The stretch. The ache. And I avoid angling for his prostate, although I'm positive I'm rubbing it regardless of trying.

Rowan looks as awed as me when I find his gaze. I shake my head a little, and his lips stretch into a smile. It's quiet apart from Alex's litany of moans and the squelch of my fist in his body. It's reverent.

He's so smooth inside, his inner muscles silky and welcoming. We already trimmed my nails down to nothing, so I'm not worried about that. I focus on Alex's body. On what his sounds are telling me. I watch the steady stream of precum leaking from his cock. And I look at my wrist, watching the ink on my skin disappear time and time again as I fuck Alex gently with my fist. I squirt another pump of lube around his hole for good measure, and I catalogue every single second of what's happening, knowing I won't forget it for as long as I live.

The minutes seem to stretch endlessly, but the truth is it doesn't take long at all before Alex starts to tremble. It's as if his whole body is shaking, and when he starts fluttering against my fist, his muscles beginning to tighten, I know he's about to come. I wait, as he instructed me to do. I keep up my shallow pumps, stretching his rim, listening to his gasps and *mmms*. And when his cock jerks and cum starts overflowing his crown like a fountain, I aim for his prostate and press.

Alex's body tightens around me like a vise, strangling my hand and my wrist, and his cock jerks harder, splattering some of his release across his stomach and chest. He keeps coming, eyes closed, mouth open in bliss, as his orgasm flows from him unendingly. It's quite possibly the most erotic thing I've ever seen.

His body tries to force my fist away, but Alex told me he'd prefer for me to wait, so I do. I keep my hand inside of him, unmoving until his legs fall lax. Until his cock stops dribbling. Until his breath whooshes from him like a broken, beautiful sigh. Until his rim relaxes. And then, carefully, and very slowly, I pull my fist free.

Alex doesn't move, even as his eyelids flutter open. Even as he stares unseeing up at the ceiling. My cock is rock hard, but I ignore it. I don't even want to come. Not right now. I grab the hand towel we readied, and I wipe Alex up with gentle strokes. I check over his face, his breathing, make sure there's no sign of pain or injury, and when Rowan gives me a little nod, I retreat quickly to the bathroom.

Something in my chest stutters as I wash up and start the bath. And when I look up at my reflection in the mirror, there's a tear below my eye. I wipe it away, smiling to myself. Feeling like I'm floating.

Back in the bedroom, Rowan is maneuvering Alex into his arms. He slides off the bed, carrying Alex easily toward the bathroom, and I rub over the bigger man's lower back as he passes.

Tub full, I turn off the water and get in first. Ro lowers Alex into the bath in front of me, and even though Alex's eyes are open, and he seems aware of what's happening, he's quiet. There's a soft smile on his face, though, and once he's in the big tub, stretched out along my chest and between my legs, he lets out a gentle sigh.

I almost think I hear him whisper "Heaven," but it's so quiet I can't know for sure.

I kiss the top of his head, mouthing a *thank you*, holding him close. And when I turn to Ro, who's kneeling beside the tub, he leans in, mouth meeting mine in a slow, soft drag.

Eyes closed, I hold my men, and my heart beats strong. Steady. And sure.

Chapter 28

ROWAN

There's softness when I wake. A whole lot of softness, like fluffy clouds.

Alex's hair, I realize.

And warmth at my back. Finn.

A smile overtakes my face before I've even opened my eyes. How did I get this lucky?

"Hey, Grizzly Bear," Alex whispers.

I hum as the smaller man shifts against my front, his fingers ghosting over my beard. "Morning," I finally manage.

His fingers brush over my closed eyelids next. "Happy birthday."

I huff a little. "Mm."

"I have a surprise for you."

That gets me to crack open my eyes. "Yeah?"

"He wakes," Alex says with a grin. "Stay here. I'll be right back."

With that, Alex plants a quick kiss against my nose and then rolls out of bed. As he pads into the bathroom, disappearing from sight, Finn's hand stirs against my hip.

"Morning," Finn says.

I huff another laugh.

"What do you want to do today?" Finn asks, rolling onto his back and stretching.

I turn to take him in, eyes sweeping over his exposed torso. I never get tired of looking at Finn. "Do you think Mojave would try to eat a rat?"

Finn blinks before turning his head my way. "Pardon?"

I run my fingers over a Phalaenopsis on Finn's obliques. The blooms are big and deep purple. "I was thinking about how I used to have a pet rat when I was younger. I always liked that rat."

"You want a rat for your birthday?" Finn asks, curling towards me. He wraps his arm around my waist, and I continue exploring the tattoos along his chest.

"I don't know. It was just a thought," I admit.

"Hm," Finn says, sucking his lip ring into his mouth. "We could certainly try it. I doubt Mojave would care."

"Yeah?" I ask, a little excited at the prospect now that I've put it out there.

Finn shrugs a bit. "Yeah. Why not?"

When the door to the bathroom opens, Finn and I look that way. Alex steps into view, cocking his hip and running his hands along the doorframe to either side of him. "Do you like my knickerbockers?" he asks.

I wheeze.

"Goldie," Finn says around a choked laugh. "What..."

Alex strikes another pose, showing off a baseball uniform that is far too tight and too short to be considered regulation, I'm sure. The top is cut high, exposing his slim stomach and belly button. And the bottoms... Well, the bottoms are so tight and white I can see every curve of his cock.

"Where?" I croak. "What?"

"You like them?" he asks again.

I nod repeatedly.

Alex bites his lip as he strolls slowly out from the door-way, letting me look my fill. And then he starts to sing.

"Happy birthday to you," Alex croons, voice intentionally breathy. "Happy birthday to you." He spins, showcasing his ass.

Hell.

Finn curses next to me.

"Happy birthday, darling Grizzly Bear," Alex sings, spin-ning back around. "Happy birthday to you."

He punctuates the last note by hopping up onto the bed, and I'm stunned nearly speechless. But there's one thing I have to make sure he knows.

"Marilyn...*and* Joe...have got nothing on you, Goldieboi."

Alex beams, crawling up over my body. He hovers there for a moment, all bright-eyed and beautiful, before lower-ing his lips to mine. "Fuck me?" he mutters, diving back in without giving me a chance to answer.

I groan, my cock definitely on board with that plan.

"You sure that's a good idea?" Finn asks gently, and when Alex unglues himself from my face, I can see that Finn is reverently stroking over Alex's ass.

I add my hand to the mix.

"It's been nearly a week," Alex replies, referring to the fisting. "I'm good to go, Ging. And you," he adds, leaning over to grab Finn's chin, continuing at a whisper. "You can have my mouth."

Finn groans, making a lunge for Alex, but Alex laughs and shoves his face away. Finn is not to be deterred. He grabs Alex around the waist, tugging him down to the bed as Alex cackles and squirms.

"C'mon, Grizzly," Alex calls amidst his laughter. "Let's get these knickers off me so you can bockers me like there's no tomorrow."

Finn growls, shoving his face into Alex's neck as the blonde man squeals.

And me?

I'm right where I'm meant to be.

"Hey, guys?" I say with some confusion. "Why are you driving me to work?"

Alex, Finn, and I did end up visiting the pet shop this afternoon after sharing a nice meal out of the house for once. The pet shop employee suggested we bring Mojave by in her carrier to get a feel for how she'd react to rodents. We'll do that another day.

But right now, Alex is most definitely navigating us toward my place of employment, and I'm not sure why.

Alex chuckles in response to my question while Finn simply raises an amused eyebrow.

"It's a surprise," Alex says nonchalantly as he turns into the parking lot of Mike's Garage.

"Another one?" I ask. The knickerbockers weren't enough?

"Trust us, Baby Bear," Alex says serenely.

I do.

Alex parks his Jeep, and the three of us hop out of the vehicle. It's five o'clock, just an hour from closing time, but the lot is packed. Far more packed than I'm used to seeing for a mid-week evening.

Alex lopes toward the front of the garage, not a care in the world, and Finn walks with me at a more sedate pace. When I give him a questioning look, he seals his lips.

Instead of going through the front door, Alex heads for the open service bay, flashing me a secretive smile moments before he slips out of sight. Perplexed, I follow. But as soon as I round the corner into the garage, the reason for his mischievousness becomes abundantly clear.

"Surprise!"

"Fuck," I mutter.

Finn rubs my back encouragingly as I take in the sight before me. Half of the service bay has been cleared of cars, tools, and equipment and is now occupied with tables of food and almost everyone I know.

Aaron shoots forward first, a big smile on his face. He holds out a drink in a clear plastic cup with a pineapple wedge along the top. "Nonalcoholic," he says. "Happy birthday, boss!"

"I, uh..."

Pauly steps forward next, giving me a big slap on the side of my arm. "Happy birthday, Grizlak. Welcome to your party."

"My... Why?" I ask, utterly confused.

"Because everyone deserves to be celebrated once in a while," Aaron answers. "You maybe more than most."

Well, shit.

Finn squeezes my arm, and I find his hand, linking my fingers with his as my throat gets tight.

Alex reappears, a big birthday hat in his hand. With a grin, he beckons me down, and I lean forward so he can secure the hat around my head. "Happy birthday, Grizzly Bear," he says again. "C'mon. Let's mingle."

Alex tugs me forward, and I shake my head as we approach the party already in full swing. Music pumps from the speakers in the bay, although not too loudly, and my coworkers and their loved ones are standing around, laughing and making a dent in the spread of food. Even Finn's sister Fiona is here, as well as Old Mike, the owner of the garage.

It's a small crowd, but it's everyone who's come to matter to me here in Vegas.

Pauly hands me a plate with what appears to be a pulled pork sandwich. I guess all of Aaron's random questions about pineapple and pork are starting to make a little more sense now.

"So," Pauly says as Alex pulls Fiona into a conversation with Finn. "Looks like everything is going good." He pointedly eyes the men standing just behind me.

I shrug a little. "What can I say?"

"I mean...anything," Pauly says with a snort. "Gimme something, boss."

I roll my eyes, but a smile tugs at my lips before I take a bite of my sandwich. "Finn has a big bed," I mumble.

Pauly barks a laugh. "Mhm. And the other stuff?"

"What other stuff?" I ask, trying the pineapple punch. It's incredibly refreshing. Bubbly and fruity.

My friend shakes his head and pats his chest. "The stuff in here, Grizlak. The important stuff."

Oh. "Yeah. That's, uh... Good."

Pauly looks fondly exasperated as Freddie joins us, bumping me gently with his elbow and wishing me happy birthday. Our conversation turns from my boyfriends to the shop and Freddie's daughters, who aren't here. All the while, I eat my pulled pork and snack on potato salad and fruit kabobs. Finn brushes a kiss on my cheek at one point for no reason whatsoever. Alex sends me flirty winks more than once. Old Mike gives me a grunted thanks for keeping his baby running. And I vaguely wonder if this is what pride feels like. Pride in my job. My relationships. My community. And myself.

It's a good feeling.

When most of the dinner food has been consumed, Aaron moves it aside and disappears into the lobby. He comes back out a few minutes later, a lit birthday cake in hand, and my partygoers break into an out-of-tune, horribly perfect rendition of "Happy Birthday."

It doesn't beat Goldie's, though.

The cake has my name on top, although it's misspelled as "Rowen." Aaron gives me an apologetic wince when I notice that, letting me know the bakery messed it up, but I shake my head.

This whole day has been perfect. I wouldn't change a thing.

You're supposed to make a wish when you blow out birthday candles, but as I look at the flames flickering over top of my cake, I can't come up with a single thing to wish for.

So, in the end, as those flames wisp into nothingness, I wish for this.

Exactly this.

I should've known something was bound to go wrong.

Everyone is settled around the tables, chatting and eating cake when, out of nowhere, Alex grips my arm tightly, squeezing with all his might. My head whips up in concern, and I take in the worried expression on his face, but he's not looking at me. He's looking out the open service bay doors.

Finn curses quietly as I swing my head in that direction, finding the source of Alex's agitation.

My gut sinks. Manny. Because why the hell not?

My ex is strolling through the garage like he owns it, expensive suit in place, face full of vitriol and determination.

No good can come of Manuel approaching me in that manner regardless of the people all around.

Conversation comes to a halt slowly, gazes swinging between me and my ex. Pauly makes a noise that sounds suspiciously like a growl, and someone turns off the music, making the stomp of Manuel's final footsteps sound loud in the echoing garage. Manuel comes to a stop a mere three feet away from me, standing on the other side of the table from where I'm sitting. His face is set in a smirk I've seen enough times to know it means trouble.

"Manuel," I greet as even-toned as I can. "What are you doing here?"

"Do you know who he is?" my ex asks.

I shake my head slowly. "What are you talking about?"

He pulls his phone from his pocket. "Your little boy toy. Do you know what he does?"

Alex's grip on my arm tightens as I grit out, "Don't."

Manuel ignores me, flashing his phone screen my way. The unmistakable sounds and sights of sex fill the hushed room, and my gut tightens to the point of pain.

"Your *boyfriend*," Manuel sneers. "Do you know he sells his body?"

Finn leans over to grab Manuel's phone, shoving it face-down on the table, but it's too late. Half the party was privy to what was on that screen.

Pulse thundering in my ears, acid churning in my stomach, I look at this man who once claimed to care for me. I thought he appreciated me for a time. I thought he was my future.

What a fool I was.

I'm no longer the man desperate for scraps, and this time, Manuel has gone too far.

"I know," I tell my ex, voice harsh even to my own ears. "I know exactly who he is."

Manuel's face flashes in surprise for all of a moment before his lips twist cruelly. "And you're okay with that? Sleeping with a slut?"

Alex's gasp is small beside me, almost overshadowed by Pauly's sharp "*Hey.*" And I reach for my boyfriend. I reach for Alex, but he pushes out of his seat before I can grab him. The next thing I know, Alex is jogging through the door into the lobby, his blonde head disappearing from sight.

And that acid inside my stomach turns to fire.

Chapter 29
FINN

I'm out of my seat the same moment as Alex, but he runs off before I can say a word to stop him. I open my mouth, gaze pinned on the asshole who thought it was appropriate to storm in here in front of a room full of people and disclose someone's personal information without their consent.

But before I can chew his ass out, Rowan speaks.

"That's enough," Ro says, voice steady and deceptively calm. "You're no longer welcome here, Manuel."

"Excuse me?" the man asks, having the nerve to sound indignant. Everyone else stays quiet, but uncomfortable looks are being passed around.

"I can take a lot," Rowan says, standing slowly. "I can take you talking shit about me"—I grit my teeth at that—"but you do *not* get to hurt the man I love. You need to leave. Now."

Manuel looks shocked, and I don't know if it's Ro's declaration or the fact that my sweet boyfriend is standing up to him at all. Either way, it's about time Manuel found out his intimidation tactics only extend so far.

The surprise doesn't last long, however, and Manuel's typical mask of displeasure slips right back into place as he scoffs.

"Rowan," he says. "You can't be naive enough to think that man loves you back."

My hand tightens into a fist. I'm not a violent person, but for my men, I'd move the world. And Manuel's behavior has me wanting to move his face from this garage.

Ro gives my arm a gentle squeeze. "Go," he says, hitching his head in the direction Alex disappeared. "Please."

Exhaling—and trusting Ro can handle this—I turn to find our third.

Rowan's voice, calmly demanding his ex leave, follows me through the garage as I head into the lobby. Alex isn't in the front room, but there's a cracked-open door spilling light behind the counter, so I beeline that way. When I push the door open fully, finding what appears to be a small employee break room, Alex is sitting on a metal chair with his knees tucked up against his chest. He gives me a wan smile.

"Goldie," I say quietly, heart clenching at the sight of the moisture that lingers in his eyes. I grab an empty chair, flipping it opposite his and sitting down close enough that I can wrap my arms around his small form.

Alex lists forward, letting me hold his weight, his breath hitting my neck. "Fuck," he says, shaking his head slightly.

"Are you okay?" I ask him, even though it's clear he's not.

"No, I'm pissed," he says.

It's not what I'm expecting.

"I'm pissed off that I let him get to me," he goes on. "I'm not that guy who's ashamed of what he does. I don't care if people know I'm in porn. It's never bothered me. But—fuck."

"What?" I ask softly, rubbing Alex's back as it expands under my palms.

"He called me a slut," Alex answers, blowing out an uneven breath. "My ex, before I became an adult entertainer, called me a slut."

"Oh, Alex," I say, kissing the hair above his ear. "It's a trash term."

"Yes, it is," he agrees, making no move to lean away from me. "It's shit. It's judgmental and shaming. When my ex called me that, he meant it. It wasn't playful. It wasn't a tease. He meant it. Because I wanted to have sex with him a lot, my own boyfriend. And instead of having an adult conversation and telling me his sexual appetite didn't match up with my own, he decided to hurt me. It wasn't okay."

"No, it wasn't," I agree, holding him tighter.

Alex puffs out another breath, nuzzling his face into my neck. "I like sex, but I've never pushed someone past their boundaries. Or cheated. I never would. I was so angry at him for that. For trying to shut me down because he was intimidated by my libido. I broke up with him after that, and I got a job at Elite 8 Studios."

So many pieces are fitting together now, and it makes me all the more determined to make sure Alex knows he's safe with me and Ro. That we'd never shame him for that.

"I shouldn't have let Ro's ex get to me," Alex goes on. "But he did. And I do worry... I worry for Rowan and you." He finally leans back, meeting my gaze with wet, hazel eyes. "I worry that things like what just happened will hurt you."

"Goldie," I say gently, wiping my thumbs under his eyes. "We're bears. We're made of tougher stuff than that."

Alex chuckles a little wetly, his pink lips tipping into a shaky smile.

"We've got teeth and nails, and believe you me, we're not afraid to use them. Ro's out there right now, claws extended. You should've seen him."

"Really?" Alex asks, smile widening.

"Mm. It was hot," I answer.

"Fuck," Alex says, shaking his head. "Can't believe I missed it."

"I'll give you a replay later," I assure him, sifting my fingers through his soft blonde hair. "Alex, we're not going to ask you to give up your job. It doesn't hurt us, what you do. It doesn't make you a slut. I hope that, if or when you do decide to quit, Ro and I will be enough for you. I want that. I want us to be everything you need."

Alex's lip trembles slightly. "No one has ever wanted to be that for me."

I exhale roughly, stroking over his cheek. If I could, I'd cradle this man in my palms so nothing could ever again crack that tender heart of his.

"Then no one knows you the way Ro and I do," I tell him firmly. "How could they and not want to give you the world? How could they and not want to have you for keeps?"

"Finn," he says softly.

"Your job is not a threat to any of us," I reiterate as Rowan steps quietly into the room, making his way toward us. "And I don't give a fuck what people think about how our relationship works. That's between you, me, and Ro. The only thing I want—the only thing I ask—is that while you're ours, we get the honor of being yours."

I place my hand on my chest, and Alex's face softens in recognition.

"Oh, Ging," the small blonde says, dropping his legs to the floor between mine. He grabs my knee and reaches for Ro.

Looking between the two of us—connected to the two of us—he says, "Don't you know? Don't you realize? I'm wildly in love with the both of you. Of course it's you. Only you two."

My heart batters against my ribcage, trying to take flight. "Goldie," I choke.

"You two are mine," Alex says, scooting to the very edge of his seat. His grip on me tightens, and I've no doubt it's the same for Ro. "You're mine. And I'm yours. And that's perfect. It's just right, the three of us. The way we fit."

Fuck.

The expression on Alex's face is so open and honest, there's no doubt in my mind he means every single word of what he's saying.

"I love you, too," I reply hoarsely, my hand on Alex's cheek. I lay my other overtop the one Ro has on my shoulder, and when I look up, Ro's eyes are glistening. "Both of you. I love you both so goddamn much."

Time stands still for just a moment. It's a dream. A beautiful reality. And then Alex is shaking my arm wildly. "You *guys*," he says. "Kiss!"

I hiccup a laugh, and Rowan leans down, connecting his lips to mine. I grip the back of his head almost roughly, desperate to be as close to him as possible. My chest *sings*, and I pour every single ounce of my *I love you* into the kiss. When we separate, I tug Alex to me next. The last thing I see before his mouth is on mine is a wide, happy smile.

I love you. I love you.

Ro crouches low when Alex and I split apart. Hands on both of our legs, he looks between each of us. "I love you," he says softly, earnestly, before shifting his gaze and repeating the message. "I love you."

Alex leans in with a stuttered breath, and he and Ro share their own gentle kiss. I rub my hand over Alex's leg. Sweep my fingers along Rowan's beard.

Perfection.

"God," Alex says, sitting back and wiping his cheeks. "Look at us. We're the fucking cutest. I can't wait to stuff both your dicks up my ass."

Ro chokes on a cough as I garble a laugh. *My God.*

I hope this man never stops shocking me.

"Trouble," I voice, giving Alex a pinch. "Such trouble."

"Oh, come on," Alex retorts lightly, swatting my leg. "You can't tell me you haven't thought about it."

No, I can't.

"Just imagine," the blonde menace continues, leaning close to Ro, lips against the shell of his ear. "You'll be inside me where it's soft, warm, and so very tight. And as you fuck me senseless, stretching me wide, Finn's piercings will be running up and down your dick. Over and over again. Driving you wild."

Alex hums as Rowan swallows, and then the little nymph turns my way, eyes blazing bright. He snags my bottom lip between his teeth, licking the ring there before leaning back just an inch. "It'll be like you're fucking both of us at once."

"Oh, hell," I mutter, shoving the heel of my palm against my dick.

Alex titters a laugh before popping off his chair. "C'mon, boys. There's a party going on. Let's get back out there."

Rowan and I share a bemused look, and I reach over, gripping the back of his neck gently. "Everything okay?"

"More than," Ro answers, nodding surely.

"All right," I say with a smile. "Then let's go."

When the three of us walk back out into the service bay, the music is on again, and everyone is finishing their cake as if the disruption called Manuel never happened. Pauly hops up as soon as he sees us coming, and he guides Alex back to his seat, chatting his ear off. Alex laughs, and I catch Fiona's eye. She tucks her hand near her heart, giving me a gentle yet concerned look. There's no judgment on her face. In fact, no one here looks remotely perturbed by what Manuel revealed about Alex's job.

I give my sister a reassuring smile, offering my thanks, and then I retake my seat amongst Rowan's family.

"Okay, but look at this one," Alex says excitedly, pointing to a picture of a very young *me* buck naked on top of a small horse.

Rowan turns to me. "Finn," he says, tongue in cheek. "I didn't realize you were such a nudist."

My gran laughs, and Alex cackles, looking delighted by this whole experience.

Why am I not surprised?

"He's always been a rebel," Fiona pipes, crossing her legs as she sips her ginger ale.

"You're all a bunch of rabble-rousers," I declare.

"Oh, honey," Alex says, patting my knee. "Are you only just figuring this out?"

I shove Alex's snack plate closer to him. "Here. Stick something in that mouth."

Alex's lips twist, and he turns his face firmly away from my gran before picking up a baby carrot and bringing it slowly to his mouth. He wraps his lips around it and *sucks*, cheeks hollowed, and then he gives me a wink.

Aw, fuck. Asked for that one, didn't I?

Fiona snickers none too quietly.

"Have you had a chance to meet Finnigan's parents?" Gran asks Rowan.

I refocus myself on the conversation as Ro shakes his head, eyes pinging to me.

"They haven't called," I tell my gran. Fi gives me a sympathetic look.

Gran huffs out a small sigh, pulling her sweater more securely around her. "Fucking idiots," she mutters.

"*Gran*," I exclaim as Alex's eyes widen.

She waves her hand in the air. My gran has never been one to mince words. "You can't tell me it's not true. What's more important than family?"

Ro's eyes meet mine as Gran turns another page in the photo album on her lap. She hands it over to Rowan, pointing to a picture of all of us—Gran, Grandpa, my parents, me and my siblings, even my aunts and uncles. We're together under the shade of a big oak tree. I don't remember the moment the picture was taken, but it was clearly a family get-together of some sort.

"Their priorities changed," Gran says, the sadness in her tone evident. "Too caught up in stuff that doesn't even matter. At least you two have some common sense." *Me and Fiona.*

"Sorry, Gran," I say softly, exchanging a look with my sister. I know she, like me, still harbors some guilt over the missed time we should have been spending in Gran's life.

"Not for you to be sorry about," Gran replies, picking at her own plate of snacks before settling on a cracker and cheese combo. "You're here, aren't you? Just promise me, Finnigan, that when you have kids, you won't let them go from your life without a fight."

This time, my eyes meet Alex's.

"Promise," I say.

Fiona clears her throat lightly. "Gran, would you like some more ginger ale?"

"Please," Gran replies.

"I'll get it," I say, popping up from my seat.

Fiona follows me to the kitchen anyways, and when I grab a fresh soda from the fridge, she rests her hip against the counter, crossing her arms loosely.

"You know it wasn't a criticism, right?" she says.

"What?" I ask her, not having a clue what she's talking about.

"The last time we talked about kids. When I questioned how that would work in a situation like yours," she explains.

Ah.

"I didn't take it that way, no," I tell her.

She looks relieved, although some tension still lines the cut of her brow.

"We'd figure it out," I say, having a feeling that's what's on her mind.

Fi nods before dropping her arms. "Do you want me to talk to Mom and Dad?"

"About?"

"About..." She waves her hand. "All this. Getting in touch with you. Being better parents."

I huff a laugh, shaking my head. "No, Fi. It's on them if they don't want to be in my life. You know I tried. I tried a lot when I was younger to get them to accept me, but as soon as I went off on my own path, that was it."

My sister sighs. She knows the story. "I hate it. How sanctimonious they can be. Dillon and Conner, too. They're turds."

"Turds, Fi? Really?"

She snorts.

"I'm surprised our parents didn't give you grief over your divorce," I note.

"Oh, they did," Fiona replies. "But since I still work at the company, they have to play nice for appearances' sake. At least when we're in public."

"That's fucked," I note.

She doesn't disagree with me.

"At least we found our way back to one another," I say. "I'm glad for that."

Fiona gives me a small smile. "Yeah. I am, too."

After a sigh, I notch my head toward the living room. "Come on. If we leave Alex alone for too long, he's bound to get into trouble. And you know Gran will get in on it, too."

Fi shakes her head lightly. "I think I like Alex's brand of trouble."

"Oh God. Don't ever let him hear you say that."

My sister huffs a little laugh, but then her tone turns serious. "They're good men, Finn. I like them. Both of them."

Both of them. A few months back, I never would have anticipated being where I am today, with not only the neighbor I'd been pining after but his former hookup, too. I wouldn't have anticipated I'd have two men to love.

I thought it was a possibility, sure—that my heart was made for something bigger. But the reality of it is so much *more* than I expected. It's vibrant and beautiful and so very right. It may not be simple, what we are, but it *is* easy. Belonging to Ro and Alex is the easiest thing.

Smile at the corner of my lips, I tell my sister, "Yeah, Fi. They're pretty great, huh?"

They're my future. And damn, I can't wait to see how our love grows.

Chapter 30

ALEX

"Oh, look at her!" I say in excitement. "She *loves* them."

"Love might be a strong word," Finn replies.

I shush him. "Our silly Ginger Bear doesn't know what he's talking about, does he? No, he doesn't," I coo to Mojave, who's lying inside her cat carrier with a bored look on her face. Yes, she does look bored, but I refuse to give Finn the satisfaction of admitting to her tepid attitude.

Honestly, it's probably for the best that she's disinterested in the small rodents.

"Love those little rats," I whisper. "Don'tcha, girl?"

Finn shakes his head, lip ring tucked between his teeth.

"What about this one?" Rowan asks, pointing to a small black-and-white rat whose paws are up on the glass. "He's cute."

"The *cutest*," I agree, watching the little rat's whiskers twitch about. "What do you think, Emil?"

The man uses his knuckle to adjust his glasses. "Um. Fine?"

"Just fine?" I ask.

Emil shrugs. "I mean, it's a rat. Why am I here again?"

I roll my eyes. "Because I invited you, silly." Leaning closer to our soon-to-be pet, I add, "And don't listen to him. You're definitely the cutest."

Rowan taps a note near the front of the cage. "It says here they suggest adopting rats in pairs, but this guy was being bullied by the others, so they separated him out. Maybe we could find him a new friend?"

I clutch my chest. "Of *course* we will," I assure them both before touching the glass. "You're coming with us, little buddy, and we'll find you the nicest friend there is. Yes, we will."

"I'll grab the salesperson," Finn says with a smirk, peeling off from our group.

"This is so exciting," I say with a little hop, looping my arm with Ro's and wrapping my other around Emil to pull him close. "Our family is expanding."

Emil looks over at me slowly. "You mean because of the rat, right?"

I give him a big smile. Emil doesn't know it yet, but I've adopted him, too. We're going to be the best of friends. "Are you done with your finals?" I ask, letting my coworker go.

He nods, hands in his pockets. "Yeah. Last one was this morning. You?"

"Yep," I chirp. "All done."

Last test finished. Projects turned in. *Done.*

"You know what this calls for?" I ask, strolling along the displays of animals before stopping with a gasp. "Here."

"What?" Emil asks, joining me.

I point. "A hermit crab. You definitely deserve a hermit crab, Emil."

"I, uh... Do I, though?"

I nod fervently. "Yes, absolutely. Treat yourself, boo."

Emil leans down, looking through the glass at the little crab sitting—lying?—in the corner. "I honestly don't know if this is a treat, Alex."

"Hey, Alex?" Finn calls. "I think we're ready."

"Here we go," I say excitedly, skipping back over to the cages where the mammals are. The salesperson is transferring our little black-and-white rat to a portable carrier, and the rodent looks just as happy about it as Mojave does. As the employee explains the process for introducing another rat down the road, I snuggle against Rowan's side. "This is a beautiful moment."

He chuckles, leaning over to kiss the top of my head. "Thanks for supporting this."

"Are you kidding?" I say. "I *love* this. We're going to be the best rat daddies there ever were."

"That sounds so odd, Alex," Emil says, shaking his head.

I hum. Sounds perfect to me.

Finn grabs Mojave's carrier as the rest of us trail after the salesperson to the counter. We have food and treats, but everything else is already set up back at Finn's house. I spent the better part of yesterday getting Casa de Ratas organized and furnished. Our new furry friend is going to *adore* it.

Before we head out of the store, Emil says, "You're off next week, right?"

"Yeah, I am." I took the whole week off as a post-finals breather. "Will I see you at the party tomorrow?"

The Elite 8 crew is getting together at the studio to celebrate my graduation. Jerome is the one who suggested it, the sentimental bastard. Heart of gold, that man. I'm convinced of it.

"I'll be there," Emil confirms.

I give my coworker a quick hug, and he chuckles, patting me on the back.

"See ya later, Kent," I call as he heads toward the door.

"Kent?" he asks, pausing.

I tap the side of my head, where Emil's glasses sit. "Not all superheroes wear capes."

"No, some of us just wear jockstraps," he shoots back.

Cackling, I give Emil a wave goodbye, and he heads out the door.

"Ready to get our new guy home?" Finn asks, Mojave's carrier in one hand, the rat's in the other.

I nod definitively, taking the rat carrier from him as Ro follows with the bags. "We need to come up with a name," I point out.

"Any ideas?" Rowan asks.

I consider that as we pack everything into my Jeep. "I think you should pick," I finally say. "This was your idea, after all."

Honestly, when I found out Ro wanted to get another pet, I was stoked. Not only because Mojave deserves a sibling. But because it was clear adopting a rat was something important to Grizzly Bear. A link to his past, in a way.

I think this is his way of bringing a piece of his parents back into his life. And of course I wanted to support that.

"What about Axle?" Ro says once we're halfway back to his neighborhood.

I raise a brow. "That cute little rat with the whiskers and pink nose? He's not a hardened criminal, Ro."

He huffs a laugh. "Strut? Sparky?"

"You're naming car parts, aren't you, baby?" Finn chirps up from the back.

I bark a laugh, and Rowan falls silent. When I glance his way from my spot in the driver's seat, there's a smile on his face.

"Poppet?" he suggests.

I gasp. "Is that a car part?"

Rowan nods in my peripheral vision. "Poppet valve."

"Oh my God. Poppet," I breathe, my grin widening by the second. "That's perfect."

"Yeah?" Ro asks.

I nod, flicking my eyes up to Finn in the rearview mirror. "Ging?"

"Sounds great to me," the man answers.

"Hear that, Poppet?" I call out to our new pet rat. "You've got a name."

When we get back to Finn's, he lets Mojave out of her carrier and then heads to the kitchen to feed her. Mo swerves around his legs, purring loudly as he dishes out her food.

"Don't worry," Finn says in almost too quiet of a voice for me to hear. He scratches along Mojave's back. "We won't ever forget about you."

A smile twists my lips. My sweet Papa Bear.

Leaving him to it, I bring Poppet up to his new home on the second-floor landing, right beside the orchids. "Look at this, Poppet," I say, pulling him gently from the carrier. The little rat is calm, letting me hold him without issue. "This is your new home."

Poppet looks enthused as he takes in his luxurious three-story condo with natural lighting and a garden view. His whiskers flick about, and he turns in my hand, scenting the air.

"I think he's going to like it here," Ro says, kneeling down next to me. His eyes are creased softly, and there's a gentle smile on his face as he runs his hand smoothly over Poppet's back.

"Of course he is," I respond, leaning against Rowan's arm. "He's got us."

Ro hums. "The pet shop employee said we should give him some time to get acclimated before being too hands-on."

"Okay," I say a little sadly, giving Poppet one last finger-pet between his ears before setting him inside his home. Ro and I watch as he starts exploring.

"I'm going to help Finn get dinner ready," Rowan says after a while, standing up.

"I'll be down in a minute," I tell him. "I just want to get a few pictures first."

Ro drags his fingers through my hair—a voiceless confirmation that has me purring—before he heads down the stairs. I pull out my phone and snap half a dozen pics as Poppet heads up to the second floor to investigate his bed. I send a couple to Anh.

Me: Look at my new baby!

She replies right away.

Anh: Aw, you're a daddy now.

Technically, Mojave is my first child, but I don't correct her.

Me: I know. Isn't it great?

Anh: By the way, here's a link to a butt plug I think you'd enjoy.

I bark a laugh before slapping a hand over my mouth. Poppet doesn't look upset by the sudden loud noise, but I still keep the rest of my laughter to a minimum as I send Anh an array of emojis to profess my thanks. After filling up Poppet's dish with the food we got from the pet store, I retreat downstairs to find my men.

The pair are inside the kitchen, Finn's arms around Ro as they look at the contents of the open fridge. Finn places a kiss against Ro's neck, his amber hair cascading to the side and the stud in his ear glinting. My heart does a complicated skip jump, and when Rowan turns his face to the side and the pair kiss in earnest, I have a sudden urge for something completely unrelated to food.

Finn, as if of the same mind, closes the fridge door, eyes flicking to me in the entryway of the room before he nudges Ro back against the appliance. Our grizzly thunks into it, head back as Finn strokes a hand up his chest and lays a kiss along his throat.

Damn.

I love the two of them together. I *want* the two of them together.

Finn holds out his hand, inviting me closer, and I grab it in an instant, letting him tug me into the fray. His mouth meets mine next, urging me open, his piercing flicking against my lip.

"Can I—" I start to ask, but Ro's mouth closes over my earlobe, and I groan.

"Can you what, Goldie?" Finn asks, his palm smoothing down my back. Lower. Over my ass.

I shiver. "Can I have you both tonight?"

Finn's grip tightens against my ass cheek, and Ro inhales softly.

"I'm off work this coming week," I go on. "So I don't have to worry about recovery time. And, fuck. I..." I roll my head to the side when Ro sucks against my neck. "I want to feel you. Both of you."

Finn grabs my chin gently, pulling my focus. His lip twitches slightly before his mouth twists into a teasing smirk.

God, I love a teasing Ging.

"Yeah, Goldie?" Finn asks, a wicked hint to his words. "You wanna be double-stuffed?"

"Like an Oreo," I shoot back.

Finn barks a laugh, his eyes lighting. Without warning, he swoops down, grabbing me around the waist. I squeal, latching on as my world goes temporarily flying.

"You heard the man," Finn says to Rowan, turning from the kitchen. "We've got a horny twinkie on our hands."

"The horniest," I agree around my laughter as Finn starts to truck me up the stairs. Ro appears in my vision, his smile wide as he jogs up after us.

"He wants to be filled with your cream," Finn adds, outright laughing.

"Oh, my God," I groan, my smile so wide it hurts. "That was the worst, Ging. You can do better than that."

As we pass Poppet, I send a silent apology for the things our poor rat might witness inside this house.

Finn clears his throat as he carries me through the doorway into the bedroom, and then he tosses me onto the bed. I giggle as I bounce atop the mattress, and Finn leans over me, hair disheveled, arms braced on either side of my body. "Our man wants us tonight, Ro," he rumbles. "*Both* of us. He wants us to stretch him wide with our cocks."

Oh, yes.

"He wants to feel it," Finn goes on as Rowan appears by my side. "Wants it to ache. Wants to be so full, so out of his mind with pleasure, that there's nothing and no one but *us*. Because we're his. And he's ours."

I lick my lips, heart thudding as I nod.

Finn traces a line down my chest and over my belly button. He doesn't stop until his finger graces the erection tenting my jeans. "He wants that sweet, little hole of his so fucked out that all week, every time he sits down, and every time he feels a twinge, he'll remember exactly who owned this ass."

"Oh fuck," I gasp, losing my voice as Finn's mouth collides into my own.

Daddy Bear is out to play.

Finn deftly unbuttons and unzips my jeans, hand curling around my dick as his tongue makes me dizzy. It's an onslaught. A beautiful, toe-curling onslaught.

When Finn takes a step back, I groan. *No.* "Don't make me beg."

"Never," he says, tugging his shirt swiftly over his head. And *damn*, with that one word, it's like he knows me.

Because he does, a voice inside says. He does know me.

As Finn shoves down his pants, my gaze swings Ro's way. The man—bless him—is already completely and gloriously nude, and suddenly, I need more of what I walked in on in the kitchen.

"I want to watch you two," I voice aloud, hastening to shove my pants the rest of the way off. "I wanna stretch myself while I watch."

Finn's predatory gaze shifts Ro's way, a wicked gleam in his eye. "That so?"

"God, yes," I say, kicking my briefs away and then tossing my shirt.

Ro, for his part, doesn't even bat an eyelash, and I feel a strong sense of pride at that. I remember the first time we were together like this, just him and me, and how hesitant he was. How unsure. Now, he's standing tall, watching Finn expectantly as the tattooed man struts his way.

Finn skirts around Rowan's body, hand trailing along skin, until he's behind our grizzly. One hand slides low, circling Ro's cock, and the other travels higher, curling gently around Ro's throat. Finn angles Rowan's head to the side, eyes on me as he nips the skin at Ro's neck.

Shit, that's hot.

"And what is it you want to watch?" Finn asks, stroking Rowan slowly. Ro moans, dropping his head back against Finn's shoulder.

"Anything," I breathe, pumping myself in time with Finn's fist. "Everything."

"Greedy," Finn says with a twisting smirk.

"When it comes to you two? Damn right I am," I readily admit, abandoning my cock in favor of grabbing the lube.

When I come back up, bottle in hand, Finn is guiding Ro onto the bed. I wet my fingers, dick jumping when Finn straddles Rowan's body backwards, his mouth poised over our Grizzly Bear's cock and *his* cock in prime position for Rowan to taste. I thank all the Heavens above that Finn has as dirty of a mind as my own. And that these men are *mine*.

Finn swallows Ro's cock without preamble, and Ro and I both moan. I slip a finger inside of my body, quickly followed by a second, working myself open as I take in the sight before me. Ro: big, strong, hairy, *kind*. So damn lovable I could burst, but also so damn sexy, his rugged body laid out below Finn like a dream. And then Finn, braced above Rowan, so colorful with that ginger hair and the bright tapestry of flowers that vine down his chest and arms. His muscles bunch as he holds himself aloft Ro, and Rowan's cock shuttles in and out of his mouth as his own disappears inside the other man's lips.

The sight makes me want to purr.

I'm up to four fingers, hard and aching, ready for more, and Finn seems to sense it. His eyes swing my way, and ever so slowly, he drags his lips off Rowan's cock.

"You two," I breathe out, moaning as I twist my fingers. "So gorgeous. I'm the luckiest twink alive. My two men. My two bears."

Finn smirks, although there's a softness in his gaze. "Ready to be fucked by your two bears?"

"*God* yes," I groan.

Finn slips off Ro's body, and I quickly take his place, meeting my grizzly's lips as I rub my cock against his stomach. He tastes like Finn. Like *ours*.

"Gorgeous," I tell him again, kissing Ro as his big hands map over my skin like I'm his most favorite treasure. "You're so good for us, baby. Absolutely perfect."

Rowan's eyes soften at that, and his fingers twine up into my hair, cradling my head. "I believe you," he says softly, and my heart practically leaps from my chest.

As I grin down at my Grizzly Bear—*such a good boy, the bestest*—the crinkle of a condom wrapper announces Finn is suiting up. His hand slides reverently along my ass, stroking, petting almost, and I widen my straddle, easing down over Rowan's lap. As soon as I settle, the blunt end of Finn's cock presses against my entrance, and then he's slipping inside. I drop my face to Rowan's chest, groaning as I welcome Finn in.

His Jacob's Ladder starts to pass over my rim as he works his way into my body in smooth, small strokes. And I know it's intentional, the way he's entering me. The way he's making sure those piercings hit me just right time and time again. It's deliriously good, and I moan my assent against Rowan's furry pec.

"Okay?" Finn asks, rubbing his hand over my back.

"Uh-huh. My God. So okay," I answer, wiggling back against him, shivering as he retreats and runs those piercings along me again. "Gonna die. It'll be a good way to go."

Finn chuckles, the sound raspy and low, and then, all at once, he's seated inside me, hips at my ass.

"*Ah*," I moan out. *Bliss.*

Finn's fingers thread up through my hair, his hand along the back of my head—a possessive hold. And then he starts to move.

I bite Rowan's chest as that ladder drags along my rim and inner walls. My Grizzly Bear grunts, and I soothe his skin with my tongue.

Licked him. He's mine.

Part of me wonders what Finn's piercings would feel like without the rubber in the way, but at least for now, the condom is a necessity. Maybe someday...

When Finn angles for my prostate, rubbing the top of his Prince Albert along the sensitive gland, I about shoot upright.

"Je-sus," I yell out, pressing back on him, my cock leaking, my nerve endings on fire.

Finn reads me like a book. He keeps up a steady pace at my sweet spot until I can't take it any longer. Until I know, if we keep at this, the show's going to be over before we get to the main act.

"Okay, okay," I say, reaching back and giving Finn a slap.

He immediately backs off, chuckling again, and when Finn slips from my body, I know exactly what he's thinking.

"Your turn," I tell Ro, easing up so we can slip a condom on his cock.

Rowan licks his lips as Finn does the honors, and then Finn drags my hips back into position, settling me over Ro. He holds Rowan's cock at the base and gives me a push down, and then my *Grizzly Bear* is sliding inside of me.

"Ah, yes," I say, tossing my head back.

Rowan's thickness stretches me wide, and I ride him, hands on his chest for balance. Ro watches me as if I hung the moon, his eyes wide and endlessly soft, his mouth parted, and his hands clutching my thighs.

I don't know whether or not it *was* fate that led me here, but I think I needed someone like Ro. Someone who looks at me as if I'm simply amazing. Someone who gives me control, and who makes me feel powerful for being my own special brand of extra. Someone who *needs* me the way I need him.

And Finn, this man at my back, whose hands are roaming over my cock and Ro's leg. I needed someone like him, too. Someone to take care of me, who knows the difference between giving and demanding. Someone who allows me to let go.

These two men—they're more than I expected. More than I ever dared dream for. Not when I was a young boy finding out about love for the first time. And not even many months ago, as a man who had learned the limitations of real-life fairy tales.

Well that man can suck it. 'Cause damn. All my wishes are coming true.

When Finn starts adding his fingers into the mix, stretching me alongside Rowan's cock, my body sings.

"*Yes*," I say, leaning forward until I'm draped over Rowan's body. His arms come around me, warm along my back, and my breathing picks up in anticipation. I blow out a breath. "Do it."

Finn's fingers disappear, and then his crown pushes against my rim. Rowan's hands spasm against my back, and his groan rivals my own keen. There's stretching. So much stretching. A distant ache that blooms pain-pleasure all along my synapses. It spreads outwards, warmth blanketing my body. I go lax, not resisting in the least as Finn's crown battles to get into my body.

"Okay?" Finn checks, not yet through the outer ring of muscle.

I nod against Rowan's chest, and fingers sift through my hair. "Yes, love," I breathe. "So okay."

Finn pulls back for a moment and adds more lube with his fingers, and then he's pressing again. That bloom. That not-quite-pain. And then...

Ah.

Finn stalls as soon as his crown slips inside my body. His exhale is loud, and he runs his palms over my skin. "Goldie," he says reverently.

Mhm.

He inches forward, my Ginger Bear, and my soul lights.

Rowan groans beneath me, saying something about the "damn piercings," but it sounds like he's speaking through cotton balls. I'm in the clouds, every inch of me buzzing, tingles spreading over my skin. My orgasm is steadily building, but it's a distant feeling, so separate from what I'm experiencing inside.

"Is this what you wanted, Goldie?" Finn asks, voice soft and lips at my neck as he comes to a rest against my ass, both he and Rowan stuffed in me as far as they can go. "You wanted to be trapped between the two of us?"

I exhale, rolling my head until my cheek encounters the sweet press of those lips. "Nowhere else I'd rather be."

Chapter 31
ROWAN

Alex's cheeks are flushed as he lies against my chest, his lips bright pink and his hair tousled around his head.

I have a brief moment of suspension. My mind flashes back to the very first time I met this man, when he was situated over top of me similarly to this. When I wondered if he was an angel.

I'm still not convinced I didn't pass out in Mike's Garage in a cloud of carbon dioxide and vehicle emissions that day. How does one go from having so little...to having *this*?

Finn holds my gaze as he starts to move inside Alex. I can do little but lie here, holding Alex's weight, lending my cock. But it's what's needed. And truth be told, Finn has it under control.

The man is situated between my spread legs, his knees against my inner thighs. Alex, of course, is between us, lying on top of me with his legs to either side of my body. My cock is maybe only half of the way inside of him at this angle, but it doesn't matter. Nor does it matter that I can't move.

Because Finn is moving. And his cock, with every stroke, is dragging all of those little metal balls and ladder rungs against my dick. Between that and the absolute vise-grip press of Alex squeezing us tight, it's everything I can do to simply weather the storm.

"Ro," Finn says, reaching for me.

I give him my hand, and he presses it to the mattress, fingers interlaced with my own. His gaze is sharp, and I don't think I've ever seen him look as possessive as he does right now.

Is he feeling what I am? This almost desperate urge to never let go?

As Finn fucks Alex—fucks against me—Alex bounces lightly on my body. He moves like a doll, and honestly, I'd be concerned if I hadn't seen him react the same way when Finn fisted him. Alex loves this, and he trusts us to take care of him when he's vulnerable in this way.

Alex may be pliant against me, but his mouth doesn't stop moving. "Fuck me, fuck me," he mumbles, so quietly it's as if he's saying it for himself. "So good. My bears. My men. *Mine*. Gonna come."

Finn catches that, and his eyes ping to me as he thrusts a little harder. Alex moans louder, his body starting to tighten around our cocks. I grit my teeth, the pressure intense, and I'd grab Alex's cock and help him along, except there's no way I can reach it. It's pressed firmly against my lower stomach.

It doesn't seem to matter. Alex croaks out another moan, turning his face down against my chest. His vocalizations rumble through me as his cock starts to stream between us, his body clamping tight around me and Finn. I rub his back, wincing as he strangles my cock to the point of discomfort, and Finn's hand tightens in my own. He stops moving, not wanting to hurt Alex while that man's body is strung this tight, but Alex's ring of muscle continues to milk us as he writhes and pants through his orgasm.

It goes on. And on. And I'd come if Finn were to move even a muscle against me. The imagery alone, the sounds Alex is making as he finds his bliss, have me nearly tipping over the edge. When Alex finally releases his tension, slumping against my chest and exhaling heavily, Finn slowly retreats from his body.

Alex scoots himself up ever so slightly, enough for my cock to slip free, and then he waves his hand backwards. "You guys," he slurs. "You guys come."

Finn, not missing a beat, strips away his condom and my own. And with Alex still lying atop my body, Finn brings our bare cocks together and strokes.

My head hits the mattress, and I groan as I rush closer to the edge. My entire body is already wound tight, just waiting to tip, and when I feel Finn start to swell against me, the first of his release coating my cock, I fall. A shout punches from my lungs as all that tension breaks, as bliss rolls over me in waves. It's flying. It's floating. It's tumbling down a ravine.

"Fuck," I mutter, my heaving breaths moving Alex up and down on my chest.

"Mhm," Alex mutters, cheek pressed against me, hands on my arms.

Finn strokes my leg, his golden gaze soft when he looks my way. His hair falls over one eye, his tattoos are bright amidst his skin, but *fuck*. It's his expression that gets me.

It's love.

"Alex," Finn says softly, brushing the blonde's hair out of his face. "Do you want a bath?"

"In a minute," Alex answers, sighing.

"Okay," Finn says, climbing up beside us and lying down at our sides. His fingers flit over my beard, and I turn my face, giving his knuckles a kiss.

We're quiet for a moment, all of us catching our breaths. I'm not surprised when Alex is the first to speak.

"So, are we going to keep two houses?" the man asks. "Or should we move into one?"

Finn and I exchange a look.

"I'm pro one," Alex continues. "That way, I won't miss either of you coming out of the shower. Although, when we have kids, we might need a bigger place."

Finn's eyes widen, although there's a smile on his face.

I know exactly how he feels.

"I, uh..." I clear my throat and try again. "I wouldn't be opposed to one place."

Finn's fingers brush over my cheek, and Alex sighs happily.

"Yeah," our Goldie says before his eyelids drift shut. "A boy sure could get used to this, you know."

"Okay, so now you want to whip it."

Alex's eyebrows wing up, and he grins. "How must I whip it?"

Finn huffs a laugh before shaking his head and answering, "Whip it good."

Alex titters, whipping the eggs in the glass mixing bowl. He starts humming, and I can't help but smile.

"Ready for your graduation?" I ask from my spot at the kitchen table. Poppet is running through the tunnel system Alex set up for him to use downstairs until we're sure Mojave has no interest in taking a bite out of the rodent.

Alex nods, shooting me a little smile. "I am. I'm kind of sad to be done, but also..." He shrugs. "I don't know. It feels good, too. Like I accomplished something."

"Something big," Finn agrees, chopping cherry tomatoes to put in the omelets.

Alex gives Finn a nudge with his hip before saying, in a quieter voice, "I hope they're supportive."

"Your parents?" Finn asks.

Alex nods before setting the whisk against the side of the bowl. "I know they'll be there, but I hope they're okay with us. Unless your parents come around, they're all we've got."

Finn runs a hand over Alex's back, shooting me a little look over his shoulder before he says, "I wouldn't hold out hope for my parents."

"Yeah," Alex says with a sigh.

"It'll be okay," I pipe up. "We're not alone, you know. We have Gran and Fiona and Pauly and a whole fleet of porn stars at our back. But even if we didn't, we'd still have each other."

Alex gives me the softest smile at that and comes over to where I'm sitting. He climbs onto my lap, and I smooth my hands to his backside, fleetingly wondering if he can still feel us, Finn and me. If he's still sore after last night. "Grizzly Bear, you sweet man. I love you, you know that, right?"

"I know, Alex," I say gently, accepting the hug he gives me with eagerness. He smells fresh from his shower and a little bit like flowers because of his hair product. I breathe him in happily. "I love you, too."

"I'm never going to get sick of that," Alex replies before saying, a little louder, "Love you, too, Ginger Bear. Don't feel left out."

"Never," Finn replies from the stove, a smile twisting his lips.

When Alex sits back, he gives my cheek another peck before standing up. Hopping over to the stove, he hip checks Finn out of the way and takes over. "Okay, tell me what to do," the blonde demands.

Finn chuckles, handing over the spatula. "Add the toppings to one side and then flip it closed."

"I got this," Alex says, distributing cheese and tomatoes into the cooking omelet, his tongue sticking out of the corner of his mouth.

Finn brushes his own hair out of his eyes, and the ink on his hand reminds me of something.

"Alex," I say. "When are you going to show us your book?"

Alex shoots me a coy little grin. "Soon."

"Will you at least tell us what it's called?" Finn asks.

Alex's secret smile stays in place, but he faces forward again, slowly flipping the omelet closed. "It's titled *Goldie and the Two Bears*."

Finn and I exchange a look at that.

I can't wait to read it.

When our late morning breakfast is done, I sneak away to run a quick errand before Alex's graduation, and by the time I get back, Finn and Alex are dressed and ready to go. Finn is wearing a simple white button-down, which makes his hair and ink pop, and Alex looks worlds away from the feisty young man he usually presents himself as. He's dressed in all black, although his shirt does have a very subtle floral pattern.

"There you are," Alex says. "Ready to go?"

I give him a nod, checking my own shirt over for wrinkles. It's light blue, and I felt good putting it on today when I swung by my own place before coming back here. When I glanced in the mirror, I saw a man who looked happy. A man with a smile and a matching set of eyes.

I saw the man I think Finn and Alex have been seeing this whole time.

"You know, you should just move your clothes over here already," Alex says.

I huff a laugh. "Think Finn's closet can handle it?"

Alex taps his chin. "Good point. Finn, we may need to convert your office."

"Into a closet?" Finn asks, brow raised. "Where will I work?"

"In the conservatory, of course," Alex answers.

There's a pause. "You mean the landing at the top of the stairs?" Finn checks.

Alex nods, slipping cufflinks on. "Mhm."

"Where the orchids are?" Finn asks.

"Mhm," Alex answers.

"And the beanbags?"

"Mhm."

"And where Poppet now lives?"

Alex gives Finn an exasperated look. "Yes, Honey Bear."

Finn bites his lip. "Do you see the problem?"

Alex waves his hand in the air. "There's plenty of room."

"Alex, there's *no* room," Finn counters. "None whatsoever."

Alex makes a *psh* sound, and Finn looks to me for guidance.

I shrug. "I've heard beanbags are very ergonomic."

Finn closes his eyes for a moment and pinches the bridge of his nose, but his lips are twisted into a smile. When he lets go, he shakes his head. "You two are trouble, and I'm so damn glad you're mine."

"Aww," Alex says, slipping his arms around Finn's waist and looking up at the man. "You're a sap, and I love it. Now let me ride you, Ginger Pony. We have a graduation to get to."

As Finn allows Alex to hop up onto his back and leads the blonde from the room with only a single grumble, I take a moment to look around. True, the closet is already full to bursting, but there's a good chunk of space on the other side of the room near the window. My dresser would likely fit perfectly in the spot.

Truth be told, I've been spending more time at Finn's place these days than my own. Ever since Alex popped into our lives, we've slowly been migrating here. Maybe it's the energy of this place, like Finn says, that draws us. Or maybe it doesn't matter *where* we are, so long as we're together. I don't have strong ties to my own house. I could see living here with Alex and Finn. Making the move official. After all, we're already living together. That much is obvious.

Sometimes, still, I wonder why I came here to Las Vegas. I wonder why the restless pull inside drew me to this very spot. I was alone. My parents gone. No family left. It was just me and my Chevy, so I drove. I drove, and I stopped here. And I never left.

Maybe there are countless paths we can take in life. Limitless possibilities. If that's true, I'm glad the road I traveled brought me here. I'm glad to have set up camp in a spot where both Finn and Alex appeared when I needed them most. Was I waiting for them the entire time? It feels like it, in a way. I was definitely waiting for something.

But now, I realize, I don't feel like I'm *waiting* at all. I'm not anticipating the next change in my life or wondering where I'm going.

I found home. I'm here. I made it.

And *woah*. Isn't that something?

"Grizzly Bear?" Alex calls up from downstairs. "Did you get lost? Do you need a rescue? I have a very well-trained horse ready to ride in and save you if needed. I can provide mouth-to-mouth resuscitation."

As tempting as that is... "No, I'm not lost." Not in the least. "I'll be right down."

Smile on my face, I turn out the light and go to join my men.

Chapter 32

ALEX

Damn, I did it. I'm a college graduate. Four years late, maybe, but so what? I'm glad I finished on my own terms. That I got the degree I wanted instead of playing it safe.

"Mr. Alex Monroe," a familiar voice calls.

Turning, I smile as I set eyes on Niko. He swoops in, giving me a fierce hug.

Dixon, at Niko's side, flicks the tassel on my cap. "You did good, kid."

I inhale, looking up at the man. "Papa," I whisper.

Dixon sighs, immediately dropping his head, and Niko rubs over his shoulder in a consoling manner.

"You did it to yourself," Niko supplies.

Dixon doesn't even counter him.

Chest full of fuzzies, I pull Dixon into my arms, squeezing with all my might. It means more than I can say that they came to my graduation ceremony, despite the fact that I'll see them again later at my party.

Dixon sighs, but he squeezes me back. "Proud of you."

Oh fuck.

"Aw, damn it," Dixon says, pulling back. "Are you crying?"

"Nope," I say, wiping my eyes and giving the man a beaming smile. "Thank you for coming."

Dixon's face softens.

"Hey, small fry," another voice pipes.

"Mali-boo!" I twist and throw my arms around my blonde friend. "Is Daddy Henrik here?"

Mal huffs a laugh. "No, but he'll be at the party later."

"Good," I say, releasing my friend. "I haven't seen him in way too long."

"You just like the fact that you can tease him and he can't run away," Mal counters.

I gasp. "Mal, that is terrible. If the man needed to run, I'd happily lend my hand."

Mal shakes his head, chuckling, and choosing, I think, not to comment on how ineffectual that move would be if Henrik—who happens to be blind—were attempting to run from *me*.

Niko gives my arm a squeeze. "Congrats, Alex. Seriously. We'll see you later?"

"You bet," I tell him, giving all three of my friends a temporary goodbye.

When I turn around, I nearly walk face first into a very familiar chest.

"Woah there," the chest rumbles.

Smile wide, I launch myself into Finn's arms. He catches me easily, even though my robe makes it hard to get a good grip around him with my legs. "Ging," I breathe out, as if I didn't just spend the entire morning with the man before my ceremony.

He chuckles lightly against my ear. He gets it.

When Finn sets me down, I find Rowan right next to him, and I hop up on tiptoes to wrap my hands around his neck. "Thank you for being here."

Rowan gives me a shy smile, kissing the side of my forehead, and when we disentangle, he holds out a bouquet of flowers.

My heart squeezes tight. So *that's* where he got off to earlier.

"For you," my Grizzly Bear says, handing the bundle over.

Bringing the bouquet to my nose, I inhale the fresh floral aroma, sharp and sweet, and make a mental note to learn the types of blooms I'm holding if for no other reason than to have a name to put to the images I know I'll be sketching the next time my fingers meet pencil and paper.

"Thank you, Grizz," I reply, hoping he hears how much I mean it.

By his expression, I think he does.

When a pair of small arms wrap around me from behind, I let loose a laugh.

"We did it," Anh says in my ear.

"We did," I say, spinning to greet my friend. Like me, she's dressed in graduation robes with a pointy, flat cap atop her head. "What's next?"

Anh gives a great, big shrug. "I don't know. Life goes on? I keep selling my mugs on Etsy until I get my pottery in a gallery somewhere?"

"You'll get there," I tell my friend.

"You know there's no guarantee of that in our business," she says.

She's not wrong. But after Professor Hughes called me into her office to give me an enthusiastic shove in the direction of publishing my book on the caveat I polish the story with the help of an actual writer, I'm more optimistic than ever that I can make something of my art. Something wonderful and gay.

"Still," I tell Anh. "I have faith in you. Oh, boo, these are my boyfriends." I reach for my guys, presenting them like the prizes they are. "Meet Rowan and Finnigan. Guys, this is my bestie, Anh."

There's a little smirk on Anh's face when she shakes each of their hands. I can see exactly what's going through her head as she makes a quick tally, noting Finn's tattoos and then zeroing in on Rowan. "What nice forearms you have," she tells my Grizzly Bear, and I have to hold back the bark of laughter that tries to break free, remembering that very first rather disproportionate sketch Anh caught me drawing.

Rowan, for his part, looks befuddled but gives Anh a polite thank you.

I, however, give Anh a little shove. "Get out of here, you troublemaker."

"That's you," Anh says, but she does take a step away. "I do have to go find my parents."

"Same," I tell her, but before Anh can take another step, I pull her back into my arms.

Her body deflates against mine. "This isn't the end," she says. "For us."

"No, I know," I tell her softly. But I don't let go, instead breathing in the subtle scent of clay that hangs around Anh's person.

When we finally step apart, Anh pinches my cheek. "Love you, dork."

"Love you, too. Brunch next weekend?" I check, even though I know there's no real need to.

"Wouldn't miss it," she replies. "I have to tell you all about my new friend, Dickolas Hoult, after all."

"Anh," I gasp reverently.

She sends me a wink. "Later, baby boy."

"Bye, boo."

When it's only me and my guys left in a sea of mingling graduates, family, and friends, I sigh.

"Ready?" Finn asks.

"Ready," I reply.

With my bears by my side, I scour the auditorium for my parents. They texted me before the ceremony to let me know they'd arrived, but I didn't have time to find them before I had to take my seat. Now, I'm not sure where they are.

In the end, I text them to meet us outside near the fountain. It takes a few minutes, but when I see them approaching, nerves hit me square in the gut.

My mom's gaze skitters between me and my guys hesitantly. My dad looks a little more even-keeled, although he does take a moment to look both my boyfriends over. I imagine he's forming some conclusions, in particular, about Finn's appearance that couldn't be more wrong. But my dad isn't the type to be outwardly impolite to anyone, so as soon as they reach us, he holds out his hand.

"I'm Arnold," he says, introducing himself to Ro first.

"Rowan," my man replies, shaking my dad's hand. "It's nice to meet you."

My dad nods, reaching for Finn next.

"Finnigan," Ging says, making my chest bubble. I adore when he uses his full name.

"Pleasure to meet you both," my dad says, much to my surprise.

Hope starts to spring.

"And this is my mom, Mary," I say, noting how her gaze is on the flowers in my hand before it shifts to Ro's arm tucked securely around me. I swear her expression softens some.

My mom accepts both Rowan and Finn's handshakes, muttering a quiet "Nice to meet you" to each man. She turns to me next—my mother: the only person in my life who meets me eye to eye—and pulls me in for a hug.

My eyes prickle as her familiar vanilla perfume wraps around me along with her embrace. "Congratulations, honey."

"Thank you, Mom."

My dad's hand lands on my back, and he pats me twice.

"Now, uh," my mom says, pulling back and glancing at my dad briefly. "We were hoping to take Alex out for an early dinner. Rowan, Finnigan, would you join us?"

That hope soars, and my lip wobbles. Just a tiny bit.

"Of course," Ro answers.

"We'd be honored," Finn adds.

As a myriad of emotions run through me, from relief to outright exhilaration, the five of us make the short trek to the parking lot behind the auditorium. We decide on a place to eat while we walk, and the drive there doesn't take long after that. The steakhouse my dad suggested, of which Finn heartily approved, is just on the outskirts of campus. Once there, Finn detours to the back of the car.

"Everything okay?" I ask, no longer dressed in my robes and cap.

"Mhm," Finn responds, opening the trunk and pulling something out from within. "Just needed to grab this."

When Finn stands upright, it's with an orchid in his hands. It's sitting in a beautiful blue glazed pot, and the orchid itself stretches almost wildly from the top, green leaves standing proudly in every direction. At its highest peak, the plant breaks into a cascading shower of flowers that hang downwards. Small, heart-shaped blooms. The ones Rowan mentioned were mottled with pink. These are pure white—stark and beautiful. Behind each balances a delicate, five-pointed star.

"A Brassavola," Finn says as my mouth hangs open. "It opened up just in time."

Hearts dancing among the stars.

"You brought this for my parents?" I ask.

"I had a feeling I'd have a chance to give it to them," he responds.

"Damn," I say, insides skipping every which way. "You are so getting lucky tonight."

Finn smirks as Rowan chuckles beside me.

"Shall we?" our Grizzly Bear asks.

"We most certainly shall," I reply, linking my arm with his.

Finn shuts the trunk, and the three of us head inside, where my parents are already seated. My mom's eyes just about bug out when Finn hands her the beautiful potted orchid, describing the type of light conditions it prefers and explaining how to care for it. My dad, as we sit down, asks Rowan about the shop. And not long after, Finn explains about his own job and how lucky he is to work from home, all while contributing to a hearty 401(k). I think that's the point my dad falls a little bit in love.

I know the feeling.

Sitting back, I take it all in, a broad smile on my face. Everything is just how it should be.

"Ow-ow!" I call out, clapping as Marco, boom operator extraordinaire, struts down the makeshift catwalk in tight leather pants and an open vest. Somehow, my party quickly derailed into a fashion show for the crew. The behind-the-scenes men of Elite 8 Studios have been picking out their favorite outfits usually reserved for the cast and modeling the results.

I am *here* for it.

Marco spins, sticking his ass out and posing before strutting back the way he came.

"Get it, honey," Raylin calls out from her unofficial judges' table. She sips from the straw in her drink before marking something down on the paper in front of her.

Cas, sitting at my side with his feet propped up on an empty chair, shakes his head. "I didn't expect this," he says.

"What's that?" I ask, giving the man my attention.

"This place," he says, fanning his hand out. "These people. When I applied for a job here, I never expected I'd feel more at home than..."

He lets the end of his sentence peter out and shrugs, but I hear what he's not saying. Cas fits here, and maybe he hasn't felt that much before. Looking past the man, I catch sight of Teddy nearby, too, chatting with Emil. I think maybe we all found some acceptance within these walls.

I give Cas's hair a ruffle. "I'm glad you found us, boo."

"Me, too," he says with a smile.

"Are you still looking for a beau?" I ask, glancing around for my own men. They're standing near the food table, waylaid on their quest to bring back more snacks. Currently, they're caught up in a conversation with Dixon and Niko. Mal is nearby, too, getting drinks. Henrik has a hand on the crook of Mal's arm, and there's a small smile on his face.

Cas shrugs slightly. "I mean, yeah. I haven't had much luck in romance, but there has to be someone out there who's made for me, don't you think?"

I hum, watching as Bill comes down the catwalk dressed in a skimpy sailor's outfit. His husband is at his side, wearing a captain's hat.

"Yeah, Cas," I tell the man seriously. "I think there are people out there for all of us. Don't give up hope, okay?"

I almost did. I'd almost resigned myself to never having that happily ever after.

Thank God for Grindr and a persuasive poly ginger.

My guys reclaim their seats nearby, and I lean into Rowan, who's closest. He has a small plate in his hands, and I steal a pretzel from his pile of food. Dixon settles on the other side of Finn, a Hyped coffee cup in hand.

I snort.

"Needed a little pick-me-up, Grandpa?" I ask.

Dixon flips me the bird. The man does love his hazelnut lattes.

"Hey, Cas," I say slowly, leaning back toward the brunette.

"Hm?"

"You work out, right?" I ask. It's a rhetorical question. The man clearly has a gym routine.

He nods. "Yeah."

"You should ask Dixon to bring you along to his gym sometime," I say.

"Why's that?" Cas asks, looking past me to where Dixon is sitting.

"No reason." *Lies.* "Just make sure you hydrate afterwards. There's the cutest coffee shop"—*and barista*—"right around the corner."

Cas nods. "Okay."

Grinning, I settle back into my seat, wolf-whistling as Nathaniel comes down the catwalk in a rather revealing leather daddy getup. Jerome, I notice, is barely managing to hide his laughter.

"Alex," Ro says quietly from beside me.

"Hm?" I respond, curling my arm around his and leaning into his side. So warm and cozy.

"This is just the start, isn't it?"

I look over at him in surprise. "What do you mean?"

He gazes down at me with those big puppy eyes, a small smile on his lips. "This. Us. We've barely even begun."

My heart pitter-patters away in my chest, emotion swirling amongst the steady cadence of *mine* and *yes* and *always*. "Yeah, Grizzly Bear," I answer. "This is just the start."

"Good," he says softly, placing a hand on Finn's knee. Finn leans forward, catching the tail end of what Ro is saying. "I'm really rather excited to live my life with you."

"Ro," I breathe out, reaching around the man to grab onto Finn, as well. I look between the two of them. Speak to the two of them. "You make me happy. So ridiculously happy. I'm one lucky boy."

"I don't think luck had anything to do with it," Rowan replies.

"No?" Finn asks, drawing Ro's attention his way.

Rowan shakes his head. "No. I think it was choice. I think love is a choice. I think it's something you keep choosing. I'll keep choosing you," he says, looking between me and Finn.

Finn cups Rowan's cheek, leaning in for a quick kiss. "I will always choose the two of you."

"Oh damn it, you guys," I cry, moving Rowan's snack plate out of the way before swinging onto his lap. I kiss Ro fiercely, grab Finn, and kiss him fiercely, too. "In all my short life, I have never loved like I love you. *Both* of you. You make me feel at home. You make me feel safe. If love is a choice, it is the easiest one I have ever made. Because it's with you."

Finn runs his fingers through my hair, eyes golden and bright. Ro's hand smooths up my back. My heart beats like a drum.

Maybe it is a choice, all of this, but the truth is I *am* lucky. My life is full to the brim.

I have a job I adore and my work family in the form of this wonderful bunch of weirdos surrounding me.

There's my art friends and new people coming into my life—like Fiona and Gran O'Conner—who I have no doubt are here to stay.

I have a degree under my belt now and a plan of where to go from here. A book that could maybe be something and other ideas forming in my head.

I have my parents, who showed up today, exactly when and how I needed them to. They supported me—*us*—even though I know it wasn't easy for them to come around to something so unconventional.

There's my children—Mojave and Poppet. The lights of my life.

And my men. There's these two men who wove their way into my life as if they were always meant to be here. Two men who love me, wholly and undeniably. Who goddamn cherish me the way anybody deserves.

They love the pieces of me just as I am, extras, bonuses, and sparkles included. I'm not too much. Not to them.

I give them each another kiss because I can.

Maybe it's not traditional, our kind of love. The way we fit.

But for the three of us, it's *just right.*

Epilogue
ALEX

Four Years Later

"Once upon a time, there was a boy named Goldie. And he was the happiest little fucker in all the woods.

"The hair atop his head was flaxen gold perfection. And the land's finest silk hugged his goods."

"You know, we're not going to be able to read this to him for much longer," I whisper.

Finn shushes me, even as he wraps his arm around my shoulder. I sigh, taking a sip of my tea as Rowan continues to read.

"Goldie, one day, he went for a walk. And out yonder he found a surprise.

"Two big bears, there they stood, shirtless and hairy. Right before his wide, wandering eyes."

I huff a little laugh.

"*Now you might think you know where this story is going. But don't come to any conclusions just yet.*

"*Because you haven't thus heard how our hero was clever. You see, Goldie caught those two bears in his net.*"

"He loves this book," Finn says quietly. "Look. He's already falling asleep."

I snort a little. "Yeah, well, he's an infant. In a few months, once he understands *words*, we'll have to hide it from him until he's thirty and married."

This time, Finn snorts. But then he sobers.

"What is it?" I ask in concern.

He looks over at me, golden eyes raking across my face for a moment. "I was just thinking what that might be like. Our family. Thirty years from now."

I set my tea down and wrap my arms around Finn's middle, squeezing my Ginger Bear tight. He smells like cinnamon—always—and a little like baby formula. Life of a new papa.

"I hope it's just like this," I tell him.

"*Just* like this?" he questions, and I can hear the humor in his tone.

I roll my eyes, but I don't let go. I leave my cheek against Finn's chest as we stand in the doorway of the nursery, watching Rowan put our child to bed. "Well, Jack will be older, of course. No more diapers," I point out.

"And us?" Finn asks.

"We'll be more rested," I tease.

Finn chuckles, his chest shaking under my ear.

"Uh-oh. Close your ears, Jack," I whisper.

"*Now here's a lesson for all tops, sides, and bottoms. Labels can teach us a lot.*

"Our heroes learned the importance of reading that day. Because the warming lube was much too hot."

Finn's chest shakes again. "How are the illustrations for the second book coming along?"

"Good," I answer, picking up my mug and taking another sip of my sleepy time tea. I've had to get used to falling asleep earlier, considering the *lack* of sleep I've been getting at night. "Big surprise, but Cinderfella's book has a strong floral aesthetic."

"Just like Goldie's," Finn notes.

"Mhm."

Goldie and the Two Bears came out just over two years ago, and ever since I published the adult fairy tale, I've had a stream of commissions coming in from authors looking for art or illustrations for *their* queer stories. Honestly, it's a dream come true. This is exactly what I wanted to do with my degree.

Goldie's book, of course, only exists because of my men. I didn't illustrate the characters to look like us, but anyone who knows me knows exactly where the inspiration for Goldie and his two bears came from.

My bears. My real-life fairy tale.

The art is simplistic 2D drawings with sharp lines and lots of color. And, of course, flowers. The Brassavola orchid features an especially prominent place in the book Rowan is reading to our now sleeping baby.

And Finn's orchids... Well, they're set up in their new home. In *our* new home, which is just the right size for our expanded family. The house we now live in is in a nice little suburb with a lot out back for when Jack is old enough to run around, and like our last home, we painted the exterior of this one teal. In fact, as soon as we moved in, Finn, with Fiona's help, set to work filling every nook and cranny of the house with color. They even retiled the kitchen floor. It's perfect.

Finn still works remotely out of his slightly bigger office space. Ro is still at the shop. And Mojave, Poppet, and our second rat child, Hemi, have their new favorite sun spots. As for me, well. I haven't told my guys yet, but I'm ready to hang up my jockstrap. Not because they've asked me to, and not because I think I wouldn't be able to raise a baby with my job.

I'm ready, simple as that.

Commissions are keeping me busy. I want to spend more time with my men, Jack included. And frankly, I'm looking forward to ditching condoms for the first time in my life. I can't wait to feel my Grizz and my Ging inside me bare.

Even when I hand in my official resignation at Elite 8 Studios, I know I'll always have my brothers. Dixon and Niko. Cas and his beau. Teddy and his hubby. Mal—even though he quit long ago—and Henrik. Plus Emil and the others.

And, of course, there's my sisters. Anh, Fiona, and the rest of our brunch crowd. Although speaking of...

"How's Fiona doing?" I ask Finn. I know he talked to her a couple hours ago.

"Good," he answers, running his fingers lazily through my hair. I lean more fully against his side. "She's still tired, of course. Her body is going through a lot of changes right now."

I nod, making a mental note to stop by again tomorrow and bring her more chocolates. The woman deserves *all* the chocolate after helping create Jack.

When Fiona sat the three of us down one day and offered the use of her eggs and body to create a life, we were floored. I might have cried. Just a little.

Okay, a *lot.*

Fiona carried Jack, who is Rowan's biological son, through artificial insemination. And now, she's the proudest aunt there ever was.

And me? I don't think I could hold any more love in my heart than I already do for that little babe cradled in my Grizzly Bear's big arms. It's scary how much I love him.

Big, scary, and amazing.

"Here comes my favorite part," Finn says quietly as Rowan flips the page, nearing the end of the book.

"*Goldie and his two bears settled down for a nap. The mattress below them just right.*

"*And even in sleep, on their faces there sat. Three smiles, all beaming and bright.*

"*Now everyone knows how a fairy tale ends. With the big ol' gay happily ever after.*

"*But this one, you see, is a little bit different. Because this is just the end of their chapter.*"

Finn sighs, tugging me close. "I love you, my Goldie," he says, whisper-soft.

My heart squeezes oh so tight. "Love you, too, Ging."

He kisses the top of my head. "Done with your tea?"

I nod, handing over the empty mug. It's a simple white design, but it's my favorite mug in the house. On it are two short words: "& Mr." The companion set, three mugs in total, was a handmade gift from Anh. When all together, they're "Mr., Mr., & Mr."

Just like us.

Finn takes hold of my chin, giving me a brief kiss before he heads down the stairs. I wait in the doorway as Rowan settles Jack into his crib. He looks tired when he finally walks out the door. Tired, but happy.

"Hey," I say softly.

"Hey," he answers, wrapping me in his arms. "Is it time for bed?"

I chuckle against his chest. "Sure is, Grizzly Bear. C'mon."

The two of us head into the bedroom, not bothering to get undressed. We'll probably be up again in a few hours.

Ro's body goes completely lax as soon as he's on his back, and I chuckle, settling in beside him. His arm wraps around me—one final plea of strength.

"Kiss?" he mumbles.

"Always," I answer, leaning over and slotting my lips to Ro's. It's soft and sweet, and his beard scratches me just right. Rowan sighs into the kiss, and I know exactly how he feels.

When Finn gets into bed on Rowan's other side, I can't help but take a moment to look over my two men.

My Grizzly. My Ging.

The absolute loves of my life.

I am one lucky twink.

"Once upon a time," Finn says ever so quietly, "there were three parents who got some sleep."

"Ooh, ooh," I say. "I know how this story ends."

And they lived.

Happily. Ever. After.

The End

About the Author

Information about Emmy Sanders and her complete list of works can be found on her website. Subscribe to her newsletter, join her Facebook reader group, Emmy's Enclave, and connect via email or social media:

www.emmysanders.com

Find online:
www.facebook.com/emmysandersmm
www.instagram.com/emmysandersmm

www.ingramcontent.com/pod-product-compliance
Lightning Source LLC
Chambersburg PA
CBHW070606300726
48975CB00006B/1734